INVISIBLES
ED SIEGLE

Myriad Editions

First published in 2011 by

Myriad Editions
59 Lansdowne Place
Brighton BN3 1FL

www.MyriadEditions.com

1 3 5 7 9 10 8 6 4 2

A CIP catalogue record for this book is available from the
British Library.

ISBN: 978-0-9565599-1-3

Printed on FSC-accredited paper by
Cox & Wyman Limited, Reading, UK

For Louise, Sam, Zoe and baby

This is just a little samba,
Built upon a single note,
Other notes are bound to follow,
But the root is still that note,
Now this new one is the consequence
Of the one we've just been through,
As I'm bound to be the unavoidable consequence of you.

'Samba de Uma Nota Só'
(Antônio Carlos Jobim and Newton Mendonça)

One

The man on the late news laughed, showing a gap in his teeth, and for a moment he looked like Joel's dead father. His body was thin, his dark face creased. He wore a soiled red and black Flamengo football shirt. He was one of a crowd watching the *polícia* flounder round a hijacked bus, and Joel didn't need to be told the pictures came from Rio de Janeiro.

The footage switched to the windscreen of the bus, on the inside of which a hostage was writing in red lipstick: 'At six o'clock, he's going to kill everyone'. Night fell in an instant as the report skipped towards its climax. Cameras flashed and sirens wailed. An anchorwoman seemed an eye of stillness in a cyclone of pandemonium. The shot panned to the crowd and there Gilberto was again, if it was him. Joel caught another glimpse of a gap-toothed smile and begged the lens to zoom in and remove all doubt, but instead it showed the hijacker being dragged into a police van. As the report came to an end, a crowd tore at the vehicle's windows, howling vengeance for the woman lying lifeless in a fireman's arms.

Joel rummaged for an old tape and recorded the footage the next time they looped the news. He played it again and again, crouching near the screen, moving from side to side, trying to find the perfect angle. He sped through the fatherless parts and watched the relevant sections in slow motion. Frozen, the frames were blurred. Natural speed gave a sharper image, but each snatch ended too soon to be sure.

1

Joel smiled when the man smiled, and ran his tongue from canine tooth to canine tooth, pausing to feel the central gap. His father felt alive in him again, in flesh and tooth and the spaces in between.

Some time after midnight, Joel turned off the television, went into the kitchen and poured himself a tumbler of gold cachaça, then sat on a step outside in the yard as the liquid warmed his guts and he looked up at the stars. He wondered just how incensed Debbie would be if he rang her this late to tell a tale she wouldn't believe. His dad was alive! Joel couldn't sleep at the best of times and these were surely the very best. He looked at his bike, sitting black and inert in its shed across the yard. Then he fetched trainers and a black jacket, manoeuvred ticking wheels down steps and launched himself along the street, pushing elation into the pedals. The air rushed cool against his face as his dark shape flew through the multicoloured streets, squeezing through parked cars, past a startled fox, then turning up the hill with barely a breath, until he was hurtling into Queen's Park Road where he turned towards the sea, speeding downhill now, rounding a chicane by the old park gate, taking the racing line across the wrong side of the road, guessing from silence that nothing came the other way. Through the lights of Edward Street and down Rock Gardens, until the road ran into the promenade of Brighton seafront, where he slithered his bike around a bend and down two ramps, then along the beachfront itself, pedalling hard again, past the chained-up Palace Pier, until he reached a groyne with a donut sculpture, which he rode along until he reached the end.

Joel stood looking across the sea, breathing the air through wide nostrils.

'I'm coming to get you, you old bugger!' he yelled.

But Joel wanted to be closer to his father *immediately* – not in weeks or days when he could catch a plane – so he swung his bike on to his back, jogged down the groyne, and strode across the pebbles. He stripped and stood before the sea, with the light of the moon on his skin and the sound of waves in his ears, and spread his arms wide. The sea lapped at his calves then up his thighs until he dived beneath the surface, emerging with a shriek. Out from the shore he swam, bobbing under waves, spinning on to his back. Joel looked towards the beach, which was dotted with clubbers and smokers and drinkers and snoggers – and every now and again he could hear a cheer or a bass beat on the wind. He wondered if Debbie was out tonight, and if she was with anybody yet – it was only a matter of time.

Jesus, it's freezing, what am I doing? Joel thought, then dived under the water a final time, letting his body sink, with his eyes open and stinging beneath the waves and the water like iced silk on his skin. He swam then hobbled on to the shore and spun a few times in the breeze to dry himself, which only made him colder. He pulled his clothes back on, feeling a little damp at the skin, and sat on the pebbles longing for a cigarette. The cold was definitely winning, so he jumped up and down a few times, then wheeled his bicycle up the beach, mounted and pedalled home.

He parked his bike in the yard, watched the video again then went upstairs and sat on his bed. He listened to his breathing until it slowed, calling 'Undiú' into his head – the song his father liked to sit on the end of his bed and sing when Joel was a kid.

Orange light slipped past the curtains. Birds hadn't started singing yet, and he was glad. He tried to sleep, but his mind would only spin Brazilian memories. Joel reached under the bed, retrieved a shoebox, opened the lid and took out a silver compass, feeling its weight in his palm. He looked at pale, round-cornered photographs of himself and a dark brown man with black hair and a gap-toothed smile. There was one of them kicking a half-deflated football in a square lined with palm trees, another of them holding green coconuts on Ipanema beach. He thought about the news footage and

3

wondered how his dad's Flamengo shirt had become so soiled. Joel sang under his breath, *'Uma vez Flamengo, Flamengo até morrer'* – 'Once Flamengo, Flamengo till I die' – a chant Gilberto and Joel had once loved to sing along with the red and black thousands, high in a stand of the Maracanã.

But Gilberto wasn't dead. He was alive, and smiling. Twenty-five years without a word and up he pops with a smile.

Bar do Paulo sat on a corner in Lapa, a few blocks from the white viaduct over which trams rattled to Santa Teresa. Seven stools lined a zinc counter which sliced across the front. The regulars were ignoring Fat Paulo's grumbles about the stupidity of the *polícia*, and chattering at a television that hung in the top left corner, looking as if it was going to tumble. The walls were adorned with Flamengo team photographs and pennants, and to the right stood a six-foot cardboard cut-out of the Pope, dressed in the red and black shirt of that Holy team. The Pope's fingers were raised to bless the enlightened patrons, to remind them to keep the faith – no matter how woeful the missed chance or crushing the loss at the feet of the Devil's team: Vasco da Gama. Part of the counter housed a window on to savoury pastries: *pasteis* and *coxinhas* and *empadas*. The glass was always visited by an ant or two and the regulars would stage races, betting on the ants' attempts to scurry to pastry heaven.

Nelson arrived at five o'clock to find a stranger on his stool. He caught Fat Paulo's eye and shrugged an appeal, but Paulo merely stared back because Nelson was way overdue with his tab. Nelson felt in the pocket of his shorts in vain. His stomach ached at him and he tried to keep his eyes off the beautiful pastries. Maybe he could win some money on the ants, he thought, though Zemané was the only man who might just lend him a stake, and Zemané wasn't on his stool – though *his* stool was being reserved. So Nelson stood back, squinted at the television and told his mouth to stop nagging him about a glistening beer.

4

The television wasn't showing football. Cameras were trained on a bus, around which policemen and reporters crouched and scrambled. The shaking picture showed a man gripping a weeping girl by the neck, holding a gun in her mouth. Someone had scrawled on a window in red lipstick: 'They cut off his mother's head'. A reporter said the hijacker, Sérgio, was threatening to kill the hostages at six o'clock. Sérgio looked drug-crazed, or perhaps he was mad from living on the street. He was talking, talking, talking – right there on centre stage, telling the cops what to do, moving the hostages around and scaring the life out of them all. Nelson was surprised they hadn't already shot Sérgio – it must be some kind of record for a black man in a siege – but there were crowds barely yards from the bus, men and women and kids, and maybe they didn't want to solve this crime the usual way in front of the locals and thirty million Brazilians watching on TV.

Nelson knew most people wouldn't feel sympathy for Sérgio, but he couldn't help cheering for him, lined up as Sérgio was against the guns and cameras of the world, and he found himself clenching his fists in empty pockets and willing Sérgio to win – to escape from the bus and get the money or whatever he wanted, whatever the police didn't want him to have. And Nelson thought, for a moment at least, that maybe *he* should hold up a bus or a car or an American and grab some money to pay off his vast debt. Perhaps he could buy himself a chance, a fresh start in a flat with a view of the sea and a place on the roof to grow hibiscus plants, somewhere he could play his guitar and refine his compositions. Secure a foundation, work hard and the rest would follow – that was what Zemané always said.

Beers were poured and pastry numbers dwindled as the regulars slouched, transfixed. Lights flashed around the bus as the moment of death drew near. Nelson watched as best he could, but his legs were aching. He was just thinking he might go home and practise guitar when Zemané arrived, cuffed him around the head, kicked the usurper off Nelson's stool and bought him a beer. Fat Paulo glared at Nelson, who raised his glass and winked. On television, pandemonium broke out as Sérgio was wrestled into a van and a limp woman was carried away in a fireman's embrace.

The regulars sat and stood and waved their arms as they argued about Sérgio. Some thought he was a hero; most shouted that he was a devil. Everyone agreed the police were to blame, and celebrated the fact with swigs of beer and a slapping of hands. Zemané dissected Sérgio's kidnapping technique and pointed out improvements to police tactics, creating a mock scene on the counter with his straw hat for the bus and a cigar for a bazooka. Nelson sided with Zemané and was rewarded with two more beers, but no one bought him anything to eat and he didn't want to say he was hungry. To be unable to afford a beer was one level of poverty; to be unable to eat was penury of a different order, and not something you showed to bar-friends. Nelson told his stomach it would have to wait until he was paid for the gig that night at the Bar das Terezas.

At nine o'clock, Nelson left his stool, assuring Fat Paulo he'd pay his tab the very next day and treat everyone to a beer – two if he won on thè ants. He walked through dark, thin streets which sloped into the beginnings of the hills, where the mansions of Santa Teresa stood silent, their shutters clammed, hoping not to be spotted by the million-eyed beast of the *favelas*. Beyond the mansions and *favelas* slept the forest. And above the forest stood the giant statue of Cristo Redentor, arms spread on the highest point, staring down on all of Rio.

Nelson climbed some steps and pushed open a door into a tall house. He took off his flip-flops and hurried up three flights, trying not to make a sound. He paused at the top of the stairs. He could hear cars, somewhere, and a television on the floor below. No sound came from his room, but a blade of light sliced from the door. He peeped through the crack

6

and saw an enormous black man in a Vasco da Gama singlet sitting in the armchair with his eyes closed. Apart from a mattress, the chair was the only piece of furniture Nelson hadn't sold. He'd kept the armchair because he couldn't squeeze it through the door, which annoyed him because someone had obviously managed in the first place. Nelson doubted the Vasco man bore glad tidings, but he needed his guitar. He tried to push the door silently, but it creaked and Vasco opened huge white eyes.

'You don't live here any more, Flamengo,' Vasco said.

Nelson grinned and scratched his wormy hair. He might be smooth broke but he still had all his hair, even at thirty-nine years old.

'*Beleza!*' he said. 'If I can just pick up my things, I'll be on my way.'

'Make yourself at home,' Vasco replied, and grinned – now he saw Nelson wasn't going to fight.

On the mattress in the corner was a tidy pile. Nelson had read in a magazine he'd found that there was a new craze in America: ridding yourself of possessions you didn't need, to let your life breathe. My life has gigantic lungs, he thought. There were two T-shirts with faded logos, a pair of black shorts the same as those he was wearing, a plastic razor with bristles between the blades, a bar of soap, a book of songs, and a photograph of himself aged sixteen with a spherical afro and his arm round his little sister Mariana. He put the items in a plastic bag.

'I was wondering,' Nelson said. 'My guitar?'

'Adolfo sold it,' Vasco replied, and closed his eyes.

Back in the street, Nelson sat on the kerb and wondered what to do. He couldn't play the gig without his guitar, and he couldn't say someone had sold it because he owed them an ocean of money. The manageress of the Bar das Terezas had only given Nelson the gig because he'd convinced her of his respectability. It wasn't any old Brazilian place she ran – though it looked like one, because that was how foreigners

7

liked it. You had to be of a certain calibre to work there, she often said, because Americans didn't want to come to a bar where some *marginal* might rob them because he was down on his luck. Nelson had lied that he worked in the smart – but fictitious – Hotel José Manoel, giving her the number for the Bar do Paulo. When she'd rung for a reference, Zemané had pretended to be the owner.

It was sad to have blown the gig, but almost the end of the world to have lost the guitar. It wasn't the fanciest one in the world, but he didn't have much left from his late aunt Zila and he liked to think he could feel her presence when he played. He could hardly bear to think of another man coaxing its strings into a melody, so he resolved to walk and walk until he found a place to pine and sleep. He looked up then down the street, and decided up was better than down. Besides, one of Zila's Eleven Commandments was: *When presented with several paths, always take the first*. Nelson had spent much of his life interpreting this by doing the first thing that came into his head – a policy which had won him friends and lost them again in equal measure; which had led him to learn the guitar and a thousand songs, but which had lost him every *real* he'd ever earned and a fair number of those earned by others.

He walked through alleys, round corners and along cobbled streets. He came across tram tracks and followed them through the heart of Santa Teresa, where people spilled from a bar or two and the smell of black beans and fishy *moqueca* slithered through the air. I'll eat tomorrow, he told himself. On he walked, past shuttered houses and high-walled mansions, until most of the buildings fell away, revealing a landscape of a million shimmering lights: *favelas* sparkled, office blocks were patched with yellow squares, and chimneys far away spat flames into the night. Turning the other way, he saw the statue of Cristo through the trees.

Nelson noticed a house standing slightly apart on the edge of the vista across the city. He didn't think Cristo's eyes had seen him, since they were looking over the bay to somewhere far beyond – America, he wouldn't be surprised. If Cristo hadn't spotted him, Nelson could hardly argue the appearance of the house was a Sign. He stood in the middle of the road and wondered how his life had come to this: hungry in an empty street at night, perhaps being shown a place to sleep by an indifferent Jesus. Life could be worse, as his aunt Zila was fond of saying – at times when it was hard to see quite how. He tried not to remember her pastries. Anyway, if Jesus wasn't helping, that was his problem. Yemanjá was the deity that really mattered, and Nelson was sure she'd be up here helping in person, if it weren't so late and he weren't so far from the sea.

Nelson took off his flip-flops and padded over to the wall round the house. The sensation of warm cobbles on the soles of his feet made him think of playing as a child. The wall was eight feet high and topped with broken glass. He wondered if there was a dog: most dogs liked him, but you could never be sure. If only he had something to feed one. He chuckled through a rumble from his stomach. If he had something to feed a dog, he wouldn't be feeding it to a dog. He eyed the wall and thought about an attempt, but noticed a wide door set at least a metre deep. Its dark recess beckoned. His blinking felt slow and his thoughts far apart. He sat against the door and, pleased to hear no sign of the potential dog, made a pillow on the step of his bag of possessions, lay down with his legs curled tightly, and fell asleep.

Two

Joel awoke early, jogged dowstairs and sat in the flooded light of the kitchen. He listened to the kettle reach a crescendo, made a mug of tea and stirred up some porridge. He ate his breakfast on the step in the yard, where yellow roses were shedding their petals and blue alkanets ran wild. Then he watched the clip again a few times, hoping daylight would help to confirm the man was definitely his dad.

At eight o'clock he called the surgery and told them he'd contracted food poisoning. When he thought it was late enough, he rang his mother.

'You up yet?' he asked.

'Very funny,' Jackie replied.

'Do you want the good news or the bad news?'

'Give me the good, go on.'

'I've got the day off and I'm coming over,' said Joel.

'Lucky me!'

'So, are you ready for the bad?'

'Bad for you, or bad for me?'

'Worse for you, I'm afraid.'

'Isn't that always the way?'

'I saw dad on the news last night – in Jardim Botânico.'

'Typical,' Jackie said with a tut.

'I've got it on tape.'

'Oh, joy of all joys.'

Joel walked along three or four streets of terraced houses with brightly coloured doors until he reached Jackie's, where he let himself in. In the living room, an ashtray spewed cigarette butts on to a coffee table and tooth-marked pizza crusts lay in a box on the floor. There were empty wine glasses bearing faint prints of lips, some of which were probably Debbie's. Joel picked up the ashtray, took it into the kitchen, threw away the butts and washed it out. He put the kettle on and watered a limp basil plant on the windowsill. Jackie came in, wearing a furry coat, red lipstick fresh. They observed one another. A trace of perfume reached him. He nodded towards a mug on the side.

'I've given you sugar,' he said.

'Well, don't blame me if you end up wth a hippo for a mother.'

'I know what you're going to say,' said Joel, holding up his hands. 'But he's there in glorious Technicolor.'

'Name your price,' said Jackie. 'I'll lay any odds you like.'

She sank into the sofa and watched the video. Joel watched her. The curtains were still drawn, and light from the television flickered on her skin. He looked for quivers in the movements of her face, but her eyelids maintained as steady a rhythm when the man who looked like Gilberto appeared as when the hijacker ranted in Portuguese, 'Are you watching this? This isn't one of those films you see on TV. This is my film! I made it myself! Just watch while I blow off her head.'

'They should blow off *your* blinking head,' Jackie said.

'Dad, or the hijacker?' asked Joel.

She reached for an ashtray, crushed a pinkish butt, then checked her make-up in a leopardskin compact mirror.

'Best be off,' she said, standing up. 'Don't want to keep Miriam waiting.'

'That's a mighty fine dress for the bookies.'

'I bet better when I look my best.'

'Aren't you even going to entertain the possibility that it's him?'

'You mean impossibility, I think.'

11

Jackie left the room.

'Instead of chasing ghosts, why don't you ring Debbie?' she called from the hall, all chance of response denied by the closing of the front door.

It was obvious she wasn't meeting Miriam, but Joel wished she'd find a less ridiculous man than Carlo to be secretive about.

Jackie walked to the corner, stopped and lit a cigarette, then looked back towards her door. She enjoyed standing on corners smoking: it felt pleasantly seedy. She winked at her reflection in the double-glazed door of number 1A. She was starting to think the coat was a mistake; it was warmer than she'd thought. Her red dress didn't really go with it, and the coat didn't really go with anything, except perhaps road-kill. But Jackie liked to look on the edge of shabby because at least it was looking *something*. Her exterior might be a little wrinkled, but underneath she was pure milk.

She wondered if Joel was ever tempted to follow her – as Gilberto had in the last months in Brazil. Joel was a man who wanted all the facts. When they'd fled to England twenty-five years ago, it had not been enough for a ten-year-old Joel to know Brazil was 'over there, petal, past the end of the pier'; he'd needed to know the compass bearing.

Life was complicated enough without the old goat playing tricks again. Jackie had one relationship to extinguish and another to set alight – the last thing she needed was Gilberto jumping out of his grave to muck it up. He was dead and he could bloody well stay that way. She felt a stab of fear for Joel. There was no need to panic, she told herself. Joel would come to his senses, she was sure. It could not possibly be Gilberto. Joel would watch the clip again, doubt would creep in, and everything would settle to its normal chaotic level. Sooner or later he'd patch things up with Debbie. There'd been plenty of rows, sure, but if you didn't row – that was when you had to worry. She told herself they'd work it out, that before you

12

knew it they'd have a couple of little ones and there'd be no more time to fret about the departed.

Jackie squashed a butt under her shoe then ambled down Islingword Road and round the corner towards town. She crossed at the lights and walked under the trees that flanked the skate-park, where whiter-than-white kids in baseball caps, trousers hanging low, slouched on BMXs at the top of ramps. Two boys watched her pass, faces set.

'I can see your pants,' Jackie yelled, which made one of them swear and the other blush.

A man with a bare chest and a dirty sleeping bag asked for change for a cup of tea, but she didn't pause because she was thinking of how best to end it with Carlo. Heaven only knew why she'd even started it. Anyone who added an 'o' to their name deserved to be given a wide berth. He'd been fun for a while and there was always something to be said for a slightly younger man. Most older men were dead from the hairy nostrils down. The trouble was that, although Carlo had initially been inflamed by her individuality, now he wanted her tailored to his design. He had started to make remarks about her Thursday nights with Miriam at the Rusty Axe. At first Jackie thought that if she saw a little less of him, he might forget about ownership and remember to enjoy the parts she was prepared to lend. But it was clear, now, that he wanted all of her, and since all of *him* didn't add up to all that much, it was time to move on. She was fifty-seven and she wasn't about to change her ways. Besides, there was a genuine prospect of something developing with Tony, a delight she'd resisted considering for several years, mainly because he was the senior partner at Joel's surgery. Tony's retirement loomed, Jackie's good intentions were withering and, more to the point, Tony seemed to be finally over the death of his old moo. Thankfully Jackie had yet to spot the woman haunting any news clips – though knowing her luck it'd be the Apocalypse by Friday and all the dead would be raised, just when life was looking rosy.

Jackie hurried through the streets of North Laine. Finally she stopped to check her reflection in a shop window, opening her coat to view the settle of her dress. Then she smiled, tied the belt loosely, turned the corner and waved at Tony.

Joel cleared a space on his mother's sofa, lay back and watched the clip again. He wished he knew what she really thought. Did she still think about Gilberto? Joel wondered how she would feel about him going back to Rio. He couldn't believe it had been so long: twenty-five years, though it sometimes felt like yesterday. Debbie had often asked why he hadn't gone before. His old mate Liam had even been working there for the best part of a year, with a flat and a spare room – Christ, Joel was the reason Liam had caught the Brazil bug in the first place.

It wasn't easy to explain. *I'll go next year*, he'd always said, and told himself he didn't want to aggravate his mother's scars. Over the years he'd convinced himself it wasn't that important, that he wasn't really fussed. Brazil was just a place he'd been as a kid, his father had died – fathers did die – big deal. What was there to gain? It had no bearing. He didn't get much holiday and he could use it to better purpose. He had a good life, a good job, a good set of mates. He was happy. There weren't any cavities to be filled.

He wondered whether his mother ever thought about the early years in Brighton, following their escape. Joel would always remember entering Britain in '75 as if descending to some nether world – a thousand white hands at Heathrow stretching to grasp returning loved ones, rows of pale faces staring until recognition sparked dead eyes. Children skipping into the arms of grannies and grandpas and uncles and aunts and sisters and brothers and mothers and fathers – fathers seemingly everywhere: filling the airport, stuffing the world, arriving and waiting and pushing trolleys piled with family luggage, while Jackie and Joel stood like boulders in a river. Joel clutched a shoebox and wore green shorts and a yellow

T-shirt; everyone else wore jumpers and coats, most of them brown or black or grey. Then, just when it seemed all colour had drained from the world, with a shriek and a waddling rush came a woman wearing an endless multicoloured scarf. Jackie and Miriam hugged and hugged and Miriam covered Joel's face in kisses, then led them through crowds of ghostly faces into a forest of concrete pillars where Joel remembered the cold moved through him in a sheet – so different from the gentle chill which sat on your skin late on a Rio winter's day.

Joel and his mum had huddled under a blanket in the back of Miriam's Renault 4, sipping sugary tea from a Thermos cup, as Miriam tried to rattle them back to Brighton before they froze. He remembered the orange strobe from street-lights which hung frozen above an empty motorway. He saw his breath like smoke, his mum's too. Their eyes met often. She smiled and stroked the back of his head.

They stayed with Miriam in a terraced house on a hill with a view of the grey sea. Joel remembered a black Christmas, his first touch of snow, nights which fell at four and rose at ten, leafless branches on rigid trees, a cold white sun, pebbles like eggs on a sepia shore. He discovered scarves, mittens and bobble hats, men with pallid skin and hairy faces, mashed potato and baked beans. No one in Brighton was anything but white. He felt like the butterflies he sometimes found flapping against steamed-up windows. A change had come over the world, like a dream – yet part of him didn't want to wake up, because he could see his mum was becoming happier.

At first, Jackie slept clenched in a ball in Miriam's spare bed. Joel was supposed to sleep on a camp bed by her side, but would sneak into the other end and coil his arms around her legs, which sometimes thrashed as Jackie dreamed. Buried under the covers he would softly snore, as if asleep, while Jackie told Miriam the tale of her past few years. As Jackie gave up her stories, he felt her limbs unfold. Over time, there was more talk of England and less of Brazil. She went for walks, a duffel-coat hood pulled up. She would ask Miriam about the news, the changes in her thirteen years away, songs she heard on the radio, current fashions. One day Miriam took her shopping. That evening they went to the Rusty Axe.

Joel remembered Miriam returning with a woman who laughed with a cackle, and he lay in bed wondering who it was until he heard her say 'my little Joel'. She came to deliver a goodnight kiss and stroked his head, her hair loose, exhaling a sharp, sweet smell. Before he faded into sleep he heard chinking bottles, a needle scratch across vinyl, music starting too loudly then turned down, Miriam whooping and his mum cackling again. Joel had a feeling they wouldn't be going back to Brazil for a few more weeks at least.

Twenty-five years of weeks and counting still.

As time went on, Jackie did her best to forget the Brazilian years and Joel tried to etch them into his mind. As she slept in, he would sit in his pyjamas at the bottom of the stairs and wait for letters to fall on to the mat. At night he would lie awake and wonder how long it would be until they heard from his dad. One day Mum will take me to one side, he would say to himself. She'll say, 'Do you want the good news or the bad news?' The bad was never all that bad; the good was normally something you expected. So the bad might be that Gilberto was still in prison (but alive!) and the good would be that he was being released. When he came out, Joel knew he would probably have to come to Britain. It wasn't so bad: it was cold, but the people were nice. The police didn't have guns, so they couldn't shoot him even if they wanted to.

While he waited for such a revelation, he kept his spirits up through nightly conversations. 'Did you go for your swim today?' he would ask a picture of his dad on the beach. 'I bet you sat on the sand and drank a coconut; I bet it tasted as sweet as it always does when your mouth is salty. I'm keeping an eye on Mum for you, like you said. Write when you can – I know you keep meaning to. When you can find the time to sit down and write a proper letter – I know how it is. We'll laugh about all of this one day, when you're freed.'

Sure enough, bubbles of conversation floated to his room. He heard Jackie arguing on the phone in Portuguese, talk of papers and once the word 'release'. He determined to be patient. His mum wouldn't want to excite him until it was confirmed. Perhaps Joel would have to wait even longer to see his father, until Gilberto had fully recovered. Prison would have taken its toll. I'll wait forever, he thought.

When spring arrived and he felt the sun on his skin, Joel came to see that England had its charms. He went for bike rides on the Downs, climbed trees, and threw pebbles into the sea. He started at school. He muddled his words sometimes and was the only child in his class who wasn't white, though with his brown skin but pale blue eyes, his curly but not afro hair, there were those that weren't sure how to label him. One girl decided he was a coon and a couple of lads preferred to call him a Paki, but most just saw another kid and gradually he slotted in between them. Parents would comment on how good he must be at football, given there was 'a touch of the Pelé' in him, and everyone wanted him in their team, until they saw him play. But Joel had to admit he liked being the foreign kid, the one they couldn't quite suss, with a secret called Brazil they could never own.

One day Joel came home and Jackie said, 'I've got some news.'

There were tears in her eyes.

She borrowed Miriam's car and drove Joel up to Devil's Dyke. She turned off the engine.

'I've always loved this view,' she said, and took a tissue from her bag and blew her nose.

Joel looked over the ever-so-English landscape stretching north below the Downs. There were one or two other cars. A few people sat on the grass which fell away off the swell of the ridge. He looked through the windscreen down the slope. Panic was close. The news was bad, he knew it. It was always bad if they didn't say there was good news and bad news. The fields below looked as far away as the bottom of the sea. He wished he were in a boat, with his dad, beyond the horizon, a million miles from here. He felt again the way he had on the mountain, Pedra da Gávea: as if his blood had turned to wire. Jackie was talking about his dad and Joel could picture him on the mountain, running away, as blades swooped from the sky and he thought of pterodactyls. The wires pulled in Joel's veins and he clutched his knees. Jackie said his dad was dead; they were sending the papers; she shuddered with tears. The money, the flat, the body was missing; the papers were on the way. The prison, the papers, the flat, the money, the body, the body, the body...

Joel stopped the video, leaving the tape in the machine in the hope that Jackie might see the light, and let himself out of her house. He turned towards the seafront, his feet falling hard as he strode over the top of the hill, down past the police station and across St James's Street. When he reached the Palace Pier he walked a short way along the promenade then shuffled down some steps on to the beach. He found a spot on the pebbles, sat, and gazed past the dying West Pier. He was glad to feel his brown forearms starting to burn and his shaved head sting. Pebbles jutted into his Brazilian flip-flops. He could hear wind tinkling in the rigging of surf-cats, summer tunes drifting from bathers' radios, screams from the rollercoaster on the Palace Pier. He stared into the molten white of the sun on the sea and remembered reading that Newton had stared directly into the sun, discovering that light scorched his vision red and black. The nutter had even wedged a bodkin between his eyeball and its socket, to gauge the effects of pressure. Joel wasn't sure what a bodkin was, but he'd happily give it a whirl. He took out his compass, breathed on the glass, polished it on the hem of his Flamengo shirt and placed it on a stone, cocking his head to ensure it was flat. The needle swung to stillness, precisely over north.

He edged round until he could stare across the sea, southwest at 219 degrees. It was 5,734 miles to Rio de Janeiro. Keeping his eyes on the bearing, he kicked off his flip-flops and walked barefoot across the pebbles, hurting the hollows of his feet until they sank into shingle in the shallows. If his old man were also in the water, in Brazil – would they not be connected by a transatlantic wave of particles? It would be eight-thirty in Rio. Perhaps he still went for a morning swim on Ipanema beach.

Joel wandered back from the sea and sat on a wall by a basketball court. He watched kids slip balls between flexing knees, corn-rowed heads bobbing. A pick-and-mix of youth in Knicks and Lakers tops, tall baseball caps set wonky. Stringy boys smoked cigarettes to the butt and flicked them to the ground. Skaters rattled their boards and scooter kids licked Mr Whippys. Tourists walked past, pointing at the piers. Suddenly Joel sensed a coolness in the air, and found himself submerged in a suspension of temperatures, hot and cold together. He turned to look across the water but the sea mist had dissolved everything.

In Nelson's dream, Yemanjá poured wine from an amphora into his mouth until it overflowed. When he awoke he found this strange, because Yemanjá was not the sort of deity to have much time for amphorae. Something a little more natural – more Brazilian – would have been in keeping: a coconut perhaps. The starry sky was starting to promise light. Nelson sat up, wiped dribble from his cheek and thought about food. Man, his stomach ached. Then he realised neither light nor hunger had woken him, but voices on the other side of the wall.

Half a leg was numb, but he grabbed his bag and hobbled round the corner. Beyond the wall a man hummed 'Happy Birthday', a woman giggled and keys chinked.

'What's the code, honey?' the woman's voice said.

'Now think, sugar,' said the voice of the man.

'My birthday! Thirteen, o-six, sixty!' said the woman.

'Happy birthday, my little cherry stone.'

'Can I really be forty?' she said with a sigh.

'And more beautiful every year.'

Nelson heard six bleeps, a high-pitched whine, a heavy door closing and keys turning in locks. Torchlight fanned behind the wall. The man was panting, dragging suitcases on plastic wheels. Nelson withdrew further as a black Mercedes pulled up.

'Perfect timing! Oh, honey!' said the woman.

'*I love New York in June...*' crooned the man as he opened the door in the wall.

'Oh! So do I, honey, I'm sure I do! And London in July!'

'*A foggy da-ay... in London to-wn,*' sang the man as a driver helped him dump giant cases into the boot.

'Oh, how I'll adore the fog!' said the woman.

Nelson peeked around the corner. The woman was as small as a bird. The man was fat and having trouble squeezing into the back of the car. Nelson heard a final giggle and a forthright command to a driver who surely already knew the destination: 'To the airport: the international airport.'

The car rolled away and Nelson emerged. He wanted to slap hands and chink glasses with everyone at Bar do Paulo – though upon reflection this piece of fortune might serve him better if kept secret. It could be the very break he'd been working so hard to find. He didn't know whether to thank Cristo or Yemanjá, so he thanked them both – as was only fair – by sticking his thumb up at the distant sea and at Cristo on the hill. He saw that the sky was almost pale and thought he'd better climb over before the streets started to trickle with people. He found a piece of wood and wedged it against the wall, then, using it as a foothold, reached up and gripped a patch which was bare of glass. He hauled himself up, on to, and over – taking care not to snag his plastic bag as he let himself down.

Nelson roamed his new domain with swinging arms. There was a yard between the house and the wall, which was cluttered with ornaments, tubs and beds of flowers. There were hibiscus bushes, gloriosas with yellow-magenta petals and the cornet blooms of *copo de leite*. At the back was a sheer drop with a view over the city towards the bay. Spilling down the hillside to the left and spreading underneath the house was the motley red-brick slide of a *favela*. Smoke rose from morning fires like steam from the hide of a beast. Radio music and cries drifted over the valley. Nelson observed it as one might a bull in a corral: not without fear; not without admiration. Borrowing a view like this, looking down on his brothers and sisters, made him feel like a rich man for a minute, until his stomach burned. It was almost light. Soon car doors would be slamming and trams waking in their sheds. Maids would already be walking down from the hills or catching buses from the edges of the city to make breakfast for richer folk.

In the yard, there were a half a dozen sandstone carvings of Buddha and a four-foot-high Ganesh. Nelson promised to worship whoever was sitting on a key, but he lifted them all in vain. The ground-floor windows had bars, so, half breaking his back, Nelson dragged Ganesh until he sat under a balcony, then climbed on to his head. He pulled himself up and over a balustrade and, keeping low, examined the french door into a bedroom. Nelson tried the handle and grinned when he found the door locked: the gods weren't dispensing miracles. But as he yanked the handle up and down he was encouraged to feel a little give, so he sat with his back braced against the balustrade and started to kick. He kicked until his feet were sore then crouched and used his shoulder, trying to time his bashes to coincide with cars, which passed more frequently as day arrived. Perceiving a definite loosening, he let himself down to the ground and hunted for something to insert and prise open the gap. He found a trowel, the tip of which he managed to worm into the hinge. He twisted and hammered and twisted until he started to hear the divine sound of splintering. With a final heave the door gave up.

Nelson stumbled on to polished floorboards and an alarm started to scream. He bolted downstairs, found the key-pad and jabbed silver keys. 13-06-60.

Silence settled on everything.

He found the fridge, which was unplugged and empty. He ducked his head under a tap and drank until he felt sick. In a cupboard he discovered a can of tomatoes and a bag of penne and said, 'How about a little pasta arrabbiata, *senhor*?' – a dish he knew from working as a waiter in an Italian place. He opened the tin and took half a mouthful of pasta and half of tomatoes, gulping the crunchy blend so fast that nausea swept it into the sink. After that, he slowed and finished off the rest.

Marble surfaces glowed in the light of dawn. Nelson wandered into a living room strewn with sofas and rugs, which beckoned him to snooze. As sunlight lit the walls, he noticed a door in the corner which looked as if it opened on to the cliff. He crept towards it, turned a knob and beheld steps down into a blazing hexagonal room with bay windows giving on to a view of half the world. In the centre he found a chair and a music stand with a book of bossa nova songs open in its arms. Against a wall, sleeping like vampires in black cases, were instruments: a violin, a mandolin – and the unmistakable shape of a guitar.

Nelson flicked the catches of the guitar case open with his thumbs and ran his fingers over red velvet. He lifted the guitar gently from its bed, sat on the chair and laid the sleeping instrument in his lap. A label inside said, 'José Ramirez, Madrid, 1975', and just by the feel of the wood Nelson could tell it would really sing. He tuned the strings, savouring the sweet cacophony of an instrument finding harmony, then started to strum a few chords, speeding up and slowing down, getting a feel for the instrument's flight until he began to sing 'Song of the Sabiá' – which seemed an appropriate melody with which to bless this latest start. Even sad Jobim songs made Nelson happy, as if singing of solitude made him feel less lonely, but this was a more optimistic number than some. He sang partly in homage to Yemanjá – for she alone could be behind this lucky day – and partly for poor Sérgio, who needed a song sung for him if anyone did; but mainly for himself. Of course, there was nothing like an audience – and now he had a guitar he could ask for another chance at the Bar das Terezas. He'd need a shrewd excuse for his no-show the night before, but with Yemanjá unrolling a magic carpet before his footsteps there was certainly hope.

As he felt the strings fall in with his fingers' caress, Nelson looked over the *favela* below and imagined he was inside an enormous eye, unblinking, surveying the world around which he had scrambled for thirty-nine years with varying colours of success. And as he gazed it struck him that there was something impudent about a *favela*. He knew this wasn't a helpful thought, given that right at this moment a million *favelados* were sweating as a squeegee boy, a maid, a whore, a pickpocket, a petrol pump attendant, a bus driver, a street sweeper or simply standing with a dozen brothers in a prison cell meant for two. But a *favela* was created by hands carrying bricks and sheets of metal up towering slopes to build a home, when the rest of the city wished they wouldn't. 'We're here,' the *favelas* said, 'and there's nothing you can do.' To make matters worse, many *favelas* had the cheek not to squat by the swamps on the fringes of the city nor to sprawl on scrubland heading into nowhere – but to sit on the central hills that made Rio the 'Marvellous City'. And these hills were so beautiful that *playboys* in the South Zone had no choice but to look up and see the brick and concrete boxes, which weren't going to vanish, no matter how much rich folk wished they would.

He could see black kids in bright shorts kicking a ball, a fat woman heaving bags up twisting steps. Nelson wondered how God came to develop the intricate logic by which it was

23

fine to sit on His celestial arse instead of helping. Still, he had to admit it was better to be up here looking down than down there looking up. Besides, Nelson couldn't help but feel a bit sorry for Him. It must be hard to be around and amongst people all the time without anyone noticing. It was bad enough at Bar do Paulo when you didn't have a *real* and Zemané was nowhere to be seen. God didn't have a Zemané; he was *the* Zemané – but it was better to be the mortal one, in a way, because he was right there before your eyes, bang slap in the middle of life. Immortal, invisible, lonely as hell: that was how Nelson perceived God. He smiled and wondered at his own intricate logic – by which it seemed better to be the bossy but generous owner of a bar than creator of the universe.

The room began to heat like an oven, so he put down the guitar, fetched a glass of water and drank it while reclining on a giant cushion. Whatever life gave or took today, it was better to start from a velvet cushion than a mattress on the floor. His aunt Zila used to say that every day you didn't make your future better was a day you made it worse – though Nelson suspected a few days doing precious little helped to lubricate the whole machine. But today was not a day to sit fat like Buddha and contemplate the beauty of it all. Nelson didn't know much about money, but Zemané was forever talking about liquidity. That meant turning this place into some cash.

Nelson's stomach burned and he considered more pasta and tomatoes – but how much better to stroll down to a restaurant, select a table under a fan and tear open a cheese-bread roll as a stew bubbled on a hob. He looked at a clock on the wall – a pretty thing with Roman numbers and a frame of silver rays – and thought: fifty *reais*. But while he might have been able to sell the clock, he *liked* the clock, and ever since he'd sold his watch to a frightened tourist for five dollars he'd been longing to know the time. Nelson had to admit he didn't really like to steal. Were he to possess a greater affinity for that

24

line of work, he'd be in a very different place in the order of the world: rich or dead, no doubt. He had the skills: with his musical fingers he could pluck a wallet like a ghost. But every time he tried to commit a crime he heard Aunt Zila saying, 'You don't have to tell me, I can see it in your eyes.' In any case, Nelson owed Adolfo too many *reais* to approach him with anything to hawk, and Zemané would insist on knowing his source. There were other faces that might help, but Nelson wasn't much of a negotiator. Besides, if he wanted money for lunch he'd have to carry his booty down the street in the fullness of morning light, and that would not be clever.

There must be some cash in a house like this, Nelson thought. A maid he'd once dated, who worked in an American's apartment, used to buy Nelson clothes with the change the man would leave in an ashtray by his bed. 'Go ahead, take it,' the man would say. She had sometimes done so but kept a note of how much, in case he changed his mind and wanted it back. Two friends of hers had lost their jobs for stealing things they hadn't stolen, so it wasn't worth the risk.

Nelson looked in the drawers of a writing desk, in scented cedar boxes and china pots painted with dolphins. He tried cupboards in the hall and storage jars in the kitchen. He loped upstairs and hunted in a dressing table then went through a dozen handbags stuffed in the top of a wardrobe. His fingers wormed into the pockets of countless pairs of giant slacks and he even tried on a pair, posing in a floor-to-ceiling mirror, holding the waistband far in front, pulling faces. Finally, inside a pocket of an enormous jacket, he felt a thin wad of notes.

'*Show!*' Nelson said.

There were six bills: green hummingbird, purple egret, red macaw, a plastic one with a bearded man and a red dot, brown Jaguar, blue grouper fish – one hundred and seventy-six *reais*. He twirled, fanning his bills like a dancer he'd seen in a soap. I won't even steal, he thought. I'll borrow the money until I get paid. I'll ask for new notes at a bank and put them back. He could feel the eyes of Zila.

'It's true!' Nelson said, spinning round. 'Watch me!'

Nelson took a shower, shaved, did thirty-nine press-ups and tried to tame rebellious coils of hair. He put on black shorts and a red T-shirt with 'Zicooooo!' fading on the chest. He laid his other clean T-shirt out on a table next to the bed in the room with the balcony, and pressed the photo of himself and his sister into the frame of a mirror. He packed the guitar in its case, picked up some keys and let himself out of the house.

Outside, a yellow tram ran past with black kids hanging on the open sides. He winked at a boy, who made a cool sign with his fingers. As the tram sped and slowed, sped and slowed, the kids played in its wake, letting their feet skip over the cobbles, swinging by fingertips from a rail. Nelson followed the shining tracks, humming a tune, feeling the world was better than a day before. He soon arrived at Largo dos Guimarães, where streets bumped into a square and overhead wires converged in a spiky web. Nelson walked down the street and through the swing doors of a restaurant he'd been passing for years.

It was a small place, with a dozen tables covered in blue-checked cloth. A radio in the kitchen warmed the air with *forró* and exhortations to *aleeegriiiiiiiiaa!!!!!* An old man slurped green soup in a corner. A freckled American couple in khaki shorts were trying to translate a menu using their guidebook. On another day Nelson might have offered his services, as he knew the English for some dishes thanks to his days as a waiter, but this was a day to be waited *upon* – a thought which made him grin at the Americans, who weren't sure whether to be flattered or terrified.

A waitress in stretch-tight jeans with a green vest tied above her navel came to take his order. She refused to be drawn on the merits of goat with broccoli, so he plumped for a feast of *carne de sol*. The waitress told him his order was meant for two, refused his invitation to share it, and wiggled off to fetch a long-necked beer, which Nelson poured slowly into a frosted glass. He observed it for a good few seconds before he took a gulp, resisting an urge to gasp.

As he waited he looked at a copy of the *Jornal do Brasil* which someone had left on a table. He read that Sérgio was dead, having been suffocated by five policemen on the way to hospital – though why they were taking him to hospital was a mystery, since he hadn't been injured. Geisa, the girl in the fireman's arms, was dead too. A policeman had tried to shoot Sérgio, but missed from point blank range and shot Geisa instead, though Sérgio shot her after that as they both fell to the ground. The biggest surprise was that Sérgio wasn't called Sérgio at all, but Sandro, though he had been christened Alex, they thought; and they didn't know much about his life except that he was twenty-one and had been on the street since he was seven. To top it all, he was one of the kids that escaped the famous Candelária massacre in '93, when the cops shot eight children as they slept outside the church. Well, you got him in the end, Nelson thought.

Nelson read the Candelária numbers. There were seventy-two kids sleeping at the church that night in '93 and, of the sixty-four that survived, thirty-eight had since died violent deaths. Five more had died of AIDS, ten were in jail, two were dealers. Nine of the survivors still lived on the streets. Make that eight, the article said. If you liked your comedy dark, there was an endless night of laughter to be found in the newspaper. Nelson shook his head at a beautiful quote from the governor of Rio, who said, 'It would have turned out better if the girl hadn't been killed.' One of the hostages said she didn't have anything against Sandro, that he was a victim too and she didn't wish him dead – only that he'd never existed. He didn't exist for twenty-one years, thought Nelson.

The waitress brought his food and Nelson managed to tickle a smile. Her name was Selma. Maybe she'll let me kidnap her, he thought. Since the meal was meant for two, Nelson wolfed the first person's portion like a starving man, then took his time over the second – as he'd seen diners do in the Italian place: red-faced old men who ate with all the time in the world. Nelson chewed individual grains of rice and felt the meat's texture with his tongue. He dabbed up every crumb. He finished the meal with a *cafezinho* and creamed papaya pudding. Selma refused his invitation to come back and plump his cushions, but, as he hopped on to a tram with his guitar, he thought there was really nothing he'd rather do than go to Bar do Paulo and see the regulars. On a day like this, there was no way he could lose on the ants.

Three

Joel's assistant, Vicky, directed light into a pink cavern. A stalactite wobbled and white rocks glinted with gold and silver. Joel aimed the hypodermic towards the gum at the back of the lower jaw and, as needle entered flesh, Mr Kenny emitted a sound like a baby bird hoping for a worm. He was a bit of a squealer, Mr Kenny, but a pleasant enough bloke, and Joel hoped the inferior block had worked. He often thought about Gilberto when he gave this injection. His father had always been proud of his steady hand; he'd once said that as he went in with the hypodermic he felt like a bullfighter with a single chance to sink the blade. His patients rarely experienced pain – at least, before his first stint in prison; afterwards his hand would shake as it neared the mouth. He took to drinking whisky to steady himself and started wearing a mask to hide the smell, mumbling curses as he willed the needle to sink in sweetly once again. As word of painful procedures spread, patient numbers waned.

When Mr Kenny had left, Joel flicked a pair of latex gloves into the bin and ran his fingers over his scalp. Eighteen mouths in an afternoon – some way to measure out your life. Still, it must have been more of an ordeal in his father's time: hypodermics large as knitting-needles, digging out teeth left and right. Nowadays it was crowns and bridges, implants and cosmetic work, fillings which set by light alone. Restoration and enhancement were the watchwords – gone was the age of the Full Clearance: all the teeth extracted at once, replaced with sparkling dentures – a popular twenty-first birthday present in its time, or a generous start to married life for a lucky bride.

Yet there was something more captivating about dentistry in the old days. As a child, Joel loved to sit in the chair in his dad's surgery, as Gilberto used the foot pump to raise him up and lower him down. Sometimes he'd sit quietly on a stool and watch him perform procedures with bare and nimble fingers, his gap-toothed smile at that time uninhibited by any mask. His dad would let him drop pink tablets of mouthwash to fizz in a glass tumbler, and Joel would play with the whizzing drill or go down to the basement, passing tanks of gas as big as World War Two bombs, to watch technicians fire bunsens to sculpt red wax mouths. Joel would take slabs of wax back to the Ipanema flat, and his mum would mould them into fishes and turtles, monkeys and pelicans.

Dentistry might have changed, but teeth still held that magic. Why were there so many odes to the eyes? Lovers did not connect through a touching of corneas – mouths sealed the moment of union or betrayal, teeth chewed the morsels which saved the hungry, while eyes wept impotent. When Joel had first met Debbie he'd been attracted to many of her physical features, but when she smiled: what beauties! White and mighty, curved in a line with a tiny kink: imperfect perfection.

When he'd changed out of his tunic, Joel knocked on the door of Tony's surgery.

'Come in,' Tony said.

Joel entered and sat in a wooden chair culled from some church hall. Tony sat at an old bureau, finishing paperwork. A few years ago Joel would have found it much more awkward to ask for time off, but Tony was retiring at the end of the year, and Vicky and Joel had noticed that he was showing signs of winding down. His skin was tanned from garden and golf course – he was taking more days off to play. His hair was still more blond than grey and seemed longer on the nape – an almost youthful look. Joel marvelled at men of sixty-odd who still looked fresh from the box. He wondered how Gilberto would have looked, had his life not been ambushed. He pictured his father and Tony together – head by head, wrinkle by wrinkle. Joel wondered if there was anything crumpled in Tony's life. He'd been through some difficult times – the death of his wife, a few years back – but to look at him you wouldn't know it.

Tony put the lid back on his fountain pen, turned to Joel and smiled. 'So, how's the stomach?'

'The stomach?

'Dodgy curry, wasn't it?'

If Joel didn't know him better, he might have thought Tony was smirking.

'All good now, thanks,' said Joel.

'So where did you get it from?'

'A prawn madras.'

'No, I mean which restaurant – to make sure I avoid it.'

He was definitely smirking. It wasn't the first time recently, either. Joel felt a little put out. Your boss wasn't supposed to guess what you were up to – or rather, he was meant to have the decency not to show he knew. How was a younger generation meant to have a sense of sin if old-timers were too obvious about having seen and done it all?

'Bengali Bungalow,' said Joel.

'Haven't heard of that one.'

Probably because I've just made it up, Joel thought.

'So, what can I do you for?' Tony asked.

Joel thought about telling a lie, but he hadn't prepared anything. 'Did I ever tell you about my father?'

Tony looked at Joel with a warm blend of care and concern. That was more like it, Joel thought. The Tony I know. 'Well,' continued Joel, 'it seems he might be alive, after all.'

'Wow – that's incredible!' the older man said. 'Wasn't he supposed to have... years ago?'

'That's right – although, it might sound a bit funny, but I was never sure, you know, I always had a feeling – '

'So how's this come to light? Did he get back in touch with you? Or with your mother?'

'Nothing like that, no,' Joel replied. 'I saw him on the news.'

'So he's over here?'

'No, no – it was a clip from Rio.'

'Ohhh!'

Tony seemed almost pleased. Joel felt a little annoyed: was Tony worried that if his dad were over here it might affect Joel's work? Surely there were more important matters at stake? And hadn't Tony considered Joel might want to go and see his dad, in Brazil? Distance didn't make a resurrection any less real.

Joel's annoyance made him shed all scruples about asking for leave at short notice.

'Do you want the good news or the bad news?' he asked.

'The good or the bad?'

'The good news is, I'd like time off to go and see him.'

'Go and *see* him?'

'Look, I know it's a pain in the arse, but it's now or never. I've been waiting for this chance for twenty-five years.'

'Of course,' said Tony. 'You must go, no question. Of course you must. Just let me know when you're thinking of – '

'That's the bad news,' said Joel. 'I'm hoping to fly out on Friday.'

'*This* Friday?'

'This Friday.'

Tony let out a whistle. 'For how long?' he asked.

'A couple of weeks, I guess. I don't really know.'

'OK,' Tony said eventually. 'Two weeks or so it is.' He stood up and offered his hand. 'Good luck,' he said, as they shook.

'Knowing him, I'm going to need it,' said Joel.

'Bring me back a bottle of that stuff – what's it called?'

'Cachaça?'

'Lethal stuff with the limes and business.'

Since when had Tony been drinking caipirinhas? How the hell did he even know what a caipirinha was? No one was indispensable, so they said, but it was supposed to hurt a little bit when you were gone. Joel had expected Tony to be considerably inconvenienced by the fact that he was leaving a full list of patients – and here Tony was, thinking about cocktails. That was the trouble with the 21st century: too many old people, with too much money, having too much fun. What ever happened to donning beige, seizing up and whining about standards? They ought to be ashamed of themselves.

Joel left the surgery and turned into London Road. He walked past electrical stores and bicycle shops, past a bus stop outside Iceland clogged with carrier bags. People waited for buses, smoking. Tattoos crept from collars, schoolkids in messed-up uniforms scrapped. A man in a suit willed the right bus to appear with eyes left empty by an office day. Another man in thick glasses nodded at Joel, and he smiled back as he passed and said, 'Hello, John.' Being acknowledged by patients made Joel feel like a proper local; he felt he had seen more of Rio than some parts of Brighton. He had read that in Rio you could take a tour of the *favelas* to learn about the real lives of the invisible millions. Perhaps someone should run a tour to Whitehawk, hidden over the back of town, to show the softer side of a Brighton ghetto: living rooms fashioned by *Changing Rooms*, gardens inspired by Titchmarsh, children with addictions no more serious than to PlayStation. Set middle-class minds at rest.

Debbie walked into North Laine, looked at a halter-necked dress in a window and wondered if it would make her arms look fat. Joel will be here any minute, she thought. Once upon a time the prospect of his arrival would have made something inside her skip; these days it triggered more of a lurch. She thought again about the final, pointless argument. It hadn't been anything like their worst and she wondered if it had any qualities which distingushed it from the rest, other than its position at the very end of a broken chain. They had been watching one of his favourite films, *Central do Brasil*. Debbie had made a gentle remark about the reluctance of Dora to mother the boy Josué, which pricked a comment from Joel about the boy's quest – to find his dad – which triggered a retort from Debbie about men being big babies, which led Joel to make a sarcastic remark about Debbie's one-track mind, which provoked a dig from Debbie about being lost up a dead-end road without his fucking compass, which led to a folding of arms, a brewing silence, a simultaneous finger-pointing rant, and to Debbie throwing a snow globe of Paris at Joel's head. The City of Love. The city that sadly arrowed past his ear and failed to crack his skull.

She felt a bit bad about the snow globe, though it also had to be acknowledged that adult life provided too few opportunities to hurl things. Whether it had helped was a different question. Chucking ornaments was not necessarily the best way to rescue the two of them from the whirlpool in which they'd been spinning: never happy enough to commit; never committed enough to be happy. They loved one another – they'd said so even as they called it quits – but they'd never quite managed to get married, have children, make plans. Most of their friends were sailing happily into the distance while Debbie and Joel had been doing the doggy-paddle. And now the father issue had re-emerged. Debbie didn't wish to form a view before she'd heard the facts, but she had always feared it would haunt him again. It had never really gone away.

Debbie looked at a cream top decorated with pairs of cherries. Destined for a younger girl, she thought, unless I feel like looking a fool. She sensed someone behind her and smelt the mildly antiseptic aroma of the surgery.

'Would you look at that and go sixty quid?' said Debbie.

'Um...' said Joel.

'I'd look at it and go twenty,' she said.

They walked through the Lanes. Joel made jokes about the tiaras and vintage armaments in the windows of shops they passed, and Debbie looked for subtext. They reached the sea near the Palace Pier and leaned against the rail, and Joel wondered when the starlings would come back to swoop and morph against the evening sky, which made him think of the very first time he'd watched them, in the autumn of '76, not long after he started at senior school, and he thought about the day he came in and sat by the window and noticed kids glancing at him. Some of them smiled, nervously, especially the girls, and he guessed his mum must have told the teacher, and his teacher must have told the class. I'm like the Man in the Iron Mask, thought Joel: the Boy Whose Father Died. He could see his classmates' eyes hid questions – how did he die? How does it feel? Was it murder? But as time went by he realised none of them was going to ask. They'd been told not to mention it, no doubt. He was grateful for that, he really was, but...

But it wasn't that simple, was it? There was no real need for sympathy – because his dad was still alive. If he was dead, where was the evidence? That was the first thing they looked for in Agatha Christie books. Without a body or evidence, or a body *of* evidence (he liked this joke), there was no proof. If his dad's body had been lost they would still be trying to find it – a corpse wasn't something you lost and forgot all about. If they had found it, they would have said so. If it wasn't lost and it wasn't found... then perhaps it wasn't a corpse at all. Books and films were full of this kind of riddle, and sooner or later a clever loner would come along and work it out.

'Have they found the body yet?' he asked his mum one day.

Jackie was drinking tea and froze in the middle of dipping her biscuit, so that it sogged into the mug. He expected one of her lectures, but instead she just said no and looked unhappy. He thought it would be a good idea to change the subject.

'Can I go to Kevin's?'

'Where does he live, petal?'

'Whitehawk.'

Jackie looked at her watch as if it was significant. 'Not today, darling,' she said.

'Why?'

'Because it's not convenient.'

Joel knew there was no way round the veto of convenience. 'Is Whitehawk a *favela*?'

'No,' said his mum sharply. 'There aren't any *favelas* here. And don't let me hear you say that again. It's very rude.'

Rudeness was another concept he was getting used to. He wondered who was really being rude.

Jackie moved from job to job. She worked in Woolies, then as a cleaner at a school. In Brazil they'd had a maid. She wanted something more office-based, so she could use her brain, but someone else always seemed to get the nod. Then in the spring of '77 she saw an advert for a cashier at a betting shop. She rubbed along well with the old-timers and found she had a knack for the odds. Towards the end of the year life started to pick up and Jackie plucked up the courage to call their lawyer in Brazil. If he could sell the Ipanema flat, she could put down a deposit on a house. She wanted to make sure Joel had something for the future.

It was complicated, the lawyer said. She would need the death certificate to transfer the property into her name. In the meantime there were months of bills and *condominio* to pay. The bank account was almost empty and he hadn't even taken all his fees. If the bills weren't paid, the flat might be seized.

A nice lady at a *cartório*, a register office, said there were complications with the death certificate. There'd been a change of personnel and filing system. She couldn't find Gilberto's file. It could take time. If Jackie came in person there would be ways of speeding it up. Every time she called, something had changed. One day she received a letter from the *cartório* asking for certified copies of her birth and marriage certificates, letters of reference from her employer and her parents. She rang to explain her estrangement from her family, to find that the nice lady no longer worked there and a new man could find no reference to her case. In a desperate moment she rang the old flat and a woman who sounded suspiciously like the nice lady picked up the phone, then hung up when Jackie started to scream at her. Jackie rang and rang, but no one answered and one day the line was dead. The money in the bank ran out and the lawyer stopped taking calls.

Through 1977 Joel allowed himself the luxury of crying on anniversaries, making a pact with his father that his parting promise not to cry could have exceptions which proved the rule of his resilience. The allotted occasions were his own birthday in July, Gilberto and Jackie's birthdays in May, and the 18th of December – the day of Gilberto's second arrest. Sometimes Joel would buy his mum flowers on these days, which she greeted with great joy – not being privy to the reason. One date he couldn't keep was that of Gilberto's death, and every date that passed which wasn't that date gave him a secret confidence. Sometimes he laughed about it with his father in his room. He made sure he kept the mementoes in his shoebox in order. He'd always felt safe in the order of his father's surgery so he kept the pictures of Brazil in a uniform pile, pressed into a corner of the box. Joel became anxious about the chaotic state of the house. He started to hoover, tidy and dust. He arranged ornaments symmetrically.

In December 1977, Joel noticed that Jackie's calls to Brazil had stopped. She no longer took him to one side, every month or so, to tell him about progress with the – certificate. Joel found it hard to understand her attitude: matters did not seem to have been resolved. She was spending more time out with Miriam. Sometimes, when they came back after the pub, Joel could hear male voices. Jackie hummed as she did the washing-up, planted flowers. And so one day as Jackie was hoovering, Joel kicked a switch on the wall and the machine whined into silence. He pulled her over to the sofa.

'I want to know what's going on,' said Joel, sitting with folded arms.

'What do you mean, petal?'

'What are we doing about Dad?'

'There's nothing we can do,' she said. 'No one will talk to me and – '

'But where *is* he, Mummy?'

Jackie looked pained. 'He's dead, darling.'

'But where's his body?'

'I'm not sure exactly, the lady said... well, she couldn't be sure – '

'But how do you *know*?' Joel rolled his eyes.

'Know what, petal?'

'That he's D-E-A-D!'

'Because they told me, honey, and you know what he said himself... oh, Joel, I *know*, I'm sorry, my petal, but – '

'You don't know *anything*. The lady lied and stole our flat, and the lawyer lied and stole our money and everyone lied to hide – '

'Oh, stop it, petal, please stop it. I know how much you'd like it not to be true, but he's gone, my petal, he's gone forever.'

'No, he hasn't.'

'He has, petal.'

'He hasn't,' insisted Joel, taking her hands, 'don't you see? He's hiding away until the coast is clear. He'll come and live with us here, when he's ready; he's just waiting – '

Jackie stood up. 'Waiting where and waiting *why*? It's been two years, Joel. *Two years*. If he isn't dead then he doesn't *want* to see us.'

Joel looked up at his mother and thought, I hate you.

Jackie sat down and took Joel's limp hands.

'He would want to see *you*, he would. But he can't, because he's dead. He's dead, petal, and you need to understand that fact, awful as it is. He's dead. I think we should talk about this more. I should have realised. I thought you were better, you seemed so much better. I can help you, petal, Mummy can help you.'

'Help yourself, *petal*,' said Joel.

He lay on his bed but he didn't cry. He felt the wires in his veins pulling his fingers tight. She was wrong and she would be sorry. He couldn't lie still. He had to get out of the house. He wanted to hurt her. He ran downstairs and put his head round the door.

'I'm going to Kevin's,' he said.

Joel slammed the door and ran up the road, over the top of the hill, round the bowl of Queen's Park and along a couple of streets until the buildings started to change. On one side stood houses which were tall, white and square at the front, some with small gardens. On the other the houses were lower and grey or pebble-dashed, grouped together in pairs with gaps between them, some of which were filled with rubble. He turned a corner and saw more houses up the sweep of the hill to the left. They had staring windows but looked all right. This couldn't be it.

He cut across the houses and up the side of a hill. As he climbed he noticed a peculiar feeling in his stomach and felt a bit sick, as if there were fear in the air, and he started to think about the mountain, Pedra da Gávea, but stopped himself. He sat on chalky earth in a copse halfway to the top and made himself look at the town below which peeped through thin and leafless trees. You couldn't see through one tree in Brazil, let alone a forest of them. Beyond town the sea glinted through the colourless trunks. Seagulls squawked above. The silhouette of a high-rise cut the distant pier in two.

Joel climbed to the crest of the hill where the wind had teased brambles across the ground like a wispy comb-over. There was no sign of Whitehawk. He wondered why they hadn't claimed the spare part of the hill. No doubt it was different in Britain but he wished his mum would clarify.

She used to explain everything, or if she couldn't his dad would make something up. A lie was better than nothing. He kicked stones along a path and wondered if his mum was looking for him. He came to a field and was surprised by the grandstand of the racecourse that looked out across a hidden valley in which lay lines of houses, most of them red brick. Joel wondered if that was it. It didn't look like a *favela*. The houses were bigger – proper homes which looked as if they belonged. In Rio the boxes clung on to the tops of hills and fell down their slopes. Joel could see cars driving up paved roads, small gardens and people scurrying, just like in other Brighton streets. He wondered why his mum had made such a fuss.

He retraced his steps to the woods. Near the path, three kids were smacking a tree with bits of iron. There was a small kid of about twelve, Joel's age, and two taller ones, of fourteen or fifteen. They were stringy boys with pale faces and ripped T-shirts and one of them had a biker jacket which was far too big for him, and his hair set in rigid spikes. Joel's heart started to beat faster as this kid caught sight of him, set his top lip into a snarl and whacked the tree harder. As Joel drew level, the other tall one stopped, spat close to the path then carried on whacking. As Joel passed, the small one said, 'Cunt.' The hairs on Joel's neck stood up as he waited to feel the slash of rusty iron.

In the following months, Joel kept thinking about those kids. He went back a few times, until, one summer's afternoon, he found the small one smoking a cigarette and trying to start a fire with a magnifying glass. Joel trapped and torched a beetle, and the kid told him his name was Liam. Joel smoked his first fag and hated it, then smoked another, inhaling after a scornful tutorial. He bought cigarettes, which Jackie confiscated having smelt smoke on his clothes. She told him off. Hypocrite, he thought.

Through the winter of '78 and into the summer of '79, Joel hung around at Liam's where they listened to punk,

40

smoked fags and watched *Death Race 2000* or *The Texas Chainsaw Massacre*. For his fourteenth birthday Joel asked for a Samurai sword or some Japanese throwing stars. Jackie asked a man she'd been seeing in secret to help, introducing him as a boyfriend of Miriam's. Mack had been in a band which had once supported Free on tour. He talked to Joel of backstage bacchanalia and roadie lore. They clashed over the merits of punk against the blues, but bonded through a hatred of disco. Joel spent less time in his room and spoke to his mum with a positive lilt to his voice. Mack taught him how to drive in his Spitfire 1500 on a friend's farm, joking that Joel was a proper little James Hunt. Sometimes Mack gave Joel advice and he considered it. One day Mack came round and they talked about going on holiday to France, just the three of them. Joel wondered why Miriam didn't seem to be in the picture. Mack knew of a hotel not far from Mont St-Michel. Mack wasn't taking Miriam. Joel could have his own room. Mack and Jackie in one room, Joel in another. Mack and Jackie in one bed. Mack and Jackie, Mack and Jackie, Mack and Jackie.

Joel had run out of the house and down to the beach. There was a sharpness to the skin of the sea, as if lifted from beneath by blades, and white horses seemed rigid as they grated across the advancing membrane. Fuck Mack and his fucking car. Shaven skulls and sick-green hair. Pins through disinterested skin. Back home that night Joel ripped the sleeves from his T-shirts and practised spitting at his face in a smashed mirror on his wall. Fuck Brazil. England was it. Joel sprayed jagged Js on the walls of multi-storey car parks, puked Merrydown cider on pavements in the early hours. He wanted to form a band called Dog Shit, but his voice could only handle ballads, a fact he kept secret. He hated his mother, hated Miriam.

'Do you really hate her?' asked faux-deathly-looking girls who hung around the littered parks where he and his songless band lurked.

'Fuck off,' he would reply.

In the summer of 1980, Liam's mum went away and he threw a party for Joel's fifteenth birthday. The taller lads were there, and Joel brought some of his own mates. They drank cider, Cinzano, vodka. They started a fire in the woods on the side of the hill, scattering when the fuzz arrived. Later a girl called Debbie turned up whom Joel had seen around. Ian, one of the tall lads, had the keys to his dad's car. Debbie wanted Ian to take her for a ride but Ian puked. Joel said he'd take her. Debbie's legs in the passenger seat seemed the longest, smoothest things he had ever seen. She blew smoke rings as he swerved the car round the bends of Whitehawk. Her skirt rode up and he saw her white knickers. He took a swig of cider and pressed his foot on to the pedal. He'd never felt so good, he thought amid the exhilaration of acceleration. He lurched the car on to the main road, careful to keep to the left. In France they drive on the right, Mack had said. But here it wasn't right to drive on the right – wasn't that it? He thought about Mack and shoved his foot down. The wires in his veins made him grip the steering wheel until his knuckles were white peaks. Debbie was rubbing his leg, thighs parted, a delicious grin on her lips. Life could not get any better than this – life would not get any better than this. Here was a perfect answer to the question of his life – he saw it now through the enlightenment of cider. It was only a matter of time before they met another car. Dad was waiting, watching, willing. Death was smiling with a gap in its teeth. Two white eyes flickered ahead, shining with approval. He turned to Debbie, their eyes met and their lips parted in the arriving light. He jerked the steering-wheel clockwise, the car filled with whiteness and metallic thunder slammed him towards his destiny.

At first he could only hear noises far away and imagined he was a whale making whooping sounds at the bottom of a dark sea. After a while the noises gained a grain, until he recognised the twitterings of Miriam and his mum, Liam talking to him about a gig, the lame jokes of a teacher he'd never liked but who 'took an interest in him' (the weirdo). At first their conversations were hard to grip, like episodes from a quickly forgotten cartoon. Then light started to appear and he found he was sitting up in a hospital room watching his mum weeping with a blend of happiness and despair. For a while he kept his eyes stationary. He felt warmly frozen. He wondered if he wanted to stay this way. The idea was not without appeal. Jackie squeezed his hand and wept and he wanted to squeeze back but didn't. Debbie came to visit and showed him her plaster cast, which she'd covered in her drawings – though Liam had got her in trouble with her mum by scrawling 'slag' bang slap across the middle. Ian had drawn a cartoon of a punk rocker. Ian's dad wasn't cross with Joel about the car, Debbie said, and the other motorist had escaped with minor injuries. When Jackie left the room Debbie kissed Joel full on the lips and he felt a pop of happiness.

One day Jackie sat by his bed and held his hand and told him how much she loved him and begged him please to come back to her and said that without him her life meant nothing. From his Adidas sports bag she pulled out his shoebox and showed him pictures of his dad and swore that from that day on they'd talk about him whenever Joel wanted and that all she wanted was to have him back, and as she put her arms round him and he felt her tears on his cheeks he found himself putting his arms round her and crying and crying and crying and crying and saying he loved her too, that it was all right now, that he was OK, that it would be OK and that he loved her, loved her, loved her...

Joel and Debbie left the Palace Pier behind, heading west, as they nearly always did, walking along the promenade by the road, watching the goings-on below: kids springing in the giant bouncer, couples whooping on the merry-go-round, three shot rallies on the volleyball court, pink heads and lager at shiny tables. Up ahead, clouds towered above Hove. Joel and Debbie passed the slumped West Pier and the rusted

Edwardian bandstand, reaching the wide tarmac between Hove Lawns and the sea. They found a bench overlooking the shingle beach and sat down.

'Do you ever think about the crash?' asked Joel.

'A novel way to get a girl's attention, I'll give you that.'

'Yeah, sorry about that.'

'I guess it beats your typical first date,' said Debbie.

'Probably wasn't the best omen, though, was it?'

'Is that what we came here to talk about?'

Joel looked at the sea and shook his head. 'I've got some news,' he said.

'So I hear.'

'Yeah, I thought she might have told you.'

'So, the old bugger's alive, you reckon?' Debbie asked.

'I take it you don't believe it either, then?'

'I haven't seen the clip.'

'I thought you might take my word for it,' said Joel.

'You're joking, aren't you? What was it Jackie told me Gilberto said? "The first time inside they take bits of you; the second time they take the rest." His words, not mine.'

'Yeah, but maybe they *didn't* kill him that second time inside. Perhaps he escaped. Or maybe they let him out when the climate changed. There were plenty of survivors. Perhaps he didn't want to contact us because he knew we'd have rebuilt our lives, or – '

'So how come Jackie's so sure?' asked Debbie.

'She doesn't want to see it, does she? It's the last thing she wants.'

'And you do want to see it, don't you?'

'Maybe I do,' said Joel. 'I don't know. But it looks a lot like him – and that's good enough for me.'

The wind had died and the sea was grey-blue and slightly luminous – a colour befitting a warmer clime, Joel thought. Where it met the shore it hardly made a ripple now, as if it was resting, perfectly balanced, its head on the pillow of the beach, its breath almost imperceptible. It seemed incredible that such a powerful being – embodied by giant oceans, its limbs stretching around the globe – should lie here with such stillness.

'Look,' said Joel, 'I didn't come here to row about it.'

'So what's the punchline, then?'

'I just wanted you to hear it from me.'

'That you're going out there?' asked Debbie.

'That too, yes. I'm going to stay with Liam for a couple of weeks. See what I can find.'

'Booked the flight, all set?'

'Leaving on Friday,' said Joel.

Debbie looked at him, then shook her head and laughed. 'It's just bloody typical,' she said.

'What?' said Joel, a little puzzled.

'All those years together and *now* you're bloody going to Rio.'

'Crappy timing, I know.'

'Staying with your best mate, a block from Ipanema beach!'

'If you came along you'd only wind each other up.' Joel smiled.

'How bad could it be on a lounger by the rooftop pool?'

'We can go and lounge next year.'

'I've heard that one before,' said Debbie. 'Anyway, I'm not in the habit of going on holiday with exes.'

'Maybe we'll patch things up.'

'Don't bet on it.'

'You won't be wanting a present, then?' sad Joel.

'Oh, yes, *please* – that would solve everything.'

'How about a snow globe? I believe they're your weapon of choice.'

'I should watch out if I were you. I might aim a lot better next time.'

They walked back towards the piers. The shutters of shops and cafés were closed in the red brick wall of the seafront, though drinkers still lolled beneath yellow Lipton Tea umbrellas. They said goodbye beside the merry-go-round, exchanging peculiar kisses on the cheek, consolidated with a hug. Joel watched her walk away – she didn't turn round and wave – then strode up a ramp on to the promenade, past the pier and over the road into a narrow street, his feet slaloming between two men holding hands, a bloke kick-starting a Vespa, a girl sitting against a wall with a cardboard sign between her feet. He walked up the hill into Hanover, pausing every now and again to look back towards the sea. When he arrived home he started to pack.

Liam's flat was on the fourth floor of Tiffany's, a twenty-storey aparthotel with a pool on the roof. From his balcony, between a gap in apartment blocks, Liam could see a slice of beach, sea and sky – white, blue, blue. He ate a breakfast comprising a *cafezinho* and chunks of tropical fruit: mango, papaya and one the name of which he'd forgotten, that he'd bought from a street stall. It amused Liam to think that growing up in England there had essentially been three fruits: apples, oranges and bananas. Perhaps pears, if you were posh. Here, Liam tried to eat a fruit he'd never heard of every week. He'd been in Brazil eight months and there were dozens more to try.

He watered the hibiscus he'd bought to make the balcony more homely. There was a roof terrace opposite with dozens of hibiscus bushes and Liam had watched hummingbirds flit in and feed. There were three flowers on his struggling shrub, hardly a feast for a hungry bird, but he lived in hope.

Liam put his cup and saucer in the sink and wondered if washing them up would undermine his maid's working rights. Having Betty to clean for him was one of a million wonderful things about this stint in Brazil, but involved a whole new etiquette he failed to comprehend. He washed, but didn't dry.

There was a buzz at the door and he opened it. Betty – pronounced 'Betchy', she had led him to understand – was short and black with straight shoulder-length hair and a golden tooth. She wore a blue uniform with a white pinafore. She laughed after most of his attempts at Portuguese and he understood almost nothing she said, except for the words *namorada, filho* and *Deus*: girlfriend, son and God. Liam had worked out that Betty wanted him to find the first, that the escapades of her son were the bane of her life, and that she thought God ought to be doing a better job on both counts. Today was the day the agency paid her for the month, and Liam wondered if she'd come early because he was supposed to tip her.

Betty said, '*Bom dia,*' very slowly, then, '*Tudo bem?*'

He said, '*Tudo...*' then hesitated because he could never remember if it was '*tudo bem*' or '*tudo bom*' or if it really mattered. She said something he didn't understand, laughed and disappeared into the kitchen.

Liam loitered in the living room wondering about the tip. The agency said people often did and often didn't. Eva, the office manager at work, shrugged and said it was up to him. He'd even tried asking Betty, but the only words he'd understood were 'God' and 'wishes'. Joel would probably tell him to leave her a big fat tip. He took out his wallet. Would ten *reais* do? Not much more than three or four quid but enough for a couple of bottles of cachaça or a slab of steak to treat the family. Ten should do it, he thought. He accosted Betty in the kitchen. She pointed at the cup he'd washed and wagged a finger. Liam held out a note and said, '*Para você, obrigado*' – for you, thank you.

Betty looked a bit puzzled, frowned, then smiled and took the money with an '*Obrigada*' – leaving Liam no wiser. 'Something something *Deus*, something something *namorada*,' said Betty with a laugh and a shake of the head.

Liam took the lift to the ground floor and said, '*Oi!*' to the men on the desk. He stood in the street and waited for a yellow cab to appear down the stretch of Rua Prudente de Morais. The Ipanema streets always made him think of

Joel. It would be interesting to see what he made of it after all these years. Back in Brighton everybody knew him as the boy from Brazil. In their teenage years and beyond it had given Joel a twist he'd played to effect, when it suited him. He'd done the drum band thing, and hosted a Latin night for a while at a club beneath a seafront colonnade. One summer, Liam and Joel had tried to run a beach bar down near the volleyball court, selling *vitaminas* and caipirinhas to beach bums and wannabe surfers stranded on Brighton's pebble shore. Liam wondered if these groups had equivalents in countries which really did have sun, surf and sand: were there kids in Bondi decked out in parkas, assuming a cockney lilt, dreaming of drizzle? The bar wasn't making any money – it was hard to make a profit selling cheap caipirinhas when cachaça cost £15 a bottle – so they'd driven to Portugal in a van and filled it with bottles of Velho Barreiro. Customs and Excise had not taken kindly to their interpretation of personal consumption and had seized the lot. The bar died gasping on the shore.

It was odd to think of Joel arriving without Debbie. Whenever Liam had thought of them coming he'd thought of *them* coming. All of Joel's stories had Debbie written into them. She'd been in the drum band, taken money on the door at the Latin night, lent them half the cash for the cachaça run. Liam wondered what the story was – he'd only heard it second-hand from people who wouldn't really know the truth. One way or another, Joel had lost the best thing that had ever happened to him in favour of someone who might not even be alive and who seemed to have done his life little but harm. Perhaps it wasn't quite as simple as that. Liam wondered what line he should take on Gilbertogate. Jackie would have denied it was him, Debbie would have given it to him straight, and everyone else would have taken the news with a fair degree of public sympathy and an equal amount of private concern. He wondered if there was any point in trying to set Joel straight.

A taxi spotted Liam's raised arm, veered across the road and pulled up in front of Tiffany's. Liam got in, told the driver the address – that much he could say – and slouched in the back of the taxi. He loved the way the tint of his shades graded the blue of the early morning sky. It was a twenty-minute ride to his office overlooking Botafogo beach. Along a stretch of Ipanema, past tanned joggers and skaters, to the long curve of Copacabana with its palm trees and volleyball courts and air of dated paradise. The beaten black leather in the back of the cab felt good. The caress of conditioned air on his slightly sunburnt scalp felt good. His suit felt as loose as his limbs. It certainly beat the Northern Line.

The car slowed to a halt at some lights and two black kids stepped in front of the car and started juggling tennis balls. Alone then together they conjured the balls in triangular arcs, mixing in a spin here, a clap there. As engines started to rev, they passed to the side of the car and Liam reached for his wallet, wondering about the correct amount. As fingers reached to tap the smoky glass the car rolled forward. Liam stroked his wallet and determined to be quicker next time.

The taxi drove through a tunnel and soon was pulling up outside a tall block. Liam skipped up the steps, spun through a revolving door, and took a lift to the twenty-third floor. He said '*Oi!*' to the office-boy, José, who said, 'Hi!' back. As Liam was starting his computer, Eva arrived.

'The bus, the bus, the bus,' said Eva, dropping a bursting handbag on to her desk. 'Oh, Liaminho, you don't know what it's like – to have to kick my son out of bed and make him breakfast – he should make me breakfast at my age, would that be too much? Then I board the bus and the driver is new, so he goes the wrong way, so we all get off and have to find another bus to take us back to where we started. Then another bus with a driver who thinks he is Ayrton Senna and nearly kills us twice. And every time a black man boards the passengers breathe in – and all because that maniac on Monday night has everyone terrified of being the next victim.'

'You've got it all wrong, Eva,' said Liam. 'Sérgio's the victim – didn't you hear?'

'What a joke, friend! Imagine! A *malandro* shoots a pregnant teacher and they call *him* a victim.'

'They're saying the police were to blame.'

'Next they'll be making him Saint Sérgio!' said Eva.

'The cops had done no shooting practice for a year, I read. No training. They didn't even have walkie-talkies – they ran the whole show by sign language.'

'Don't talk to me about the police,' said Eva. 'My husband was an officer – I divorced that subject long ago.'

'So I guess you're not looking for a presidential cop?'

'Oh, Liam, friend, when *are* you going to find my president?'

'I'm doing my best,' said Liam. 'They're pretty thin on the ground.'

'Oh, my God!' said Eva, suddenly looking at him. 'What have you done to your head? I've never seen a head so red!'

'I might have overcooked it a little,' he said, opening his briefcase and taking out a present. 'But that aside, happy birthday.'

'You remembered!' she said, and kissed him on each cheek. 'Forty-six, can you imagine? Before you know it I'll be *fifty* and not a president in sight.'

'Forty-six is nothing, Eva – what's that expression you taught me?'

'An old hen makes good soup, but a young chicken makes an old cock crow?'

'That wasn't the one I was thinking of.'

Eva tore off the wrapping paper and examined a purple handbag, which Liam had bought at a market. She set the new bag next to her old one and stood back.

'Your time has come,' she said to her old bag. 'Your successor is fit to become the bag of a president's wife.'

'Let's take it president-hunting on Joel's first night,' said Liam.

'Let's go dancing!'

'Let's take him to Lapa. He was born for Lapa.'

'You know the best place on a Saturday night?' said Eva.

'Bar das Terezas?'

'You're learning, Liaminho!'

'Let's give them a call.'

'You can't book like that. It's not the Royal Alfred Hall.'

'Let's drop by later, then,' Liam proposed. 'Before it all goes pear-shaped, the least we can do is show the man a proper night.'

Jackie drove Joel through town in her small white car, past shoppers and down-and-outs on London Road, past Preston Park – full of lush trees and summer sports – until they were curving through the Downs and into the carefully rural fields of Sussex. At Heathrow, Joel checked in while Jackie went for a wander. He found her drinking a glass of red wine, playing a fruit machine.

'I'd better go through,' he said.

'Still time to change your mind,' she joked.

'Can't let the old git escape again.'

'Just don't bring him back, whatever you do.'

'I might throttle him, you never know,' said Joel.

'I shan't pretend I'd disapprove.'

They stood and looked at one another.

'Give your old mum a hug, then.'

They hugged then walked to the queue at Departures.

'Send us a postcard.'

'Better go,' he said.

'Go on!'

He followed the snake of barriers, gave his papers to a woman in uniform and turned to see Jackie had gone. He passed through security and sat by a window near his gate watching planes come and go as daylight faded. Twenty-five years since their plane had landed on one of those strips out there. Twenty-five years since three had become two.

Although Joel knew several kids who were better with one sorted mum or dad than they would have been with the feuding pair of them, the subtraction still hurt. Nevertheless he had to admit they'd done OK, he and his mother. It was odd to think he'd ever been at war with her, and it made him wonder how common it was to fight the person who fought for you. There was no formula that balanced a mother's love for a child with the love a child returned, and yet whatever he'd given had always seemed to be enough for her, no matter how minuscule. He felt a touch of shame at having been anything other than her champion. Perhaps antagonism was easier for a mother to bear than indifference; perhaps a greater fear was that a child should disappear or fade into a person she couldn't understand. He was glad that, for all his adolescent truculence, he'd stayed close to her, and that ever since his car crash their conflict had been jovial, in the main.

Joel boarded, squeezed into his seat and buckled up. The plane took off and he looked out of the window at the disappearing land below with its patches of dark woods and clusters of glowing orange and filaments of flowing lights. He thought about Jackie again and how he'd started to view her properly only after the accident. He remembered being released from hospital and telling her he saw more clearly. He continued to look at the contents of the shoebox now and again, touching the photographs with a smile and reverent fingers. It was funny to think he'd ever talked to a photograph. 'My dad's dead,' he'd say, and after a while he could say it with hardly a pause.

From then on, life had started to slide on smoother rails. He did better than expected in his O-levels, especially in the sciences. He took particular care over cross-section diagrams of the eye, the heart, the jaw. He knew what he wanted to be when he grew up. He and his mum grew closer. They came to love the differences between them. He started to look after her chaotic finances: he opened savings accounts on

52

her behalf, and they agreed allowances for her vices. Jackie refused to talk about the possibility of a love life, though Joel said he felt differently about it now. He even called Mack once, but the phone went dead as soon as Joel said his name. Jackie talked about their old life in Brazil, bought imported bossa nova LPs and began to cultivate a kind of tropical exoticism – dressing in animal prints, filling the house with thick-leaved plants, blessing the living-room with a Rousseau print of a tiger creeping through jungle on the eve of a storm. Joel sent away for Brazilian Portuguese language tapes and would sit at the kitchen table as his tongue traced lost routines: shushing the 'x' of *abacaxi*, enjoying the soft final 'd' of bittersweet *saudade*. He felt that if he kept the words alive the things they represented would continue to exist; as if mentioning Ipanema beach would ensure Atlantic waves continued to stroke its sand. They talked about Gilberto, and, while Jackie omitted some details of the darker years, she told him about the times which followed the first night she saw him at A Gaiola, when he stepped into a circle of light and music flowed into her life. Their conversations never spoke of a live Gilberto, and neither did Joel's dreams – not often, at least.

As Joel stared out of the window to where the illuminated outline of departing Britain was giving way to a dark sea, it was hard to believe he was finally on this flight – not finally after the length of the week, but finally after the whole of his life. Brazil! If only Gilberto knew Joel was speeding towards him. He whistled 'Samba do Avião' to himself, ordered half a bottle of champagne and said, '*Obrigado*,' to a British stewardess, who looked a bit puzzled. He changed his watch to Brazilian time. Joel wondered how many miles he was closing every minute. Far away on the other side of the sea Liam would be stocking up the Velho Barreiro, a taxi would be winding its way round town ready to make its way to the airport, and his dad would be spending his final afternoon on a different side of the ocean from his son.

When all was black outside but for blinking lights, Joel pulled down the shade and closed his eyes.

Jackie drove the motorway alone. Cars sped by on the outside. She listened to the radio then turned it off. She enjoyed the occasional noise of the indicators. She wondered how long it would be before she went back to pick Joel up. He will return, she thought, he *will* come back. She tried to remember some of the advice she'd been given in her life. There was something almost comforting about the way it never did any good. How could advice really help when some apparently important decisions were without lasting consequence, while others – made casually one day – changed the course of your whole future. She had simply decided to go to Brazil. Not the smallest decision – granted – but never one meant to herald irreversible change. Yet it had scarred her life and was lacerating her son's.

She swung round a slip-road on to the M23. When Joel was born she'd had such hopes for another chance to wipe the grime of history away and fashion something clean again. How wonderful to feel a baby look at you as if you were a goddess; how terrible to find you carried on making a dirty mess. One day the little angel would see the truth – the gap between you and godliness being as infinite as it was obvious. It was only a matter of time. The question was: had she made Joel's life better or worse than it would have been with another mother or no mother at all? Romulus hadn't done too badly with a wolf. Jackie laughed. A man in an overtaking car frowned. Laughing alone in an empty car – lock me up, she thought. She wondered what good motherhood even meant. Was it better to throw them out of the nest and expect them to flap, or to coddle them and hope they weren't chewed to bits the minute they left?

In the darkness, she drove round twisting bends. The road shed lanes. She wondered which versions of history would be unlocked: the good years or the bad years; the mad father

54

or the tender one. She squeezed the car into a space outside her house, and looked in the rear-view mirror to see if her mascara had run. She sat for a while and thought about going to the Rusty Axe but didn't feel like being with people. She didn't feel like being alone either, that was the trouble. She tutted, hauled herself out of the car and entered the house.

'I'm ho-ome,' she said to no one.

Jackie poured a glass of red wine from the end of a bottle, drained it then fetched a wet flannel. She lay back on the sofa under a tiger-print blanket and put the cold cloth over her eyes. She tried to imagine meeting a resurrected Gilberto but the images refused to segue into a narrative. She couldn't believe it was the remotest prospect. She wondered what Tony was doing. She wondered what his late wife would say about their affair. 'I knew he'd go to pot,' most probably. Jackie poked her tongue out. A week ago she'd been expecting to melt into the rest of her life without major challenges. Perhaps her affair with Tony would really soar; perhaps she'd wake one day to find a lump. She'd assumed she would accept her fate, good or bad, and slip away with plenty of tears and plenty of laughs.

What if Joel was right? The whole world would change. Her life was full to the brim without Gilberto, so everything would be squeezed. The mere fact of his being alive, in Joel's life, even if she tried to repel him to the very edges of hers, would take up so much space. She wondered if Tony would be able to find room; if he would even try.

She stood in the kitchen looking across the dark garden at the lights of Brighton. You couldn't call the view over the valley pretty: some houses, the rooftops of commercial buildings, the odd church, a couple of high-rises. She sat down on the sofa. She could feel the beat of her heart. The silence seemed to hum. There was still hope for Joel and Debbie. She had no god to pray to, so she screwed her eyes tight and made wishes to nothing: that Gilberto was lying peacefully and permanently in his grave; that Brazil would give Joel answers to his vital questions, dead dad or not; that Joel and Debbie would see sense, settle down and give her grandchildren. By the time the buggers were old enough to see the balls-up she'd made of her life she'd be long dead. I'll drink to that, she thought.

Nelson observed his racing ant. He wondered if the creature knew it was being watched. It certainly seemed unaware it was in a race. Fat Paulo's ant looked more alert and, though it wasn't exactly sprinting towards the finish, at least it was scuttling in the right direction. The eyes of ten men were glued to the ants and there was a hush between the exhortations of the start and the crescendo of the finish. Nelson perceived an unusual tension. Fat Paulo hadn't raced since *Carnaval* when Zemané beat him seven times in a row, triggering rumours he was an ant whisperer. But today Paulo had been more than keen to pick an ant and lay down a cool twenty. Nelson didn't turn up every day with crisp banknotes, and he was kicking himself for making his change of fortune so apparent. The tension reflected questions to which he hadn't yet invented answers. Zemané – sitting on his stool, smoking a thick cigar, twisting a wedding ring round a finger – would be the one to phrase them.

Nelson's ant swerved to the right and darted towards the finish. Paulo's ant, upon which the bulk had been wagered, responded with a spurt of pace. A moan rose in the throats of the audience and turned into whoops and laughs. Nelson started to grin as faces crowded in and the tumult rose. His ant started to sprint over the glass but, just as it was on the verge of crossing the line, a glass spilled a tide of beer over the field and washed the ants into oblivion.

Stools toppled, fingers were pointed and arms waved as the argument fell into the street. Nelson swore he'd seen Fat Paulo nudge the errant glass; Paulo grinned and claimed that in the event of an abandoned race all money reverted to the bar. There was shouting and a shaking of heads, until voices were silenced by the chinking of a lighter against a glass. Zemané put the lighter back in the top pocket of his short-sleeved shirt, threw a cigar stub into the road and said, 'Nelson won, so pay the man.'

Paulo watched Nelson as he skipped from man to man holding out his hand, into which bills were reluctantly slapped. When all the money had been paid, Nelson spun to the bar and said, 'Two beers for everyone!' – sparking smiles and slaps on the back. Zemané drank his first beer in one swig, then sipped his second with his eyes fixed on Nelson, who was starting to look for another ant.

When his glass was empty, Zemané stood up and said, 'Let's go for a walk.'

Nelson drained his second beer, picked up the guitar and tried to catch up with Zemané without looking like a child summoned by its mother. They wove through vendors on the pavement selling sweets, bootleg CDs, plastic pens, leather bracelets, toy cars made from tin cans. They walked along a street lined with trees with thick waxy leaves, until they came to a scrubby square with a bench which overlooked parked cars.

The light was starting to fade as they sat down.

'What you need, Nelson, my friend, is someone to take care of you.'

Nelson knew the dirty response to this, but not the serious one, and it was hard to find the right remark when his vanity was swollen by the word 'friend'.

'That's probably true,' said Nelson nodding in a manner he hoped appeared wise.

'And none of those *popozudas* I've seen you chasing at *Carnaval*. A woman who'll stop you spending that money on fools and ants.'

'Look,' said Nelson, 'the money – '

'Doesn't belong to you. Those notes are cashpoint-smooth and I don't believe you have an account. You must have... inherited them since I saw you yesterday, because

you're far too happy. I don't *think* you've mugged anybody
– there's not enough guilt under that smile – '

'You're right,' Nelson started. 'I've found – '

'Don't tell me. If you tell me I'll want to stop you or help
you or get a percentage. But let me give you some advice: if
this is any kind of chance, then stay away from the bar until
you've made the most of it. Those *bobos* will ruin everything
they can.'

'Not if I ruin it first,' said Nelson, hoping his friend
would laugh.

'Find a woman to give your life a spine. It doesn't even
have to be a woman – I'm not old-fashioned – a man or a
woman, it doesn't make any difference. A man alone is a fish
without bones, isn't that what they say?'

Perhaps Zemané was right. Nelson had to admit a little
rala-e-rola would be nice, but not with some dead-fly girl
who did what she was told. It would take a fine fish to fill his
plate. Nelson thought about the house and wished plans came
to him as easily as melodies.

'I have to take my wife to her class,' said Zemané, standing
up. 'Remember, word has a habit of getting around. Adolfo
was asking after you. Came by the bar with that Vasco shit.
If he finds out about your fortune...'

Zemané rolled off down the street.

At first Nelson had been careful to record the rent he
owed Adolfo, confident that a few more gigs would balance
the books. But one day he'd whistled up the stairs only to
receive a lecture from Adolfo on interest rates, payment
penalties and the threat to his *bunda* if he didn't start earning
faster. Nelson had made three quick payments, enough to
keep Adolfo happy – until Adolfo had discovered it wasn't
Nelson's skill with a guitar that was earning him sheaves
of *reais*, but the sale of his own furniture. Nelson wasn't
surprised Adolfo had kicked him out, but it was strange he
hadn't taken the opportunity to dispense a little violence.
In the days before Zemané bought Bar do Paulo, Vasco had

knifed a man before the eyes of the regulars, while Adolfo stood by with his hands in his pockets.

Nelson carried the guitar through darkening streets until he emerged by the high white arches of the viaduct. He bought an *empada* from a stall and sat on a step close to the Bar das Terezas. At seven-thirty – to the very second, Nelson wouldn't have been surprised – he saw the manageress arrive. She wore a tight black suit and her blonde hair in a ponytail. Her roots were dark, her skin was brown, her nails were red. Perhaps the leather folder under her arm held blueprints for the next bar in her trajectory. When she unlocked the door, he reached from behind and pushed it open.

'That must be Nelson *malandro*,' she said, strolling through and switching on the lights. 'I can tell by the smell of sweat and failure.'

This knocked Nelson, because he knew there were only the odours of beer and victory upon him at that moment, fresh as he was from his triumph on the ants.

'You have every right to be cruel,' he said.

'The truth is sometimes tragic,' she said, and turned on a heel, not quite as skilfully as she might have liked. 'If you've any sense you'll grovel quickly then get lost.'

'Before I apologise for my no-show,' he said holding up his hands, 'which I admit is the worst crime a musician can commit, worse even than stealing someone else's tune – which after all is inevitable given that Mother Music gave birth to only a small family of notes, many of whom do not get along with one another – '

'Nelson, why are you *here*? You're not here when you should be, and you are here when you shouldn't be. Were you put on earth to wind me up?'

'I'm here because there's something I'd like to show you.'

'I can't imagine you have anything I'd like to see.'

'You might be right. But then again... let me ask you one question. Which is more important: the musician or the instrument?'

59

'Nelson, I don't have time for – '

'Just humour me for a final minute.'

She looked him up and down. 'OK,' she said. 'The instrument.'

'Are you sure? Surely a good musician is what really counts?'

'Look, Nelson, I'm not saying you aren't a good musican. Everybody likes it when you play – I even like it when you play – but nobody likes it, at all, when there's nobody here to play. That pisses everybody off, especially me. Instruments don't fail to show up.'

'So what if your patrons could listen to the finest instrument in the city?'

'Is there a point to this?'

'The other night, when I should have been playing here, I was trying to secure the use of the most supreme guitar in Rio de Janeiro: a Spanish guitar, from Spain. I now possess that guitar – the best example of its kind in all Brazil – but the tragic truth is: I've been sacked by the very person most deserving of its sound.'

Nelson opened the case and took out the guitar. He sat on a chair in the middle of the stage and started to pick the first notes of 'Dindi', a song he knew she always liked to hear. The manageress stood with arms folded, her face still. As he started to sing, Nelson wondered if she could hear the instrument's quality. She watched his fingers and his face and he thought he saw ambition in her eyes. If this was the finest guitar in the city, perhaps it would give her bar an edge... When the song finished, she came over and studied the guitar. Nelson watched her eye the label inside and run her fingers over the cedar top and along the ebony fingerboard.

She groaned and said, 'You've got one shot. Saturday night: you and the magic guitar. You'd better not let me down again.'

On his way out, Nelson was almost bowled to the ground by a foreigner in a stripy suit with a scalp of tortured pink.

As Nelson swayed out of the way, a far more pleasing figure stepped into the light. Yemanjá, Nelson thought, and, though this woman wore a white suit instead of the dress he'd seen in a thousand representations, the spring of her long black hair and the way she rolled like the sea when she walked left him in no doubt. He watched from the doorway as she joked with the manageress and said something he didn't quite catch about the president or something. The pink man smiled as if he didn't understand and produced a fold of bills when the goddess touched his arm. The manageress pointed to the centre of the floor in front of the stage and promised the finest guitar in South America. The pink man stuck up two big thumbs.

Four

A trolley wheel squashed Joel's toe and he woke into a plane bustling with morning readjustments. He pulled a shutter up and saw a broccoli carpet of forest far below. Jesus! He squashed his face to the glass: trees and trees and trees and a brown worm of a river wiggling here and there. He noticed himself grinning. He tried not to grin and grinned at the fact that he couldn't stop. Brazil!

The horizon still held dawn's multicoloured stripes. As light brightened on to the trees they became patched with scrubby pasture and red earth. A shack, a road, a village, pasture, savannah, forest, a village, a factory, towns – until the whole earth seemed to be covered in tiny cells. Joel's vision scurried across every detail and he was suddenly conscious of a multitude of lives ticking along on this side of the ocean, as his life once had also ticked. And he was aware that Brazil had not been frozen for all these years in which he'd dreamed of it, but warm and alive and getting on perfectly well without him. He felt he had a lifetime of catching-up to do, as if he was duty-bound to find out everything Brazil had been up to since the last time they met.

After what seemed an age, the cells spread along a plain and into a valley, filling a basin fringed by ridges and plum-stone mountains, until suddenly there was the sea shining beneath the brightest blue of the sky, then a glimpse of Guanabara Bay, as the plane sank circling like a bird, turning the landscape on its side, until it was running faster over water and green land and the wheels bounced on to the ground. Brazil! Joel thought, and applause swept through the plane.

He stood in the aisle with his bag – come on, come on – then the plane unclogged and he ducked from the door into thick Brazilian air. Brazil! As he took the steps, his eyes roamed over the edges of the airport and he tried to match this arrival with his memories of departure. A few palm trees waved fingers beyond the tarmac. Low buildings looked asleep. The blue sky was disappearing over the mountains leaving a soft grey. Then, with a step he wanted to proclaim like Armstrong, Joel stepped on to Brazil for the first time in twenty-five years. Brazil! Such a simple thing – walking on Brazil – but Joel enjoyed every glorious stride towards the terminal.

At Passport Control the guard looked long at Joel's photograph. He can't see too many brown Englishmen in Flamengo shirts, thought Joel. As Joel waited for his suitcase he realised the glances of locals dwelt on other foreign passengers, while the foreigners' eyes were careful how they alighted on him, unsure if he was friend or foe. The doors slid open and taxi offers rained on pallid passengers, while Joel cruised through. Just as he was starting to think there really was a touch of samba in his stride, he heard a voice shout, 'Joel!'

'Liam!' said Joel and the two men hugged.

'Ready to roll?' said Liam.

'Never readier.'

They lounged on the leather back seat of a yellow cab as it hurtled towards the city. They drove past mangroves, over flyovers, passing close to the da Penha church on its little mount – Joel talking nineteen to the dozen of this or that forgotten feature as he feasted on the view. Past thousands of red-brick boxes, then tower blocks and offices, and suddenly it was a city Joel remembered as with a shout he caught a glimpse of the Maracanã away to the right. Then through a long tunnel until they shot out in front of the lake to career round its shore, with Cristo Redentor high on his hill at their backs. Finally, they darted into the tree thick streets of Ipanema.

The cab slid up a ramp in front of Tiffany's. Joel and Liam got out, Joel paid the driver with a cheery *'Tchau!'*, then they pushed through huge glass doors into a marble lobby. The desk clerks spoke to Joel in Portuguese and slapped his back and smiled a lot and complimented him on his choice of football team.

Up in his flat, Liam showed Joel his weedy hibiscus plant and the slice of sea visible from his balcony. Joel took a shower and changed into a Brazil shirt, long shorts and flip-flops. He put his compass in his pocket. They took the lift to where a pool sat under a retractable roof. From the terrace outside was a view of the length of Ipanema beach, at the end of which the twin mountains of Dois Irmãos nestled against one another, low cloud hanging over their shoulders. Joel wondered if he would be able to see the giant outline of Pedra da Gávea beyond, if it weren't for the cloud. Liam talked about a place called Bar das Terezas, where they mixed a mean caipirinha and barmen crushed the ice with pestles in the palms of their hands. Joel leaned on a rail and looked at the sweep of the waves. He'd always imagined this view with a blue sky and sharp lines, but instead the air was moist and the edges of buildings looked almost soft.

They walked round to the back of the terrace where the view across the rooftops was of the lake, backed by forested ridges which jagged along to where Cristo stood on his peak. Closer to them, not much more than a couple of blocks away, stood a small hill covered in a *favela*. Joel looked beyond the hill towards the lake. Somewhere across the other side the hijacked bus had stopped, though buildings blocked the view of that section of the shore.

'You know where the hijack happened?' he asked Liam.

'Near the Parque Lage, wasn't it?' he replied. 'Over that way somewhere.'

'Do you have a map?' asked Joel.

'There's an *A–Z* in the flat.'

'I wrote down the street names from the news clip.'

'Nasty business, that hijack,' said Liam. 'Why they didn't just shoot the maniac I'll never know.'

'Were you watching it live?'

'I think the whole country was.'

'Well, there's your answer,' said Joel.

'I didn't think they cared enough to pass up a chance to shoot a nutter. It's not like people don't know the cops shoot people.'

'Yes, but live on TV?'

'So why didn't they clear the cameras and *then* shoot him?' asked Liam.

'They ballsed it up, there's no doubt about that.'

'Still the guy got what he deserved in the end.'

'I don't know,' said Joel. 'Sounds like he had a tough life: he'd been living on the streets since he was seven.'

'Um... maybe – but did you notice he shot a pregnant woman?'

'Well, he didn't exactly, did he? I mean, the police shot her first.'

'You're joking, aren't you?' said Liam. 'The man was a lunatic. He'd already been inside loads of times. Drug-dealing, armed robbery, assault – '

'Yeah, but not till *after* he escaped being shot with all those kids at Candelária.'

'I don't see how that makes any difference. His life wasn't all bad. They say he was an orphan, but what about that woman – Elza – who says she's his mother?'

'They don't know if she is his mother,' said Joel. 'They don't even know his real name.'

'And that makes it all right for him to shoot the place up?'

'It makes it lot easier for them to wipe him out.'

Liam shook his head and smiled.

'So, did you come all this way to stick up for a dead man?' he said.

'You're right,' said Joel. 'Let's go and look for a live one.'

Joel and Liam took the lift to the ground floor and stood in the street, where the leaves looked swollen on the trees and the air was thickening into rain. They hailed a cab and soon were riding along the curve of Ipanema, passing cyclists and joggers running in lanes by the fringes of the beach, where serious men and women in trunks and bikinis hurled themselves on volleyball courts. They drove past kiosks hung with coconuts like giant bunches of grapes, at which locals lounged in singlets and flip-flops sipping a beer or reading a newspaper. As the soft points of the mountain Dois Irmãos were looming above, the taxi swung to the right into Leblon, where brown people shopped and walked dogs or strolled dressed only in bathers towards the beach. Joel studied the face of every man he saw, and twisted round once to let his vision follow one old fellow. On they drove, past the white back of the Jockey Club, past rows of Imperial Palms in the Botanical Gardens, until they reached the Parque Lage. The taxi slowed to a halt.

Joel paid the driver with a *'Tchau, 'brigado!'* and stepped on to the kerb.

Liam and Joel stood beside a telephone box next to which the hijacked bus had parked five days before. Nearby on the pavement there were flowers, candles and messages on cards. A postcard of Sugarloaf sat on top of a wreath. There were drawings of the dead girl Geisa on the pavement, underneath one of which had been written 'Cause of death: incompetence'. Some people stopped and looked at the spot where she died and crossed themselves; others crouched with heads bowed, lips moving and eyes closed.

Joel scanned the scene, walking around, trying to merge the details of the real place with his memory of the clip. One of the cameras must have been here, a motorbike somewhere there, the crowd standing not far back. Joel looked over at a place on the pavement, near some trees.

'That's where Dad was, I think,' Joel said.

He stood on the spot and looked at the ground, wondering where Gilberto's feet had taken him when the crowd dispersed. He looked up and down the street, across the road, over at the people looking at the tributes to Geisa. If only his compass had his father for a pole.

Joel took a wad of papers from his bag and handed half to Liam. On each sheet were two photos of Gilberto – a faded photograph from the end of their time in Rio, and a blurred shot from the newsreel. Underneath were Liam's phone numbers, and a message in Portuguese and English:

Son seeks long-lost father – Gilberto Cabral

REWARD OFFERED

If you have seen this man *please* call
Ask for Joel Cabral
Thanks

Joel taped a poster to the trunk of a tree and Liam fixed one to a lamp-post. For the next couple of hours they visited houses and apartment blocks on nearby streets, giving the sheets to desk clerks, maids and delivery boys, to passers-by and taxi drivers playing cards at a table by a rank. They taped copies in phone boxes and left others under the wipers of cars parked across pavements. They found a small café and watched the owner pin one on the wall. He stood them a beer, and they ate a couple of savoury pastries, before he sent them on their way, saying, 'A full stomach has sharper eyes.'

Joel bought some lilies from a kiosk and laid them by Geisa's shrine. He wondered if there were flowers anywhere for Sandro. Two kids came along, black boys in faded T-shirts and bare feet. One juggled tennis balls then balanced one on his forehead while the other inspected Joel's poster. Liam gave the juggler five *reais* and they grinned and ran off.

They searched the Botanical Gardens, lest a down-and-out-man with a gap in his teeth was sleeping on a bench. Joel imagined his nine-year-old self darting between the trees. They walked around the lake, handing posters to passing people, until they arrived back in Ipanema again. By now it was five o'clock and dusk had started to colour the air, so they strolled along the beach in the falling evening, admiring the shawl of twinkling *favela* lights which lay across a shoulder of Dois Irmãos. At the Leblon end of the beach, they came to the Caneca 70 bar, where they drank a few beers and watched the Flamengo game. Vasco scored before half-time to many cries of '*Brincadeira!*' – what a joke! – but Flamengo equalised after the break and Tuta sealed victory for the red and black tribe, so that soon passing cars were blaring their horns as patrons sang '*Meeeeeengoooo!*'. Joel and Liam toasted the win with caipirinhas, and shared a colossal steak served on a metal platter.

And all the while Joel watched the faces of men that passed, in case his dad should happen by, and listened to the Portuguese the locals spoke, to try to get in tune. It was hard to believe he was finally here, and wonderful to watch a Flamengo game again in the city the team was from, and to laugh as the locals larked in the afterglow of victory. There were half a dozen foreigners in the bar, some of them wearing Flamengo shirts, and the locals taught them amusing phrases and bits of chants, only some of which they grasped. Joel got the gist of everything, though he found there were also words he didn't understand and one of the waiters spoke to him in English, which he hoped was more for Liam's benefit than his own. When they'd finished their drinks they paid the bill, bid *tchau* to the waiter, and wandered back along the shore to get ready to go out.

Jackie awoke late on Saturday morning and lay in bed with her eyes glued shut beneath a leopard-print eye-mask. Her mouth longed for anything wet, her teeth for minty smoothness. Half of her wanted to wallow in tortured thoughts of her Brazilian past, the other to run outside and allow a busy day to chase them from her mind. But she could tell it would be bright outside, that was the trouble with day, and she dreaded her hangover slightly more than her memories. She hadn't thought about her own voyage to Brazil for a long time. She could hardly believe that Joel was really there. Besides, Brazil would be easier to forget completely if she could deny that the early days in the Marvellous City had been the happiest of her life.

In 1962 Miriam and Jackie had been nineteen – nineteen! – and both working as secretaries in a firm of chartered accountants. Miriam didn't have a bloke but Jackie was entertaining two: Malcolm, sporter of starved ties and skinny suits, and Edward Squires, the boss's nephew, a twenty-six-year-old graduate of Cambridge University, destined for brilliance in the accountancy firmament. Then Miriam met a man called Frank at a do for clients. Frank was pushing his forties, he said – though they were never sure from which side of forty he meant. He was a large man with fingers like sausages, with which he loved to maul piano keys into a ragtime tune. He sang in a barbershop quartet and wrote poetry.

Frank spent a lot of time away on business for a mining company, and, the week Miriam declared to Jackie that she was in love, Frank declared he'd been offered a full-time post in Rio de Janeiro. He wanted Miriam to follow him. He said he could pull a few strings and find her work. At sunset one summer's evening, in the the back of his car at Devil's Dyke, he mentioned the word marriage. Miriam pressed him excitedly.

'Love is not a pie to bake in a day,' he said.

Frank left for Brazil and Miriam waited. For months he wrote to her of palm-tasselled beaches and coconut cocktails, of pudding mountains and blancmange sunsets. Miriam would sit on her bed and draft replies, while Jackie looked up words in Roget's *Thesaurus*. They wrote of the imperious Palace Pier and the decadent domes of the Pavilion, of the unctuous curves of the Downs, multifarious pebbles on the beach.

Frank's replies made promises and promises, until, just as they were starting to wonder if his feelings for Miriam were veritable, Frank wrote that he'd found a small flat three blocks from Ipanema beach. If Miriam felt nervous about coming alone, he wrote – why didn't she bring Jackie? The two of them could live like birds of paradise by the turquoise sea.

Jackie thought about it for a few seconds then said, 'Where on earth will I find a bikini here in December?'

'Oh, Jacks!' said Miriam. 'You can't, can you?'

'You're not leaving me alone in this dump.'

'But what about Edward? I thought – '

'I'm sure there are plenty of Eduardos.'

The girls squealed and hugged. It felt so right. They drafted their acceptance of his most felicitous invitation and, that freezing December evening, ran barefoot to the postbox, ensuring their fate was sealed before they changed their minds.

Jackie hummed all the way home, almost skipping down the hill lest she be late for supper. As she opened the front door she heard men's voices in the living room. She put her coat on the hat-stand and listened. She could make out her father talking, laughing, and another man's quiet assent. Her first thought was that her father must have been promoted. Twenty-five years of loyal service and never a day's work missed. Jackie could smell sweet pipesmoke. She could hear the hiss of the pressure cooker. She was wondering if she should change into a frock with a longer hem, when the door to the sitting-room opened and her father stood in the gap, managing to grin and speak while biting on his pipe.

'Here she is!' he said. 'I thought I heard something. Not losing the old hearing yet.'

He always filled out his Sussex lilt when he wanted to impress. Perhaps it was Mr Le Marchant himself. Jackie sagged at the propect of an evening being patronised and ignored. Her father held the door and she entered, a compliant smile already forming, to find herself surprised: beside the mantelpiece, cigarette askew in poiseless fingers, stood Edward Squires. He wore a green cardigan and shiny brown shoes and his cheeks burned a pretty red. Jackie adjusted her grin. What was *he* doing here? Oh, God! Did this mean her father was going to start talking about 'courting'? Would her mother take her aside to warn her of men's ways? The only ways Edward knew, Jackie had taught him herself. She felt a spurt of annoyance as she took his hand, with intentional weakness, and said, 'Edward.' She normally teased him with 'Teddy'.

Over a dinner of boiled ham, mashed potato, carrots, onions, cabbage and parsley sauce, Edward did try very hard not to talk about accountancy, but her father seemed determined to enlighten some imaginary audience with a discourse on the fruits it bore the civilised world. 'Bore' was certainly the word, Jackie thought, as she rubbed her toes on Edward's brogues. To be admired were men with the bravery to fight the dragon of fiscal chaos, brave souls with the resolution to subject savage figures to their rule. Jackie watched her mother eat neatly and dispense the occasional smile. She longed to know what she really thought. The ham was beautifully cooked and – perhaps noting Jackie's glances at her mother, or simply because he was well brought-up – Edward complimented her on it. He even shot Jackie a conspiratorial glance during one of her father's diatribes, and Jackie winked back and remembered that he was not without a sense of humour. As her mother poured parsley sauce on to Edward's seconds, Jackie thought of a new trick to teach him later. As her mother offered home-made lemonade, she thought of the lime cocktails Frank had mentioned in his letters. She wondered how she could ever tell them of her Brazilian plans.

Her mother brought cheese and port. Jackie detected an acceleration in proceedings. Cheddar chunks were set on crackers and consumed before they were settled. Port glasses were left isolated on the bleached tablecloth. Father disappeared to help Mother with the washing-up – never known before. Jackie found herself in the living room with Edward. He stood ten feet from her, hands behind his back. He coughed, rouged and sank to one knee.

Jackie wanted to laugh and to throttle him. The melodrama of his action was accentuated by the distance between them. He reminded her of a man proposing up on a stage in some dreadful farce. But the black box he produced was not for some other reluctant heroine.

'Jacqueline,' he said with trembling lips, 'will you marry me?'

All was quiet in the house.

'Oh, Teddy,' she said. 'I simply can't, I'm sorry. You see – '

'Now wait a minute, young lady,' said her father, entering from the hall, followed, a little sheepishly, by her mother.

'I'm sorry,' Jackie said. 'But I just can't. Teddy, darling, don't you think you should have mentioned this – ?'

'Don't be so bloody silly,' said her father. 'Talk to her, Audrey, for goodness' sake...'

Audrey and Jackie looked at Edward – everything a father could wish for, a father like hers at least. Edward was still on one knee and didn't quite know what to do with his hands, now that the box had dropped to the carpet, and given that his only ever sweetheart was not about to be mantled in his arms. Jackie saw that her mother gazed upon Edward with the same eyes as herself: full of pity, but lacking even a grain of doubt. She felt heartened that her mother didn't want her to have this man, no matter how well his books balanced.

'I can't marry you, Teddy,' said Jackie, looking her father in the eyes. 'Because I've accepted a new position. In Rio de Janeiro.'

Across town Miriam told her parents about Frank's offer. Her mum wept into her bread and butter pudding. It was so far away; when would they ever see her? Miriam and her mum sobbed on the sofa and her dad made them tea. Miriam was to tell him every detail, he said. Of what the job consisted and where they would be living and how the arrangements were to be made. He said he'd talk to people he knew in the foreign service, from his days in the '50s in Hong Kong. He imagined Rio to be similar in many ways: a beautiful city by a bay, plenty of potential, an expat life. Men like Frank had put the Great in Britain by trading in places just like these. South America was the future. He would talk to Frank himself, make sure all the 't's were crossed. Play her cards right and Miriam could live in the lap of luxury. It had a ring to it: Mrs Miriam Duff. She'd fallen on her feet this time, no two ways about it. And if Jackie could tag along – so much the better. It was always good to have a friend at hand.

The friend was at hand sooner than expected. Within the hour he opened the door to find Jackie with a suitcase, a cut lip and mascara trailing down her cheeks.

A month or so later, in January 1963, Frank met them at Rio airport and a driver took them to their Ipanema flat, which was small but bright, on the third floor of a block, with a view of the sea if you craned your neck. It was hard to pick out the details of that first day in a city which became so familiar over the years. She remembered thinking how round and mossy the mountains looked, that she could feel the sun burning within minutes on her skin, that there were more trees than she'd expected in the streets and that the sea seemed to lurk round every corner. But the first night she would remember forever. Frank told them they were going to see a friend sing at a club, where Frank himself tickled the ivories every now and again. He mushed caipirinhas in their tiny kitchen as they put on short frocks and low heels, then, feeling distinctly tipsy, they walked away from the beach a few blocks until they emerged from a leafy street on to a road by the shores of a lake. Here and there the slopes of the mountains glittered with tiny lights, and beyond the water, illuminated on the point of a peak, stood the famous statue of Christ, looking away to the right.

To the left was a two-storey building with a neon sign which read 'A Gaiola'. They climbed narrow stairs, feeling a lift of anticipation as they brushed posters that told of a thousand shows, including the bill for that very night, headed by *O Rouxinol de Ipanema* – the Nightingale of Ipanema. A hostess greeted them with a 'Hi, Frankie!' and three kisses on his cheeks, then led them to a table at the front. Six feet away, in a spotlight on a low stage, stood a red velvet stool and a table upon which sat a thin glass of beer. Jackie watched the bubbles in the golden liquid rise as the room flowed with murmurs.

A hand reached out of the darkness and picked up the glass. The hand was dark and extended from a white cotton shirt. Onto the stool he slid, smiling with mouth closed unto the multitude, which hushed. From behind him came the clickety-click of a stick on hollow wood, then a few high notes were plucked on a mandolin. As a flute joined and swept the ensemble into a rhythm, the Nightingale showed the gap in his teeth and started to sing.

On Saturday morning, Nelson decided to get a better feel for the famous guitar, so he sat on the chair in the music room and played 'Aguas de Março' and a few of his own compositions. As he played he told himself it had not been the biggest lie to say this was the best guitar in Brazil. It was the finest Nelson had played, and he'd played many. There was no doubt Yemanjá was working on his case: first the donation of the guitar, then the appearance of her very incarnation at the Bar das Terezas. Nelson didn't believe in Fate – it was hard to have faith when it dealt you losing hands. But perhaps the cards were better this time. One minute Zemané is telling him to find someone; the next a woman in white swims into his life. It fitted together like sugar and limes.

Nelson took a cold shower, ate some papaya then watched the news. He thought about songs and wondered how many Americans would come. When his stomach persisted with its gurgles, he walked down to the restaurant and ordered *carne de sol* for the third time in four days. He watched the waitress wiggle through a beaded curtain into the kitchen. He heard the cook's low voice, her giggle and then silence. If Nelson ever ran a restaurant – it was possible, he thought, the way things were going – he would make certain there was no canoodling between cook and waitress. Even if Selma did prefer the cook to him, the dissemblance of possibility could have added magic to his lunchtimes. In his restaurant Nelson would ensure the waiters and waitresses never broke diners' spells.

There was a newspaper on a table again, and Nelson looked for more pieces about the hijacked bus. Man! – the police were taking a hiding, which made him slap the table in joy. There were allegations that the officers who'd strangled Sandro had tried to persuade the doctors to hide the cause of death. One report said they'd wanted to enter the morgue and fill the body with bullets. Someone had tampered with the wagon in which Sandro died, and there were now more bullets in the gun fired by the policeman who shot Geisa than when it was first seized. Nelson swigged his beer and read some of the letters. An ex-policeman said killing Sandro was in line with the thinking of the cop around the world: that he was born to kill the outlaw. Nelson couldn't speak for the rest of the world but it was hard to argue in Brazil: 289 killed by the cops last year in the state of Rio. The governor's view was that this showed they were beating crime – ridding the streets of undesirables, shooting the city clean. The governor was a one-man comedy show. At the very moment the hijack was taking place he was giving a speech about how violence and police brutality lived only in the imagination of journalists. Meanwhile thirty million Brazilians were watching this 'fiction' with their own eyes. The letters were full of anger and sadness. Solutions were proposed – a lady from Singapore argued for the death penalty. We already have it, *babaco*, thought Nelson. To counter the claims of incompetence, the police were already in action mode – there were blitzes on the buses, six hundred officers manning roadblocks, and already this week at least one man shot dead. Nelson asked himself how many people being searched would be black and how many white, and he knew the answer well enough, just as he knew the blitzes would cease once the memory of Sandro died, and that nothing would ever really change.

Nelson scraped the last sandy *farofa* from his plate and called for the bill. Selma appeared, unashamedly flushed. He searched his pockets but could only find a couple of notes, which covered the meal but left him with only coins.

As he stood to leave, Selma said, 'I almost forgot – your friend was looking for you.'

'*Beleza!*' said Nelson. 'My friend Yemanjá or my friend Cristo?'

'You shouldn't joke about them,' she said, 'they can see everything.'

'Even into the kitchen?'

'Ha, ha, ha,' said the waitress, rolling her pretty eyes.

'Was he a round man in a straw hat?' asked Nelson hopefully.

'More of a mountain in a Vasco shirt.'

'How lucky I am to have such caring friends.'

He scampered home. If they'd traced him to the restaurant it wouldn't be long before they found the house. That was the trouble with the gods – always giving with one hand and taking away with the other. Ours not to reason why, ours just to be mucked around. Fat Paulo said they were all the same: gods, politicians, women. But Nelson thought that was fuzzy thinking. Each god was weird in his or her own way, each politician was more corrupt than the next, and no two women were alike. Life for a spiritual, poor, single man was about as easy as making ice on Ipanema beach.

Nelson practised for a few more hours, expecting a knock on the door at any time. He laid down the guitar as darkness jumped on the city and lights flicked on across the panorama.

He stood at the window and wondered whether he'd ever stop running. Running, running, running – every day since Zila died and he and little Mariana moved into a shack in Chácara do Céu. Running from one job to another: shining the shoes of tooth-picking businessmen on the pavements of Centro; cleaning cars in a back-street in Catete; collecting tin cans in a rickety cart with a rhythmic squeak. The best job of all had been working as a delivery boy for a supermarket in the South Zone, wheeling trolleys home for rich people and unloading groceries on to cool tiled kitchen floors. Sometimes the Americans had given him a *refrigerante* – a Coke if he was lucky – and they would often tip far more than Brazilians. Some of the Americans who spoke Portuguese would try to engage him in conversation: 'Where do you live, *moço*? Do you live in a *favela*? Do you like soccer? Who's your favourite player? I hear that Zico guy is awesome.' Nelson lost that job owing to the theft of a bottle of cachaça, which the boys all knew had been stolen by a security guard.

Running faster still since Mariana died. Cities, towns, hills, shacks – until here he was on a Saturday evening in June of the new millennium, looking over a world he'd never stopped tearing round. There were only two ways out of the race: you won or you lost. No one could keep on going forever. Nelson wondered how close he was to the end.

He turned from the window and put the guitar in its welcoming case. He clapped his hands and did a little dance. Well, however close he was, there was no doubt it was going to be quite a night. Centre-stage in front of a crowd, playing an instrument he adored, singing songs of his choosing, amusing Americans with his anecdotes and taking their eagerly proffered dollars. If it was to be the finale – if Adolfo or Vasco did show up – then so be it. If he could choose a final night on earth, this would be the one.

Nelson watched the Flamengo game sitting on a big cushion. He drank a couple of bottles of beer, though they didn't taste quite as good as a freshly poured *chopp* at Bar do

Paulo. It felt odd to have neither mates with whom to yell at the players nor hands to slap when Tuta's goal went in, so Nelson leapt around slapping imaginary palms and laughing with fantasy friends, which did not feel half as strange as it must have looked. In fact, it was nice to have some space in which to roam, and he found he could be more flamboyant now there were no eyes to evaluate his moves. When Nelson had lived on the street, he'd often felt invisible to the world, but also that he had no privacy. The world watched him when it wanted to and ignored him when it didn't. With a place of his own a man could choose. Nelson saw Flamengo's victory as an omen and wondered which of the gods was in charge of football. He didn't think of Jesus as a football man – though, if he were, Nelson suspected he'd play like an Englishman: with rudimentary skill but prepared to be crucified for victory. Buddha would play like a Brazilian, since all the neutrals loved him and he never went out to do his brothers harm. As for the Devil, everyone knew he played for Argentina – a fact from which the Argentines no doubt drew great pride.

He changed into white cotton trousers and a white shirt he'd bought at a street market. Americans liked the look of a black man in white, as if it made him less of the animal they feared. Nelson checked the mirror to ensure his curls were in order, then skipped downstairs, scooped up the guitar and hit the street. It was a beautiful time of night, an hour when disappointment seemed impossible. As Nelson walked downwards, downwards, he felt he might break into a run at any moment. He walked round cobbled corners and down cracked flights of steps as the view of the city sank up to meet him, until he emerged behind the arches of Lapa, which already teemed with night fish. Chords and gentle beats floated though the crowds from open-windowed bars. Some youths stood hard-faced on corners; others snaked through the hordes holding hands. Nelson weaved through partygoers and pavement vendors, taking a final sniff of the night before he stepped through a door.

Inside, the manageress was setting out plastic chairs.

'One more minute and I'd have sacked your *bunda*,' she said.

The dawn woke Debbie and she couldn't sleep, so she sat at the breakfast bar of her new flat and looked out of the window across Marine Parade at the early light on the sea. Somewhere over there Joel was searching for his father. She wondered if he'd made any progress. She wondered if she'd ever look at the sea and think of someone else. Life is never simple, she thought. Isn't that its joy? You don't choose who you love, not if you own a properly functioning heart.

Still, they weren't together any more. They'd given it all they could over the years, that was what they'd said. It would be for the best, in the end. It was a good thing he was in Brazil – and very apt. At least it meant he couldn't walk through the door. She wished she could remove him from her thoughts, but nearly twenty years together had painted pretty well everything the colour of their relationship. There was little left from a time when life had just been hers.

Over in the corner, under the window, was a box containing some of his possessions, a few stray items she'd found among her own. He'd been meaning to pick it up. She'd been thinking of throwing it out. She knelt beside it and opened the lid. As she observed the artefacts an idea came to her and she laughed to herself: what's the harm? It won't solve anything, but it'll feel good. She selected a couple of dog-eared Brazilian novels, a few postcards and a sarong someone had bought for Joel on Ipanema beach. She considered picking out an old diary but thought better of it. She found a pair of Flamengo socks and a poster showing the *bonde* route through Santa Teresa. She took a can of lighter fluid from the kitchen and a wooden tray of Joel's she'd never really liked. 'These'll do,' she said aloud. 'No need to go overboard.'

She put the lot in a bin bag and strode across the road. She crunched across the pebbles to the edge of the sea, glad her flat was to the east of the pier where fewer people were likely to complain. She tipped the contents of the bag on to the tray, ripped the sarong in two, tore up a book and squirted lighter fluid liberally. She pushed the tray on to the waves and threw a match towards it. It missed, but a second one hit and flames started to wave from the low heap, until fragments floated over the water.

'Look, Mummy!' shouted a little girl.

'Cool!' said her mother, and lifted her daughter up to watch the pyre bob further from the shore.

Two small boys started to throw pebbles – ploop, plop – rocking the burning tray. A direct hit roused a cheer from passing students who joined in. Burning pages scattered, water shipped on board, until with the clatter of a boulder from on high the vessel capsized. The crowd applauded and Debbie took a bow.

Later she took a shower, spending time over her hair, washing it slowly as she steamed. She brushed it for a long time, dried it with care then did her make-up differently: darker eyes, wetter-looking lips. She curled her lashes and put on a dress she'd been eyeing in a shop for weeks which fitted like a garment easily cast off. She checked all angles in the mirror, knocked back a tequila shot, turned off the stereo, put on her silver shoes and left the house.

She met Emma at a cocktail bar – all smooth edges and chocolate-coloured sofas. They sipped flavoured martinis served in smoked glasses. Debbie knew they mixed a wicked caipirinha but decided it was not on her menu. Before she could stop herself she wondered what Joel was doing at that moment. Brazil was four hours behind. Getting ready to go out on the town, no doubt. In Rio de-bloody-Janeiro, the little sod.

They moved to a pub and drank a couple of pints. The male specimens looked weedy or vain or ragged around the edges, or seemed to have a desperate look in their eye. She shook her head when a smiling pair quizzically eyed the other half of their table. A balding man doused in sandalwood asked her if she wanted a drink.

'What do *you* reckon?' she said.

They knocked back a couple of tequila shots and talked about Emma's latest near miss with a relationship. The bloke she currently fancied was married. Debbie said she didn't understand how someone in love with someone – if they really were *in love* with someone – could sleep with somebody else. Perhaps because he was more in love with himself, she mused. Emma told her not to be naïve. Debbie said she certainly couldn't imagine doing it with any of these cretins, love or no love, and 'doing it' seemed about the most glamorous way to describe it. It would not be the stuff of poetry. Better to have lost in love than never to have loved at all? Debbie wondered if there was a pat proverb to shed light on loving someone who was unquestionably deranged but who still seemed better than any living alternative.

'Those chairs taken?' asked a bloke with pointy facial hair.

'No,' said Debbie.

'Mind if we – ?'

'Yes,' said Debbie.

She couldn't quite believe it when they scuttled off. What was wrong with a good old-fashioned pointless argument?

'You're not really in the swing of this, are you?' said Emma.

'Limbo is all very well as a dance,' said Debbie.

'Shall we move on?'

'I can't think of anywhere I'd like to go right now. If I see anyone enjoying themselves I might just punch them.'

'We could call it a night, if you like?' said Emma.

'How about Beachy Head?'

'Or there's always Casablanca's?'

'God, has it really come to that?' grinned Debbie.

'You know you love it,' Emma replied.

At Casablanca's, they drank pints of lager with Tuaca chasers. Debbie's limbs felt loose and her stomach warm.

They found a dancefloor and lurked at the fringe. What a bunch, thought Debbie. Everyone looked happy, though. The music was hardly cutting-edge, but in this state neither would be her moves. She laughed at the suggestion that they ever had been, eased into the flow of a summer disco tune, spun on her heel, pointed at Emma and they were off. Dance, dance, dance, she thought. She shimmied with strangers and was relieved that no one tried to grope her. The old legs were a bit wobbly, down there far away from her waggling head, but they seemed fairly under control. She managed to turn a couple of staggers into quasi-moves. She guessed most of the words to a '70s song she'd forgotten she even knew. They boogied until the club shut.

Outside, the crowd shrank as the final punters headed home. Debbie insisted they say goodnight to the sea.

'Come on, honey,' said Emma. 'Let's get you to bed.'

'Give me a minute,' slurred Debbie. 'The night's not quite over the hill just yet. Only in its thirties. Plenty of life in the girl.'

They meandered across the road and leant on the rail of the promenade. Stars shone. The sea was nearly calm; they could hear a gentle whoosh over the boom boom beat of the serious clubs under the arches below. They walked very carefully down some steps to the beach. Debbie led Emma over the pebbles towards the lap of the sea, where they sat for a while on Emma's denim jacket, fidgeting for comfort on the stones.

'A man overboard at night is a man dead,' said Debbie.

'I'll bear that in mind,' said Emma.

'You wouldn't catch me dead in the sea, even in the day,' said Debbie. 'Bloody fish.'

'What have you got against fish?'

'Slimy, never-blinking eyes, lurking.'

'If they don't close their eyes,' asked Emma, 'how do they sleep?'

'Maybe they gather under the pier, looking up at the stars and roosting starlings.'

'Darling starlings,' said Emma.

'Rio lies at 219 degrees from here,' said Debbie. She sat up a bit and pointed. 'That's that-a-way, to the layman.'

'Layman? There's a joke there somewhere,' chuckled Emma.

'He's in love with another – did I tell you?'

'Another what?'

'He's in love with a woman called Brazil,' slurred Debbie.

'He must be nuts.'

'If you crack another joke like that I might have to swim from this island myself.'

'Isle remember that,' said Emma.

'I don't suppose he's sparing me a moment's thought.'

'That's OK, because we're not thinking about him, either.'

'I like your thinking,' said Debbie.

'I think we should go home.'

'I think you're right.'

At ten o'clock in the evening Joel and Liam took a cab to Copacabana. They buzzed at the gate of Eva's block. She took a few minutes to emerge.

'Sorry, sorry, sorry,' she said. 'How do I look?'

'Fit for any president,' said Liam and kissed her twice on the cheeks.

'Are we sure about black?' asked Eva, twirling. 'I didn't feel like white tonight. I'm not so pure – I have hidden treasures, riddles, *mystique*.'

Soon the taxi was skirting the curve of Botafogo beach. Sugarloaf stood plump and pointy across the water, crowned with half-lit buildings, its cable necklace dangling. The lights of yachts scribbled squiggles on the bay. The taxi sped between the low trees of Flamengo park, where in the shadows at the edges of the road, on the grass beneath low trees, children huddled under blankets, their eyes catching the light like cats.

Joel wondered if his father searched for somewhere to sleep at night or whether he had a place to stay.

The taxi slowed as the arches of the viaduct appeared and suddenly the world outside whirled. Young black men and women flowed in all directions, their limbs brushing the car as it drew to a halt. Stepping out, Joel saw the kerb was crowded with vendors, squatting with stoves or baskets of food, others standing with sizzling carts or dispensing drinks in plastic cups. The air was thick with a rhythm of beats from bars overlaid with vendors' cries, and smelled of smoke from stalls and the perfume of passing girls. Joel wanted to dive into the crowd, trailing his hands to touch all things Brazilian. Liam looked nervous and waited for Eva to swing her legs from the car and Joel saw that sharp eyes flicked to him, as Liam's eyes sought to look at nothing.

'Let's go!' said Eva, and Liam followed her into the mêlée, as Joel strode behind, his eyes ranging, until they darted through a simple door. They bought handwritten tickets stamped with the image of a mandolin, then brushed through a gap in curtains to a room laid out with chairs in which a man in white was tuning up with a group of musicians. A smiling woman in a linen suit pointed to their plastic seats.

The man in white sat on a low stage only feet from their place in the front row. He dished out smiles and nods to the audience as they settled into their chairs, and he chatted with the other musicians: a bald guy on mandolin, a plump woman on flute, a young guy in a singlet on percussion – *cuíca* drum and *agogô* – and there was a grey-haired man with a tambourine and an accordion at his feet. To the tic-tac, tic-tic of a stick on wood they slid into a rhythm, heads moving in time, elastically bound. They played a *chorinho* tune, whose plucked notes fell from the strings of a mandolin as the sad voice of the guitarist belied his happy eyes. What perfect seats they had, Joel thought, since between songs the singer seemed to address his anecdotes almost entirely to the three of them. He rambled through topics from religion to Flamengo – via a brief discourse on ants – and the audience were warm to his words, though eventually the linen-suited lady ran a finger across her throat. The band swung into the ebb and flow of a *forró* tune, which Joel recognised as 'Esperando na Janela'.

'Debbie was mad about this tune,' Joel said merrily. 'I played it to her once and then she was always putting it on.'

'Can you dance *forró*, Joelinho?' Eva said.

'Very badly,' said Joel.

'Come on,' said Eva. 'I'll teach you. Then you can wow her when you get home.'

'Right now, I don't think she'd take kindly to me treading on her toes.'

'Better the right man all over your toes than the wrong man waltzing you off your feet,' said Eva, catching Liam's eye.

'Now you mention it,' Joel said, 'I'd been meaning to ask – do you know where I can get a snow globe in Rio? She likes to throw them at my head.'

'Where I come from that's an act of love,' said Eva.

She rose and they pushed a space between the chairs.

'Like this,' she said. 'One two, one two, to the side, that's right...'

'How about you, Eva – I hear you're on the lookout for a president?'

'There is a serious lack. One would think a bar like this – not too authentic, not too inauthentic – would be heaving with presidents big and small and in between. The problem with presidents – and I tell myself this time and again but I never listen – is they don't like dancing. A president can't afford to make a fool of himself, and you can't dance unless you can be a fool. I know, I know – how can I even think of falling in love with a man who doesn't dance? I confess – it's a problem, there's no way round it. But I think that with a little love dancing feet can be put on the legs of any man.'

Another song started. Joel and Eva danced closer to the stage. Though Joel was pleased he'd managed to grasp the basics, it was a joy to watch locals flex more elaborate routines. The music came to a halt and the band started to rise. The singer grinned and hopped from the stage.

'May I trouble you?' he said to Eva in Portuguese.

'Of course, my friend. You play like an angel!'

'Thank you, my goddess,' Nelson replied with a little bow.

'If I were really a goddess, I'd have a president on my arm and a full glass in my hand. Nothing else would I change tonight, even with divine powers – though I might arrange for these boys to have their hearts a little fuller. So many bad men in the world, and these two good ones going to waste. Joel here even *has* a goddess back at home, he's just not been very good at worshipping, so she's sent him to Purgatory for a while.'

'If this is Purgatory, I'll take it,' said Joel.

'I guess we aren't too far from heaven or hell,' said Nelson. 'Both are just around the corner in the Marvellous City.'

'Well in the absence of any angels bearing drinks,' said Eva, 'we'll have to go the the bar ourselves. Besides, we need to soak a little rhythm into those English legs. Come on, Liaminho, it's your round.'

Eva and Liam headed for the bar. Joel and the singer stood for a moment, then the singer clapped a hand on Joel's back in a half embrace and asked him in Portuguese, 'What's your name, brother? Mine is Nelson.'

'Joel,' he replied.

'*Americano?*'

'English,' said Joel, in Portuguese.

'You speak pretty well for an English guy.'

'Maybe not so good for a kid who grew up in Ipanema.'

'In Ipanema? *Que legal!*' said Nelson. 'A brother Carioca.'

'I aim to be by the time I leave in a couple of weeks, that's for sure. Just twenty-five years of catching up to do.'

'Where better to have twenty-five years of fun in a fortnight?'

'I'll drink to that!' said Joel, and drained his glass.

'So are you back to visit old friends, the family, your lover, the goddess...?'

'Eva?' laughed Joel. 'No, as a matter of fact, I'm here to track down my father.'

'It's always good to look out for your family,' Nelson said, and patted Joel on the shoulder again.

'I've waited half my life to hear music like this,' said Joel. 'Do you play here every night?'

'I would if she let me,' said Nelson, nodding towards the manageress. 'Listen, if you like the music, maybe I could put on a show one night. I wouldn't ask for much – '

'Two caipirinhas!' said Eva, handing a tumbler to Joel, and another to Nelson.

Nelson grinned and they all chinked classes and said, '*Saude,*' but the manageress was mouthing to him now, so he stuck a little thumb up to them, thanked them for the drink, and went to speak to her. Joel watched Nelson circulate, though he didn't stop to talk to any of the others, and Joel wondered if the attentiveness of the singer came as part of their prime pitch in the middle of the floor. It was a shame he'd moved on. Joel liked the sound of a private show – or was it one of those tourist scams you were meant to avoid, even though it sounded like you'd be missing out?

'So tell me, Joel,' said Eva, 'what are you doing about your father?'

'Well, we've been back to Jardim Botânico, asked around, put posters up. I guess we'll hit the streets again tomorrow, stop by the old flat in case anyone in the block knows him – '

'Listen, Joelinho, I have a friend at a ministry. I can ask if she can find some record of your father. But you have to promise me you'll be careful – you can't go wandering the streets like locals, darling – listen to your aunt Eva and don't be a hard-head.'

'I promise – though it's a bit easier for me than for Liam – at least I look Brazilian.'

'A bit Brazilian, not a lot Brazilian, *querido.*'

'Wait till you see me in a Flamengo shirt.'

'I can tell you're a *gringo* from twenty kilometres!' Eva said.

'Now you're exaggerating,' laughed Joel.

'I could tell blindfold!'

They drank and danced, more and more, as the music slowly quickened. The room became crammed, the chairs scattered, as into the early hours the band played on. Joel and Liam danced *forró* with Eva and friends of hers and strangers. The world became a whirl of staggers and steps, while Nelson sat above on the stage, his eyes seeming to follow their moves. Until finally even Nelson was on his feet and dancing as the band slammed off the night with a quickening version of 'Aquarela do Brasil', the chorus of which was chanted by everyone – '*Brasil! Pra Mim, Pra Mim, Brasil!*' – until long after the band had laid down their instruments and bowed a final time.

When the chanting finally stopped and the public started to slip away, Nelson tried to speak to Eva again, but the manageress collared him to stack up chairs. Joel led Liam and Eva out of the bar and they roamed the streets for a while, squeezing through the crowds, their blood racing too fast to quit just yet. Liam felt bolder now that he was full of cachaça, and Joel felt more Brazilian too, which was an odd thought, he realised, since he *was* Brazilian, and he couldn't help but wonder where he'd be that same night if he'd never left the country of his birth. So he studied the locals for a while and imagined he was them, until it seemed this was a drunken line of thought. Perhaps I'd be singing in a bar like Nelson, Joel thought, though why the geography of his upbringing should effect miracles on his vocal cords he couldn't explain. In the end they all tired, so, pausing to watch one more song from a band playing at a table on a pavement, they headed for a taxi rank and took a cab home.

Five

On Sunday morning, Nelson played guitar in front of the blazing windows, but his mind wouldn't settle on a tune. There had to be a way to earn some real money. He'd made ninety-eight *reais* from his fee and tips, which wasn't bad, though hardly enough to change his fortunes. A couple of gigs a week might keep the rumbles from his belly, but there was no chance of earning enough to sate Adolfo. The foreigners are the ticket, he thought. Yemanjá has led them to me. It's just a question of making the right moves.

He thought about the moment the goddess arrived at the gig, just as the chairs were starting to fill, slipping through the curtains with her two male sidekicks. The brown one – Joel – was a riddle. He looked so like a Carioca but his shirt screamed '*gringo*' and he walked with glue in his legs. Joel and Eva didn't seem to know each other well, and yet sometimes they left the pink man looking as lonely as a fish in a bucket. More to the point, Joel had sounded interested in meeting up, which might have served the double purpose of earning Nelson some money and securing him more goddess time, had opportunities not been thwarted by the manageress.

Nelson had been saddened to see the goddess in black, though perhaps it meant there were games to be played – and what was the point if there weren't a few of those? Eva, she was called. She had looked far too little at Nelson and far too much at the other members of the band – who were excellent musicians but not romantic prospects for a deity. Nelson had done his best to grab her attention in the gaps between songs: talking about his love for Yemanjá; touching on the triumph of good over evil – as exemplified by Flamengo's victory; stressing the importance of sticking to a straight path – like the truest racing ant. Eva had seemed more intent on conversations with the foreigners, so Nelson had moved closer to the edge – and heard her talk about the president, Nelson thought, so he hoped he wasn't falling for a politician. He wanted action as well as talk from his lover, and only as many lies as were reasonable.

He also remembered Joel saying he was hunting for his father, though it wasn't clear what his father had done. From what he'd been able to overhear as he passed by, it had something to do with poor Sandro, and Joel had put Wanted posters up around Jardim Botânico. Nelson couldn't help but hope his father got away. But then again... if Joel wanted to search for his dad, maybe Nelson could be his eyes – and earn a few *reais*. Nelson might even find him – with Yemanjá guiding his every move, there had to be a chance. The posters were the key: with a little more information he was certain he could spin a simple plan.

He left the house, skipped down the street and jumped on to a tram as it slowed to take a bend. He walked through Centro, down Sunday streets of offices with frozen windows, past banks and dormant sandwich bars. He passed the church of Candelária and thought about Sandro and the massacre on those steps. What kind of a life had that boy led? To live in the shadows of the streets, with half the people ignoring you and the rest wishing you didn't exist. On a radio show that morning, the callers had been burning Sandro: he was just another drugged-up *marginal*, a criminal who got what he deserved. Of course, it was tragic to have seen his mother's head severed before his eyes, the callers said, but these kids have choices just like all of us. They don't have to live on the street and not all of them end up killing pregnant women. Look at João X and José Y, the office boys in our company – born in the gutter but making a living the honest way, not like those rats with knives down in Copacabana. It annoyed Nelson to hear them equate street kids with drug gang members, *favela* inhabitants with criminals, as if they were one and the same. And Nelson asked himself: if a child of seven must live on the street, who's the criminal? He walked faster and faster, chasing thoughts of his sister from his head because now was not the time to be coming to a boil.

He boarded a bus at Praça Mauá. He noticed the driver's gaze lingering on the eyes of arriving passengers. Every man and woman on every bus was wondering if it could happen to them this time, and they studied the others a bit more closely than before. There was something good about that, Nelson thought. Through half-closed eyelids, he viewed the bay, parks with thick green leaves, shops and apartment blocks. Women in long T-shirts walked dogs; men with bare chests begged for change. A bus wasn't a bad place to spend part of the day, he thought, going round and round the city catching episodes. Nelson dreamed himself into the lives of beautiful passers-by until his eyes closed, and when he awoke he found the bus was quivering to a halt near the Jockey Club. He jumped off. Nearby, rich kids and red-faced foreigners stood on the pavements and in the road, drinking beer and admiring one another. Nelson considered blending with this gallery but, though he was sure to be bought a few drinks for his oh-so-zany-Brazilian act, he needed money not beer, and the idea forming required his full attention. He imagined Zemané pointing a stubby cigar at him, pressing the merits of careful planning. Zemané said he had a map of the future in his mind and often strolled around the remaining years of his life – no doubt in cayman-skin loafers. Nelson had trouble imagining much beyond tomorrow, but for the first time in a while a plan was taking shape.

Nelson strolled alongside the Botanical Gardens until the road ran past the Parque Lage and he found the junction where the hijacked bus had stopped. He crossed and looked at the shrine to Geisa, which made him think of his little sister Mariana again, so he snatched his mind from melancholy thoughts and hunted around for one of Joel's posters. Sure enough, taped to a tree a few yards down the road was a piece of paper, which read:

Son seeks long-lost father – Gilberto Cabral

REWARD OFFERED

If you have seen this man *please* call
Ask for Joel Cabral

Thanks

What was the *right* thing to do? He could feel his aunt Zila watching and knew he shouldn't really just take Joel for a ride. But he thought of what Zemané might say – 'When I have a need and you have a need, that's business' – and besides, how could Joel hope to find a father in a city like this when he couldn't look in half the places one might live?

The sun was smarting on his skin and his stomach was starting to complain. He entered a phone box, slipped a coin into the slot and dialled. A foreign voice came on the line.

'Hello? Um – *bom dia?*'

'Joel Cabral?'

'One moment! I'll get him.'

Nelson heard a foreign man call, 'JOEL! For you, quick!'

A new voice said, '*Alô?*'

'Joel Cabral?' repeated Nelson.

'*Sim!*' said Joel.

'I'm calling about your poster,' said Nelson in Portuguese.

'That's what I was hoping!'

'The man in the picture? I think I might know where to find him.'

'You're joking! That's amazing! Have you seen him, then? Do you know him? Is he all right – ?'

'The business is the following: I know a place where they cook for the gods. Buy me lunch and I'll tell you everything.'

'It's a deal... but listen, can you tell me a bit more? I mean, how come you – ?'

'All in good time, brother... How are you fixed for today?'

'Today is good, very good.'

'Largo dos Guimarães, Santa Teresa. You know where that is?'

'Sure.'

'Wait on the corner by the tram stop, around one o'clock.'

'How will I know you?'

'I'll know you,' said Nelson.

Nelson hung up, walked to the square, found an empty table outside a bar and ordered a beer. Time for one, he thought, to rouse persuasive spirits. He watched happy youngsters tucking into *feijoada* stew while their foreign friends picked out the bits they didn't fancy. His stomach, roused by the beer, could smell the black beans. In a little while we'll eat like kings, he told it. As he savoured the cold liquid Nelson mulled over the main wrinkle in his plan: the issue of coincidence. Was it absurd that one day he should be playing guitar in front of Joel and the next should happen, purely by chance, to see his poster? On the face of it, yes. But coincidences made the world go round – if the lucky Earth hadn't chanced across a ball of fire, people wouldn't be bumping into each other at all. He wasn't sure Joel would believe his innocence and he was almost certain Eva wouldn't, but it had to be worth a try.

He finished his beer, ordered another for the sake of harmony – one was a lonely number – realised he'd better hurry up, drained the glass, paid, ran to a bus on the point of closing its doors, boarded and sailed across town.

Debbie lay flat on her back with her head lolling to the side and concentrated on a small tear in the curtain which was allowing a ray of light into the room. It had not been many minutes since fixing her vision on that spot, and that spot alone, had been the only way to fend off spinning nausea, and she still felt an attachment to that ray of light, so she resolved to keep her eyes on the tear for a little longer.

Her mouth tasted of chewed cigarettes and Tuaca. She wondered what Joel and Liam had got up to last night and hoped they were feeling similarly afflicted. Two single boys in South America. She and Joel might no longer be together, but she hoped he'd consider how she might feel. Thinking of him now, as she lay there sick and low, she felt blind and without rights. Twenty years must surely leave a legacy; she hoped he'd act accordingly. Liam was pretty together now. They had plenty of friends who still burned the oil like a well on fire, and others whom mid-life angst had panicked into setting themselves alight. But Liam was far too sorted these days to feel any obligation to lead Joel astray. She and Joel had joked, only the other week, that Liam's progression was a kind of microcosm of the ascent of man: from banging bits of iron against trees to working for a corporation in Rio de Janeiro. None of his friends knew what he did, and he said it was too dull to explain, but they seemed to pay him for whatever it was and the present gig was particularly good: living in Ipanema, all expenses paid.

Even in her current state, she had to acknowledge she liked Liam, on the whole. There was a bond between them, a kind of equal opposition and attraction that held them at a comfortable distance, a connection maintained by a combination of affection and suspicion that went with loving the same person from a different vantage point. They'd spoken about it on various drunken nights. She couldn't think of a better best mate for Joel, and yet Liam had got Joel into a lot of trouble in his time. Liam had told her he couldn't imagine Joel with anyone else, but that sometimes the ways in which she'd tried to shape Joel had annoyed him. Fortunately, Liam hadn't managed to kill Joel and Debbie hadn't managed to change him much at all, so they were both pretty happy in the end. She knew Liam would be equally worried about the current predicament – much had been spoken and unspoken on that subject over the years – and she felt pretty sure he'd be keeping a close eye on Joel. If she couldn't be there, it was the next best thing.

Debbie reached over the edge of her bed, grabbed a magazine, rolled it into a tube – all without moving her eyes from the tear in the curtain – and lashed out at a fly that had just stopped buzzing around the room and settled on the wall. Then she used the magazine to fan herself a few times, hoping it might change things for the better, which it didn't. She dropped the magazine on the floor. The fly took to the air again. It was going to be one of those days.

'Let me speak to him!' said Eva.

Liam put down the phone and fetched Joel from his room, where he was was trying to look as Brazilian as he could. He'd bought a bead necklace at the hippy fair in Praça General Osório, which he wore with his Flamengo shirt, long board shorts, flip-flops and a pair of wraparound shades.

'How do I look?'

'Like you're trying a bit too hard,' said Liam.

Joel removed the sunglasses.

'Eva's on the phone,' said Liam. 'Wants to talk you out of it.'

Joel picked up. 'Eva, listen – '

'Go,' she said. 'Go and meet this *marginal* you know nothing about. Let him take you down an alley and shoot you!'

'Look, I'll be careful, but what can – '

'I bet he's not even *seen* your father. *Nossa!* Just make sure he kills you today so I don't have to worry when it's going to happen.'

95

'We're just having lunch. I'll be careful, I swear. I'm going to listen to what he has to say, that's all. No alleys, I promise.'

'But you don't know anything about him. You didn't even ask his name, who he is, what he does, why he is wandering about the place looking at posters then wanting to meet you in Santa Teresa – one minute he is by the lake, then he is in the hills – it doesn't make any sense, *querido*.'

'Maybe my dad is in Santa Teresa. I pay this guy a few *reais* and he takes me to him...'

'Joel, *I* can help you, like I said. I *know* people – maybe not presidents, but we can find him without lunches with *malandros* in parts of town you don't know – '

'It's Santa Teresa in broad daylight, not Rocinha.'

'A gun doesn't care what part of town it's in, not in this city, my friend.'

'I really don't think he's going to shoot me, Eva.'

'Well, however he does it, I just hope he makes it quick!'

Joel took a cab to Carioca station and caught a tram. As the yellow tramcar reached the end of the arches and started to climb, three black kids sprinted along then jumped up and clung on to the side. Joel almost leapt from his seat, expecting some kind of assault, but the kids just hung on as the car took the twists of the roads. Soon the tram was running over cobbles high above the city. A few shops and cafés appeared on the right, the kids jumped running into the road behind and the car drew to a halt. Joel stepped down and stood at the stop. A few people ambled by but no one seemed to be waiting. Joel wondered from which direction the caller would come or if he was already watching. His eyes followed a couple of men as they walked along the road but they continued on their way. He looked at windows and doorways. He looked up and down the tram lines, feigning waiting for a tram. Joel thought of Eva's comments about him looking foreign, and wondered if it was true that the locals could see he wasn't one of them. It occurred to him that the harder he tried to look natural, the less natural he'd look. So he tried not to try, which he suspected would make things even worse.

Nelson saw Joel on the corner. He was standing with his hands in his pockets looking like a man who was trying not to look as if he was waiting. His body was still, but his eyes shot this way and that. Nelson looked at Joel and wondered what kind of deal he might be able to cut. He hadn't really thought about figures.

'Think of a price and treble it,' Zemané would say.

He could see Joel moving from foot to foot now, his eyes roving. He suspected Zemané would eat a man like Joel alive. Nelson walked slowly closer and stood on the pavement opposite him. Joel's eyes settled upon him and Nelson grinned at Joel and crossed the road.

Joel watched a man approaching. As he came closer, Joel thought he recognised him. It looked a lot like the singer from the bar. What a coincidence! Joel felt a tiny bit pleased but also a rush of irritation: now was precisely not the time to be making friends. What if Nelson's presence scared the caller away?

'Joel?' said Nelson, taking Joel's hand and patting him on the back.

'Nelson?'

'What a coincidence!'

'Great to see you!' said Joel, trying to ensure his eyes were attentive, at the same time as glancing round. 'Look, I'd love to talk but – I feel really bad about this – I'm meeting someone, right now, and it's really important... do you have a number, or...'

'Hey – I'm meeting someone too – isn't that weird? I saw this Wanted poster when I was hanging out in my old neighbourhood. Turns out – '

'Wait a minute – you've come to meet a guy about a poster?'

'Sure.'

'It's *my* poster.'

'You've got to be kidding!'

'This is incredible...'

'Now that really is a coincidence!' said Nelson. 'You see me play... I see your poster!'

'Coincidence isn't even close.'

'There's magic on every block of the Marvellous City,' Nelson replied with a smile.

Sometimes Joel had the feeling life possessed a will of its own. He far preferred it when it followed his own plans. Events sold as Fate were usually pure coincidence, but happenings sold as coincidence were mostly nothing of the sort. The trouble was, he couldn't discount the possibility that he wasn't being taken for a ride. At least they were going to sit down – weren't they? – in a place full of people. Nelson could hardly shoot him over lunch. He would sit, listen and try to work out the angles. If he didn't believe the story Nelson told, he'd tell him to get lost.

'OK, so what's the plan?' Joel asked.

'Let's go and eat and I'll tell you what I know.'

They walked down the street and through swing doors into a restaurant with checked tablecloths and photographs of footballers on the walls. The tables were full of brown locals and foreigners slowly devouring cod balls or chicken *à passarinho* or sucking drinks through straws. A radio played *forró*. A waitress wiggled through a beaded curtain and showed them to a table.

'You again, *malandro*!' said Selma, though she said it with a girlish smile and kissed Nelson three times on the cheeks instead of two. Nelson was sure her trousers were tighter than he remembered.

'Chef not in today?' said Nelson.

'New chef,' she said.

'Not up to the job?' said Nelson with a wink.

'Boss caught him being over-familiar with a waitress,' said Selma.

'You must have been upset?'

'The bitch was sacked too,' she said and touched his forearm softly.

Joel looked at the menu and thought about Nelson. He was thrilled to see the names of forgotten dishes, and pleased to find he understood most of the words. But it was hard to concentrate on choosing when he was trying to judge if Nelson was taking him for a ride. Joel hadn't the first idea what kind of person he might be – he was written in a language Joel didn't completely grasp. In Britain he liked to think he could look after himself: he and Liam had been in some dives in their time, and he reckoned he could sense a dangerous man the minute he walked in. Joel had watched dozens of films about Brazil, but he knew next to nothing about the real world of the *favela* or the street. Nelson played guitar and smiled a lot; he was friendly, but it was impossible to guess his thoughts. The coincidence was great... but could he believe Nelson was simply here to fleece him? Perhaps he didn't want to believe it.

Nelson looked at Joel and thought about the menu. He wanted everything but knew it was better not to show he was hungry. If he thinks I eat like a king each day then maybe he'll pay me like one, Nelson thought.

'What would you recommend?' said Joel.

'It's all good,' said Nelson. 'I'll have whatever you're having.'

'Are you hungry?'

'No more than usual.'

'I could eat a horse,' said Joel.

'We don't eat a lot of horse round here but there's always the *carne de sol*,' said Nelson, chiding himself for showing his desire.

'Let's have two of those, with a caipirinha on the side.'

Joel waved Selma over and ordered. When she left them alone again, Joel asked, 'So, what's the story?'

'The business is the following,' said Nelson. 'I am not a hundred per cent certain I know where your father is. I don't

99

know him exactly. But, from what I can tell from the pictures – and you've got to admit they're not the very best – he looks like a guy I used to see around.'

'And what's the deal?'

'Buy me lunch,' he said. 'Pay me to find him.'

'I'm happy to talk about money,' said Joel. 'But please don't lie to me. I've been hoping to find him for twenty-five years, so I could do without being given the runaround.'

Nelson nodded. That was the problem: how to string him along without at least a couple of lies? He supposed it depended a bit on definition – after all, Nelson did know the kind of places a man like that might roam, and he *might* even have seen Gilberto somewhere, he couldn't swear he hadn't – and if he couldn't swear he hadn't, surely it wasn't an utter lie to say he thought he had?

'If I don't find him, you stop paying,' said Nelson.

'How much do you want?'

'Say... one hundred and fifty *reais* a day?'

'That seems a bit steep,' Joel said. 'Where are you going to look?'

'I'm going to start in Cantagalo.'

'The *favela* by Ipanema?'

'Right.'

'That's where you saw him?'

'Where I might have seen him.'

Cantagalo made some sense, Joel thought: it was the nearest *favela* to their old flat. Perhaps it was the natural refuge of an Ipanema man fallen on hard times. Only the day before, he'd been standing on Liam's roof looking towards the very place. It was hard not to wonder if his dad had been gazing back. Joel thought about the money: fifty quid a day. Nelson seemed so loose in the movement of his limbs, so bright in the engagement of his eyes, that Joel found it hard to be certain he had an agenda, though he surely did – the coincidence was just too great. It was a lot of money, but maybe it was worth it for a couple of days – as long as there were results. It wasn't going to bankrupt him, and in the meantime he could take up Eva's offer too.

Nelson wondered if it was easier to lie to foreigners than Brazilians. Cantagalo had been a flash of inspiration. Nelson had never actually been there, but its location would make it easier to meet Joel without having to run all over the city. He could still look for the missing father where he chose, but it was better to put somewhere in Joel's mind as the searching ground. Nelson suspected he was the type to ask lots of questions and be picky about the answers. He didn't really plan to go to Cantagalo – whoever ran that hill might not appreciate a stranger turning up with a photo asking questions. But since Joel wouldn't be able to go there either, it didn't matter much.

'OK,' said Joel. 'A hundred and fifty.'

'*Beleza!*' Nelson said.

'But I come with you.'

'We'll never find him if you do.'

'What difference does it make?'

'A stranger asking questions in a place like that can only be a cop.'

'Even if I'm with you?'

'They'd probably shoot me too,' said Nelson.

Joel smiled at Nelson and took out his wallet. 'OK. Half now, half tomorrow night,' he said. 'Let's see what you've managed to find out. But if I'm not happy then, we'll call it quits.'

'OK,' said Nelson. 'A hundred and fifty now, and a hundred and fifty tomorrow.'

'Wait a minute, I make it seventy-five?'

'You're forgetting today, *cara*. The meter's already running.'

Joel paused for a second before counting out the money.

'No progress, no more cash,' he said as he handed the bills to Nelson.

'Be tranquil, my brother,' said Nelson. 'I might even bring your father tomorrow night.'

'I'll drink to that,' said Joel, raising his glass. 'So where shall we meet?'

'How about Porcão? The one in Ipanema, nine o'clock.'

'OK. Sounds good.'

The two men observed each other. Joel wondered if he'd ever see Nelson again, though he supposed he might be able to trace him through the bar where they'd seen him sing. If he didn't show up at Porcão there wasn't a lot of point. Nelson looked at Joel and wondered if he'd ever see another *real* of his money. How could he show progress when he was more likely to find a polar bear in Copacabana? Especially if Joel's father didn't want to be found.

'So why do you want to find him, anyway?' asked Nelson.

'I'm sorry?'

'What did he do?'

'Do?'

'He must have done something or you wouldn't be after him.'

'He died,' said Joel. 'At least I thought he had, until – '

'Bummer,' said Nelson. 'My mother died and my aunt died – and then my sister too, that was the worst.'

'I'm sorry to hear that,' said Joel.

'Do you have a sister?'

'I'm an only child.'

'Well, I guess you can't have everything,' said Nelson. 'You never had a sister and I never had a father. We might not have a full team but we still have to play ball.'

They finished their food and ordered *cafezinhos*. Joel asked Nelson how he learnt to play guitar and Nelson told him about the one Zila saved to buy. And Joel understood most of the story Nelson told, if not every word, and he hoped that as days went by he'd come to understand everything he said.

Nelson wanted to tell Joel that Adolfo had taken the very guitar Zila bought for him, but he wasn't sure where the story might end, and feared he'd tell Joel about the house, the Spanish guitar and the money from the fat man's trousers – because, once Nelson started, he sometimes couldn't stop. It felt strange to be keeping so many secrets, even from a stranger like Joel, but he suspected that if he said too much he'd wind up on the poor end of the deal.

'Keep your eyes awake and your mouth asleep,' Zemané had told him once. 'The loser always talks the most.'

They left the restaurant and stood awkwardly by the tram stop. Nelson patted Joel on the back, grasped his hand and said, 'See you tomorrow,' then walked up the hill and round the corner. Joel caught the tram to Centro where he took a taxi. He sat in the back with his head leaning against the glass, listening to a Chico Buarque song on the radio, watching sights slide by as he thought about Nelson's question. He's my father, he said to himself, of course I want to find him.

Jackie took a taxi to Tony's. She wore a red dress with a plunging top and a rearing bottom, new heels and tiger-print knickers. She wondered if he'd made an effort. How did a man of his ilk ready himself for a date? She imagined him lathering his face with a badger-hair brush, running a black comb he'd owned since childhood through his hair, ironing a stripy shirt in his socks and Y-fronts. She wondered if he wished his wife were still alive to iron for him. He wouldn't look in the mirror to see if he looked all right, nor fret over whether the shirt he'd chosen would find favour. He'd just prepare himself the way he always had, in a manner he deemed proper, without any fuss.

She had all but given up on men of Tony's age. The embers barely glowed in most of them. Many liked the idea of sex, but not the reality. They made a good enough fist of it in the early stages but, as soon as there was a semblance of a relationship, out came the slippers. Jackie might have written off Tony too, had he not been quite so beautiful – it was the only word for him. She felt challenged to prove that an animal lurked inside even such a preposterously decent man. The second time she'd been to his house in Hove, he'd been planting a row of runner beans. He'd wanted to stop, change into something smarter and take her to 'a wonderful French place he knew', but she'd insisted he carry on, and sat in a deckchair while he pushed tools into the earth. She'd poured him caipirinhas from a Thermos flask, which they'd drunk from crystal glasses as she admired his brown arms and clinging gardening slacks.

For three dates he'd failed to lay a finger. The anticipation might have been something to relish, had she been surer there was anything to anticipate. She wasn't going to jump on him: she didn't mind taking charge once they were off, but she wanted him to do her the honour of a first move. Then, on their last rendezvous, the day she'd fled the wretched video clip, as they were walking along the seafront past Hove Lawns, Tony had placed his hand on the very small of her back and pressed, all without so much as a flicker in his lips, as he talked of tickets he'd bought for a Stoppard play. Then he'd slid his hand across her back and smoothly into her palm – as if he had been doing the same for aeons. The plunge was close.

As the taxi crawled through traffic, Jackie thought of Joel and hoped he was being careful, of course, but taking time to have fun, no matter why he was there. He knew how to enjoy himself, that was for certain, and she couldn't think of any greater blessing. There could hardly be a better place than Rio for that, and what was the sense in going there only to think about the past?

Jackie tried not to think about Gilberto but, Joel's mission aside, she was going on a date – and she always found it impossible to think about a new lover without old lovers posing questions. The most awkward ones were set by thoughts of the good times with Gilberto. She couldn't kid herself such times had never existed, but how much easier if they could be forgotten. It was hard to live with the fact that her life was so defined by him, someone she'd known so many years ago, a person with such significance that he'd split her life into Before and After. When she thought of it like this, she sometimes wondered upon which instant the irrevocable change in her life had found its pivot. Hours before she had first seen Gilberto at A Gaiola, sitting with Miriam on a plane to Brazil, there had been no possibility of a connection between Gilberto and herself. Later that night, as she'd lain in his bed, there could never again be any doubt of one. When had it swivelled? Had it started the moment he opened his mouth to sing 'A Quiet Night of Quiet Stars'? Had it been the second their eyes first met? Joel liked to joke that it was when she first saw his teeth. Initially he'd appeared to be singing to everyone and no one, as he gazed into the sea of the crowd, but gradually his vision had seemed to focus closer and closer to Jackie – until his songs became their songs, until even when he moved his eyes to others, for the sake of politeness if nothing else, she could not take her eyes from him. She would swear it was certainly sealed before he stepped down from the stage and Frank presented them to one another.

They had kissed cheeks and she'd moved her lips closer to his than she would normally have done. Later that night in his room she'd put these same questions to him as she tapped the rhythm of 'Love Me Do' on his smooth brown chest with bright pink fingernails.

'It didn't start tonight at all,' Gilberto had replied. 'We've always been connected, like two fishes on the same piece of line. We just needed to reel each other in, my angel fish.'

The next day he'd surprised her by turning up in his starched white tunic to take her walking along the seafront in the sun, where he was the subject of admiring glances from many a local woman, making Jackie feel the luckiest girl in the Latin world. He was a dentist by day and a singer by night, a cocktail of light and dark. He was the first man she didn't have to guide, the first to give her more pleasure than she knew how to give herself. It made her skin crawl to think of the limpness of English men with their clattering rock and roll, their skinny trousers and ties, hanging about with drooping fags in their lips, like so many mangy cats.

She had to admit those first few months were the finest of her life. She felt like a renegade, thousands of miles from home in the bed of a man who sang like a nightingale, living through the infancy of a religion: as the God Samba raised the Holy Son, Bossa Nova, in the Holy Land of Rio de Janeiro. And as the world dreamed of the Girl from Ipanema, Jackie was that girl right there, tall and tanned and young and lovely, walking to the beach by day, listening to the Nightingale by night.

Soon it was 1964 and even the coup seemed gentle, stealing in on April 1st, baring only baby teeth. They read of tanks in the streets that year – but also of Bardot in Búzios, where Jackie and Gilberto would spend weekends in a place with windows that opened over the waves. Gilberto had mostly sung covers of Sinatra and Davis, Bennett and Presley, but now he took to singing the compositions of Lyra or Lobo, Vinícius and Jobim, Menescal and Bôscoli. And, even if his own songs did not go down so well, it was great to carouse the city by night and see Nara or Bethânia singing in a show, to feel Gilberto was part of a scene to rival any in the world.

As Jackie's taxi cruised through Hove, she asked herself: how could you truly love again when you'd had a time that could never be beaten? No matter how distant an island those months were, no matter how bad the years which followed, you could not alter the fact of them. She was a different person now, she told herself – as different from the person she was then as one woman is from another.

She knew this was only partly true, but there wasn't a way to make it look any better, so this line of thinking did the trick, most of the time.

Jackie stepped carefully out of the cab and asked the driver if her seams were straight. She stood at the end of the gravel drive and smoked a final cigarette. Tony had never mentioned her smoking, but she somehow imagined he disapproved. She crunched up to the door of the detached red-brick house and pressed a finger to the bell. Beyond circles in the panes she saw a distorted shape move through the hall and after a few beats he opened the door. He smiled and kissed her upon one cheek, then the other (on their first date he'd shaken her hand). He wore a dark suit, shiny shoes and a lilac shirt without a tie, revealing a hint of a sandy curl. He smelled faintly of citrus. They crunched down the drive to where a black car purred. Tony opened the door for her. They settled into the cream leather back seat.

'To the marina, please,' Tony said.

Tony's instruction induced mild panic in Jackie, and she hoped its ripples didn't show. Carlo ran a bar at the marina. Tony frequented three restaurants where the waiters used his Christian name, all far from the marina; she'd assumed they would dine at one of them tonight. Although it was not too late to request an alternative, she couldn't do so without raising questions, and with their affair so deliciously poised she feared a deviation might set them back weeks. Jackie took Tony's hand and squeezed. The risk of discovery might even sprinkle the evening with a sugar of excitement. Besides, what were the chances of actually meeting Carlo? She made a mental note: tomorrow I'll tell him it's over.

The Palace Pier slid by. Golden drops of electric light streamed down the helter-skelter as the evening sky turned peachy. The car smoothly rode a bend and Jackie swayed closer to Tony. Tall white Regency houses made everything look grand. She felt a lifting inside. Of course, you could never again feel twenty-one, but not so long ago she'd thought all relatives of such sensations had died with the carefree Jackie who boarded that plane in '63.

The car rolled to a halt next to the less than fashionable shops of a marina arcade. Jackie and Tony entered a hotel and took a lift to the second-floor restaurant, where they were shown to a table with a view over the marina. The sun had set and the masts of sailboats were painted with dark bright colours. They ordered kir royales, chinked glasses and took a sip.

'So, what are we going to do about Joel?' said Tony.

Jackie took his hand.

'We'll have to tell him about us sooner or later,' she said.

'Bit of a shock, don't you think?' asked Tony.

'He's thirty-four.'

'Yes, but... your boss and your mother?'

'He did introduce us,' said Jackie.

'Not with this in mind.'

'I suppose that depends on what you mean by "this".'

Tony put a hand softly on the back of her head. The kiss started lightly and rolled on, lasting longer than Jackie expected. Three dinners, two walks along the seafront, a movie, two freezing stints on park benches, innumerable pecks on the cheek and finally...

A loitering waiter intervened. They composed themselves and ordered.

'I expect you were wondering...' said Tony, looking happy.

'...if you were ever going to get round to it?'

He laughed. It was absurd, though in the sweet mist of her present mood it didn't vex her as it might have. She did feel twenty-one and he acted fifteen, yet between them they had a hundred and twenty-one years. Hadn't they learned anything? They had learned it and forgotten it again, she supposed, and if that weren't true this wouldn't feel half as good. Other people, sophisticated people, seemed to become more accomplished as they grew older and Jackie was tempted to marvel at them – though she didn't. How dull it looked to have it all worked out.

'So when *are* we going to tell him?' asked Tony.

'When he's back from Brazil.'

'You must be having kittens?'

'About him being there?'

'About Gilberto. I mean, if he's alive, doesn't that – ?'

'He's most certainly not,' said Jackie squeezing his hand. 'Look, I think it's something Joel needs to get out of his system – he probably should have gone years ago.'

A waiter brought their starters. Jackie looked out of the window. A solitary seagull sat on a mooring post. Jackie took a gulp of champagne and tried to keep a lid on old feelings. She looked at the lights of the boats. Dead he was, dead. Yet because of that dead bastard Tony was no longer pressing his knee to hers and she was drinking faster than she ought to. She wanted so badly for Tony to take her to bed and yet, no matter how sweet it would feel, in some small way it would always be *in spite of* Gilberto. He might be dead but he was always lurking.

'Let's talk about us,' Jackie said.

'I'll drink to that,' said Tony.

'Tell me how great you are.'

'I'm bloody marvellous.'

'Give me some examples,' said Jackie.

'They've gone clean out of my mind.'

'Give me some dirty ones, then.'

'I can see where your son gets his terrific sense of humour,' said Tony.

'He despairs at my sense of humour.'

'Maybe there is some hope for him, in that case.'

'I don't care what he thinks,' Jackie lied.

'So why don't we tell him about us?'

'We will.'

'When he comes back?' asked Tony.

'When there's more of an "us" to tell him about.'

Tony looked at Jackie and Jackie studied Tony. He had more wrinkles of happiness than of pain, she thought. She liked the fact that she didn't have a clue what he'd say next. Perhaps it was always like that at the start, but it was thrilling nonetheless.

'When did we start lying to our children?' he said with a chuckle.

'We've always lied to them.'

'Speak for yourself!'

'Once upon a time,' said Jackie, 'they didn't poke their noses into our business.'

'Perhaps our business was simpler then.'

'There's no harm in a bit of complexity,' Jackie said.

'Sounds good,' said Tony. 'Though I'm not so sure it's true.'

The main course came and went. They drank a bottle and a half of red wine, which stained their teeth. They shared a chocolate pudding, finished their coffees and Jackie insisted on paying the bill.

'Consider it a thank-you, on behalf of my son,' she said.

'All right,' said Tony. 'But next time's on me.'

'You can take me to the bar and buy me a martini, with an olive. Then you can take me back to yours.'

When rehearsing this sort of moment, Jackie had expected Tony to look ruffled. Instead he looked happy, and she felt it was going to be a wonderful night. Tony led her to the bar. Jackie devoured her cocktail olive and tried not to gulp down her martini. Tony called a taxi for Hove. Jackie finished her drink, put on her coat, allowed Tony to take her arm and turned to the door.

Through the door walked Carlo. He wore a polo-neck under a double-breasted jacket and tan loafers with tassels. What folly, Jackie thought on seeing Carlo next to Tony. Life could play its tricks, but the worst by far were those you played on yourself.

'Jackie?' Carlo said. 'Miriam's poker night?'

'Last-minute change of plan,' said Jackie.

'An old friend, no doubt,' said Carlo, holding his hand out to Tony.

'Something like that,' said Tony shaking his hand firmly.

'Got plenty of friends, our Jackie,' said Carlo.

'So I'm learning,' said Tony.

'Full of surprises!' said Carlo.

'We'd better be getting away,' said Jackie.

'Nothing like an early night,' said Carlo.

The sky was dark outside and the air cool. Jackie and Tony stood apart, trying to find words before they opened the taxi doors.

Tony smiled and shook his head.

'Look – ' he started.

'It's over between me and Carlo,' said Jackie. 'Dead and buried. I swear.'

'Another man who thinks he's rather less dead than you make out.'

'It's *over*. I meant everything I said. It doesn't change anything.'

'That's a matter of opinion.'

Tony held the door open and Jackie climbed inside. He told the driver to make a stop in Hanover. The taxi drove slowly along the seafront. Jackie felt anxiety inflate. It made her want to scream – to have felt so electrified. One more day, a simple phone call to Carlo, and there would have been no further need for deception. She had been minutes from the chance of a relationship with a man with a little decency about him – and how many of those were there aged sixty-four with the body of a younger man who seemed to want more than someone to do the ironing? She could not help but feel that here was the hand of Gilberto again. Maybe Joel's trip would serve some purpose other than his own; perhaps if Joel proved Gilberto was dead the bastard would stop haunting her. She knew he was dead, she could feel he was dead, and yet... God! What did she need – to see his corpse?

It has nothing to do with Gilberto, she told herself. Face facts: you've made a mess of it, again, full stop. History didn't exactly argue otherwise.

The taxi stopped outside her house. Jackie stood on the pavement and Tony came round to her side.

'It's been fun,' he said.

He gave her a hug. A bloody *hug*, she thought. She felt a brush of stubble against her cheek. Their mouths were close but they didn't move together.

Jackie pulled away and smiled. 'It can still be fun,' she said.

Tony climbed into the car. As she stepped towards her door she felt a moment of panic, fearing she'd never again feel as happy as earlier, let alone have the chance to feel happier still. The moment passed. If it really was right with Tony, then everything could be resolved – couldn't it? She scrabbled for her keys. She watched the car drive away, let herself into the house, took out her cigarettes, sat at the bottom of the stairs and lit up. She undid the tight buckles on her shoes and wiggled her cramped toes. When she'd finished her cigarette, she wept.

Nelson sneaked up behind Fat Paulo, put his hands over his eyes and said, 'Guess who?'

'Dead Nelson,' said Paulo.

'Very much alive,' said Nelson.

'Until Adolfo finds you,' said Paulo, and went back to polishing the counter.

Nelson sat on his stool. Soon more of the guys turned up and Nelson took their friendly slaps and bought them beers with one of Joel's notes. Then Zemané arrived, wearing a Panama hat which looked too new and turned out to be a present from his wife. He sat on his stool smoking a cigar, observing Nelson joke around, wearing a look Nelson wished he could read.

While the boys were looking for ants, Nelson bent to the ear of Zemané and said, 'I know I shouldn't have come, but – '

'You might as well,' said Zemané. 'The word is out: everybody knows you're rich.'

'Hardly rich – '

'Rich enough to open the eyes of sleeping debts.'

'It'll be OK, you'll see,' said Nelson, twisting hair between his fingers. 'I'll be able to pay him something soon. I've made a plan and it's working, I'm earning every day – '

'When a debtor without money doesn't pay, a creditor gets disappointed,' said Zemané.

'Sure,' said Nelson, 'I understand, but – '

'When a debtor *with* money doesn't pay, he gets angry.'

'Right, yes, but – '

'Adolfo is bad enough when he's happy. Now...'

Nelson wanted to buy Zemané a beer to make things seem all right, but the phone in the bar rang, causing everyone to turn in surprise and watch Paulo hunt behind the Pope. When the phone had been installed, Paulo had called it his hotline to heaven. It hardly ever rang, so the regulars joked that his place had been booked in hell.

'Hotel José Manoel?' said Paulo when he found the phone. 'One minute...' He passed the phone to Zemané.

'Good day,' Zemané said. 'Senhor José Manoel? Speaking... Yes, I remember Nelson – the finest worker we ever had... And who might you be? ... He always spoke most highly of your establishment, I must pay a visit soon... As luck would have it, he just dropped by... I'll pass you over.'

Nelson took the phone. 'Hello?' he said.

'Whatever is going on,' said the stern voice of the manageress, 'it better not be trouble. I have someone to speak to you.'

'*Malandro!*' came the low voice of Eva.

'My goddess,' said Nelson, tossing a wink to the crowd, causing a ripple of hand-slaps.

'When I get my hands on you – '

'So why don't we combine for a chat? The stars are shining and – '

'If I wanted mumbo-jumbo I'd sit on my *bunda* all day watching soaps. But I don't, *malandro*, oh, no, I don't. I go to work, in an office, in a suit, with people who also like to earn a living. Not like some *vagabundo* spending another man's

113

money, pretending to lend him a hand. Well, Joel might stand for it – poor boy, if his mother could see him now – but I won't, *malandro*, I won't.'

'All is not always as it seems, my goddess,' said Nelson, making gestures of 'no problem' to the crowd, who'd started to laugh at the audible shrieking. 'Meet me at Carioca station, at five o'clock. I'll show you something that'll change your mind.'

'Take a tram ride with you? Yes, please! Take me into the hills at dusk! Murder me in an alley – '

'Send my regards to the manageress,' said Nelson, and hung up.

The phone rang again and, when Nelson signalled he didn't want it, at a nod from Zemané Paulo pulled out the cord. A murmur of exclamations splintered into half a dozen conversations, as the men round the bar analysed the call. Theories sprouted. Nelson had never been one to share details, and many had suspected there were no details to recount. Yet here was a hysterical woman on the end of the phone who wasn't his mother, and that could only mean one thing. They looked on Nelson with new eyes. Telling them he was off to prepare dinner for a goddess, he left the bar with whistles ringing in his ears.

Nelson caught a bus to a market, then hauled his catch home. He dug out a tablecloth and tall cream candles, vacuumed rugs, swept floors and arranged the music room. He tuned his guitar and practised a few songs, then set about preparing dinner. It was a while since he'd cooked for somebody else and it made him think he must surely be rising in the world, given that barely a week ago he hadn't had the means to feed himself. He took ingredients out of bags: eggs, a brown coconut and sugar for *beijinhos;* milk, butter, eggs, flour and *queijo de minas* cheese for Zila's receipe for cheese-bread. Since the sea was the realm of Yemanjá, Nelson assumed his goddess would not object to a bit of cod, with broccoli on the side and sandy *farofa de ovo*. He chopped and mixed for nearly an hour until, as the squares of sunlight on the surfaces slanted into longer shapes, neat pyramids of ingredients sat waiting in bowls. Nelson threw cloths over them, then quickly showered and shaved with a new razor without bristles in the blades. He took his white outfit off the washing line and, scented with the fat man's cologne, let himself out of the front door and hurried down to the tram stop, where he jumped on a tramcar just before it left.

The afternoon sun had passed behind the hills, though there were patches of light on the city as the shadows spread. The tram rattled over the viaduct and was soon pulling into Carioca station. Nelson could see Eva waiting on the platform with her arms crossed, dressed in white, refusing to smile as he hopped off. He went to kiss her on both cheeks but she stepped back.

'Come for a ride,' he said. 'Give me a chance.'

'Are you totally crazy? Don't answer that, don't. What am I even doing here when the sun is about to go down and I have a million better things to do? I've just come to say: stay away from Joel – do you understand? I would ask you to give the money back – I know you won't – but at least you can disappear. Go back to your guitar and leave that boy alone.'

'I don't care about the money,' said Nelson. 'Here, have it back. Give it to Joel and say I'm sorry. Perhaps it's better if I don't help. Maybe you're right.'

Nelson counted out a hundred and fifty *reais* and held them towards Eva. This is what Zemané would call a calculated risk, he thought. He wondered if she'd take the money. He didn't think she would and hoped he was right. After paying for the cod, the rest of the food and even a bottle of sparkling Chandon – a drink Nelson knew Zemané drank with his wife – he was left with less than twenty *reais*.

Eva took the money and put it in her bag. Nelson watched her fingers squeeze the clasp shut.

Eva had to admit she was surprised. Poor men and criminals did not give refunds. She had expected a fight, bad language,

115

maybe even threats. She'd envisaged a long campaign saving Joel from the clutches of a villain. Now she had the money, a worry jabbed her heart. What if Nelson really did know how to help? What if she'd scotched the only chance Joel had?

Perhaps there was a better way. If she did go with Nelson, she could find out what he really intended. Who knew what a desperate man might do in the hills at night – but Nelson didn't seem the type to jump a woman just like that, and he was going to too much trouble if that was all he had in mind. It was risky, there was no doubt – but she would do it for her boys; there was no other choice.

'Just one evening, that's all I ask,' said Nelson. 'What do you have to lose?'

'My time, my patience, my handbag.'

'Do muggers usually dole out money?'

'Perhaps it's a calculated risk,' said Eva.

'I must be cleverer than you think.'

'It never pays to assume anyone is stupid.'

'Come on,' said Nelson. 'You never know – we might have fun.'

The yellow tram was starting to fill.

'What do you have in mind?' said Eva. 'I can't believe I'm asking. Someone please explain why I'm asking.'

'A little dinner, a little music. Come and see.'

The driver was calling for final passengers. Nelson watched Eva look at the yellow car, shake her head and walk towards it. He followed close behind and helped her climb inside where they settled next to one another on a wooden bench. The tram lurched and soon they were riding over the high Lapa arches. Daylight was really dying now, lights were coming on and Eva had never seen the city from this climbing angle at this time of day. The office blocks looked softer and the cut-off cone of the cathedral looked more like a crown than a bucket in the evening light.

They got off the tram near the house and walked up the street. Nelson let Eva through the gate and ushered her inside before she could wander the flowering yard and catch sight of the view. He showed her into the living room and watched her look around.

'Don't even try to pretend this is your house,' said Eva. 'Don't even think about that one, no way.'

'Didn't I tell you I was a president?'

'Of the United States of Malandro?'

'The house belongs to a friend,' laughed Nelson.

'You have rich friends for an unreliable musician.'

'The rich, the poor, the occasional goddess.'

'If I'm a goddess, how come I'm so far from heaven?'

'If you follow me, I'll try and make things a little more divine.'

Nelson showed Eva to the kitchen, hoping she'd be impressed when like a conjuror he pulled back the cloths on bowls of chopped ingredients. She leaned on the door-frame as he took out a chilled bottle of Chandon. He watched her face for signs of the surprise she must surely feel – that a man like him should be deftly popping the cork from a bottle and filling flutes. He tried to remember the last time he'd waited on someone who wasn't paying. It felt good to feel her eyes observing, perhaps seeing him as more than just another poor man trying to swim his way out of a swamp.

They chinked glasses, said, '*Saude*,' then Eva watched him put cubed potatoes, cabbage, *repolho* and onion into a dish, add spices and oil, olives and chopped hard-boiled eggs, then thick slices of cod. As he worked, he talked about anything that came into his head, hoping he might chance across some magic words which would turn him into a man with whom she'd want to stay.

'My aunt Zila used to call this dish *Bacalhau Leandra* – after my mother – and as she prepared it she would have me sit on the kitchen worktop while she told me stories of their childhood in Recife. Zila used to say cod was an honest fish which never tried to play tricks on you, unlike the men who caught it. Though in truth she preferred to cook fish whole rather than in slices, because she liked being able to see the entire beast on her plate. "When you can look your food in the eye you can eat with a clear heart," she used to say.'

Nelson was worried the reference to fish eyes might put Eva off her meal, and was thinking about steering the conversation on to a finer subject, when Eva asked, 'Did you ever eat anything you killed?'

'Only chickens and fish,' said Nelson.

'Do they taste any better?'

'The first few times.'

'Did it give you a thrill?' asked Eva, her eyes widening.

'I can't say it did.'

'I could kill a chicken. I just never had to.'

'Perhaps it's harder if you don't really need to,' said Nelson.

'You're probably right.'

'I could buy a chicken next time, if you like. We could kill it in the yard.'

'You never know,' said Eva. 'I might be good at it. Maybe I could go into the chicken trade. God knows what else I'm going to do when they throw me on the street.'

'You'll never be on the street, not a woman like you.'

'Like me? Like what? They're talking of making us redundant, Nelson.'

'So find another job.'

'It's not so easy, Nelson, for a woman not far from fifty – I won't tell you how close because that's my secret – when the bosses all want younger women to adorn their days.'

'Not all of them are like that,' said Nelson. 'Besides, you have... *qualities* which younger women don't.'

'I'm glad you noticed, Nelson, you're kind, and I appreciate that, don't think I don't, but what chance does a maturing woman really have? Men will tell you the woman is worshipped – don't shake your head, that's what you all say – that they love their mother, love their daughter, love their beautiful wife. But they also love the *gatas* on the beach with

118

their swollen *bundas* on display, and they'd rather have one of them decorating the office than a woman closer to falling from the tree. What chance is there for a woman in her prime without even a simple husband, let alone a president?'

'I don't understand why you're so obsessed with presidents.'

'Why shouldn't I have the best? I'd be a president myself, were such a thing allowed, but this is a man's world, friend, so let's not even pretend.'

'Do you really think some rich guy is going to solve all your problems?'

'It's about equality,' said Eva. 'I want my equal. It's not about money.'

'It never is if you have some.'

'Even the fat can be hungry, friend. But I'm not greedy, not me.'

'I'm just saying: a president isn't the only type of man that could make you happy.'

'Do you think you could make me happy?' said Eva, raising an eyebrow.

'You'd need to give me a chance.'

'There's no harm dreaming,' said Eva. 'You have your dreams and I have mine.'

Nelson browned onions then mixed in eggs, stirring a bit harder than was necessary. He added manioc flour and salt, then when the blend was loose he set it aside and topped up their glasses. Tonight is a pearl, he said to himself; let's make sure it shines. He raised his glass and said, '*Stop dreaming, stop breathing*, that's what Zila used to say. Number one of her Eleven Commandments.'

'Eleven's a funny kind of number, Nelsinho – weren't ten enough?'

'She thought mankind ought to have moved on since Moses.'

'You'd better tell me what they are,' said Eva. 'I might have been breaking some.'

'Number two: *Do unto others what they would do unto you if they didn't have any shoes either.*'

'What about if their shoes are nicer than yours?' said Eva. 'I'd like to put a curse on those witches.'

'Number three: *Life should be a string of pearls. Find as many pearls as you can and string them all together.*'

'Pearls?'

'Tonight is a pearl,' said Nelson.

'I take it one man's pearl is another's pebble?'

'Number four: *Never hit a woman.*'

'Bravo!'

'Did anyone ever hit you, Eva?' asked Nelson.

'No, they didn't. Thank God, they didn't.'

'Do you think presidents hit more or less than other men?'

'I should think about the same. I'm not saying they're saints.'

'Number five: *Never say sorry for something that's not your fault.*'

'I need to tell Liam that one.'

'Six: *Believe in no gods before yourself.*'

'I take it Zila wasn't a religious woman?'

'She thought gods were mainly for emergencies and special occasions.' Nelson finished his glass and looked at Eva. She was smiling. It felt good to feel her waiting for the rest of the commandments. She wasn't about to run away. Whatever might or might not come of the night, some of it had gone his way.

'I've forgotten the others,' he lied, because he didn't want to give all his secrets away on the first date. 'But let's drink to number eleven: *Never forget your aunt Zila.*'

Nelson led Eva into the living room and swept out an arm to indicate the door in the corner. As she stepped down into the hexagonal room she squealed, '*Caraca!*'

The room was lit by dozens of candles – their flames reflected in the windows – and outside a thousand lights of

120

the city shone. In the centre of the floor was a round table laid with a white tablecloth and gleaming cutlery. Nelson pulled out a chair and Eva sat down. She touched her cutlery and the stem of her glass, then looked up at a grinning Nelson, who stood apart, his hands behind his back.

'Is everything to your satisfaction, madam?'

'Oh, my little *malandro*!' she said. 'Show me a president's wife who dines in half the style!'

Nelson brought the food on a silver platter and served Eva, then switched sides to fill her glass. For a while they sat and ate without a word, and Nelson recalled his wonder at the silence of dining couples he'd waited upon. He used to think rich people must have so much to be excited about, yet there they would sit, eyeing other diners, twiddling their wedding rings, swapping diluted smiles. He guessed money couldn't buy you conversation. But Nelson and Eva's silence felt like one of indulgence rather than emptiness, and in any case it was never going to last.

'Would you like to know a secret?' Eva said. 'Subordinates are the death of the imagination: as soon as you have someone to run around for you, you lose your spark. Believe me, I've seen presidents in action: ordering this for their wife, ordering that for their mistress. A monkey can order.'

'It must be nice to order, to have things ordered.'

'Nice but *chato*. Boring, boring, boring. What I wouldn't give for a president with your imagination.'

'Imagination can also get you into a lot of trouble.'

Eva put down her glass and looked at him for a moment.

'You surprise me, Nelson. I didn't have you down as a pragmatist.'

'I guess I've dreamed myself into a lot of situations over the years.'

'It can get you out of trouble too, *querido*.'

'I don't know about that,' said Nelson. 'Some troubles cannot be dreamed away, you know that, don't you? Like those problems of your own.'

121

'I can't see how a little imagination can do any harm, no matter the predicament.'

'It didn't help Sandro much, did it? He showed plenty of imagination on that bus.'

'Does it take imagination to put a gun in a woman's mouth?' asked Eva.

'Maybe he was imagining how it would feel to have a little power for once, to feel the eyes of the world upon him for a change, to be a star.'

'I think you may be the one imagining things.'

'Can you put yourself in his shoes for a moment, Eva? Is his predicament so hard to see?'

'All I see is a girl killed because of him.'

'And what about Sandro?'

'I see a *marginal* who got what he deserved.'

'I see a black man strangled in the back of a van,' said Nelson.

'Not every picture is in black and white, Nelson. Have you thought there might be a different story here?'

There was silence for a while, then Eva started talking. Nelson watched her talk about her lazy son, her shaky job, her gorgeous handbag. She told stories about Liam and Joel to which he half listened. There was every chance they could be friends, but nothing more, he knew that now. They viewed the world in different colours and he liked the shades he saw. He was sure she felt the same. He thought about playing one of the songs he'd rehearsed, but it didn't feel right any more. He wasn't in the mood to sing for friendship. So he listened and laughed and told her jokes, until there were only bones on their plates.

Nelson cleared the table and made a *cafezinho*. They stood before the windows, eating *beijinhos*, looking at the nightscape of the city. Lights chequered distant offices. Neon logos were printed on the sky. As Eva talked, Nelson wondered what the pinnacle of the dream had been: perhaps the tram ride, perhaps cooking, maybe seeing her reaction

122

to the candlelit table. When Eva appeared to have run out of words, he said, 'I'll call you a taxi.'

'A taxi! Now who's acting like a rich man?'

'You can pay me back when you find that president.'

Eva realised she'd quite forgotten to cross-examine him about Gilberto. She felt annoyed with herself for a second, then realised there was no need. Did crooks prepare feasts and pay for taxis? More than anything, he was a man who listened, Eva thought, and she wasn't going to hinder one of those.

'Here,' she said, opening her bag. 'Have the money back.'

Nelson's hand was desperate to dart towards the bills, but he kept it motionless. Eva put the money on the table, smiled and said, 'Take it. I had you wrong, Nelsinho. I'll tell Joel to rest assured.'

Now the cash was sitting there, Nelson felt a little ashamed to be taking the money back when he really hadn't a clue how to help Joel. Still, it was nice to be trusted, even if he didn't deserve it. He could almost feel Zila's eyes opening to give him one of her looks, so he told himself he really would earn Joel's money. He couldn't see how, but he'd find a way.

The taxi came, they kissed twice on the cheeks and said goodbye. Eva said she'd see him at Bar das Terezas – and that he must come to dinner – soon! He closed the taxi door and watched the car round a bend.

Nelson went into the music room and snuffed out all but a couple of candles. He picked up the guitar and played 'Chega de Saudade'. The night had been a little pearl but it was time to thread the next. He could feel the money in his pocket and for a moment he wished she'd kept it, but then he thought: I'm going to find Gilberto. I'll look for him and I'll find him. I'll earn this money and then some more. There are other goddesses. I'll make a meal for one who wants to savour every morsel. I'll play a song for one who wants to listen to every note. How hard can it be to find something if you really open your eyes?

Six

When the light of Monday morning woke him, Joel opened the door to his balcony and looked out towards the beach, then back up the block towards the body of Ipanema. Cantagalo lay not far away and soon Nelson would be up there looking. The sky was blue and the air already bright. He could hear breaking waves, Liam singing badly in the shower, CNN from the living room.

He washed, dressed and joined Liam for breakfast.

'So,' said Liam. 'All set?'

'Raring to go,' said Joel.

'I'll talk to Eva,' said Liam. 'See about her friend at the ministry.'

'Cool. If you have any other bright ideas, let me know.'

Joel stuffed a few posters in a shoulder bag and left the flat. Standing outside the aparthotel, he could already feel the direction of the old flat. With his back towards the sea it lay away to the left, at about ten o'clock. He wondered if he could reach it blindfold.

He turned right, into Praça General Osório, resolving to find his way there slowly, hoping to wind up a pleasant tension until the moment when his finger would hover over a buzzer which might not have changed for twenty-five years – a buzzer his father's finger also used to touch. Joel wondered if such objects still held fragments of his dad – skin flakes or dead cells or molecules of flesh. For how long did traces remain? Perhaps his dad was present throughout these streets, layering pavements he'd once trodden, his particles floating in the Ipanema air.

Joel bought a *vitamina* shake at a juice bar studded with rows of fruit. He walked along Visconde de Pirajá, past a supermarket, clothes shops, restaurants. He turned towards the lake, aware the flat was away to his left now, and closer. The streets looked similar to those he recalled and yet they were shorter or longer, or lined with more trees, or set at slightly different angles. Little by little, reality reshaped crumpled memories – until the roads welled with their original colours and looked just like those he remembered. He saw the quiet street down which he used to ride his bicycle, the corner on which he used to wait when his dad was due home from work. Some of the buildings had changed, but many were the same. Finally he turned into their old street.

The trees were thicker with foliage than he recalled and the road didn't seem as wide. The flat was down on the right-hand side, a block and a half from the lake. He walked a few yards then crossed for a better view. Further up, he could see the spot where his father had been shoved into a van on the day of his second arrest, Joel's last day in Brazil. He walked closer, his eyes on the very patch of tarmac, trying to focus on the solemnity of the occasion: here he was in the last place he'd seen his father. He felt hungry and cursed his stomach. He stood for a while, refusing to let the moment end. It felt peculiar to be standing in a memory. A soft breeze moved the leaves. A car passed. A woman walking an ornamental dog eyed him.

He reached their old apartment building. There was a new electric gate and a sentry-box, inside which a guard sat reading a paper. The block looked almost the same, although the flats seemed to have new windows. Joel approached the gate, wondering what he should say. He'd expected an old *porteiro*, someone like Senhor Neves who used to let Joel sit behind the desk and buzz in residents.

'*Bom dia*,' said Joel through the bars.

The guard came out of his box and stood on the other side of the gate. 'Yes?' he said in Portuguese.

'I wondered if you could help me – I'm looking for someone who used to live here.'

'What's his name?'

'Gilberto Cabral.'

'Where did he live?' asked the guard.

'Apartamento 203.'

'That's Miss Albuquerque's flat.'

'Would it be all right if I spoke to her?'

'It would, but she's at work. You could come back later.'

'Do you have her number?' asked Joel.

'Yes. But I can't give it to you without her permission.'

'Can I leave her a note?'

'Sure.'

Joel took out a poster and wrote on the back of it: 'Dear Miss Albuquerque. I used to live in your apartment when I was a child – until 1975. As the poster says: I'm looking for this man, my father. If you happen to know anything about his whereabouts, please call.'

The guard took the poster through the bars and read the note. 'You used to live here too, brother? Why didn't you say so?'

'It's a long story,' said Joel, and told him some details.

'I'll make sure she gets it, no problem.'

Joel asked about some of their old friends in the block, the Saavedras and the Soleres, but the guard hadn't heard of them. The young man ran through the names of other residents, but they weren't familiar to Joel.

'Could you put a poster up in the lobby?' Joel asked.

'Of course,' said the guard. He took a poster from Joel. A phone rang in his box and he went to pick it up. Joel hung around until the guard was off the phone, but he didn't come back. Joel called 'thanks' through the bars. The guard flicked up a little thumb and said, '*Valeu*,' without raising his eyes from his paper.

126

Joel walked back towards the sea and caught a glimpse of the red-brick boxes of Cantagalo to the left, crowning the hill. Nelson will be up there now, he thought. He might already have found Gilberto. Joel turned that way, and walked a couple of blocks until the shacks were nearer, almost above his head. There were some trees down at the end, near the foot of the hill, and it looked as if there might be a way up – though he could almost feel a line, at the entrance to that world, which he knew he had better not cross. It was strange to be so close to a place and yet to feel it lay so very far away. He had flown 5,000 miles but he couldn't walk the final hundred yards. There it was, Cantagalo, right before his eyes, and yet his father might as well be on the moon, for all that Joel could venture there. He wondered how he'd search in such a place if Nelson weren't looking on his behalf.

Joel walked back to Rua Visconde de Pirajá, busy with morning shoppers and workers and traffic. He found a phone booth by a bikini shop and called Liam but there were no new messages. He bought a passion-fruit juice and ate a pastry at a place on a corner, sitting out of the rising heat of the day. He watched people walk by – black, white, rich, poor – and made guesses about their lives he knew would not be right. When they were away on holiday, Debbie always liked to prophesise about the secret lives of sunbathers or hotel waiters. Joel watched women looking in shop windows, men in shorts and flip-flops walking dogs, taxi upon yellow taxi gliding by.

Since he wasn't sure where to look specifically, he started to walk. Maybe I'll just happen upon him, Joel thought. He walked through Ipanema, turning left and right as it took his fancy, then on into Leblon. After a couple of hours he thought he owed his feet some lunch, so he headed back to Garota de Ipanema restaurant, where he took a table at the edge by a wooden balustrade which looked down on to the pavement. Outside, a group of street kids were playing music with home-made instruments and he leant down and handed them a couple of *reais*. He ordered a beer and a steak. He could see the beach a street away and it made him think of Sundays in the early seventies, when a million brown bodies crowded on the sand. He wished he could remember those days with more precision. He had a few memories of the good times, but now he was in Brazil he expected reinforcements. Would finding his father loose a great stampede? It was maddening the way he remembered such apparently random, trivial things: a peculiar ant he'd watched roll along on a hillside outside Tiradentes, a toy car he would play with on the swirling black and white pavement of the Ipanema seafront. Much of the big stuff seemed to have gone missing – how many rollable, bounceable memories did Joel really have of his dad? From a torrent of bedside lullabies he could pan only half a dozen songs; from dozens of Flamengo games, he could picture his father celebrating only two of Zico's goals. He wished he'd made more of an effort at the time to fix significant happenings in his mind. If only someone had told him he'd leave Brazil when he was ten years old, he could have acted as if the clock were ticking towards the hour – instead of assuming the hand would sweep round forever.

Joel wasn't even sure he trusted the memory he did possess of the first time they took his dad away, when he was nearly five years old. He had an image of men in suits arriving at breakfast, of sitting at the kitchen table drawing a picture of the mountain, Pedra da Gávea. But he had a feeling the details had come from his mum. Was it true that his dad was a changed man after his first time inside? Were the fights rooted in trauma, or a normal part of married life? Perhaps it was the same for every kid: Santa was a lie and your parents fought like cockerels. He couldn't swear the fights were all that savage – sometimes he thought he'd dreamt of evenings hiding his head beneath his pillow, trying to block the sound of clatter and yelp. Yet he was certain he remembered the aftermath – when they would come and sit on his bed and his mum would stroke his hair and his dad would sing 'Undiú' until Joel fell asleep.

Joel finished his lunch. He wondered if he was getting anywhere. He'd put up posters and paced the streets. He was thankful the posters had yielded Nelson – assuming for a moment he wasn't a charlatan – and Eva was asking her friend to look in the files, but it felt wrong to depend so much on the efforts of others. He paid and strode to Liam's flat. He logged on to the internet and looked up all the Gilberto Cabrals in an online phone book. There were twenty-two in Rio, but none he hadn't called before. So he looked up the numbers for government departments and started dialling.

Jackie ate an egg and bacon sandwich and watched *Trisha*. She wasn't a fan of daytime television, but she watched it anyway. There'd be racing after lunch then *Judge Judy* later in the afternoon. As she watched a woman in a sweatshirt fold her arms and spit a comment at an ex-lover, Jackie wondered if she and Tony would get another chance. Their situation wasn't all that messy; surely all relationships came with complications by the time you were their age? He would call soon – by tomorrow at the latest, she reckoned. She was interested to note the confidence with which she made predictions on the behaviour of men, given the spectacular failures of the past.

The programme came to an end and she played the hijack clip. She paused it on the face of the man Joel claimed was his dad. There was certainly a look in his eyes, whoever he was. He might be drunk, she thought, or a bit mad. But it wasn't the same as Gilberto's look, the one that used to ghost into his eyes without warning, just when you'd forgotten it existed. She remembered the first time she'd met that look. They had been standing on the balcony of his flat, on a humid evening in December 1964, and Jackie had been wondering how to tell him she was pregnant. You look so happy, she remembered thinking, standing there, talking to me about your music. Little do you know how much happier you'll be in a few minutes. She'd waited for a break in the flow, barely listening to his words, as he paced and waved his arms, talking of a song he'd heard, dismissing a new singer he didn't rate. Finally she said, 'I'm pregnant,' the words just spilling out when he was halfway through an anecdote, because she couldn't keep them inside any more or think of a way to dress them up.

Gilberto finished his sentence and stood, his arms suddenly frozen in front of him, with a look in his eyes she could not translate. She remembered feeling, suddenly, that there was someone else behind his eyes she had not seen before, as if there were another man inside him too, who had only now decided to show her a glimpse of himself, perhaps even as a warning. For the instant this feeling lasted, Jackie felt frightened, and she felt a touch of embarrassment too, so that she blushed, to have revealed her secret not only to the man she loved but to this lurker. Gilberto walked towards her with his hands raised, held her face with his fingers and said, 'The world is changing – why not us?' and broke into the widest smile.

The day after Jackie's revelation, they met Miriam for lunch. Jackie talked and talked and talked about their plans. They were going to get married next November, she said, in a pink church in Tiradentes, when the baby was a few months old. Miriam would be her maid of honour and Frank could give her away. There was so much to be organised and... Jackie saw that Miriam had started to cry.

'Frank is seeing someone else,' said Miriam.

'Impossible!' said Gilberto.

'I walked in on them,' said Miriam.

'Why didn't he tell me?' said Gilberto.

'That's hardly the point,' said Jackie. 'Is he... *seeing* her, or was it just... I mean.'

'I've had my suspicions,' said Miriam.

'Why didn't you tell me?' said Jackie.

'You're so happy, Jacks. I didn't want to – '

'Oh, Miriam!' said Jackie.

'I want to go home,' Miriam said.

Gilberto and Jackie looked at one another.

'But you can't go now!' said Gilberto. 'Back to cold rain and men like dogs. What you need is a *Brazilian* man. I know the very one for you; why didn't I think of it before? I know the very man – '

'I mean it, Jacks. I want to go home.'

Gilberto slid his arm round Jackie's waist.

'But you *can't* go!' said Jackie. 'We're in this together... what'll I do without you – ?'

'I'll write every day,' said Miriam. 'I'll come and visit – '

'We can come and see you in Brighton, one day,' said Gilberto.

'I'll rent a place with a view of the sea,' said Miriam.

'You *can't* go,' said Jackie, tearfully.

'The heat brings me out in a rash,' said Miriam, trying to laugh through her tears, 'the food repeats on me, I can't understand a word anyone says, and it's not much fun being next to you in a bikini.'

In June 1965, Gilberto wrote a song for the coming child which he was convinced would break the big time. It wasn't imperative to write songs yourself: look at Elis on *O Fino da Bossa* – her own weekly show for little more than an *interesting* voice, not even a refined one. But songwriting would give him an edge. It would show there were more strings to his bow than singing and dancing and raising a laugh with his Sammy Davis brows. He bought a television, so that the swollen Jackie could keep her eye on the latest musical trends. It would help to keep her occupied too, while Gilberto walked the clubs and stalked the record producers. Stars were bursting every night – take that kid Paulinho da Viola: he was huge because of *Rosa de Ouro* – Rose of Gold – though Gilberto preferred to call the show *Rose of Shit*. Gilberto would stagger home and tell Jackie his own ideas for a show: *Carioca Cowboys* it would be called, with a Wild West feel, some American class. He'd play the host, *O Duque* – the Duke – there'd be gunfights and Elvis covers, *choro*

131

tunes sung to cowgirls beneath a tropical moon, dancing girls. He'd pen a new song every week to end the show.

Joel was born in Ipanema Hospital, on the 17th of July 1965. Jackie and Gilberto had been sitting on a bench in the Botanical Gardens, beneath an arcade of weeping cypresses, talking about plans for the child, their wedding, Gilberto's career. He wanted to go part-time to devote more hours to his music, reasoning that the head of his dental practice was a musical man himself and would be sure to understand. Jackie recalled looking at the ground as she searched for the perfect words to draw the focus of the man she loved to his priorities. As she spoke of security, as he paced with alien eyes, a fleshquake started to ripple inside. Soon Gilberto was helping her hobble down endless paths through wild palms and trees with mighty trunks – and into a taxi, flagged dangerously in the street, which speared round the curve of the lake as she puffed and prayed to Cristo high on his hill that she would reach a bed before it was too late.

The baby was born at five to midnight, as Gilberto was singing 'Only for You', a song he'd written in its honour, in a new venue in Copacabana. He arrived at dawn and together they gazed through tired eyes at the swaddled infant, then Gilberto sang 'Only for You' in his softest voice, as Jackie clasped his hand and felt full to the brim with hope. They decided to call him Joel, in honour of Jackie's late uncle Joseph and Gilberto's all-time favourite Flamengo player.

Joel grew, crawled, walked. He said his first word, 'mama', on a Sunday afternoon to a song by Caetano Veloso and Gal Costa called 'Sunday', which Jackie took as a sign of great intuition, though it made Gilberto crush the limes for a caipirinha with extra vigour – at the thought of those Bahians inspiring his own child. Wasn't it enough, he ranted – as he smashed ice wrapped in a towel against the kitchen worktop – that this *báfia* was stealing the livelihoods of musicians in Rio, without them thieving words from the mouths of children? Why did the world revolve around Bahia? What was wrong with the music of Minas Gerais, his homeland? If you weren't from Bahia, if you didn't dress like a freak, none of the producers was interested. Caetano! Bethânia! Gil! Gal! With each name he smacked the ice-stuffed towel.

Life was hard for a man with a small child, Jackie's new friends said. She was managing so well, they told her, mastering Portuguese much faster than the other expat wives. In her white bikini she looked just like that Bond girl, they said, if a touch plumper and with redder hair. You could hardly tell she'd had a baby. It was tough for a man, they said. Sometimes Jackie and Gilberto went out together, but she didn't always feel comfortable leaving Joel with a babysitter. Often Gilberto went out alone – after all, there was his singing career to think about, and who knew when he might catch the ear of an impresario and land himself that crucial deal.

Joel toddled and stars were born, but Gilberto wasn't one of them. Gilberto and Jackie were finally married in Tiradentes in November 1967, three streets from Gilberto's childhood home, in a simple service with a couple of Rio friends and a few of his old neighbours. Afterwards they dined in the garden of a mansion where candles burned under Brugmansia trees pungent with trumpet flowers. The locals adored Gilberto's songs and lauded him for his success on the Rio scene, and Jackie was happy to humour them.

Jackie loved watching father and son together. When he played games with Joel or read to him, Gilberto seemed a different man from the one who kicked the door closed late at night – the same door Joel would run towards when he heard Gilberto's key in the lock upon his return from work. They looked so similar to one another: the brown of their skin, their pale eyes and uncontrollable hair. How could you love one and not the other? She would always remember the time they rode up Sugarloaf in a cable-car Gilberto had hired just for the three of them. Joel had run round and round inside, as the glass box soared above views of the city, the beaches, the sea. She remembered Gilberto pointing out that the trees on the slopes below had leaves of more than one shade of green – predominantly dark but daubed here and there with shades of lime, which gave them a livelier feel than uniformity could have achieved. Sometimes when she looked at trees, Jackie still thought about that ride.

'Look at the big mountain, Daddy!' Joel had said, jumping up and down at the top of Sugarloaf, pointing at the distant anvil head of Pedra da Gávea.

'We'll climb it one day,' Gilberto said. 'Like two mountain lions.'

1968 was a year full of promise, in spite of the new military regime, and though at times it was frightening to be stopped at roadblocks, to be asked for papers, to read of punishment and disappearance, trouble seemed largely removed from their own lives. Gilberto was earning more and they moved into a larger apartment with a maid and a service lift, nearer the lake and closer to A Gaiola, where Gilberto would sing his own songs to warm applause. They became part of a loose crowd which hung around beaches on the fringes of Rio at weekends and spent evenings in Copacabana. Gilberto sang a couple of times at Teatro Jovem and once was complimented by Aloysio de Oliveira. One Sunday afternoon a melody came to him, and then a rhythm, and he started to sing a song to Joel which he knew at once could become a sensation. 'Jardim, Jardim' it would be called, a ballad of love and fatherhood in a garden, with a smooth vocal, a hint of samba, a sexy rhythm. He would show them all: it would be the making of the Minas sound.

One night Gilberto sang 'Jardim, Jardim' at A Gaiola. When he came back, far into the night, he opened the door with soft hands and unleashed a tropical storm of kisses upon a sleeping Jackie. He told her that by chance a patient of his had been in the audience – Angelica Branca, the wife of a major in the army, a woman with first-class connections in the music scene. Angelica was ahead of her time, Gilberto said, one of those modern women: neat skirt, flat shoes, flat-curved American hair. Jackie said she knew the type, though she wasn't sure she did and was pretty sure she didn't want to. He said that Angelica knew an impresario, with a club in Copacabana, who was on the lookout for modern talent. Angelica couldn't promise anything but she would have a word in his ear, she said, because there was something fresh and original about Gilberto's music. Angelica liked the fact that he came from Minas – Angelica's father came from Ouro Preto – because Minas folk were dependable, prudent, not given to advertising themselves but supremely *deserving*.

Over the next few weeks he saw Angelica frequently. Angelica knows the business, he would say; she's teaching me how to play the game. Then one day he announced that Friday would be the night. He would meet Angelica for dinner, she would brief him and they would hit the club where the impresario would give Gilberto a private audience. If all went well, he would sing 'Jardim, Jardim' to the public that night. There would be TV people in the audience, she said, and record company boys from Odeon and Philips. Gilberto chirped all week about Angelica, his prospects of a record deal, his dreams of playing Carnegie Hall.

When Friday arrived, Gilberto spent an age slicking his hair and making sure his clothes looked just right. Jackie wanted to come along, but he said this was business, not pleasure, that there would be plenty of opportunities for them to bathe in the moonlight of his success. So when he left she closed the door behind him and sat on the balcony smoking cigarettes she'd secretly bought, listening to people pass in the street talking excitedly because it was Friday, because they were Brazilian. And Jackie remembered asking herself how she had come to be a person who listened to other people being happy. On the very night their lives were supposedly taking a turn for the better, she felt further from home than ever before. She stood and looked into the street then went and sat on Joel's bed and stroked his hair and watched his stirrings for a while. How easy it would be, she thought, to fetch my passport from the drawer, take some money from the safe and get a taxi to the airport. All it would take would be for my legs to make me stand and my hands to collect the necessary things on my behalf. I could change my life back to the way it was before. Joel would miss me, but he'd be all right with his dad. It would be a good place for him to grow up. His life might well be better without the burden of an unhappy mother. One day he would understand. But it wasn't possible for her legs or arms to make that move because they were frozen by her love for Joel, and no matter what suffering it meant she knew she could never leave him behind, and she couldn't just take him away without organising a million things, so she'd simply have to make the best of it. But there would be no siblings to go with Joel, she decided that night, out on the dark balcony at the end of her packet of cigarettes. She would not bear Gilberto another child, no matter how well this business with the music went. She would take the Pill, whatever the risks. She would give her true love to Joel and a cover version to his dad.

When Gilberto returned not long before dawn to breathe fermented breath on the back of her neck, Jackie pretended she was asleep. He hummed one of his tunes and pressed himself into her. For the first time Jackie thought, 'I hate you,' and it burned her beautifully to think the words, whatever nonsense anyone said about love, love, love – so she thought them again and again and again until she fell asleep.

Jackie turned off the video, made a cup of tea and smoked a cigarette. She had a bit of a headache so she fetched a wet flannel and lay back with it over her eyes. It wasn't quite the same as when Joel did it for her, but it still felt soothing. Get me, she thought. Dredging up the past, running fingers over my scars.

'Scars are your stars,' Miriam always said. 'Make sure you steer by them.'

She wondered what Tony was doing. Probably in the garden, she thought. I bet he always gardens when there's something on his mind. In her dreams she'd be running to Tony, not lying here with a wet flannel on her face. How dull it was to consider consequences. She was tempted to throw off the flannel, run upstairs, pick that red dress up off the floor, shake it down, peel off her jeans, slip smaller underwear up her legs, put on a lacier, cuppier bra and wriggle her arse into that blasted frock. She imagined hooking a pair of heels from the wardrobe, fastening their tiny clasps – then wishing she'd done so at the bottom of the stairs, as she half twisted an ankle on the descent. She'd do her lipstick in the hall mirror. She'd look good, though she'd feel less than comfortable – it never did to rush the donning of impractical garments. She would ride across town in a cab and they'd scream at each other and end up screwing the dregs out of their conflict.

But she didn't rush upstairs. She remained on the sofa enjoying the flannel even though it was hardly cool any more. She groped on the table for her cigarettes and lit one. She smoked it then climbed the stairs. In the bathroom she ran the taps and washed her face with soap and cold water. My face looks old, she thought, too old to be playing games. If Tony didn't call soon, she pledged to brush her hair and put on her tatty coat, to go and tell him everything – apologising for the twists and turns. Perhaps this was the start of something, she thought, not the end.

'Perhaps it's just the start,' she said to the mirror.

She sat in the lounge with the TV off. She looked at the phone but she couldn't pick it up. If she called and he said it was over, then... it would be over. She dreaded bringing on that moment. Joel was in Brazil and perhaps he wouldn't come back and then she'd have lost him too and what would she have? She'd always imagined life would be perfect one day. She was running out of days.

Nelson went to sleep with Joel's money under the pillow and dreamed of walking the streets of Paraty with a woman in a white dress, who was not anything like Eva, who talked a lot less than her and looked at Nelson with pretty monkey eyes while a *choro* band played soothing tunes. It felt divine to be in Paraty, a place he'd always wanted to visit, though after a while it became uncomfortable because the sunlight became painfully bright. As the light shone more insistently, he saw a man in a Vasco shirt holding a torch, a man who had no right to be in his dreams and certainly no business slapping him round the face and throwing him on the floor.

'You're in big trouble, Flamengo,' Vasco said.

Adolfo stood over Nelson with his hands in his pockets. He wore a white shirt rolled to the elbows and shiny shoes. He didn't look a violent man, with his almost delicate build, tidy black hair and eyebrows neat enough to have been plucked.

'A man who owes me money has no place ordering taxis,' he said. 'If it weren't for Zemané, you'd already be in the boot of a car. I know a lovely spot across the bay where they say the water is deeper than the ocean.'

'I have some money,' said Nelson. 'And more on the way. I can pay back hundreds by the end of the week.'

'Two thousand *reais* you owe me,' said Adolfo. 'And you can thank Zemané for persuading me to charge a preferential interest rate. Your *bunda* is mine, my new delivery boy, until you work off that sum or die – whichever comes later.'

'Surely even a delivery boy is allowed to dress in private?' said Nelson.

'Five minutes,' said Adolfo, and to Vasco, 'Guard the door.'

Vasco stood outside, but it was no great testament to the intelligence of the mountain nor his boss that they neglected to think of the balcony. Nelson slipped into black shorts and yellow T-shirt, stuffed his cash in his pocket, took the photo of his sister from the mirror, shoved belongings into a carrier bag, shinned from the balcony, bolted through the gate and ran as fast as he could. As light started to tinge the edges of the sky, his feet seemed to glide over the cobbles. Once he was sure he wasn't being pursued, he strolled towards

138

Centro, reaching it as the sun was blaring white through the gaps between buildings. There was a trickle of shoeshine boys and street vendors with bags stuffed full of wares. The shutters of cafés and kiosks were winding into position and the first cars and buses of the morning tide were rolling down the road, still able to go at a pace they chose because of the emptiness of the streets. As light bloomed he saw the first suit, then two, and soon the pavements were full of people with purposeful strides. The more he thought about it, the more he liked the fact that he had a mission. It wasn't every day you had the chance to bring a man back from the grave. He joined the morning flow down Avenida Rio Branco, stopping for a *misto quente* and a *cafezinho* at a corner café.

As he ate, he tried to think about how to find Gilberto. There was no point chasing his lie to Cantagalo. Perhaps he should start instead where it all began, he thought. So he caught a bus back to the hijack spot, found one of Joel's posters taped to a tree and took it down. He set about talking to concierges, maids and security men, to people walking down the street and waiters in bars and restaurants.

After a couple of hours he was about to find a place to eat and think of another plan, when a concierge said, 'Yeah, I know him.'

'You *know* him?' said Nelson with a grin.

'I've seen him, yes.'

Edinho was thin, with white hair and a white moustache. Behind his counter were pictures of his wife, two granddaughters and a dog with a red bow.

'Round here?' asked Nelson.

'Not far away.'

'Recently?'

'Who wants to know?'

'A man with money.'

'You don't look like a man with money,' Edinho said, glancing at Nelson's plastic bag.

'I'm working for him,' said Nelson.

'So what kind of money are we talking about?'

'That depends what you have to tell me.'

'I know a place he goes at the same time every week,' said Edinho.

'A place round here?'

'That would be telling.'

'I'll give you a hundred *reais* if you tell me where,' said Nelson.

'That's not a lot of money for a man with money.'

'It's not bad for sitting on your *bunda*.'

Edinho looked at Nelson and shrugged.

'A hundred *reais*?'

'Fifty now, and fifty if he's where you say.'

'How about a hundred now and fifty if he's there? That way I don't have to worry if you forget about the fifty.'

'All right,' said Nelson. 'Where does he go?'

'A restaurant on the other side of the lake: O Paraiso,' said Edinho. 'He goes there on Thursdays at lunch.'

'Every Thursday?'

'As far as I know.'

'And how do you know?' asked Nelson.

'I go there sometimes. It's a bit of a walk from here, but the doctor told me I have to exercise. And I like the pizzas. They make them properly, with lots of tomato.'

'You're sure it's a Thursday? You're sure it's him?'

'It's not the best photo, but I'd say so,' said Edinho.

'He doesn't look like the type to lunch.'

'No, but there you go. I guess he helps them out or something, and they feed him. Maybe they just feel sorry for him, I don't know – I never asked. Always sits at a table at the back by the kitchen.'

'Do you know his name?' asked Nelson.

'Gilberto Cabral.'

'That's amazing! Oh, I can't tell you – '

'That's what it says on the poster,' chuckled Edinho. 'That's who you're looking for, right?'

Nelson gave him a hundred *reais*, promising to pay the rest at the end of the week, then walked up and down the block and around the surrounding streets, taking posters down from lamp-posts, phone boxes and bars. When he'd removed all the posters he could find, he strolled round the lake until he found O Paraiso. There were three tables on the pavement and a couple of dozen inside. Nelson sat at the bar, drank a beer and studied the layout. There was indeed a table at the back by the kitchen, though no one was sitting there today. He considered showing the poster to a waiter, to check Edinho's story – but what if they told Gilberto his son was looking for him? Perhaps he'd disappear for good. This is my fish to land, Nelson thought.

He wandered from the bar and found a bench by the waterside. Across the lake, the pale tower blocks of Leblon spread before the peaks of Dois Irmãos. Nelson counted his money – forty-three *reais*. If he was going to solve his problems with Adolfo, it was time to raise the stakes. It was a pity to take advantage of Joel's situation, regrettable to give him the run-around until Thursday, but what else could he do? It might be Nelson's only chance to save his skin. Besides, one could argue it was only right for Joel to gain a sense that they were really *searching*. Having travelled across an ocean, it might be an anticlimax to find treasure under the very first X. The more he thought about it, the more he liked the idea of a little journey out of town, and it wouldn't be such a bad idea to leave the city for a day or two, now that Adolfo had a spot marked out for him at the bottom of the bay.

Nelson found a phone booth and called Bar do Paulo. He heard stools scrape and voices hush as Zemané came to the phone. 'So he hasn't killed you yet...' said Zemané.

'Thanks to you,' said Nelson.

'But now you've run. Even I have only so many favours.'

'I understand... and if you turn me down, well, who would blame you? But I wondered... if you could help me one last time... I've thought of a way to solve everything.'

'Will it cost me?' asked Zemané.

'No.'

'Will it stop me having to bail you out every half an hour?'

'One thousand per cent!' said Nelson.

'I'll believe it when I see it.'

'There's a free dinner in it too – a *churrasco*, at Porcão.'

'I'm listening,' said Zemané.

In the afternoon, Jackie went for a rare walk. She headed along Queen's Park Road to Race Hill, then past the hospital and the allotments above the cemetery, skirting the side of the racetrack with the grandstand to her right looking over the valley in which sat Whitehawk. She turned across the track and there in front of her was the sea, impossible to escape and seemingly larger from this height, with patches of light falling on it through the clouds. She walked down through Sheepcote, alone in the scrub of the valley but for occasional dog-walkers.

Jackie couldn't chase Brazil from her thoughts. As a younger woman she would never have imagined the scabs would last for decades. She supposed some people simply healed more quickly, just as some ran faster or ate more. She wondered if there was still a trace of hatred in her heart. That curdling of love was the saddest thing: so impossible to foresee, so very hard to reverse. Those Angelica days had been the hardest; that was when it had really turned.

Gilberto's concert had been a success, so he'd said. He'd been allowed to sing his song, and the record company boys had seemed impressed by his vision for the Minas sound. It was true they'd talked a lot about *Tropicália* and *yê-yê-yê*, but they'd been very much on his wavelength, Gilberto told her. The television people had promised to be in touch. Angelica had the nerve to call Jackie and purr that he'd been marvellous.

Gilberto had dinner with Angelica frequently and the news she relayed was always positive. Sometimes they would meet first at an apartment she kept on Vieira Souto, overlooking Ipanema beach, so he could sing songs he was developing for an album, to be called *Jardim!* The record companies were still keen, she said. It was a matter of timing: selecting a slot between releases, estimating when the public was ready for his radical sound, finding the perfect date on which to let a single fly like a hot balloon.

Jackie began to *enjoy* hating him. She tried to ensure she and Joel were out when he came home from work, leaving vague notes about their whereabouts and time of return. She wore long skirts with Gilberto and short skirts without him. She cut her hair. She took tennis lessons with a coach with a reputation for pillaging wives. She became friends with a sculptress from Bahia and hung out with people from the artistic left. When Gilberto dined with Angelica, Jackie left Joel with the maid and went to Le Bateau or Sucata, where she saw the Bahians play.

One night she came home late to find Gilberto on the balcony swigging a glass of whisky. She poured one for herself, sat across the table, lit a cigarette and waited for him to start one of his rants.

'She's robbed me,' he said.

Jackie laughed. 'I'm sorry?'

'That bitch has robbed me.'

'Don't tell me – stole your heart and sold it cheap – '

'Money, you idiot,' he said. 'She's taken my money.'

'You were *paying* her?'

'It was for the record company. She told me there were costs.'

'And you're calling *me* an idiot?'

'She said there was a lot of competition.' Gilberto's voice trembled. 'They liked the sound, there was never any doubt about that. There were ways of jumping the queue...'

Jackie started to laugh. 'To think I thought you were screwing her... and she was shafting you!'

'I rang them. I thought it would help if I rang them – the record company boys. They said they would have called had

143

they been interested. They said they liked my voice but they were looking for something a bit more revolutionary. They mentioned Caetano and Gil. They said the Minas angle was already being covered by Milton Nascimento – his sound is black gold, they said. I asked them about the money, but they didn't know what I was talking about.'

There was despair in the wideness of his eyes, desperation in his broken voice.

'I went to her flat,' he said, on his feet now. 'The concierge wouldn't let me up. He gave me an envelope with my name on it. Inside was a card: "My husband suspects".'

'So much suspicion upon such innocents!'

'She *robbed* me! Don't you see? I've been *conned*! My dreams – '

'What about *our* dreams?' sad Jackie, jumping up, slamming down her hand.

'They *were* our dreams! I wrote those songs for you, for you and Joel.'

'And you fucked her for us too, I suppose?'

Gilberto turned in his stride and swung at Jackie, though she managed to sway backwards so that he missed. She remembered thinking, he just tried to hit me. Did he just try to hit me?

She clenched her fists and screamed at him, 'It's over, you son of a bitch! I'm going back home!'

'Don't say that!' Gilberto took a step towards Jackie, who backed against the rail. 'All I want is you, my love!'

'Well, I'm all you can never have, *filho da puta*!'

'I never slept with her, I swear to God. I never even kissed her. You *must* believe me, honey, say you believe me – '

'Oh, pull the other one!'

'Not once!'

'A frigid thief – you know how to pick 'em!'

'I'll make it up to you, you'll see. I've been negligent, I can see that. I was blind. I'll work hard for you both. I'll give up singing – '

'I'm not asking you to give up singing.'

'I will, I'll give it up. I'll give it up for you – '

'I'm not asking you to give up singing.'

Weeks passed. Gilberto rose early every day and went for a swim on Ipanema beach. He brought Jackie tea and fruit in bed, gave Joel his breakfast and set off early for work. He squeezed a couple more patients into his day and ceased stopping at the *botequim* for a beer on the way home. He would cook or they'd dine out. He stayed away from the clubs. Only once did Jackie see him rabid. In December '68, Gilberto Gil and Caetano Veloso were arrested. The night they heard the news, Gilberto bought a bottle of old cachaça to celebrate. He sat on the balcony sipping golden liquid from a tumbler.

'Where's their *Tropicália* now?' he said. '"Be a criminal, be a hero" – isn't that what they said? Let's see how they like it in a cell full of heroes.'

Jackie couldn't deny that things were on the up. Joel turned four in the summer of '69 and Gilberto spent a lot more time with him. They would kick a football around in a square, or spend hours playing in the surf. Jackie remembered glorious afternoons beneath the umbrellas of Castelinho on the Ipanema seafront, wearing a favourite white bikini Gilberto had bought her, watching the buzz of the beach. 1970 also started well, with Joel at school and Jackie starting to work part time in an office on Visconde de Pirajá. At times it was frightening to hear friends talk of the abduction of a cousin, the torture of an acquaintance. It made Jackie angry that Joel should have to grow up in a land where the police were to be feared more than criminals. But no matter how dark the regime, the sun still shone and Gilberto could take Joel to the Maracanã and forget about the troubles of the world as they cheered a goal by Liminha or Doval. Jackie and Gilberto talked about having more children, and Jackie agreed that it was time, feeling proud to have a man with the strength to defeat the devil inside.

One May morning at the surgery, Gilberto picked up his daylist to find Angelica's name at the top. He kept his back to her as his nurse prepared her in the chair, then filled a tooth of hers with gold without meeting her eyes. Her bottom lip was swollen and split. When the procedure was complete, the nurse left. Gilberto washed his hands in the corner and prayed Angelica would leave.

'I wish we'd really given the bastard something to be jealous about,' Angelica said in a quiet voice.

'If you're selling sympathy, I'm not buying,' said Gilberto without turning round.

'We could have had a ball, darling.'

'If I'd fucked you for the money you stole – wouldn't that make you a whore?'

'Is that what they told you, *querido*? Those record company boys are smarter than alligators.'

Gilberto turned round.

'Even if I had the time, which I don't, you'd be wasting your breath. I'm happy, Angelica. Can you understand that? I'm happy. You've taken quite enough already, you and your alligators. Leave me alone.'

At least, that was the version he recounted to Jackie that night. She didn't believe it was the whole truth... but there was little she could do and, well, they *were* happy, weren't they? Whatever had or hadn't happened. The present truth was the only truth that mattered, wasn't it?

At the end of May, Gilberto and Jackie took a bus to Paraty to celebrate her twenty-seventh birthday. It was the first time they'd been away without Joel. Inseparably they roamed the narrow streets, or lay together in a hammock in their *pousada* chirping stories of their lives before they met. Gilberto hired a schooner and they dived for starfish in the bluest shallows then sunbathed in a circle of them on the beach. On the bus home, as the mountains of Rio loomed, Jackie kissed him and said, 'Why don't you see if you can sing one night at A Gaiola?'

'I'm not sure,' he said, with excited eyes. 'I mean, are you sure – ?'

'We could go together, like the old days. Oh, let's, Gil!'

The next Friday they gave Gilberto top billing. Old smiles met his every gaze. There was warm applause as the spotlight lit him for the first time in over eighteen months, and happy murmurs as the band played the first bars of 'Samba do Avião' and regulars recalled past nights with this voice at their heart. Gilberto sang three Jobim songs, a slow rendition of a number by Jorge Ben, and finished with a much applauded version of 'Jardim, Jardim'.

In a back corner, a portly man sat on his own with a tumbler of whisky and a fat cigar. From his place in the spotlight Gilberto could discern few details of the crowd but he noticed the shape of this man, the peculiarity of his solitude, the fact that he kept his eyes constantly upon him and that he used his hands only to smoke and drink and not to applaud. Gilberto later recalled the irony of the thought that raced around his mind: that here was a real mogul from a record company. Perhaps whispers of his return had slithered from ear to ear, spurring a powerful man to seize his chance to hear the Nightingale again. Gilberto was almost certain he recognised his face. Had he seen his picture in a magazine? he wondered.

Only later did he make the connection with photographs in Angelica's apartment.

The following morning the doorbell rang at five o'clock. Two men in brown suits waited politely while Gilberto and Jackie dressed. Jackie made coffee for the federal policemen and tried to open a vista of friendship, but they would go no further than to state with neutral smiles that the authorities would like to ask a few questions. The men drank their coffee and checked their watches. Gilberto told Jackie not to worry. There was nothing to worry about. He would set matters straight and would see her later. Perhaps she should stay at home in case he needed her to pick him up. He gave her the keys to the Beetle, kissed her on the cheek and left with the men.

When Jackie arrived home from her walk to Sheepcote, she made sausage, mash and beans, mashing the spuds the way Joel liked to do it – with butter, cream and basil – though it was a bit fancy for her taste. She ate in front of *Judge Judy* then washed up.

As she was finishing, the phone started to ring. She dried her hands quickly on her jeans, walked into the lounge, smoothed her hair and picked up the receiver.

'Hello?'

'It's Tony,' he said.

'So it is!'

'Look... I won't beat about the bush... I think we should cool things for a while...'

'Do you have a period of "while" in mind?' asked Jackie.

'I mean... for good.'

'That is a long while.'

There was silence but Tony did not put down the phone. Jackie could not help but think that, if he really wanted to end it, the onus was on him to hang up. She wasn't going to. Perhaps he was too polite. Perhaps he didn't want to finish it, even if he thought he did.

'I'm sorry, Jackie. I just can't see a way – '

'It's perfectly all right. You don't have to explain. We're grown-ups. Why don't I come over this afternoon and fetch my things?'

'Your things? Right, of course. This afternoon's no good, I'm afraid, but I'm not sure – '

'Then leave me a message and let me know when's best.'

Jackie put down the phone.

She made a cup of tea and watered the wilting basil plant on the windowsill. She wondered if there was something peculiar about falling for two such very different men as Gilberto and Tony. Did the disparity suggest a lack of

148

honesty about what she really wanted? Did she just like Tony – love Tony? – because he was so different from Gilberto? Was it the difference or the man himself? She hoped she was beyond such crude reactions – at her age, after so much time. But even though she didn't think about Gilberto every day or even every month, his shadow still fell across her love life. Yet you couldn't run your fingers across the skin of a shadow. A new skin ought to beat an old ghost every time.

Joel walked the few blocks to Porcão and took a table at the side of the large windowless restaurant. He watched waiters armed with skewers of meat weave between tables laid with white cloths. He looked hungrily towards a giant buffet. Just as he was wondering if Nelson would come at all, a waiter brought him over.

'Mind if we join you?' said Nelson.

With Nelson was an older man with lightly slicked-back hair, a blue shirt and a Panama hat.

Zemané introduced himself.

'Not your father, I'm afraid,' he said, and shook hands with Joel.

'A friend of Nelson's?' asked Joel.

'More like an uncle,' said Zemané.

Nelson put his bag on a chair and Zemané parked his hat. Then they all took their plates to the buffet, which was crowned with a pig's head carved from a melon. Joel picked up salad and quail's eggs, some sashimi, curls of ginger and a smudge of wasabi. They returned to the table and Joel flipped over a disc, so that a green cartoon of a pig showed instead of a red one. A circling waiter swooped with a joint of *picanha* on a skewer. He carved a sliver as Joel held it with a pair of tongs. Zemané tucked a napkin into his collar and spooned rice and beans on to his plate. Joel ordered drinks. Caipirinhas arrived and waiters presented more cuts of beef. Zemané accepted some chicken hearts and Nelson waved over a waiter bearing sausages. Joel took a couple then turned the discs from green to red. Waiters swished passed, their eyes on the discs in case of a change.

'So,' said Joel, sitting back. 'What's the story?'

Zemané finished his mouthful, wiped his mouth, took a sip of his drink, sat back and said, 'The business is the following: I saw your father last Friday in Paraty.'

'In *Paraty*? That's miles away,' said Joel.

'In Paraty,' Nelson said with a nod.

'Are you sure?'

'Ninety per cent,' said Zemané.

'Ninety per cent?' said Joel. 'What about the other ten?'

'I'm never a hundred per cent about anything,' said Zemané.

'So where did you see him, I mean, what was he doing?'

'Walking in the street, sitting in the street... later on he was lying in the street.'

Joel looked at Nelson and said, 'What happened to Cantagalo?'

'I guess he must have moved on,' said Nelson, his eyes darting to Zemané.

'He must have been in Rio last Monday,' said Joel, 'because I saw him on the news.'

'I guess he left town,' said Zemané, and turned a disc to green.

Waiters carved more slices of rare beef. Zemané ate slowly, as if nothing in the world were at stake. Nelson made another trip to the buffet, before diving on his food again. He cast smiles at Joel, who wondered what to do. It was hard to believe they were telling anything like the truth. He wondered if there were people who could verify Nelson was lying simply from the way he smiled: interrogators or poker players perhaps? To the learned eye a thousand signs... but Joel's eye was not well schooled and all he could think of was the ninety per cent, though he knew he ought to be worrying more about the ten.

'OK,' said Joel, and smiled. 'I'm really grateful for the tip-off. If you could tell me exactly where you saw him, I'll head to Paraty.'

Zemané put down his cutlery and turned the disc to red. 'Why don't you go with Nelson? He can show you.'

'Do I get the feeling that's more than a suggestion?'

'Let me sum things up,' said Zemané. 'You want to find your father. You're happy to pay but you don't want to pay for lies.'

'Obviously not.'

'So, you and Nelson take a trip to Paraty. You pay him just like before – what did you agree – a hundred and fifty a day? Nelson will take you to where I saw the man and he'll help you look round. Maybe you'll find him tomorrow, or the next day, or the next. If he doesn't show up by the end of the week, you stop paying and carry on alone... Are you understanding?'

'All right, I get the picture, but – '

Zemané held up his hand. 'Of course, when we find him, there's the reward your poster mentions... I expect you had a sum in mind?'

'Of course,' said Joel.

'Shall I tell you if you're close?'

'I'm guessing it's more than I intended,'

'How about two thousand *reais*?' said Zemané.

'You must be bloody joking!' said Joel. 'Do I look like an idiot?'

'Just over seven hundred pounds,' said Zemané. 'Not a bad price for a father. I bet you earn more in a week.'

'That's not the point – '

'I think it's a fair price – fathers are in short supply these days.'

'I preferred Nelson's prices, personally.'

'My friend prefers mine,' said Zemané.

'I thought he was your nephew,' said Joel.

'Nephew, brother, friend,' said Zemané. 'It's all the same to a Carioca.'

Nelson shrugged and smiled apologetically, as if to indicate he would have cut a more generous deal.

Two thousand *reais*, thought Joel. What did they take him for? Maybe he *could* afford it, but it was a lot of money to ask. Ninety per cent certain: were he a betting man he still wouldn't take the odds... but could he turn down *any* possibility of finding his old man? Besides, Joel would only have to pay if they did actually find Gilberto, so perhaps it wasn't as bad as it seemed. It might be a lot of money, but nothing compared to the prize.

'OK,' said Joel. 'Two thousand – if you take me to him, in person, no stunts. All on delivery – not half now, half later – and nothing if you fail.'

Joel held out his hand. Nelson looked at Zemané, who nodded, so Nelson shook.

Zemané turned a disc to green and waiters descended. The three of them ate more meat, with rice and beans and chips and cheese-bread. When they'd eaten their fill, a waiter took their plates, and another wheeled a dessert trolley to the table. They chose puddings. Zemané ordered a brandy and lit a cigar. They talked about Flamengo's recent results and the latest news on Sandro and the hijack. Joel tried to find meanings hidden in their words and glances, without success.

When they had all finished, a waiter brought the bill. Joel glanced at Zemané, who showed no sign of paying for his friend or nephew or himself, so Joel paid for the three of them. Zemané thanked him for his generosity, wished him the best of luck, then ambled to the door. Joel and Nelson followed shortly afterwards and walked to the front of Tiffany's. Nelson wanted to ask if he could stay, but feared his credibility might be diminished if Joel knew the gravity of his predicament, so, telling Joel he was staying with a friend in Cantagalo, he headed instead for the lake, and followed its shore until he found a suitable bush. It had been a few years since he'd slept under branches, and it made him think of the life his sister led after she ran away. It made him ache to think of her sleeping without walls to protect her, without a roof to shelter her pretty head. It hurt more than anything to know he hadn't been there when her moment had come.

Seven

Jackie sat in a deckchair in the garden. She read a book, drank tea and checked the signal on her mobile often. She wondered how long it would take Tony to call. There wasn't much to pick up: a bracelet she'd taken off to replace with one he'd bought her, a red bikini she'd worn while she watched him garden, a pair of leather gloves, a book she'd finished and three bossa nova CDs. It was always handy to leave a few things at a lover's house.

She didn't think he'd leave it very long and, in any case, this minor torture was nothing next to the disembowellings of the past: to have a husband in prison, probably maimed, possibly dead, while you feared every knock on the door of your sweltering flat and tried to pacify a child who only wanted his daddy back. She had received one letter during Gilberto's first stint in jail. She'd found it sitting quietly in their mailbox in August 1970, over two months after his arrest, as if it were the most natural thing in the world for a letter to arrive from a man she'd thought she might never see again. The letter was written in black ink on fine paper decorated with leaves and oranges. Having been petrified on his behalf, having been tormented by a lack of news, having spent days berating staff at police stations and government offices, it felt absurd to receive a letter of such elegant appearance.

Gilberto wrote that, upon leaving the flat, the two men in suits had shown him into the back of a van, in which there were two more agents. There were no windows, though weak light from the windscreen half lit the indifferent faces of his captors. Gilberto had tried to memorise their route but it was hard to see much from where he sat and he soon lost track. The agents had chatted about football and plans for the weekend as if Gilberto were not there. As the van stole him further from home Gilberto remembered his casual remarks about repression – a cloud he'd assumed would sit overhead for a while but rain only on others – and felt sudden sympathy for imprisoned artists, solidarity with missing writers. He felt for the Bahians. He feared he might vomit.

As Jackie read the letter, she wondered how it could have arrived in such a pristine state and how a man suspected of agitation – she assumed this was the charge – could be allowed to post such thoughts?

An agent had taken Gilberto's arm and pulled him roughly out of the van. Gilberto remarked on the peculiarity of being handled with hostility and realised that in the course of his life he'd been touched a million times with Brazilian affection but never once by a man who meant him harm. He was made to sit in a corridor on a plastic chair, where he waited for hours, ignored by passing soldiers and clerks in spite of requests for a glass of water. Once a soldier had taken him to the bathroom, remaining behind him as he peed. At the end of the day he was taken on a long ride in another van with two military policemen who told him not to look at them. They talked about a new lieutenant nicknamed Martelo – 'Hammer' – who'd made a *malandro* sing like a bird the night before. Gilberto wondered if they knew he was known as the Nightingale. He kept his eyes away from the eyes of the guards but it was hard not to look at their black machine guns. He had the feeling that even to touch them would hurt.

Gilberto was marched though a compound with one guard in front, and another behind nudging a gun in his back. He was taken into a block four or five storeys high, the outside of which was studded with lines of bars through which black arms flailed like antennae. He was ordered to empty his pockets, remove his watch and take off all his clothes except his underpants. He was kept standing as papers were examined. There seemed confusion over his category and, although the soldiers were in favour of putting him in one of the large cells with the *malandros*, the sergeant decided that even if the reasons for his incarceration were not typical, were unclear even, it was preferable to lodge him with the political prisoners in the solitary section, since the papers had been signed by the major, and the sergeant didn't want to be responsible for spoiling the prisoner, in case the major had his own plans.

For two months, Gilberto lived in a cell just long enough to lie down in, with a dirty mattress and a dribble of a shower in a corner beside a toilet which was often blocked, making it hard to escape a stench of shit. The heat was almost unbearable, with only a tiny window high on the wall and a hatch in the door for ventilation. He was fed a chunk of hard bread and a mug of coffee in the morning, water every now and again, and a slop of chewy meat and beans at lunch, into which the more humorous guards would sometimes drop a cockroach – though after a while he retched no more from the embellished food than the unadulterated. Some of the guards would talk to him through the hatch – about Flamengo, the news, their families. Gilberto loathed hearing them speak about their children. Others would talk of how they were going to put him in with the *malandros* and tell them he'd raped a little girl. Sometimes Gilberto was able to talk to those in neighbouring cells, though the teacher on the left would only talk about God, and a journalist on the right was taken away crying one night. After a while Gilberto started talking to himself, taking on the role of Jackie or Joel, imagining them in the Botanical Gardens on a Sunday afternoon after lunch at a *churrascaria*. Joel would talk about school or Flamengo, or they would plan the promised trip up Pedra da Gávea. Gilberto swore that when he was released they'd buy a compass and a map, pick the perfect day and tackle the ascent – just as soon as he put on a bit of weight again and built his strength up. Jackie promised to cook his favourite meals: *fricassê de galinha* or *cabrito à caçadora* with mountains of *farofa* and cheese-bread still warm and sticky in the middle.

Every few days Gilberto would be taken out of his cell and marched round the compound with a gun at his back. Once or twice he was allowed to sit on the grass in the sun. He took great interest in the hazy blue shapes of mountains on the horizon and tried to write a song in his head about the longing for freedom they inspired, but all he could conjure was an endless string of notes which refused to settle into a melody. One day he was led at gunpoint into a low building in which a radio was playing Bach, where a tall lieutenant handed Gilberto his clothes. When Gilberto had dressed he was shown into an office and told to sit in a chair behind a broad mahogany desk. A soldier stood in a corner, holding a machine gun across his chest.

'Your wife is here to see you,' said the lieutenant, his voice thick with disapproval.

'My wife!'

'It's not for me to question the major's orders,' said the lieutenant. 'But bear in mind that if you rise from your seat you will be shot.'

'After all the beautiful times,' Gilberto wrote, 'it might seem odd, my darling, that I have never felt happier than at that moment: sitting in a chair in clothes which seemed to have grown, with a soldier in the corner watching me with black eyes and a finger on a trigger. How terrible then – you must believe how truly sickening – to hear light footsteps on the tiles and raise my eyes and catch sight, not of you, but of Angelica...'

Angelica said she had come to repay him for the trouble she'd caused. She had thought of the idea while walking in the Botanical Gardens, she said, a place she knew was a favourite haunt of his and Jackie's. The notion had struck her immediately as being perilous but brilliant; foolhardy, but worthy. How better to repay Gilberto and his poor wife than by typing an order on the major's headed paper and forging his signature – thus securing permission for Gilberto's 'wife' to visit him, and thereby gifting Gilberto the ability to write a letter? Angelica had brought him paper from Tuscany and a Swiss fountain pen belonging to the major. She pledged to deliver the letter the very next day, swearing she would leave it sealed.

Gilberto wrote that another good thing had come from Angelica's visit. She'd told him the major was away but would soon be back and would interrogate him personally – and that he knew very little about their friendship, despite what he might claim. If Gilberto answered simply and told the truth – that they were innocent – she was convinced her husband would set him free.

'He is a fair man,' she said. 'He believes that only the deserving should be hurt.'

When Jackie had read the letter, she walked into the bathroom and vomited. She wished she were a witch with sores to unleash upon her rival's flesh. She paced the Ipanema seafront throughout the following weeks, hoping to catch Angelica leaving her apartment – though she was ignorant of its precise location. She scoured the appointment books at Gilberto's surgery but found only a phone number, which she called and called. She got through once and screamed curses down the silent phone in her foulest Portuguese.

Jackie heard nothing more that year. 1971 arrived and she became convinced of Gilberto's death. For the first time in years she thought about returning to England. Life in Brazil without Gilberto could never be the same and she worried the wrath of the major would always hang above them. The regime did not write happy endings. Might it harm the children of its enemies? Even if Gilberto *were* set free... could she be sure that he and Angelica would leave each other alone? Jackie started to plan for a newer, safer life on the other side of the sea – where Joel could grow up in a town cradled in the Downs, in which the majors were retired and the policemen mostly on your side.

One Sunday afternoon in February 1971, Jackie opened the door and in Gilberto walked. She was reminded of drawings in medical books of muscle and sinew stripped of fat and skin. He had skin, but so much less beneath it. Wrinkles spread from all corners of his face and his eyes were those of another man: darting, angry, beseeching. Most striking of all, his head looked far too small for his giant white teeth.

They stood apart and looked at each other. She knew they ought to hug, but neither of them moved.

'I'm so glad you're back,' she said.

'What's wrong?' he asked.

'Nothing.'

'Joel?' said Gilberto and moved towards Joel's room.

'No,' she said grabbing his arm. 'He's at the Saavedras, he's fine.'

'Then what?'

She stood between Gilberto and their bedroom. As if he'd read her thoughts, he tried to pass. She blocked his way. His eyes flared and he pushed her aside so that her hip cracked against a table.

'If there's someone,' he growled, 'I'll kill...'

It was impossible to hide the fact of the suitcases, packed and waiting by the bed. Two leather ones of hers and Joel's Winnie-the-Pooh knapsack.

'How could you go?' he said, his voice quiet.

'I couldn't bear it any more – the waiting, the – '

'And take Joel away?'

'I thought you were dead,' said Jackie.

'You hoped I was dead.'

'That's not true!'

'To think: the thought of seeing you both was all that kept me alive.'

159

'I'm sorry, Gil, I was beside myself. I'm glad you're back, I really – '

'Save it,' he said. 'I need a drink. I'm going out.'

Jackie would never admit it to Joel, but sometimes she thought it would have been easier for them all if Gilberto *had* died that first time in prison, or if he'd come back that day to find they'd already caught their flight. Perhaps it was harsh to wish away a child's chance to know his father, but how much simpler it would have been to dig out memories with weaker roots.

Nelson woke at first light, bitten half to death, which was half as much as he'd been expecting. He brushed his fingers through his hair, picked up his plastic bag and headed along the shore of the lake. High on the hill, Cristo was wrapped in a white cloud and Nelson smiled to think that he too might sleep in soft sheets that night. I'm still in the game, he thought. I might be a few goals down but I'm still in the game. He crossed the road into quiet Ipanema streets and soon arrived at Tiffany's, where Joel was coming out of the high front door. Upon seeing him, Nelson felt a pang of guilt at the ruse he was playing, consoling himself that he *would* take Joel to his father, just not for a couple of days.

Joel noticed that Nelson's hair was clumpy and that he wore the same clothes as the night before. He wondered where Nelson might have slept. He put down his small rucksack, gripped Nelson's outstretched hand and patted him on the back. He had to admit he was glad they were going away. This wasn't meant to be a holiday, but Joel had always wanted to go to Paraty. Besides the night before he'd dreamt in Portuguese for the first time in decades, and it made him want to dive into Brazil.

They took a yellow taxi to the Novo Rio bus terminal. Joel chatted to Nelson as the city sights flew by, and he could feel Brazilian phrases coming quicker to his tongue and words he didn't realise he knew sprouting in his sentences. Nelson talked about his Aunt Zila and her eleven commandments, and Joel found his understanding almost always kept pace with the speed of Nelson's words.

They arrived at the terminal, queued for tickets, then had a *folhado* and a *cafezinho*. Nelson disappeared to the bathroom, so Joel sat and watched people of every shape and colour walk loose and fast across the station. The day already had a rhythm, and it made him feel calm to sit quietly in its midst. And he did feel calm, sitting there, watching the world, knowing there was nothing more he could do at that minute to find his father. I might as well enjoy it while I'm here, he thought. So he sat and watched and tried to remember everything he saw.

Joel was unaware of it, but Nelson had darted off because he'd spotted Vasco ordering a large *vitamina* from a stand. Nelson was fairly sure Vasco hadn't seen him, but there was no sense in taking chances. He sat on the toilet and said a prayer to all the gods he could remember. Adolfo's eyes were sharper than Nelson could fathom. They seemed to know his every move. He tried to keep his breathing quiet and pushed his thoughts on to Paraty. He hoped Joel wouldn't want to ask the police if they knew of his dad. Nelson didn't fancy setting foot in a police station. It had been thirteen months since his last dealings with the *polícia*, the longest gap since he was fourteen. He'd enjoyed seeing the back of that particular relationship, but the police, like love, had a habit of biting when you least expected it. The time would come, as surely as the rain he could hear starting to rattle the skylights above his head.

When the departure time was near, Nelson emerged. He darted behind Vasco as he turned to buy a hotdog, and ran to where Joel was waiting by a growling bus. If Joel looks at that watch one more time in a place like this, he'll soon be looking at an empty wrist, Nelson thought. They showed their tickets and boarded.

Rain rapped a thousand heavy fingers on the roof of the bus as it drove through the misted streets of a Rio storm.

Joel pressed his face to the glass and watched water pound the street. He wondered if it was raining in Paraty and where his father might be sheltering. He tried to picture himself finding him, perhaps in the porch of a church or under a giant mango tree. Would Gilberto be pleased to see him? Might he run away?

Nelson sat with one foot on the seat, watching the rain too. 'Every storm is the chance of a fresh start,' Zila used to say, which he'd never really understood – but which cheered him up when it rained. Joel looked so serious, staring at the splashes in the street. This father-hunting business was heavy, there was no doubting that. Nelson had no idea what it was like to lose a father, even if he'd said he did. Losing a mother and a sister and an aunt was all very well – perhaps more painful, perhaps less so, it was impossible to say – but mothers and sisters and aunts were not the issue. Nelson made a note to remember as much. 'Empathy is the fifth virtue,' he remembered reading in a magazine Zemané had borrowed from his wife because it had an article on Zico. Nelson wasn't sure what the original four virtues were, and was a little surprised that empathy hadn't found its way into the starting line-up, but resolved to show as much of it as he could. Joel might be a little obsessed, but he was tenacious; he might be a little dry and picky at times, but at least he didn't talk down to Nelson and was happy to sit right next to him, like an equal. *Nossa!* – Nelson had wondered if Joel would want to sit with him at all.

Joel and Nelson sat side by side and, although they didn't say a lot, neither of them felt the silence. As they looked out of the window, their eyes fell on the same things. And Joel thought how amazing it was to live in the modern age, where a man could catch a plane to a land across the sea, where within a week he could be on a bus with a man whose life was as different as a Martian's. Yet there were people they both knew – musical gods and film stars – and songs they'd both enjoyed, and jokes they found funny, and opinions of the way the world was run that were not as far apart as their homes or levels of wealth.

Brazil rolled under the wheels of the bus and the two men watched it pass. Hills moved up and down, houses appeared and disappeared, and with them children and women and men and dogs and cars and bicycles. The clouds left too, leaving sharp light on forests that were mostly ever-so-green but which were occasionally dotted bright pink or white or blue by a tree in blossom. Joel wondered how a Brazilian tree knew what season it was. It was the twentieth of June, almost midwinter's day. There were plenty of rebellious trees which had decided it was spring. As they drove on, they were met by views of the inlets and isles of the tropical coast. Tankers and liners sat squat on the blue, tugs chugged and sail boats were pinned in clusters here and there. They passed forests, docks and rural towns, until, turning from the road, at last they twisted through a few streets and into Paraty bus station.

They walked into the old part of town, where the buildings were white and low, with chunky red brick tiles and flowers in their gutters. The cobbles were as large as tortoise shells and the streets curved in arcs towards the sea – which, Joel had read, had once allowed defenders to ambush invading pirates. As they walked the curves Joel hoped his father would lie round every bend. At a gift shop, Joel bought Nelson a small red rucksack, into which he transferred his plastic bag of worldly goods. Then they walked a couple of streets to the *pousada* Joel had booked.

Nelson grinned as they filled in their registration cards. Not having an address, he put down that of Bar do Paulo. They walked into a courtyard filled with palms and heliconias, with flowers like sheaves of orange fishes. Hammocks hung beneath verandas close to a swimming pool. There were alcoves in the shade with leather chairs in which a few silent guests sat reading well thumbed paperbacks. Joel and Nelson sat for a while, listening to trickling water, enjoying the sight of a black and white hummingbird dancing over the pale blue.

This father-hunting business is not so bad, thought Nelson. He tried out three hammocks and was on the verge of stripping off his T-shirt and diving into the pool when Joel suggested they should dump their stuff in their rooms then meet in the bar. Joel went off, but Nelson remained swinging to and fro, feeling a bit like he used to when Zila told him to put down his guitar and help her chop vegetables. This place is just the right amount of messy, Nelson thought. He'd been in cheap white hotels and luscious pink love motels, and most of them had a practised cleanliness that reminded him of hospitals: cleaned to be soiled to be cleaned. He'd been in plenty of even cheaper places which had long since given up the battle against filth, with mud in the corners and cockroaches that crunched beneath your feet at night. This place was casually perfect: corners looked dusty, without dust; stems fell about with pretty disorder; even the hummingbirds looked slackly choreographed.

He found his room, which was white with old brown furniture and an en-suite bathroom. He turned a knob on the wall and classical music seeped into the air. Nelson laughed and jumped about. Wait till I tell the guys, he thought; they'll call me President Nelson. He unpacked his bag and put all his possessions in a drawer. He rather liked his rucksack, particularly the newness of it. Only something new could be that red. When was the last time someone had given him something new? When was the last time anyone had given him anything? Nelson checked out the complimentary toiletries, brushed his teeth with a free toothbrush, rearranged some tufts of hair in the mirror then went to meet Joel in the bar.

Down the corridor, Joel dumped his own bag by the bed. The hotel was truly beautiful. Debbie would love it. He wished she could see him in Brazil, where he felt another side of himself was coming alive. He loved the way that speaking another language changed the way he moved, making Joel feel like an actor playing himself in a slightly different way. He checked out the bathroom. He looked in the mirror and wondered if this was the last time he would see himself before he saw his dad. He flicked a little thumbs-up at himself. When you start grinning in the mirror, he thought, it can only mean trouble, so he went to find Nelson.

Joel found him reclining in a leather chair with his hands behind his head. He was looking at the menu for room service and laughing to himself. 'Are you hungry?' asked Joel.

'Let's eat on the paw,' said Nelson.

'You know where Zemané saw my dad?'

'I can see the very street before my eyes.'

Nelson didn't know the street because there wasn't a street to be known, so he reasoned it could be whichever street he chose. They turned left out of the *pousada* towards the centre of town and came across a wide street with a church at the end. Nelson stopped. 'This is the place, my brother.'

'Have you been here before?'

'Never.'

'Then how do you know?' asked Joel.

'He told me.'

'Are you certain?'

'Must you be so English?'

'It's hardly peculiar to look in the right place.'

'There's looking and looking, my brother,' said Nelson. 'Go ahead. Be all *scientific*. You won't find anything by science here. You're looking for a Brazilian man in a Brazilian town, and he's going to be lost and found in a Brazilian way.'

'So what do we do, just hang around till he shows up?'

'Didn't you meet most of the people in your life that way?'

'That doesn't make any sense.'

'You just don't want it to.'

Joel took some posters out of his bag and handed them to Nelson. 'Let's do it my way for now,' he said. 'I'll take the left, you take the right.'

Joel walked towards a bar on the left side of the street. He looked over his shoulder and was pleased to see Nelson enter the first place on the right. Joel talked to the barman for a couple of minutes but the barman didn't recognise the man in the picture, so Joel left him with a poster and the number of the *pousada*. He did the same in the next place and the next. Back in the street there was no sign of Nelson, so Joel crossed to see which bar he was in. He found him in the very first one, sitting on a stool towards the back grinning at a waitress, who had folded one of Joel's posters into a fan with which she was cooling her burning cheeks. On the table was a plate of fresh *pasteis* and three beers, one of which Nelson indicated was for Joel.

'Look – ' started Joel.

'Just listen,' said Nelson. 'Rosa here has seven little brothers and sisters. Give each kid some posters and five *reais* and you'll have a flock of detectives flying to all the bars in town. We sit here and wait for the mountain.'

'That's very kind of her, but I can't not look for him – '

'What if they bring him here and you're out there?'

'I haven't agreed they can help. '

'They're already on their way.'

'I'd be happier if we looked too.'

'We *are* looking – with eyes more likely to see than our own. What if he doesn't want to be found? It'd be easy to hide from you. You're so evident.'

Joel stood up. 'Humour me,' he said.

Nelson followed him outside. There was a dusty smell in the air, a swollen look to the clouds that slid across the sky.

'The kids will be here any minute,' implored Nelson.

No sooner had he spoken than a boy came running round the corner of the church, followed seconds later by a stream of kids of smaller sizes. They came to a halt in front of the bar and stood close around Joel and Nelson.

'Which one's the American?' said the eldest boy.

'The one that isn't smiling,' said a girl.

'He's English,' said Rosa from the doorway.

'What's the difference?' said a very small boy.

166

'They play *futebol*,' said Nelson. 'Not like Americans.'

'Manchester United!' said a medium girl.

'I prefer Flamengo,' said Joel.

'Fla-*merda*,' said another kid.

'Tiago!' said Rosa and cuffed him.

The eldest kid put out his hand. Joel gave him a wad of posters.

'And the money?' said the kid. 'Forty.'

'I thought it was thirty-five,' said Joel.

'Management fee,' said the boy.

The kid shared out posters and the children looked at the photos. 'Which one is he?' said a little girl.

'Both of them, stupid,' said an older boy.

'Are you a policeman?' said a small boy.

'He's a dentist,' said Nelson.

'Look at my teeth!' said an older girl, and bared them at Joel.

'Perfect!' said Joel with a smile.

'Now scram!' said Nelson.

The ring-leader formed the kids into a huddle and then, after a few explanations and complaints, they exploded in all directions, little ones stumbling over the cobbles.

'Let's eat,' said Nelson.

Eva looked out of a tall window at Sugarloaf across the bay. The boss's office had the most beautiful view in the world, but Eva knew beauty was never a guarantee of kindness – she might even say it was a warning sign. In her experience, being enthralled by something beautiful normally meant something ugly was about to creep up and kick you in the *bunda*. She had been expecting the meeting from which she had just emerged – there had been rumours for months. But the expectation of being kicked did nothing to lessen the bruising. Besides, there was always *talk* of cutbacks – that was how they kept you on your toes. It didn't mean the day they cut you back would really come.

What was she supposed to do? Jobs like this did not grow like coconuts. The office-boy has greater job security, she thought, as he handed her a tissue. It's a miracle I managed to last this long in a world of roving eyes and ageing wives. Eva could see the fat cats' boats bobbing on the waters in front of the yacht club. What I wouldn't give for a submarine and a dozen torpedos, she thought. Liam was in there talking to them now, bless the boy. It would do no good and they both knew it. He might buy her a week or two, and she supposed she ought to be grateful. She *was* grateful, to him at least.

She left the window and strutted round the room. A big celebration was required, a night out, that very evening or very soon. They'd go to Casa da Mãe Joana, the whole gang – Liam, the girls, the Americans, Joel – Nelson too, if he wanted – the more the merrier. She flopped down at her desk, ruffled her keyboard and pulled a face. What was the point of bothering? Reports to type, the office budget to do... screw them, Eva thought.

She picked up the phone and dialled.

'Who's speaking?' said the voice which answered.

'It's me, my friend. Eva.'

'Eva!' said Marisa. 'How *are* you?'

'*Tudo fatal*, my friend. But I'm not going to speak about it now. Too much trouble, too much, my sister, what can I do? But just listen... I want to ask you a favour: I have a friend who's looking for a man who lived here years ago, who may even have died here, in '75 perhaps. I've tried a few people, I won't go into details, but no one can find him. Then I started wondering... do you think you could dig around in the files and see if there are any records?'

'I'll try, my friend, I'll try,' said Marisa. 'I can't promise anything, but you never can tell. I'll have a look here and ring around. Give me his name and what you know.'

When the call was over, Eva lay her head on her desk and listened to the sigh of the air-conditioning, the occasional rattle of the photocopier, PCs bleeping and people down the corridor chatting on the way to grabbing a *cafezinho*. When Eva opened her eyes, Liam was walking towards her desk, hands in pockets.

'Do you want the good news or the bad news?' he said.

'Buy me a couple of weeks, *querido*?'

'Six,' he said. 'End of next month. I'm so sorry.'

'Rule five: *Never say sorry for something that's not your fault.*'

'English curse, I guess.'

'There are worse afflictions,' she said.

At lunchtime, Liam and Eva walked up Avenida Rio Branco. The sun was high and hot and wetness from the morning rain had burned away. They passed newspaper kiosks with dailies pinned to arms spread wide, wove through vendors selling shampoo and toothpaste, pirate CDs and batteries on the pavement. They turned into a side street and sat outside a restaurant with other people in suits.

'Can you expense this?' said Eva.

'Just let them try and stop me,' said Liam.

'Then I'll have the biggest steak in the house and a caipirinha.'

'Me too,' said Liam.

Eva's mobile buzzed across the table ringing 'All You Need Is Love'.

'Marisa!' she said. 'What a quick friend you are! Don't tell me you've found him already?'

'Found him here, no,' said Marisa. 'But someone up there must be saving smiles for you. I spoke to my friend in the 5th District *cartório*, and she thinks she might have found something. She's going to check it out this afternoon.'

'Progress?' asked Liam.

'It's probably nothing,' said Eva.

Eva felt bad about hiding the truth from Liam, after all he'd done. But she thought it was better to keep news from him until it was really news. If he spoke to Joel and told him half a truth, it might just make things worse.

The steaks and drinks arrived. They chinked tumblers and took a suck of caipirinha through their straws. With a flourish, Eva banged down her glass.

'So,' she said. 'Do you think his dad is dead or alive?'

'Alive,' lied Liam.

'Why?'

'I don't know. If he weren't, I don't think Joel would think he was.'

'He's pretty crazy about his father.'

'What do you think?' asked Liam.

'Either he's dead,' she said, 'or it's better if he is.'

'Why do you say that?'

'There's only one thing worse than a dead father and that's a bad one.'

'Perhaps he's reformed,' suggested Liam.

'So why didn't he get in touch?'

'There could be a million reasons.'

'A million reasons you can't give are not much better than none,' said Eva.

'Perhaps he thought he was protecting Joel. Or maybe he lost his memory, or his marbles.'

'That's all very logical, logical, Liaminho. But don't you have a *feeling* about it too? Scare off all those sensible thoughts. What do you really think, *querido*? Can you imagine him alive?'

Liam sucked down the last of his caipirinha and twirled the mush at the bottom with his straw.

'If I were a betting man...' he said.

'Yes?'

'Don't breathe a word of this to Joel.'

'Never,' she said.

'Then I'd have to say... I think he's dead.'

'That poor, poor boy!'

'Let's hope we're wrong.'

They sat and looked at their empty cocktail glasses for a few seconds.

'If we're so convinced he's dead,' said Liam, 'why did we let Joel catch a bus with a bloke we hardly know?'

In the middle of the afternoon, Eva stood by a tall window again and looked across the bay to where cable-cars swung slowly up and down the wires which stretched to the top of Sugarloaf. It was years since she'd taken that ride. She remembered an old friend's wedding reception, at a restaurant on the Morro da Urca, halfway up. Standing there, on a day like this with clouds hanging from the sky, a glass of champagne in one hand, her heels in the other, laughing at a story the bride was telling as they looked out over the Marvellous City. The bride was in Miami now. It took Eva a minute to remember her name – a name that once upon a time she must have spoken several times a day. There had been an era – hadn't there? – in which they'd all been going at the same speed; yet here Eva was, still in Rio, forty-six, divorced and redundant. She was glad she was still in Rio, but the rest of it could have gone a little faster, smoother, better.

Liam's phone rang and she left it. Her mobile rang and she answered it.

'Who's speaking?' said Eva.

'It's Marisa, Eva. I have some news for your friend.'

'Already?' said Eva.

'I know, I know, there are miracles every day. The *cartórios* are so very organised these days. Somebody filed this one properly too, all perfect, perfect. My friend looked up the name and found it – *voilà*!'

'And what did she find?' said Eva.

'I am sorry to say it, but... the certificate of death.'

'Oh, my God.'

Marisa said her friend wasn't really allowed to make a copy, but she liked to break the rules. Marisa would send a boy for it in the morning, and he'd bring it over to Eva.

Eva stood by the window, not daring to move, wondering how to inform Joel. She wasn't even sure how to tell Liam.

171

Perhaps he'd want to let Joel know himself – but was it right for Joel to hear it second-hand? She decided she would think of the perfect words, as only a woman of her experience could. The graveness of the situation superseded the demands of friendship – even regarding someone as dear to her as Liam. I'm sure Liam will understand, she thought. Would he really want to be the one to bear the news? She called the *pousada* in Paraty and left a message for Joel to call.

The sun was high in the Brighton sky, and Jackie's skin was starting to blush in the places she'd missed with the sun lotion. She went inside and rummaged under the stairs for a parasol. She found a black umbrella.

'You'll have to do,' she said.

She sat up in her deckchair and fiddled with the radio, letting an afternoon play speak gently in the background as she allowed her thoughts to drift back to Brazil. If her memories were determined to come calling, she might as well invite them in and give them cake.

Over the weeks following Gilberto's first release, Jackie had learned, piece by piece, of his treatment following the return of Major Branca. Gilberto had refused to talk about his ordeal when Jackie asked, but instead fed her revelations piecemeal, sobbing in the middle of the night or, gripping his cutlery, across the white tablecloths of once favourite restaurants. Major Branca had put Gilberto under the supervision of Martelo. Sometimes Martelo put him with the *malandros,* sometimes he tortured Gilberto himself. 'You wouldn't believe the things a man can think of doing to another,' Gilberto said. 'But he never touched my face. The major had left clear instructions.'

One day Gilberto was helped across the compound, the afternoon sun flashing into his nocturnal eyes, and taken into a room with carpets and a ceiling fan with giant blades. He was made to stand in front of a desk, behind which sat the major. It was peculiar, Gilberto told Jackie, to see him smart in his uniform, a fish comfortable in his tank, so different from the man who'd sat in the corner at A Gaiola.

'Do you know why you're here?' asked the major.

'I'm innocent,' whispered Gilberto.

'Of what crime?'

'I haven't a clue.'

'Aha! Then how can you be sure?' said the major.

'I always steer clear of trouble.'

'Artists *are* trouble.'

'I don't like artists. I sing a little, that's all. I'm a dentist, first and foremost.'

'My wife's dentist.'

'Your wife?'

'An actor as well? Bravo!'

'I hate actors,' said Gilberto.

'I hate liars.'

The major stood up and nodded to a soldier, who strutted across the room and placed the tip of his gun against the side of Gilberto's skull.

'I know about your affair with Angelica,' said the major. 'I've had better men shot for less.'

Gilberto decided to say nothing. It was hard to think with metal pressing against his skin and he wasn't sure how his voice would emerge. He also knew that he could lie well to those who wanted to believe him, but that it was harder to lie to someone who didn't. At a nod from the major, the soldier removed the gun from Gilberto's temple and started to move around. With each wandering step Gilberto feared a blow.

'Perhaps you think your silence will convince? Like a trapped spider hoping to be invisible. Let me spare you the humiliation of an exposed lie. Men of mine followed you to our flat, observed you together at concerts – '

'Then they will have seen we never touched.'

'Why else meet the wife of another man in secret?'

'It wasn't a secret – I told my wife.'

'Secret from me.'

'I didn't know you.'

'Was Jackie pleased?'

Gilberto told Jackie how much it hurt to hear the major say her name.

'No,' said Gilberto.

'If you were prepared to harm her, why would you not betray me?'

'I didn't mean to hurt anyone. I thought Angelica could help me.'

'Did she?'

'She robbed me.'

'Ha! Ha! Took your money, my beautiful witch! Robbed you of your liberty too – you fool. Took your freedom, your marriage – perhaps even your life.'

'She didn't take my marriage. My wife still loves me.'

'Only last week she paid a visit to a travel agent. I hear she was very interested in the price of tickets to London. One-way tickets, for an adult and a child.'

'You're a liar!'

'I'll wager she's packing her bags as we speak.'

'She'd wait forever!'

'She might have to.'

Gilberto didn't hear the swing of the rifle butt, which sunk a shard of pain into the side of his head.

'Be very careful with his face,' said Major Branca.

Gilberto expected blows to hail but he was taken back to his cell. In the middle of the night he was woken by a guard with the face of a child and led to a room with a single chair to which he was tied with a dog's muzzle over his mouth.

'*Assim*,' Martelo would say, as he swung the broken handle of a sledgehammer. Like *this*. '*Isso!*' he would say when the youngster got it right. Like *that!*

Gilberto was moved to a comfortable cell in a light and airy wing where they dressed his wounds and fed him palatable food. When he could stand, from the windows he could see the mountains. One afternoon when the sun was high and a cool breeze stroked the leaves of the mango trees in the yard, Gilberto was marched across the compound and taken to a room where he was made to sit in a dentist's chair. A nurse laid out instruments without meeting his eyes and a tall, thin dentist washed his hands in a corner sink. Gilberto spotted five types of forceps and an elevator. Major Branca entered and stood by Gilberto's side.

'I'm sorry to see your teeth have suffered slightly during your time under my wing. A dentist can't be allowed to have bad teeth – such a poor advertisement to his patients. Neither does a son want to see his father with brown teeth, and your wife will want to kiss you if she hasn't caught that plane.'

The nurse tilted back the chair so that Gilberto looked up into the nostrils of the major. A soldier strapped down Gilberto's arms and legs, lifted his head to slip a brace under his neck then tightened a strap across his forehead. The nurse put a prop in the right hand side of his mouth, wedging it open.

'I know Angelica came to see you, here in my own prison. She was very clever – forging my signature, lying to the lieutenant. I would still be blissfully ignorant, were it not for your wife. I was at the Ipanema flat one afternoon when the phone rang and your darling wife called. She has quite a vocabulary!'

As the major talked, Gilberto followed the assistant with his eyes. She laid out the different forceps on a table and moved the aspirator unit nearer to the chair. The aspirator was new – Gilberto had seen a similar one in a catalogue from America.

'A dead lover is certainly a sharp warning against infidelity,' said Major Branca. 'But Angelica has a short memory for dead lovers. You are lucky, in a way, that you are not her first. I have come to the conclusion – call it trial and error – that a lover maimed might serve as a more durable reminder.'

The dentist and his assistant nodded to one another. She turned on the aspirator and moved the nozzle closer to

Gilberto. The dentist approached with an elevator, which he inserted into Gilberto's mouth, between the upper molars, and rotated. Gilberto yelped.

'You're strong. Not everyone survives Martelo. We'll look after you well. You'll recover sooner than you think. And, lest you worry about shocking your poor family, we've made you a lovely new set of teeth. They've even got a gap in the middle just like yours. Call it a parting gift. I hope you'll think of me every night when you take them out, and every morning when you put them in. '

Where was the syringe? Please God, thought Gilberto, let there be a syringe. The dentist stopped separating the rear molars, the nurse cleared some blood, and the dentist approached again with a pair of molar forceps.

'They say the pain is at its peak with the first extraction, when it comes as a surprise. After a while one becomes accustomed – though I hear the canines can be a bitch. They tell me the molars can be troublesome too, with three roots or even four. I'm sure you're quick with your patients but, if all doesn't go to plan, I hear a testing molar can take minutes. You'll lose quite a bit of blood, I expect, especially without an anaesthetic, but there's plenty to spare in a hot-blooded man like you.'

The dentist gripped an upper molar between the jaws of the forceps and pulled.

'My wife will see how pitiful you are, how broken,' the major continued. 'She'll come to see you for an appointment every now and again. I will insist. She'll see you only because I order it. And one last thing: if I ever hear you've so much as hummed a lullaby, I'll have you back here quicker than you can say *jardim*!'

In spite of Gilberto's revelations, in spite of her near-departure, Jackie and Gilberto tried to pick up where they left off. They would walk by the lake in the evenings or sit on the Ipanema shore and look at the sea. They would try to talk about other things. Gilberto stayed away from bars, turned off the radio, threw away his records. He worked hard. Contrary to the major's words, Angelica did not come for an appointment, or so Gilberto said.

'Let's go away for the weekend,' he said one day. 'A second honeymoon.'

So, at the end of March 1971, they went to Búzios and rented a room in a *pousada* on the beach. They dined one moonlit night on the sand itself, at a table lit by candles feet from the shush of the waves. They drank caipirinhas and ate fresh fish. Jackie's mouth tasted of limes and the sea.

When they had finished eating, Gilberto ordered another whisky and asked, 'Why did you suggest I go and sing that night?'

'What night, darling?'

'The night at A Gaiola, the night the major watched me.'

'I wanted to hear you again, honey. You're so happy when you sing.'

'Did you tell the major I was going to be there?'

'No! Are you mad? I've never even spoken to the major – '

'Apart from when you called his flat and told him about Angelica's visit.'

'I didn't, darling. I've told you: I tried to call her, but I never spoke to anyone.'

'He said you used filthy language.'

'But I didn't talk to him, I just shouted. I thought it was her. I didn't mention the visit at all, I just called her a whore and a – '

'How did he know you were going to leave Brazil?'

'I have no idea... I wasn't really going to leave, I couldn't have gone through with it – '

'Just bought your tickets and packed your bags. Weren't going to use them – not in a million years.'

There was a sharpness to his eyes. He drained his whisky, then told her he was going to find a bar. Jackie went back to the room.

Gilberto woke her at two in the morning.

'Want to know where I've been?'

'Drinking, by the smell of it,' said Jackie half-sleepily.

'Been to see a man sing. He had a beautiful voice, like a songbird. They were all applauding, even the soldier in the corner. I watched every note that came from his mouth, especially the ones he held a bit longer than he really should have, because they felt just oh-so-good. Do you know how it feels to be a singer who cannot sing?'

'I can't imagine, darling. It must be terrible.'

'You took my voice away,' said Gilberto standing over her.

'No, Gil, that's not true. All I ever wanted was for you to sing to me.'

'All you ever wanted was to own me.'

'I wanted you to sing, honey. To *me*... to me and not that bitch.'

Gilberto beat Jackie that night for the first time. 'Not the face,' he said, 'not the face,' as he hauled her up and punched her down. She screamed at first, but the hotel slept. It felt as if the whole world was asleep.

Jackie went back into the house and forgot what she'd gone in for. She dug out a floppy summer hat she'd worn to a wedding not long before. It struck her as the kind of hat Tony might like, she wasn't sure why. She pottered about for a bit, unable to settle. It had been years since she'd put herself through that memory, and she felt a little shocked: sometimes things are dug up that you thought long buried. She wondered what made a person stay in a relationship when it was mortally wounded. You knew it was going to die one day and its daily decay was causing you pain – and yet you clung to every breath until the end. It was incredible to think that four and a half years had passed between that first assault and her flight from Brazil. She wondered how their story would have ended if they hadn't locked him up a second time, or if he had lived.

178

Jackie still found it hard to believe in the existence of cruelty. She preferred to believe that evil was a branch and not the root. She read the papers and saw she was wrong, and yet she couldn't make the leap to believing it was so. There *was* hope. One day the world *would* be a better place. If they could just change this and that... though who 'they' were to do the changing she didn't know – the ones with power were the worst of all. But she had to believe the world would be better when Joel was her age, when his kids were born. Wasn't it better now than for her mother? It was just too terrible to believe it would never get any better, that there was evil at the core of the world, malice in its eyes, like malice in that look of Gilberto's, a hunger for destruction.

She wondered how much of the blame was hers. What if she'd never made that call to Angelica's flat, or if she hadn't packed her bags? Of course, there was no excuse for beating your wife, but she did wonder what he would have been like had she been more... what? Impassive, she supposed, or compliant. Perhaps they would have lived an ordinary life. Joel would be where he was now, in Rio, and she would be there too. Perhaps she would have had more kids. Maybe she'd have grandchildren. Gilberto was always an angel with Joel – she would always remember the way he would sit on the end of his bed and sing 'Undiú'. He'd been an angel with her too, for a few years, though a devil for the rest.

Throughout the afternoon, Rosa's brothers and sisters flew back, to be fed Guaraná and *coxinhas* by Joel if he was there, or by Nelson if he wasn't. Joel visited a few bars and shops, was wished luck by two elderly ladies, winked at by a girl with braces on her teeth and prayed for by a priest who let him put up a poster in the entrance to his church. It darkened around six and rain fell hard. Joel walked through the sodden town until he reached the bar again, where the children were making paper aeroplanes of his posters and throwing them at a snoozing Nelson.

Joel woke him and thanked Rosa and the kids. Then Nelson and Joel walked back to the *pousada* with their shirts pulled over their heads against the rain. As soon as they entered the lobby, Nelson saw a note sitting in Joel's pigeonhole and, turning him by the elbow, managed to hustle him into the street.

'Joel,' said Nelson in a low and serious voice. 'I'd like to show you something very personal.'

He won't refuse, thought Nelson. He's a boy with a good heart and – in spite of the lack of progress – he's the type that wants to believe I'm honest, even if his heart feels I'm not.

'Can't you show me inside?' said Joel. 'It's kind of raining...'

'Trust me,' Nelson said, with what he hoped was a winning grin.

Nelson led him down a couple of streets, past a church on the waterfront, to a long jetty with flanks thick with sleeping vessels. The rain came to a halt. Lights swayed slowly on the masts of fishing boats, which gave way to larger schooners as they walked further over the planks to where the end of the pier stood them before a vista of the bay. Alone but for a boatman here or there, they found a couple of crates on which to sit. Nelson stared pensively across the water and thought of how to begin.

'I came here once with my sister Mariana,' he lied. 'Will you wait here? I'd like to show you a picture, to bring her back to life.'

Nelson ran back to the *pousada*. I'm sorry to use you, Mariana, he thought as he ran, but I couldn't come up with anything else. I'd like to think that, since I was by the sea, Yemanjá gave me the idea with your blessing. I hope you are helping me willingly but, if you are not, forgive me also for the sneaky crime of turning an apology into an excuse.

Back at the *pousada*, Nelson asked for his key and the note, which he said his companion had asked him to fetch. In his room, he sat on his bed and unfolded the paper.

180

It read: '*I've found out about your father. Call me – Eva.*'

Nelson called the number.

'Joel!' said Eva.

'Not exactly,' said Nelson.

'*Vagabundo!*' shrieked Eva. 'What have you done with him?'

'*Tranquilo!* He's sitting happily by the sea – '

'I need to speak to him *now*!'

'If the news is urgent, Eva, let me pass it on.'

'Tell a *malaco* like you!'

'Even goddesses should be careful who they call names.'

'You know very well his father's not in Paraty!'

'If I knew that, I wouldn't be here, sister. But if you have information, my goddess, if you have news, I'd be happy to pass it on – '

'Never!'

'Then I guess we'll keep on looking.'

'You'll never find him!'

'We will.'

'You won't.'

'We will.'

'He's dead!'

'Dead?'

'Dead. Oh, my God!' said Eva. 'Why am I telling *you*? What shame! A boy's father is dead and I'm telling a crook!'

'He can't be dead, I know a man who saw him last week.'

'And I know a woman who's found his death certificate.'

Nelson had to admit a death certificate was hard to argue with – but if he was dead, who was the man who lunched every Thursday at O Paraiso? Perhaps there was some mistake. There had to be a lot of dead Gilbertos in the world, and there were sure to be a few with the name Gilberto Cabral.

'Have you seen this certificate?' asked Nelson.

'My friend can read, you know.'

181

'But what if you're wrong? What if it's another Gilberto?'

'The facts all fit, *malandro*; we're not so stupid, stupid.'

'But I know a man who saw him alive!'

'Impossible!' said Eva.

'Do *you* want to tell him his father's dead before we're sure?' said Nelson.

'I *am* sure.'

'One hundred per cent?'

'Ninety-nine.'

'And what about the other one per cent?'

Eva sighed and Nelson let the silence weigh on her.

'Listen, my goddess. Maybe your paper is right – maybe my man is not Gilberto – but don't you think Joel would prefer to see for himself?'

'If you're lying,' said Eva, 'I'll kill you, I swear.'

'I'll be honest,' said Nelson. 'I might be mad, but I'll tell you the truth. But you can't tell Joel. Promise me you won't tell him.'

'I'll promise once I know what I'm promising.'

'Gilberto's in Rio. He'll be in a restaurant on Thursday and I'm going to take Joel there.'

'In *Rio*! So what are you doing in Paraty?'

'It's complicated...'

'Complicated! Our piece of paper is very simple.'

'I'm in trouble, Eva,' Nelson said. 'More trouble than you could even imagine. My situation is really *trash* and – '

'That's *your* problem. That boy does not deserve – '

'I know, I know, and you're right. But I do know where his father is and all I want to do is take him there – but I can't take him till Thursday and if I'd stayed in Rio I might not be alive. I need two days, Eva – two days, that's all. If I take him to his father, Joel will give me a reward, I'll be able to clear the trouble I'm in, and everybody is happy.'

There was silence, and Nelson thought that maybe this time the game was up. It was hard always living close to the cliff-edge, knowing you might just step too far and plummet. At times he felt jealous of those with their lives pasted smoothly on their bread. But it was exciting too, making a mess of things – it meant every day was *interesting* – and sometimes he would lie awake in the night and smile at just how alive trying to keep his balance made him feel.

'Two days?' said Eva.

'Just two days,' said Nelson.

'I'll sleep on it,' said Eva. 'I'm not making promises. Perhaps I'll wake up and think I was mad to get even halfway through this conversation.'

'You won't regret it,' said Nelson. 'If I don't deliver his father on Thursday, you can show him your piece of paper.'

'If I don't tell him before then.'

'There's no point telling Joel he's dead while there's even a hope.'

'I hate to hope you're right,' she said. 'But I hope you're right.'

Eva hung up. Nelson wondered what to do. It would be an intolerable night if he couldn't be sure she'd keep the paper secret. He picked up the phone and called Bar do Paulo. After a long minute Zemané came to the phone. Nelson explained.

'All it needs is a little lunch and an edible proposition,' said Zemané.

'I don't know, this time. I just don't know...'

'I'll invite her to the Confeitaria Colombo for lunch. The Wednesday buffet is my favourite of the week.'

'Do you think she'll listen?' asked Nelson.

'I suppose it depends if there's anything she needs.'

'She's not a woman who thinks she needs anything. Except a president, and I don't suppose you can give her one of those.'

'I've never met anyone who didn't need a little extra happiness,' said Zemané.

'I don't think making her happy is easy.'

'If I play it right, perhaps she'll tell me how.'

Nelson put down the phone, closed his eyes, said a prayer to every god he could name, grabbed the picture of his sister and ran to the pier.

Joel walked around on the pier, looking in all directions across the bay, hoping no one came along and asked why he was there. With Nelson for company he felt Brazilian and hardly thought about where they went; on his own he felt distinctly English. The sea was calm, the wind lighter now the rain had stopped, and as the clouds slid away they revealed a lighter sky with a thin slice of moon. He wondered if his mother and father had ever stood on this pier at night. He wondered where Nelson was. He was taking a long time to fetch a photo.

As he looked back towards the town, he realised he found it hard to believe they would find his dad here. He wondered if he should go back to the *pousada*. He started wandering towards the start of the pier, then he spotted a figure jogging in his direction and watched as it became distinguishable as Nelson, until finally Nelson stopped in front of Joel, panting. He pulled a photo from his shorts. They sat on the crates and Joel studied the picture. The young Nelson was wearing a brown suit with an orange tie and had enormous hair. Joel recognised him from his smile. A shy girl, wearing a white dress printed with hibiscus flowers, leaned into Nelson's side.

'Dig the suit,' said Joel.

Nelson knew he'd have to say something about what happened to his sister – but telling people what happened to his sister wasn't his favourite way to pass the time. Now he'd accomplished his mission and held off Eva, he felt he'd sold Mariana's story cheaply. Using the first idea that came into his head might have been a good way to keep Joel out of the *pousada*, but Nelson wished he could sometimes wait for the second idea to come along.

'You don't have to talk about it,' said Joel.

'Thanks,' said Nelson. But not talking was not something in which he was very skilled, and so he said, 'We were happy that day, that's for sure.'

'You look it. And young! Don't you wish you could be that age again?'

'You've got keep moving, that's the key. Don't ever think you're old. Keep on moving those legs, that's what Zila used to say. If you're going to die, die like an insect, with your legs waggling.'

'*Até a morte, pé forte*, my father once said to me.'

Nelson had always liked this expression, but it was funny to hear it from an English guy, though he supposed Joel was really half a Brazilian guy, so maybe it wasn't so strange. But he had to admit he was starting to wonder if Joel was laying a little too much significance on a single relative – albeit one of the more important ones. Joel had a mother who was alive, not a quasi-aunt who was dead, and, if he didn't have a sister, at least he hadn't lost one either. 'Are you really sure you'll be better off, my brother?' Nelson asked.

'What do you mean?' asked Joel.

'What if he isn't the father you want?'

'Better than none at all.'

'What if it doesn't make any difference?'

'I think it will.'

'What if he's dead?'

'We're here because you said – '

'I know, I know – but what if he was?' said Nelson.

'Even that would be better than this.'

'Than what?'

'Not knowing,' said Joel.

'Are you sure? Is it really better to know he's dead than to wonder if he might be alive somewhere, hidden and happy?'

'Look, I know what you mean, but I just need to *know*. My mum's being saying he's dead for twenty-five years – but I just don't buy it, I don't know why. Sometimes I wonder if I could believe anything less than a corpse.'

'You don't mean that, *cara*!'

'Sometimes I wish I could see him dead, touch his cold skin.'

'Now you're freaking me out!' said Nelson.

Joel laughed and Nelson shivered. Then he took the photo back from Joel and looked at it.

'I had an interview, the day they took that photo of me and Mariana, for a job as a *boy* in a big American firm. I borrowed a suit from a man down the street and I remember it was big for me. I was only sixteen. They gave me the job and Zila made us have our picture taken to commemorate the occasion. We all went out for a *churrasco*, to a place in Flamengo we used to like, and that day we ordered *everything*. It seemed the finest day of my life – and the sad thing is to look back now and think that maybe it *was* the greatest day, when it should only have been the best day until another came along.'

'There's still time,' said Joel. 'Don't go all English on me.'

'You're right,' said Nelson, smiling. 'You're learning.'

'So how was the job?'

'The week before I was meant to start, my aunt Zila was shot. Shot outside our house in Santo Amaro with a bag of shopping in each hand. The *polícia* said it was the gang and the gang said it was the *polícia*. She'd been to the market with Mariana – she'd saved to buy a piece of *picanha* to fatten me up for office life. Americans like a boy with meat on, she had said. The bullet hit Zila in the neck. She lay in a pool of blood, blinking up at the sky with her mouth opening and closing like a fish, blowing bubbles, so Mariana said.'

'Jesus,' said Joel.

Nelson stood up. He walked round in circles for a while, rubbing his hand over his mouth. He had to admit there was something comforting about Joel. He was good blood. He couldn't imagine him deceiving anyone intentionally – there was a lot to be said for that – though Zila used to preach of virtues more serviceable than honesty. True friends were those who would lie to anyone's face to make your world a better place, she used to say, sometimes even to your own. If they stabbed you in the back every now and again, it was important not to make too big a deal of it. Nobody's perfect, she would say, and if you're going to tolerate the imperfections of anyone, who better than your friends? But Joel wasn't going to stab anyone any time soon, and, though Nelson wished he'd kept a lid on his secrets, there were worse people than Joel to see them.

Nelson turned to Joel and, shaking his head, said, 'I'm sorry.'

'Rule five,' said Joel.

Nelson laughed and said, 'Listen, about your father – '

'Save it for tomorrow,' said Joel. 'How about a drink?'

'It *would* be a shame to waste a night in this beautiful place.'

They walked back into town. The clouds had cleared and cobbles gleamed beneath a sky which had sprouted stars. They found a bar where a man was playing guitar. Joel kept an eye out for his dad and they talked about Flamengo, Sandro and Brighton. As they listened to *choro* tunes, Joel thought about Nelson's question: whether it really would be better with his dad alive. It *would* be better, he thought, he knew it would. But he couldn't help thinking of the darker side of his dad – perhaps because of the violence of which Nelson had told – and he wondered what the truth was about his father and mother, and whether their story was really as bleak as Jackie said.

'It isn't a story,' Debbie used to say. 'If you pretend it's a story, you're taking his side.'

He hated it when she said that, because he didn't want to take sides between his parents; he didn't want there to be sides between them at all. Over the years he'd decided it was better if he didn't think about it any more than he had to, but he would not be able to shove it into the dark if he met his dad, that much was certain. So he hoped his dad was not as bad as his mum made out, or that even if he had been, once upon a time, he was improved now, or better still repentant, and that the darker stories – history – could be gradually forgiven.

As the singer played, Joel thought about the idea of his father inflicting pain on his mother and let it loiter in his mind for longer than he usually allowed. Joel held pain in his fingertips every day at the surgery, and sometimes thought of the power this gave him. Only once had he been tempted to use it, on a patient called Mr Lions whom he'd overheard using the word 'nigger' in a pub. When Lions next came for an appointment, Joel had made a concerted effort to control his fingers, even though he'd wanted the patient to suffer. He remembered thinking: if I were to slip and cause him pain, could I be certain it was an accident? And this made Joel wonder, then and now, what unseen forces controlled the urges of his fingers. They seemed so detatched at times: wiggling instruments sheathed in rubber, knowing their own mind.

But Joel had not hurt Mr Lions. And, while the shadow of pain was always there in the widening of patients' eyes and tensing of their muscles, he had never knowingly hurt anyone, at least not since the car crash. In some ways, though, Joel wasn't against the *idea* of pain – it wasn't the devil some painted. Pain was a manifestation of life, a proof against illusion – proof, in his own case, that his dad was more than just a photograph. There'd been a time when Joel found self-inflicted pain cathartic. But pain was not something you dished out along with love – love was supposed to be an antidote. When Joel thought about his dad and the pain he'd caused his mum, he knew there was a sum that didn't add up, no matter how many times he tried to work it out, though most of the time it was easier not to try. I'll be able to ask him soon, Joel thought. Hopefully there'll be a missing number I hadn't spotted which will make the whole equation balance.

The singer finished his songs and Joel and Nelson headed into the street, where it felt as if their limbs were gliding over the glistening cobbles. They found another bar where they shot some pool, then another where a drunken man from Curitiba bored them about his factory, obliging them to run for it when he went to the gents. They burned their feet round town until there were no more bars to find, when, given no sign of fathers either, they floated home to bed.

Eight

A phone was ringing in Joel's dream and kept on ringing as it woke him up, until he realised it was not coming from downstairs in Brighton but from next to his bed in Paraty.

'I'm sorry to call you with the early birds,' said Zemané. 'But I have news I thought you'd want to know.'

'Why does that make my heart sink?' said Joel.

'Perhaps your heart has a hole in the bottom? In any case, the good news is, your father has been sighted. It turns out he isn't in Paraty – '

'Why am I not surprised?'

' – but in Rio, after all.'

Joel let silence sit on the line.

'Wouldn't you like to know a little more?' asked Zemané.

'I'm waiting for the punchline.'

'Nelson will take you to your father on Thursday. No jokes.'

'Did you have a sudden premonition?' asked Joel.

'A confirmed sighting.'

'A hundred per cent this time?'

'Ninety-five,' said Zemané.

'Why do I still feel hope? Somebody tell me why I still feel hope.'

'It must be the Brazilian in you.'

Joel dressed and knocked on Nelson's door. Nelson was lying with his hands behind his head. His bed was made, his bag packed.

'Are you ready to go?' Nelson said.

'For someone who's always dreamed of coming here, you're in a great hurry to leave.'

They walked to the bus station, bought tickets and ate a few *salgadinhos* in a café. The bus left as the morning was starting to heat up. They watched Brazil roll by in reverse, as the bus dived in and out of towns and swathes of countryside.

'So what's today's foolproof plan?' asked Joel.

'Tomorrow we go to the place where he eats each week.'

'And you know this because…?'

'A man told me he saw him there,' said Nelson.

'When?'

'Each week. Every Thursday.'

'No – when did he tell you?' asked Joel.

'Why?'

'Why did we go to Paraty?'

'Do you think I'm lying?' said Nelson.

'Would *you* believe you?'

'I do believe me. I'm telling the truth.'

'Like you told the truth about Paraty?' said Joel.

'Like I told the truth about Zila.'

'You know, I really hope you aren't just wasting my time.'

'Hasn't it been interesting?' said Nelson.

'I didn't come here for an education.'

'If I want to rob you, why don't I just march you to a cashpoint?'

'I haven't worked that out yet.'

Nelson looked at Joel with a still face, trying to blink as infrequently as he could, hoping the look would show he was serious. It was true he was deceiving Joel, and yet he wasn't. It was hard to prove the body was honest when some of its limbs were lies. 'I promise I will take you to your father tomorrow,' he said.

'Maybe Eva will find him.'

'Maybe she'll find he's dead.'

191

'At least I'd know the truth,' said Joel.

'Sometimes it's better to be ignorant.'

'What about your sister? Didn't you want to know the truth about her?'

'You don't know anything about my sister.'

'I know something pretty bad must have happened.'

'You must be right,' said Nelson. 'You know all the answers.'

'But say you *didn't* know what happened to her? You'd want to find out, wouldn't you?'

'Whatever you say.'

'Come on, Nelson. Be honest, for once. Imagine if it was your sister. Some truths *demand* to be known.'

Joel talked and Nelson watched land flee behind the bus. More land rushed to meet them as they drove, then fell behind just like the rest. It was hard to keep his eyes on any particular thing, hard to hear any particular word – though 'sister' and 'truth' and 'hunt' and 'death' were certainly repeated. Nelson felt the surge of a feeling inside which made him want to grip that English son of a bitch's throat and throw his words back in his face. Nelson could imagine Zila wagging a finger at him, reminding him that if you get angry you only screw yourself, a notion Nelson agreed with ninety-nine per cent of the time. For the other one per cent it riled him to see so many people succeed by injecting a little anger, which made him wonder if every now and again he should take a shot at it too.

'...and if they did kill him,' Joel was saying, 'I'm not proposing to take vengeance, but maybe I'll try to find the men who took his final breath, to see if they can be brought to justice. Those days have gone, I know, now the military aren't in power, but if there are questions to be answered I'm going to ask them.'

Joel appeared to have finished, so Nelson turned in his seat to face him and, keeping his voice running slow, said, 'The army don't rule, but the war isn't over, my brother – are you understanding? I've been in a jail, fifteen to a cell, too many to lie down, sleeping in shifts, beaten for breakfast, lunch and dinner. The army might not rule but there sure isn't peace.

'Not long after Zila died, I lost the job at the American firm. It was too hard to juggle work with looking after little Mariana. One day I stole a wallet from an American in Copacabana – ten dollars it had inside – and they sentenced me to two years. Are you understanding? Zila always said you reap just what you sow, told me never to steal no matter what. Even the hungry must have morals, she said, because if we don't, how will anyone think we deserve to be fed? But morals don't fill your stomach. One wallet, two years. Are you understanding? And what was Mariana supposed to do while I was inside? Seven years old and alone in the world. When I came out I couldn't find her. I checked all the street-kid haunts but nobody seemed to know. You're right, brother, I didn't stop, because I too wanted the truth. Are you understanding? So I looked and looked, until one day I found a little boy, Cesar, who wouldn't look me in the eye when I said Mariana's name, and it turned out she'd taken this fellow under her wing. He'd been on the street since he was five. At first Cesar wouldn't talk to me, but I hung around with him for a few days and eventually he told me that he and Mariana had found a group that used to sleep in a bit of park in Glória. He said she'd spoken about me all the time and told him how, when I came out, I'd be the brains behind a scheme she had in mind: to sell sweets on Avenida Rio Branco. They found the perfect spot, with no one selling sweets on any piece of pavement for several streets around. They weren't sure how to get started and were scared to ask the other sellers. They wanted me to be the boss and my sister said I'd know how to do it right. To familiarise themselves with the area, they started sleeping up there too, in the doorway of an office block where the guard was kinder than some of the other guards and didn't shout at them or threaten to shoot them. One night a car parked up the street and a guy emerged. Cesar was awake and lifted his head while Mariana slept. Cesar didn't see the face of the guy but could see he was wearing cowboy boots and carrying something heavy in his hands, which he raised above his head as he staggered the last few steps, and, just as Cesar realised what was going to happen, the man dropped a paving stone on my sleeping sister's head.

'So I learned the truth about Mariana – are you understanding? But behind every truth another lies hidden. I wanted the truth about that man, but there are a lot of men in cowboy boots in the world. I begged the police to hunt for him, but what did they care about another dead street kid without any papers? With a brother freshly out of jail – surprise, surprise. One less invisible kid in the city – not there one day, not there the next. Maybe the guy with boots was even a cop, just like the ones who shot up Vigário Geral, just like the ones who killed the kids at Candelária, just like the cops that squashed Sandro in the back of that van last week. Are you understanding, my brother?'

Joel looked at Nelson's face and saw that his bottom lip was fighting a quiver. He wished he could put his words back in his mouth. Silence split the two of them as their eyes fixed on different aspects of the world outside. Joel could think of nothing but a man in cowboy boots with a paving stone and a sweet girl dreaming of her brother's return.

After a while they reached Rio, and the bus crept through the city, hitting a midday rush-hour, though there didn't seem much rush. Off a flyover it crawled, past a railway station littered with people, then round the back of sheds from which the multicoloured limbs of Carnival animals waggled into the air. When the bus reached the station, Joel said, 'I'm really sorry – '

'Oh, don't worry about it,' Nelson said, finding a smile. 'My words escaped my intentions for a minute, same as yours.'

Nelson glanced round as they left the bus. It was almost impossible to believe, but over by a hotdog stand, cramming three-quarters of a frankfurter into his mouth, was Vasco, with ketchup running down his chin and a look of pleasure on his face. Nelson was glad Joel looked fairly Carioca. With a little ducking and keeping still, Nelson managed to keep out of sight, and by the time Vasco realised the bus was empty, Nelson and Joel were reclining on the back seat of a taxi which eased into the traffic of early afternoon.

Eva arrived at the Confeitaria Colombo at two o'clock and was shown to an old accordion lift which took her to the first floor, where tables in the gallery gave a view on to the heads of patrons far below. Her heels clicked across the tiles, as she walked in a manner she hoped was elegant towards a round table dressed in fine white cloth, where Zemané sat talking on his phone. A smart young waiter pulled out her chair. Eva sat down and looked at the stained glass ceiling above, admiring a cherub framed in a heart of roses, scolding herself for having a sentimental turn.

Zemané ended his conversation, apologising with a roll of the eyes. 'Thank you for coming, Eva,' he said.

The man was more corpulent than Eva had expected, but taller. He had slightly more hair but it was longer and darker. He looked less like a rodent and smiled more. He looked almost elegant in a white shirt, trousers and waistcoat. He wore a wedding ring.

'I have a soft spot for this place,' said Zemané.

'So do I... though my ex-husband used to bring his mistress here.'

'We can walk down the block if you like. I know another – '

'It's fine, really,' said Eva, touching his hand. 'Every time I'm here without him it becomes a little more mine.'

'Had I known you before, I could have poisoned his food.'

'Now you're just trying to butter me up.'

'That's the idea of this meeting, after all,' said Zemané.

'I should warn you – I'm not a woman easily buttered.'

'Would a little wine increase my chances?'

'No, but it might make my refusal easier for you to swallow.'

Zemané ordered a bottle of Miolo Reserva and sparkling water. Eva regretted mentioning her husband. She didn't want to seem any kind of victim, and although she knew she would never be totally cured of her divorce she tried not to advertise the fact, especially to strangers. But sometimes a feeling simply popped out, as if of its own accord, and she supposed there was a reason this occurred, some healing benefit perhaps, so she tried not to be hard on herself when it happened.

'So,' said Eva. 'You'd like to buy my silence?'

'We hoped you might keep a secret for a day or two, but what we'd really like to buy is...'

'Is?'

'The certificate,' said Zemané.

'The *death* certificate?'

'The death certificate.'

'I thought for a moment you might be frightened of the word,' said Eva.

'Certificate?'

'Can one be frightened of those?'

'If you don't have the right ones it can be terrifying,' said Zemané.

'And why do you want it?'

'If the man at the restaurant isn't Joel's father, I'd like Nelson to give it to Joel.'

'How do I know you won't just burn it?'

'What would be the point?' said Zemané. 'You'll tell Joel anyway, if Nelson doesn't.'

'Don't you think it's time Joel knew the truth?'

'A boy like Nelson doesn't fall upon many chances to earn two thousand *reais*. A chance encounter with a foreigner who won't notice the absence of the money – is he supposed to turn his back in the name of Truth? He could be dead inside two days. That's another truth. He wants to help Joel, but in the process he'd like to help himself, because he's no fool.'

'He's looking a lot wiser from where I'm sitting, there's no denying that.'

'This was his idea, not mine.'

'So why doesn't he ask me himself?' asked Eva.

'He doesn't have anything you want.'

'And you do?'

'That's what I'm here to find out,' said Zemané.

'And what if I don't want to help?'

'Then Adolfo will kill him.'

'That's a lot to lay on the doorstep of a woman you hardly know,' said Eva. 'If Nelson's in such trouble, why don't you bail him out?'

'I bailed him out a few times,' said Zemané. 'I can't do that forever.'

'But you're here?'

'I'm here to help him help himself.'

'To Joel's money,' said Eva.

'If he takes Joel to his father, everybody wins.'

'Or shows him my certificate?'

'Right,' said Zemané.

'And for that you're going to pay me?'

'The important thing is to see that you emerge with happiness.'

'Happiness can mean a lot of things, but I appreciate the thought.'

Zemané gazed at Eva for a while. She thought he was on the verge of a pronouncement or a threat but he said, 'Shall we attack the famous buffet?'

There were salads of *feijão fradinho* with fresh tuna, fresh palm hearts with basil pesto and chicken with green coconut. There were *mineira* beans and Marimbondo rice and at the heart of it all was a roasted suckling pig. It was a thrill to lunch in a restaurant with a spread like this, where the glasses bore coats of arms and the plates were ringed with gold. But although Eva took a tiny portion of fried okra salad and a smudge of pureed yam with gorgonzola – even a woman with the will of a goddess could surely not resist – she was determined not to be bribed with fine cuisine. She would eat properly another time, at her own bidding, in circumstances altogether more celebratory. She vowed she would come here with Liam and Joel. If the certificate was wrong – how tempting to hope it was – they might even come here with Gilberto.

Eva watched Zemané tuck a napkin into his collar. If an elephant had hands they'd be like his, she thought. She watched his sizeable fingers peel a quail's egg and regretted not selecting more to eat. Eva wondered how many years of her life she'd spent watching men do things: eating, sleeping, playing stupid games, scratching assorted parts, working a little, making a lot of noise about work, and snoring, snoring, snoring. She must have spent twice as long watching them as they'd spent watching her, in spite of all her efforts. In her experience, they could only keep their mind on a woman for so long before they found another focus – usually something another man was doing, or television.

But Zemané seemed a man with a good heart – it might be a little soon to judge, but she liked to judge – and she needed to think his heart was good, because she had to admit that losing her job was starting to freeze her up inside, and she wasn't a woman who wanted to be even partly frozen. She certainly wasn't averse to an offer of happiness, now that misery was looking likely. So while she didn't like to give in to a man who was used to holding all the cards, now was not the time to be making life more difficult in the name of pride. Supply and demand were the yin and yang of the modern world – and too much of the time she was stuck in the little black hole of demand. If she helped them and they helped her and Joel found the answer, then, in the end, what was the harm? Perhaps it was even one of those win-win situations

Liam was always mentioning, to which – as far as she could tell – she'd never been party. So, as she waited for him to finish, she decided to give Nelson the benefit of the doubt, which made her happy, though she was careful to retain a tightness in the lips – which she hoped made her look like a woman not to be trifled with, but which she suspected made her look a bit like a fish.

When Zemané had cleared his plate, she said, 'There *is* something I need.'

'Name it,' said Zemané.

'A president and a million dollars and a condo in Spring Palms – wherever that is.'

'I'm sad to say my spells are on a smaller scale.'

'I need a job,' Eva said.

Zemané smiled, touched her hand and said, 'Then I might be able to help.'

They dropped in on the buffet once again, where the ribbon of Eva's resolve snapped and she piled her plate high with éclairs and chocolate millefeuilles. Back at the table, she devoured her haul while Zemané smiled on. When she had finished, the plates were cleared and they ordered coffee.

'Why do you care about Nelson so much?' asked Eva.

'I'm sentimental. I like his singing.'

'But really? I mean, the two of you are hardly similar.'

Zemané asked if he could smoke a cigar, and lit one when she said it was fine.

'I wasn't always so up,' he said, 'and he wasn't always down. But his aunt was killed, his sister was killed. It can be hard to stick to a nine-to-five after that. So he moves around trying to sing it out, bet it away, sell it with other people's furniture, smile it away to a thousand casual friends who'll never ask too many searching questions.'

'But why him? I mean, there must be millions of Nelsons.'

'I used to dine alone a lot at an Italian place, after our daughter died. My wife and I were lost in a terrible silence.

199

We couldn't find a sentence to make it better. But Nelson used to wait my table and I found I could talk to him a little, and he would talk a lot – about what Zila would say or what Yemanjá was going to do to right our wrongs. He always had a theory. Then, one day, I heard him play. If you've heard his voice you'll know what I mean.'

'Yes,' said Eva.

'Of course he lost that job, but I found out where he went to drink – I wanted to buy him a beer and thank him. I liked the bar where he drank, and as I didn't have a bar myself it became my bar as well, as an occasional drinker, at first, and then as a regular. When the owner, Paulo, ran into trouble with Adolfo – Nelson is far from alone in that – I bought the bar for a very nice price. And the rest, as they say...'

'It's a lovely story, no doubt about that, but I hope there aren't too many Nelsons in your life. Others might take you for more than a ride.'

'Everyone needs at least one Nelson, don't you think?'

'Don't get me wrong – I'm as sympathetic as the next woman. But this week everyone seems to be going sympathy-crazy. Murderers are victims and hijackers are saints. If I don't break the law soon, they'll come and lock me up.'

Zemané laughed. 'You know who I feel sorry for in that bus business?' he asked.

'Surprise me.'

'The policeman, the one who shot Geisa.'

'For a successful man you're quite the softy,' said Eva.

'He took a chance, that boy, the way I see it. He took action, tried to solve everything in a stroke. OK, so he missed the hijacker and shot her by mistake – '

'Some mistake!'

'Quite a mistake, yes,' said Zemané, 'but with better aim he'd be a hero.'

'You must be kidding me, friend! There are a zillion others more deserving of sympathy.'

'He was a thoughtful man, I read, who liked to play the piano and paint. He made a mess in front of the world and now he can't eat or sleep.'

'Some mistakes have to be paid for. You can't just shrug off the shooting of a woman. He's not testified yet, because the doctors say he's ill; the five that squashed the hijacker are claiming a right to silence; the commanding officer at the scene is going to be cleared. They shoot and kill – *bangue-bangue* – and when do they ever pay?'

'They're poor kids too, a lot of them. Would you like to be a cop?'

'Not all of them are poor. These guys were supposed to be Special Forces. Do poor kids play the piano like your little favourite?'

'They don't train them properly, that's the trouble,' said Zemané. 'They send them into the hills to fight a war.'

'They need to train them better, I agree,' said Eva.

'There's a murder every two hours – they need to do something.'

'They need to do something, I'll drink to that.'

Eva realised she'd enjoyed the cut and thrust. She was able to be herself without him spitting out his pips. She was damned if she was going to play the weeping woebetide to find a helping hand, but he didn't seem to want that. He showed no signs of wanting to get on top of her – in any meaning of the phrase. He might not be a bad boss, she thought.

She put her handbag on the table, undid the clasp, took out the folded certificate and handed it to Zemané.

When Joel got back from the bus station, he called Liam's office.

'How was Paraty?' Liam asked.

'A beautiful dead-end,' said Joel.

'So what now?'

'I don't suppose Eva's had any news?'

'Sorry.'

'Nelson still reckons he knows where my dad is. I'm going to go with him to some restaurant tomorrow. If that doesn't work out, it's back to the drawing board, I guess.'

Joel wondered what else he could try, if it wasn't his father at the restaurant. Perhaps he could talk to some of the news people, a reporter or cameraman at the hijack scene. It might be worth a try. He watched television for a while then went for a swim in the pool on the roof. He walked round the rooftop, looking at the view: Corcovado, the lake, the twin mountains at the far end of the beach. Behind their embrace, its face hidden, Joel could see one side of the summit of Pedra da Gávea. It was hard to believe he'd ever been up there. Joel leaned on the rail and looked at the faded blue edge of the distant mountain and thought about that final day with his dad.

It had started with the phone ringing him from sleep and his mother shouting at whoever was on the line. Joel had sat up in bed and listened.

'It's the end,' he heard his father say.

'Can't you run?' said Jackie.

Joel thought there was sobbing, though it didn't sound like his mum.

'To where?'

'I don't know... Belo, Argentina, the forest – '

'I'm not a fucking monkey – '

'This is no time to be funny.'

'I'm not!' hissed Gilberto.

'I'll go and see the major,' said Jackie.

'I'll talk to Angelica.'

'Don't you think that bitch has done enough?'

'She's nothing to do with – '

'You liar!' bellowed Jackie.

'Shhhhhhhh! This *isn't* going to help, not now. Go on, then, go and see the major – '

'OK, OK! You take Joel, find somewhere to hide for the day – '

'Take Joel?'

'I'm not taking him to the major,' said Jackie, 'and we can hardly leave him here. What if they come?'

'We'll climb the mountain!'

'Today! Are you *mad*?'

'They'll never find us there,' said Gilberto. 'Besides, I promised him, for his birthday.'

'His birthday's not for seven months!'

'I might not be around in seven months.'

Joel heard Jackie in the bathroom, opening wardrobe doors, emptying her handbag releasing coins which spun on the kitchen worktop. The closing of the front door sealed the flat in a moment of silence.

Gilberto came in and sat on Joel's bed.

'Who's coming?' Joel asked.

His dad smoothed creases in the sheet.

'No one.'

'Is it the *polícia*?'

'Perhaps,' said Gilberto.

'Let's climb the mountain,' said Joel.

Gilberto smiled and ruffled his hair. From behind his back he pulled a present wrapped in paper covered with hummingbirds. Joel slid a fingertip under the sticky tape and folded open the paper. A black box. He felt its weight, its edges. He opened the lid, gasped, took the compass in his hands and stroked the smooth of its silver. Keeping it flat, he flipped it open and turned it until the needle settled on north.

'*Bacana!*' he said with a bounce into his dad's arms.

They took the yellow Beetle, Joel in the front seat for a treat, his eyes on the swinging needle and the N, telling his dad what bearing they were on. Gilberto kept up cheerful responses, his eyes on the road in front, on the streets to the side, on the cars roving through the rear-view mirror. He'd forgotten about the checkpoints on the Barra road. Would they be on the lookout? Surely there were bigger fish.

Joel remembered the heat in the rattling car, air rushing through wide open windows. They drove round bends which swept past the ocean – so blue, so huge – until, dipping down, they spotted a cluster of vehicles ahead and came upon a soldier, flagging them down. Joel remembered Gilberto trying to joke with a military policeman whose eyes were hidden behind aviator shades.

'Where are you going?' asked the man.

'Barra beach,' said Gilberto.

'In walking boots?'

'We might go for a walk later, when it cools.'

'Day off work?'

'That's right.'

'It's all right for some,' said the policeman.

He looked at Gilberto's papers then took the documents over to where a fatter officer sat in a jeep. The Beetle's engine chuntered. There seemed to be some debate. Joel started to hum one of Gilberto's tunes but his dad told him to hush. Gilberto watched the men from the corners of his eyes, setting his face relaxed.

The policeman returned.

'They're looking for a man,' he said. 'For all we know, it might be you. They didn't say anything about a boy. Park up on the right. We're seeking clarification.'

Joel remembered jumping at the sudden roar of the engine as Gilberto hit the revs. By the time the guards reacted, the Beetle was round a bend and soon had turned off the main road. He remembered parking down a track and looking up through trees at the vast mountain, black above them.

'Don't be scared,' said Gilberto. 'We're safe now.'

Gilberto and Joel drank water, then grabbed their knapsacks and dived up a path through the forest. Joel gripped his dad's hand as up and up they climbed, Gilberto panting and Joel pulling along behind, holding roots and trees as they scrambled, catching sight of the sea through the forest whenever they turned. They climbed and climbed, sweat sheening their skin, though at least it was cool under the canopy.

'There's an easier way,' said Gilberto. 'But this is the proper way.'

After what seemed like hours, they reached a flat clearing where they sat on the ground.

'I'd like to see the *polícia* climb that,' said Gilberto, breathing hard.

'No chance,' said Joel.

They ate bread and ham and a chocolate bar. They drank water from a canteen. Their breathing became calmer and they could hear birdsong. It was past noon now and all of the cloud had cleared from the sky.

'Shall we get going?' asked Gilberto, standing up.

'I like it here,' said Joel. 'If they do come, we can hide in the forest.'

'Don't you want to stand on the mountain's head?'

'I do. But let's stay here a bit longer.'

'Do you remember the story about the Sphinx?'

'No,' said Joel, though he did.

They sat against a rock in the shade and Gilberto told Joel the story, making up a few new twists as he always liked to do. Joel listened to his dad's voice, feeling the grain of its varied tones and enjoying every strand. He listened too for the sound of soldiers, though all he heard were the rustle and creak of trees in the wind and the songs of birds.

After a story or two they stood up, stretched and turned on to the path towards the mountain, which, itself like a sphinx, appeared to be reclining, its head turned back on itself with one eye on the city, as if looking out for their pursuers. They stared up at the black face of the rock and Gilberto put Joel on his shoulders for a few seconds, and Joel remembered feeling like the highest being in the world, there above the forest, looking down the plummeting shoulder of the hill to the vast blue sea and the Marvellous City. On they strode, turning round the head of the mountain, where the path led to the bottom of an outcrop of rocks, by no means vertical, but seeming steeper than they were because of the great drop of a slope beneath them. Joel paused at the foot of the rocks and looked up at the cracks that would aid their ascent, then back down at the fall of the mountain below and then at his dad who wasn't smiling any more, but was shading his eyes and squinting into the sky. Joel watched his dad's face, half-lit by a high sun, shadows deep in its lines, and looked across at the profile of the mountain, which seemed harsher from this angle, blank-eyed and indifferent.

'We've got to get up these rocks,' said Gilberto. 'There must be somewhere we can hide.'

'It's really steep,' said Joel, sure he couldn't reach the cracks, thinking they'd need a rope or something. Then he heard the rotor-blades, still distant, but growing louder.

'We have to climb, Joel, it's not far, we're just high, that's all. It's only a small slope. Just keep your eyes up, not down.'

Joel looked down. The slope looked steeper still and he felt the altitude in his stomach for the first time and thought he might fall from the very spot on which he stood. He looked up to where his dad was, a few feet up the rock and holding out his hand. Joel felt frozen. He could hear the blades closer and had the feeling a pterodactyl was going to swoop on him at any moment, like the ones in books his dad used to read to him when he was little.

'Please, Joel,' said Gilberto, his voice serious. 'I'm with you, it's safe. Trust me, Joelinho – just to the top of this bit, then we're safe.'

Keeping his eyes on his dad, Joel climbed, grabbing the rock and cracks, using his dad's hand every now and again. It really wasn't a difficult slope, he told himself, no worse than those at the foot of Sugarloaf, up which he'd clambered a thousand times. They reached the top and scrambled towards the final cliff below the summit, hunting for somewhere to hide. The helicopter was close. Had it seen them? They found an overhang and crouched beneath it. A whirr of blades was thickening the air. Then they heard the metallic voice of the machine.

'*Come out, Gilberto,*' it shrieked. '*Come out or we'll shoot you dead.*'

The machine called and called for Gilberto alone, which was strange to him and Joel, since they felt themselves fugitives together.

'Crawl along and hide,' Gilberto said. 'They don't know you're here. Wait until they've gone, then go back the way we came. You can do it, Joel. You've got to be brave. I have to do what they say.'

Joel started to crawl. There was a tree a little way along, where he could hide. He turned but his dad had gone. The blades throbbed in the air and the tree shook. Joel pressed his face into the dirt. The wind grew gentler, until he could only hear common sounds: insects, birds, the wind, his heaving breath. Joel knew he should move or open his eyes, but it felt good to lie with them screwed tight. If he couldn't see the mountain, the cliffs, the drop to the forest and the sea, then maybe they didn't exist. He knew this was a state of playful thought he'd abandoned many years before, but it felt more comforting to regress – he almost sucked his thumb – lying as he was near the head of a beast of a rock, separated from a father who was probably being shot. No, he thought: they're not going to shoot him. My mum will have persuaded the major. After a few formalities they'll allow him to come home. I can't just lie here. I need to get back. Whatever is going on, they'll need me, and they'll be worrying.

He scampered down until he stood near the top of the steep slope again. He couldn't bring himself to the very edge. He had to sit before he could raise his eyes to the view. How could the world be so far below? There was no way he could go down. Every time he looked at the slope it seemed to tilt to a steeper plane.

Perhaps there's a way down the other side of the mountain, he thought. He looked behind him and suddenly thought:

how good it would be to say he'd reached the peak. He stared at the profile of the beast which had let his dad be taken. How great it would be to stand on its head, like its slayer. Joel walked back to the cliff and along its face, then, finding a gully, he climbed until he found himself on a scrubby plateau at the top. Hardly believing he was there, he walked across the sloping ground to the edge of the summit, where granite rose like the lip of a crown. He stood a few yards from the edge, staring at a world too far away and beautiful to be real. He took out his compass and took bearings on all the points his dad would have pointed out: the green pinnacle of Agulinha, the curved cranium of Pedra Bonita, the sloping back of Dois Irmãos with the city beyond.

Joel realised he would never be able to descend. To look down made the world slide underneath, as if preparing for his somersaulting fall. He sat down. He noticed that the shadow of the rock was stretching across the land. The blue of the sky was darker and the shades around the horizon were thickening into colours. There will be so many stars, he thought. No longer able to look at the view, he lay back near the peak of the rock and closed his eyes. He didn't hear the rotor-blades until they were suddenly above him. He opened his eyes, surprised himself with a scream and ran. He ran as fast as he could, bounding over rock and scrub. He ran for the gully, as the helicopter wheeled round and he heard its metallic shriek again.

'Joel Cabral Burns,' it said. 'Stop! Don't run. Shit! Don't run, moleque!'

Joel was down the gully in a flash and haring to the top of the steep slope of rocks, which twisted under him again. The helicopter wound into view and the voice was telling him not to be afraid, but he lay tight in a ball with hands over his ears, waiting for talons or bullets, feeling his blood had turned to wire which pulled him tight. The air beat on his face, the metallic voice screeched and Joel screamed as he felt a grip on his shoulder.

He opened his eyes to see a soldier.

'Major Branca says it's time you came home,' he said. 'Your mother is worried.'

He pulled Joel to his feet. The helicopter hovered. The paratrooper grabbed a harness in one hand, Joel in the other, and they were lifted twirling into the sky, high above the world, to be pulled into the machine and flown to a landing pad near the lake. Joel was driven home in a Jeep, arriving to find his mum pacing the pavement in front of the flat. A police van sat a few yards down the street, with its doors open and two agents in the back.

'If you've touched him,' his mum shouted at the soldiers in the Jeep, 'if anyone has touched him, I'll *hunt* the lot of you down!'

In the flat, Gilberto was sitting at the kitchen table drinking a glass of beer. Joel remembered he looked calm. Joel could hear his mum in the bedroom, opening cupboards.

'There's no point packing me a case,' he called.

Gilberto beckoned Joel to him and said, 'Keep an eye on your mum for me. Always take care of your mum. Think of me when you're by the sea. I'll think of you there too. Good lad... now don't cry... promise me you won't cry... you're the man of the house now... good lad, good lad.'

He stood up. He didn't pick his keys up from the bowl on the side, nor grab the linen jacket he wore in the evenings. He bent and did up a shoelace. He smiled at Joel. He said something to Jackie about the major, then laughed. He opened the front door, turned and winked at Joel and said, '*Até a morte, pé forte* – strong foot, until death,' then left the flat.

Jackie came and knelt beside Joel, who was still looking at the door.

'Listen, my love, we've got to get out. They won't let us stay. There's a plane, soon. I know how terrible this is, but we'll have time later... We need to be quick. I've packed us a bag. See if there's anything else – '

209

Joel ran to the door. He darted down the stairs with his mother's voice echoing after. He ran into the street. Along to the right, the jaws of the van were swallowing his father's back.

'*Papa!*' he shouted, but the doors closed.

Joel stood in the road and watched the van drive away. Jackie seized his hand and pulled him back inside. He didn't cry. Jackie was in a flap.

'Just a few things,' she said. 'I've brought a blanket, it'll have to do. If there's anything you want, grab it quickly. How about a book? Why don't you – ?'

'Where are we going?'

'We're going on a plane, sweetheart,' she said.

'Where to?'

'I'll tell you on the way, petal.'

'Are we going for long?'

'Just until things are a bit easier.'

'Is Dad coming to join us?'

'We've got to be quick, Joel. Come along!'

From a shelf in the living room, Joel took some photographs Gilberto had been meaning to put into an album. He fetched his lucky Flamengo ticket stub and his compass and gave them all to his mother.

'Is that it?' she asked.

'You said be quick.'

'What about your cars, some books? Don't you want anything else?'

'I don't want to go to England, if that's where we're going.'

The intercom buzzed from the front desk and they heard the lift start.

'Quick!' said Jackie.

She put Joel's stuff in her case and took his hand. They left by the back door and took the service lift. They emerged into a side alley and hurried to a street at the rear, where they flagged down a cab.

Joel stared out of the taxi window at the sights of a city he was losing. He tried not to blink. He wanted to open the door and roll to a stop in the road, alive or dead. They drove along the Ipanema seafront, the last light smouldering over the sea, street-lights illuminating palm trees, neighbours enjoying a beer. Through into Copacabana and round the great sweep of the beach, past street kids looking for a bite, a pocket, a fix, a place to rest away from harm. Through a tunnel, along Botafogo beach, past Sugarloaf, through Flamengo park, past the airport of Santos Dumont, past high-rise blocks and *favelas*, catching a glimpse of the Maracanã which made him think of where his father might be now and whether the cops were giving him a chance. The car was flying towards a plane he didn't want to take and he hoped the police would catch up and escort them back and throw them all in a cell and do whatever they wanted – how could it be worse? We'll be back, he told himself. We'll come back. The major will realise he's made his point. A lesson learnt – that's the important thing. Whatever that lesson might be.

Jackie clutched Joel in the queue for check-in. He wanted to break free, to shout at her, to tell her they could run *inside* Brazil, hide somewhere with one of their friends. Perhaps they could go to Tiradentes, stay with Gilberto's family. There must be somewhere. But he didn't know how to shout at his mum, so he glared at her.

'I'm angry too, darling,' she said. 'But we've got no choice – '

'I don't understand,' Joel said. 'Why can't we stay?'

'They won't let us, honey. The major said we have to leave *today*.'

'But what can they do?'

'Whatever they like!'

'*You* want us to go!'

'I do honey, you're right, I do. I'm scared, Joel, we're not safe – '

'But what about Dad?'

'Don't, petal, don't.'

'You don't want to help him.'

'I tried, honey, I tried.'

'You didn't try hard *enough*.'

'Don't say that! This isn't easy, Joel. Oh, Joel!'

Joel stood and watched the sun set from the roof of Tiffany's. Down by the beach he could see three street kids passing along the seafront pavement far below, pushing one another, bouncing a tennis ball, asking passers-by for change. They went down on to the sand, where one of them stopped to show the others his juggling, then the other two took it in turns to try, without success. The two non-jugglers formed a shoulder pyramid, upon which the juggling kid teetered for a while, until they all fell into a heap and wrestled one another.

He went back to the flat and mushed himself a caipirinha. It would be good to see Liam. He didn't want to think about the past. He sat on the balcony as the light died and was pleased to hear the lift open down the hall and Liam's voice at the door.

Debbie wandered over to Jackie's. Jackie made a pot of tea and they sat on the sofa cradling mugs as Jackie talked about Tony.

'What are you going to do?' Debbie said.

'I don't know. I suppose I've got one last chance, when I go and get my things. Maybe it's not too late for him to change his mind.'

'I've not seen you like this, Jacks. There was a time when I wondered what you saw in him.'

'I've known enough bad ones to know a good one,' said Jackie.

'He certainly seems to have got you hooked.'

'A bit too good for the likes of me, that's the trouble.'

'Don't talk nonsense!'

That was the trouble with dating an honest man, Jackie said to herself: you could be more confident they wouldn't mess you around but God, you had to stick fast by the rules. She wondered how a man like Tony could play it straight and waltz through life unscathed. Surely even he had skeletons?

'Let's change the subject,' said Jackie. 'What are we going to do?'

'Brighton's your oyster,' said Debbie. 'What do you feel like doing?'

'We could go for a walk?'

'I've always found walking without a destination a bit pointless.'

'We could walk to the Rusty Axe?' suggested Jackie.

'Now you're talking.'

The Rusty Axe sat on top of the hill on the edge of Hanover. From a yard at the back it had a view over the city to the west and along the curve of the coast. Jackie and Debbie bought drinks and found a table with a good view of the pub. They liked to watch people come and go and discuss which famous people they resembled. The cast was far from stellar, so they gave up and played the Bullseye quiz machine.

'You can't beat a bit o' Bully,' said Jackie.

Bully beat them soundly. Debbie wondered what she would have thought in her younger, more sophisticated days – whenever they were – had she gazed into a crystal ball and spied herself playing a Bullseye quiz machine with a woman nearly twice her age who wore dark glasses inside and swore a lot. Debbie suggested they try their hand at darts, but it turned out Jackie was rather better on the oche than she'd bargained for. The day was heating up, so they moved outside to sit in the sun. They ordered pie and chips, ate their food in a serious silence, then leant back with fresh glasses of wine and looked out over city roofs and tower blocks towards the sea.

'Let's face it,' said Jackie, 'it's not the prettiest view in the world.'

'How can you say that!'

'Don't get me wrong – I could look at it forever – but it ain't Ipanema.'

'Ipanema's got tower blocks too,' said Debbie.

'And twin mountains, and views of forest, and a curve of sand.'

'Well, I wouldn't change it for the world.'

'You know what I really like in a bit of coast?' asked Jackie.

'No.'

'Rock pools. I used to love mucking around in them when I was little.'

'They'd invented Majorca by the time I was young, thank God.'

'You don't know what you've missed.'

'No matter how hard I try, Jacks, I can't imagine you mucking about in a rock pool.'

'Was a time you couldn't keep me out of them.'

'When I think of you holding a little net, the only image that comes to mind is of fishing battered cod from a frier.'

Jackie laughed.

They chatted more as they looked at the town and the sea, and Debbie thought how strange it was that the sea always made her think of Brazil, even though she'd never been there. She hoped Joel would find Gilberto, hoped it would make him happy, hoped it might bring him back with... what? Certainty? An end to the wait-and-see-and-give-it-a-bit-more-time-to-be-sure? Debbie had never seriously considered giving up because, unlike a lot of men she knew, Joel didn't think he was more than he was. Delightful in a child, to be expected in a teenager, the tendency to think oneself bigger than the rest became more tiresome the older a man became. At some point he had to acknowledge he was not much more than nothing. If he saw himself in this way, then the something could be really cherished. This was how Joel thought, or how she'd thought he thought when she met him. She'd since discovered he didn't think about himself in these terms at all, which could have been great if it weren't for the fact that he thought a lot more about his dead and psycho dad than he did about his live and loyal lover. This had made things difficult for the best part of twenty years, but then Debbie couldn't imagine herself in a relationship with someone easy – what would be the point? There had been few dull moments. Besides, the easy ones were never as easy as they seemed. Better the git you know, she thought.

Jackie's mobile rang, but by the time she'd fished it out of her bag it had switched to voicemail.

'It's him,' said Jackie, then listened to the message.

'Tony here,' it said. *'Wondered if you'd like to come over and collect your things – think I've rounded them all up. Give me a bell if you can, I'm in all day.'*

'Wish me luck,' she said.

'Good luck!' said Debbie.

Jackie hurried home, ran a bath, washed her hair, shaved her legs, put on a long white skirt and a white shirt with loose buttons down the front. She put a touch of make-up on, a paler lipstick than normal. Wearing none would be making too much of a song and dance. She grabbed her shaggy coat, dug out the floppy summer hat, egged herself on in the hall mirror, then sat in the lounge looking at the phone. She wasn't sure what her strategy should be. She lit a cigarette and dialled.

'I'm popping over,' she said. 'I can't stay long, you'll be pleased to hear.'

On the radio in the taxi they were talking about how many years of one's life were spent asleep. Jackie wondered how many she'd spent in these turquoise and white cabs. They hadn't been bad times, as portions of her life went. She was usually riding to or from an engagement to be excited about. As she lounged in the back she liked to spy on other women who were driving family cars or sports cars or being driven by their husbands – and most of the time it felt good to be the one being whisked somewhere. She wondered how many women like her were circling town, warmly stretching conversations with a jolly assortment of drivers whose attire tended to blend into the upholstery.

The cab dropped Jackie at the foot of Tony's drive. She stood by the gate, out of sight, and smoked her customary cigarette. Were she the lady of the manor she'd get rid of that gravel, she thought. She wondered if she'd stand outside this gate again or if this would be her final, final cigarette. She crunched up the drive. Tony opened the door as she raised her hand to the knocker. She kissed him on one cheek and then the other. He smiled and stood aside to let her pass.

'Time for a coffee?' he said.

'I can squeeze one in.'

Jackie led the way to the kitchen, where she sat at the old wooden table. She wondered how many of the scratches had been made by his wife. He put the kettle on and handed her a shoebox.

'I think that's everything,' he said.

She put the box on the table and removed the lid. All there. In another situation, with a different man, she might have made a show of checking the items. Perhaps she would have refolded the bikini slowly or put on the bracelet. She closed the lid.

'Thanks,' she said.

Tony handed her a mug of coffee. He stood leaning against a marble worktop in a blue cotton shirt with rolled-up sleeves. He smiled at her kindly. She smiled back. Jackie had expected him to be a bit more ruffled. Wasn't he going to ask her questions? Where were the words thrown back in her face, the promises unstitched? All she sensed was an ironed sheet of disappointment, and for a moment she did wonder what on earth she saw in him. He might be beautiful to look at, but didn't he care?

'Aren't you going to say anything?' she asked.

'About what?'

'What do you think?'

'Listen, Jackie, let's not – '

'Argue? Why not? What have I got to lose? It's obvious you couldn't give a flying fuck for our relationship – '

'Relationship?'

'You're not even upset!' said Jackie, rising from the table.

'I am upset!'

'So why don't you *show* it?' she said with a stamp of her foot.

'You don't have a right to demand *anything*!' Tony moved away from the counter and folded his arms.

'He stirs at last!' she said. She stepped closer, so that she stood a foot away. Hands on hips, she looked up into his face. He was looking to the side slightly, at the ground. 'I don't want it to finish,' said Jackie, moving a hand towards his cheek.

'Well, I bloody well do,' he said, and stopped her hand.

Jackie held his hand for a second, before he pulled it free.

'I'm sorry,' she said. 'I should have told you about bloody Carlo. It was over between us, because of you, though I admit it was foolish of me not to tell him quicker.'

'Foolish!' said Tony and moved away. 'Christ!'

'I've never been very good at ending things.'

'Can't say no – is that it?'

'Not to you,' said Jackie.

'Now you're sounding corny! I preferred it when you were merely devious.'

'Tell me you don't feel anything for me and I'll go.'

'That old chestnut!'

'Tell me I'm a bitch and you hate me.'

'You're really something, Jackie – I'll give you that!'

'Tell me *something*, can't you? Tell me to piss off or drop dead. Tell me you never want to see me again. You can't just give me a shoebox and show me the door.'

'I can do it however I bloody well like.'

'Well, *do it*, then!'

Tony coughed and put down his mug. 'I think you should leave now.'

'Tell me it's over.'

'It's over.'

'You're making a mistake,' she said. 'I've made a mess of it, I know, and for that I'm very sorry. But we have something that could keep us spinning along for the rest of our days.'

'Well, we'll just have to do our best without it.'

'Don't you want a bit more than that?'

'I'm fine, thank you very much.'

'Liar.'

Jackie refused a taxi or a lift. It would feel good to walk for a while, she thought. Maybe she'd head for the sea.

'Your box!' he said as she reached the door.

'Burn it,' she said.

Joel left Liam's flat and hailed a cab, which took him to a bar on a corner with a black and red sign that read 'Bar do Paulo'. Zemané shook his hand and Nelson clasped him in a hug. He sat on a free stool and ordered beers. Paulo slopped them down and eyed him as he wiped the counter.

Nelson put his arm round Joel's shoulder and said, 'How about a little race?'

'I'm up for that,' said Joel. 'Whatever "that" may be.'

'Find yourself a speedy ant, my friend. The best are not too big and not too small – watch for the ones that seem most true to their course. Like a sort of English ant – that's the kind you want – that gets from A to B without much messing around. Avoid the twitchy ones which tend to bump into other ants and dance around and forget entirely what they came for. Be careful when you pick up your little racer – let him come to you, don't force him – those legs are fragile and he'll need all six of them.'

Joel scampered out on to the pavement, enjoying the feel of Carioca asphalt on his palms, and he thought how strange but wonderful it was to be scrabbling in the street with the smell of Brazil in his nose. For a moment, the indolence of traditional holidays struck him as absurd: perhaps everyone should travel with a mission – leading to red-herring bus rides to colonial towns, and insect races against scheming local guides. He selected an ant he thought looked suitably alert but which also appeared to have an eccentric streak – tending to turn in a circle before sprinting at double speed. If my ant is going to win, thought Joel, he must have unusual qualities – attributes which might win or lose a race, but which at least will give him a chance.

The ants of Nelson and Joel were studied by the referee – Zemané. A man from Florianópolis once won with an ant-like spider. Six legs were the minimum and maximum allowed. Joel's ant was larger than Nelson's and a touch more brown. Nelson's was slim and jet-black. Zemané approved the ants and placed them under a shot glass on the counter, from where they had a view of the golden pastries below. Hands reached into pockets, wallets flapped open, bills were plucked from the side of cigarette packets. The regulars waved *reais* at Paulo, who took them and scribbled down bets. The majority put their money on Nelson's ant, though Zemané was one of a minority with faith in Joel's.

'Are you ready?' said Zemané, placing his hand on the glass.

The patrons closed on the counter, pressing against Nelson and Joel, whose eyes were on the shot glass in which the ants were running around.

'*Pronto, à postos... Vamos!*' said Zemané and lifted the glass.

Joel felt the crowd surge and braced himself, keeping his eyes on the ants. Joel's ant turned a half-circle and darted across the glass at right angles to the finish. Nelson's loitered for a while, apparently in no hurry, then sprinted towards the line, stopping short to inspect a stray crumb.

'Nooooo!' cried Nelson.

Joel's ant turned and sprinted in the right direction, overtaking his distracted rival. When Joel's reached the line the majority let out a groan, while the minority whooped and Joel laughed into the air. He slapped hands with winning punters, counted his money, then proclaimed he was buying everybody a beer. This seemed to draw new patrons from the very tarmac, though Joel cared little as he stretched to pay. The regulars crowded round, asking how an Englishman who looked so like a Brazilian could end up in their bar, so Joel told them about his dad and the news clip, which started them arguing about the hijack again. Joel was enjoying the friendly conflict when he felt Nelson grip his arm. The voices around them slowly went quiet.

Adolfo and Vasco stood in the middle of the road. A black car sat nearby with its boot open and engine idling. With his hands in the pockets of his slacks, Adolfo raised his eyebrows before saying to Nelson, 'I have eyes everywhere, *malandro*.'

'Only God has eyes everywhere,' said Nelson.

'Then it's a shame he's not looking out for you.'

Vasco looked at his boss, taking his cue to walk towards the crowd in front of the bar. He reached beneath his Vasco da Gama shirt, into a pocket of his baggy shorts, and pulled out a reel of gaffer tape. Nelson started to climb off his stool but Zemané put a hand on his shoulder and pressed him down.

'Nobody is taking a friend from my bar,' Zemané said.

'We had an arrangement,' said Adolfo. 'He broke it.'

'He's going to pay you back, tomorrow.'

'Tomorrow is my least favourite day.'

'I'm getting the money tomorrow, I swear,' said Nelson.

'If I have to wait another day,' said Adolfo, 'then I'll need a little blood to keep me happy.'

'I like my blood where it is,' said Nelson.

'I can't take yours. How can you pay me tomorrow if you're dead?'

'Then you'll have to wait,' said Zemané. 'He'll pay tomorrow, like he says.'

'Take your pick,' said Adolfo to Zemané. 'Your choice, you made the deal. I can kill anyone you like.'

'There's no need to kill anybody,' said Zemané. 'You'll get your money.'

'Anyone you like: what about Paulo? He's a grumpy son of a bitch. How about him?'

'No!' said Zemané.

'He's been working for me – did you know that? Keeping tabs on Nelson... didn't do a very good job, mind you – the cockroach kept scuttling away. Want me to kill Paulo? I don't need him any more, he's a real snake and he takes up a lot of space.'

'I don't want you to take anyone.'

'Paulo it is, if you can't come up with another name.'

'I'm not going to name anybody,' said Zemané.

'How about the foreigner? Don't think we ever killed an English guy. The foreigner or Paulo – the choice is yours.'

'If you kill Joel, you won't get your money,' said Zemané.

'OK, then, Paulo it is.'

Adolfo nodded at Vasco, who grinned and approached the bar. A couple of regulars moved to block his path, so he reached into another pocket and took out a knife. The patrons parted. Vasco waggled the knife at Paulo, who came out from behind the bar. Vasco pushed him to the floor, kneeled on his back, severed a length of tape with his teeth, bound the screaming man's hands, then wound the reel round and round his head until his eyes were obscured and his cries muffled. Vasco pulled him to his feet and led him to the car. He took a truncheon from the boot and hit Paulo on the side of the head, which made a frightening cracking sound. He caught Paulo's body as it fell and heaved it into the boot.

Vasco closed the boot, turned and said, 'I'll be back for you, Flamengo, same time tomorrow.'

The regulars watched as the car drove off.

There was silence.

Zemané said, 'I'm closing up,' and everyone drifted away.

Joel felt frozen. He'd seen abduction in a hundred gangster films, but to see a man bound, coshed and taken before his eyes left him questioning his own vision. Was a man really being taken away to be killed? Yet here he was still sitting on his stool surrounded by silent regulars. He couldn't help but think of the image of his father being pushed into the back of a van all those years ago – except that wasn't the story here, it wasn't about him and his dad, but about Fat Paulo, a bit of a grumpy bastard but surely not a man who deserved to be killed – killed! He was going to die tonight – Joel couldn't believe it – and worse than that, worse than anything, Nelson might die tomorrow. Whether Gilberto was alive or dead, whether they found him or not, Joel couldn't let that happen.

'We have to talk,' said Joel. 'You need to tell me what's going on.'

'There's nothing to worry about, my friend,' said Nelson. 'I'll meet you at Tiffany's at noon.'

'I need *more* than that,' said Joel. 'Tell me about the trouble you're in, the money... I can help you, *cara*. I want to help.'

'Let's take a walk,' said Nelson.

'Where to?' said Joel.

'I want to show you something.'

Joel followed Nelson down the street, through a square where old men drank on the benches and children slept in the shadows. They strode into Lapa, along Avenida Mem de Sá and under the arches of the viaduct to where a crowd was swelling up the slope in front of the arches and down Rua Joaquim Silva. Nelson went to buy two drinks from a vendor, but Joel stopped him.

'What are they going to do to him?' Joel asked, agitated.

'Who?' replied Nelson.

222

'Who do you think?'

'I don't know.'

'Don't give me that!'

'Do I need to spell it out?'

Nelson dived into the crowd, with Joel following, until they came to a bar where an ensemble of assorted men with instruments was sitting at a table, swinging a tune into a rhythm. Nelson stood for a while, in a trance, then started to move a little, but Joel hadn't finished.

'Why don't we *do* something?' said Joel.

'About what?'

'To help Paulo!'

Nelson stopped moving and turned to Joel. 'Like what? Call the police?'

'Why not?'

Nelson laughed.

'It's not funny. Jesus! There must be something we can do. Don't you even care?'

'I'd give more of a damn if he hadn't tried to get me killed. Tomorrow Adolfo might just grant his wish.'

'How much do you owe him?'

'Two thousand. Same as you owe me... is it starting to make sense?'

'What if we don't find my father? What if I don't pay you?'

'We'll find him,' said Nelson.

'What if we don't?'

'We'll all be dead one day.'

Nelson was starting to dance as he spoke – in fact, Joel was the only one who wasn't moving at least a little.

'How can you dance when you might die tomorrow?' pleaded Joel.

'Can you think of a better reason?'

'Nelson, come on, talk to me, stop.'

'I can't tell you any more than I have,' said Nelson, shrugging.

'I need to know what to do.'

'There's nothing else to be done.'

'What if I give you the money now?' said Joel. 'I'll give you it now, tonight, and you can find Adolfo and make everything all right.'

'What about your father?'

'You can still take me there tomorrow. If we find him, we find him. If we don't, we don't.'

Nelson came to a halt. He wondered what Zila would say. On the one hand she would probably encourage him to keep to his agreement. On the other she'd want him to save his skin.

'Do you have the money here?' asked Nelson.

'Shit! No. I was going to go to the bank tomorrow morning. Damn!'

'Perhaps it's for the best. I'm not sure where to find Adolfo, and I'm not sure I want to see him any sooner than I have to. He might just kill me tonight and then you'd have lost the money and not know where to find your father either.'

'You could tell me now and I'll give you the money in the morning.'

'And miss out on taking you to him? No way, *cara*!'

'Fuck!'

'Let's stick to the plan. I'll give him the money tomorrow night and it'll probably turn out fine.'

'Turn out fine? Jesus! It's just total madness!'

'Come on,' said Nelson. 'There *is* something I want to show you.'

They squeezed through the flowing masses, rounded a corner and took off across the Largo da Lapa, leaving the crowds and the viaduct behind. They reached Avenida Rio Branco, where high-rise blocks stretched towards the distant bay. There were people leaving bars or arriving at clubs, and the odd foreign businessman hurrying nervously towards a taxi rank. Joel saw kids curled sleeping in a doorway, a woman in rags sitting on cardboard against a wall. After a while they turned down a narrow street to the right, where Nelson stopped in front of an office block.

Nelson and Joel stared at the entrance to the building. A security guard was watching television. An empty soft-drink can and three cigarette butts lay on the step.

'If I die tomorrow,' said Nelson, 'remember this place for me.'

They looked at the spot for a while. There was no chance Joel would forget the place, that much was certain, though it was hard to absorb the fact that here someone had died. Perhaps there are spots like this all over the city, Joel thought, and he tried to imagine a world pocked with black marks where all the dead had fallen. Except that this girl hadn't fallen, but had died asleep, without a chance. And she wasn't any victim, but Nelson's sister. Lord only knows what he must feel, thought Joel.

After a few minutes sitting on the step, Nelson said he wanted to head off. They found a cab, and Joel offered Nelson a lift, but he refused. Through the back window he watched Nelson walk back down the narrow street and wondered where he would go that night. Joel watched the city slide by. Kids slept under trees in the park as the cab rode red lights for fear of hold-ups. The taxi slid past deserted beaches and silent high-rises, dead kiosks and frozen palm trees, shooting Joel towards his bed with visions of Mariana on his mind. And Joel realised that he felt angry – angry for Mariana, mainly, but for Nelson and Paulo too, for a day containing so many tales of violence. And it made him think of his father's violent side again, though he didn't want to, and it made him feel ashamed to have a violent dad, and ashamed that he found it hard to be honest about the fact. And he wondered about himself. There were things he shared with his father and things he didn't. Perhaps it was just genetics, but was there something else? Part of his failure to understand the possibility – OK, the fact – that his father was a violent man came from the fact that there wasn't a violent streak in Joel. Joel had never really been in a fight, and, although he could think of plenty of people in the world he'd like to punch, he simply couldn't conceive of hitting Debbie – even if she did throw snow globes. How could his father hit his mother? What made someone drop a paving stone on a sleeping girl?

Perhaps his father could answer. There had to be some kind of reason – not an excuse, there was no excuse – but some explanation as to *why*? He wanted to ask his dad about that darker side. When had it started? Had he always felt that there was rage in him? Prison must have lanced the boil of it all over them, but was it as simple as that? Were there no earlier traces? Had he hit another woman, another man, in earlier days? There were always stories of frustrated men, or addicts, or men with secrets being unable to control themselves. Of drink prising them apart and shattering them into violence. The Bests of the world got too much sympathy, Joel thought. Any sympathy was too much. Joel wanted to hear his father's side: to listen to him talk about the cause, or trigger, or catalyst. He dreamed of him saying sorry.

Perhaps nothing could explain it. Perhaps it was intrinsic, just the way he was, the same way that he could sing or had a gap in his teeth. It hadn't come over him at all; it simply *was* him. Or, worst of all, perhaps it flashed one day like lightning on a sunny day, without storm clouds to warn, just forking into their lives, then vanishing. A flash like that would worry Joel. What if the same spark hid in him? What if another man lurked, like the man his mother said she'd seen sometimes, hiding behind Gilberto's eyes, mocking her almost, waiting for his chance to spring into her life with fury? Could Joel be sure this man would not emerge? Perhaps he was sleeping now, or watching, waiting – plotting the right time. What if he leapt out once Joel became a father? It was hard to believe that such a beautiful event could trigger something quite so ugly, but it did make Joel wonder about a darker side of himself. He thought about the white beauty of his car crash,

226

and he wondered if violence could look white to him, as death had that night, when it had shone before his eyes and seemed the most beautiful light.

Sometimes the human capacity for evil scared him. He'd been to Birkenau and seen the sunken ruins of the murder factories, where men had shovelled the bodies of thousands into ovens, every day. Men could do that to other men; his dad could hurl a fist into his mum – who was to say Joel couldn't hurt another person, perhaps one unexpected day when the world just started to turn wrong. Would he climb upon another man to save his neck; could he send a woman to the gas chambers? He didn't think he could; it didn't seem like him at all. But was there any man who could be sure?

Nine

Joel woke at dawn and lay in bed wondering whether his dad was also awake. Today their parabolic curves would intersect. He wondered whether his dad had any inkling – had he risen with a feeling the day was somehow different? Perhaps blurred images of Joel had wandered into his dreams. Later they would talk of omens, noticed before but now understood, of remembered years and forgotten years and the years to come.

He got up and showered, dressed, and went to the kitchen where he made coffee. He sat at the table outside. He looked at his watch. It was half-past seven.

Liam emerged, showered and suited. 'The big day,' he said.

'The big day,' said Joel.

'Got your compass?'

'Check.'

'Speech?' said Liam with eyebrows raised.

'I'll wing it.'

'Handcuffs?'

'Handcuffs?' frowned Joel.

'Can't let the bugger get away again.'

'If he tries I'll kill him myself.'

Liam left and Joel tried to watch television. CNN, the cartoon channel. He watered the hibiscus on the balcony. He called his bank in the UK, then when it was late enough he went into a branch on Visconde de Pirajá and withdrew money. He went back to the flat and put the cash in an envelope, sealed it and wrote 'Nelson' on the outside. He put it in a money belt which he tucked into his shorts.

At twelve the buzzer went.

Nelson was waiting outside with his red rucksack over his shoulder. They started walking. They stopped near the corner of Praça General Osório for a coffee and a juice and ordered two *folhados*. Joel made himself eat. When they had finished they walked a couple of blocks and turned towards the lake. They reached it and headed round to the right. Beyond the lake stood Cristo and the mountains. The sun was high. Joel wished he'd worn a hat, then wondered what he'd have done with a hat when he met his dad. Would he have taken it off and clutched it out of respect? Perhaps it was better to be loose and unencumbered. Joel's shirt stuck to his chest and his palms were sweaty. He wiped them on his shorts. He wondered if his dad would really be there. They must be only minutes away. They walked on further, trying to stay in the shade, then Nelson brought them to a halt. Fifty yards ahead was a restaurant with a yellow sign that read 'O Paraiso'. There were a few empty tables outside.

'Are you ready?' Nelson said.

'Is that it?'

'That's it, my friend.'

'OK,' said Joel. 'Let's go.'

He strode towards the restaurant, conscious of every step and swing of his arms. How will I look when I walk through the door? Joel asked himself. Will he recognise me? Joel wondered if a father could look at a son and not know it was his child. Perhaps he'll know me with the eyes of his heart. Twenty-five years and thousands of miles were now all down to a few yards and a couple of minutes. The moment would pass and they would be on the other side of it. God only knew how that would feel.

Nelson hurried to keep up. Oh, Zila, he said to himself. Oh, my goddess Yemanjá! Oh, Jesus and Buddha and you with the many arms and the elephant's head – let Gilberto be there. Nelson knew he had a piece of paper in his hand which looked as if it held the truth that Joel sought – but what was a piece of paper to the gods, who must have a thousand miracles in their pockets, a dozen resurrections at their fingertips? What was a piece of paper they could torch with a fork of lightning in an instant? They had the power to *make* this man Joel's father, even if he wasn't. If you ever grant me a miracle, Nelson thought with his eyes closed tight, let it be this.

Joel stepped inside and scanned the tables. A waiter in a waistcoat put a menu under his arm and started to approach. Nelson caught up with Joel and stood behind him. Joel could hear him breathing a little heavily. A ceiling fan moved slowly round, pushing a breeze over Joel's face, lightly stroking a shadow over the tablecloths and clusters of people having lunch. Joel could hear a Gil song on the radio, the chink of glasses and cutlery, a clatter from the kitchen, the sound of conversation and laughter. The waiter was on them now and asking if they wanted a table. Joel shook his head, his eyes searching. To the left there were tables with two or three people having lunch; to the right there was a business party of eight or nine. Joel had a feeling he couldn't see because he was looking too hard. Then, as Nelson touched his arm and raised his hand to point, Joel saw a pillar with a bare leg behind it, towards the kitchen at the back. He moved to his right, stepping past the waiter. Close to the door of the kitchen he saw a ragged man sitting with his cheek supported in a half-closed fist. He had matted white hair and wore a Flamengo shirt and shorts. His eyes were closed.

Joel moved closer, slowly, not daring to wake the man, and he saw that on his table was a plate which looked as though it had been licked clean. Joel stopped six feet away and studied the face and form of the man. Was this really his dad? There was no thunderbolt. How was he meant to feel? Perhaps the eyes of his heart were blind. The man looked peaceful. He reminded Joel of a painting by Vermeer – of

230

a maid sitting alone in a corner, stealing forty winks. Joel moved closer, wondering if he should reach down and touch skin he hadn't touched, perhaps, since he was a child. The man opened his eyes.

They looked at each other for an age, or so it seemed to Joel. The shape of the face was right and the hair. His shirt was dirty, like that of the man in the video clip. How was Joel supposed to know how his father might have aged? This man could have been sixty or ninety, though he looked worn more by hardship than by time. Like those photos of men at Auschwitz, thought Joel – thirty-year-olds turned sixty in a couple of years. The man's eyes were right, and there were lines of joy and sorrow spreading from their corners.

It could be my dad, thought Joel, it really could be my dad.

He was about to ask his name, when the man released a beaming smile.

Joel could have believed the lies of eyes, but not those of teeth. There was a gap – yes – but too much of a gap, in fact a missing tooth. It wasn't the only tooth missing and nor were the teeth that uniform, and in fact there was little doubting the fact that what remained of this man's teeth were his own.

'Forgive me,' said Joel.

They left the restaurant. Joel walked a few yards then sat on the pavement with his back against a wall. Nelson stood close to him, trying not to shuffle, wondering what to say. He felt the gods had let him down. Could a dead man not be hauled from his grave on a Rio Thursday? Not for a son who'd travelled five thousand miles? I hope you'll understand if I'm a little irreverent for a while, thought Nelson. What can you expect when you make it so hard? He couldn't help but think the gods were like spoilt children: announcing themselves with a tantrum here, a catastrophe there, as if the human race were simply there to mop up. Yet come the hour you wanted them to repay your devotion: surprise, surprise – they were nowhere to be seen.

He crouched next to Joel. 'I hate to do this,' he said. 'But there's something I have to show you. Eva's friend did find something. We persuaded her not to show you until we'd come here, hoping it might be wrong. I'm sorry if that wasn't the right thing to do.'

Nelson took a piece of paper from his pocket and handed it to Joel.

Joel unfolded it. He saw that it was a *certidão de óbito*, a death certificate. On it was Gilberto's name and a statement that he died at four a.m. on the 21st of December, in the year one thousand nine hundred and ninety-five, in this city, at his home address in the Rua Otávio Correia, Urca. The cause of death was blank. The place of burial was listed as the Cemitério São João Batista and in the space marked 'Witness' was the name Angelica Branca, of the same abode.

'Jesus fucking Christ,' said Joel.

He read the date again. 1995. His father had died five years ago. He'd lived for twenty more years, and not a word. Twenty years living with a serpent.

'Do you know where this address is?' Joel asked.

'We can find it, sure.'

'Let's go and see if Angelica is still there,' said Joel.

'You know her?'

'I know who she is.'

'You want to go now?'

'Yes.'

They flagged a cab which took them to Urca, under the plum of Sugarloaf, where the houses were well kept, the gutters clean – the only neighbourhood free of a *favela*, they said.

Joel stared out of the window silently, gripping the handle of the door, and Nelson watched him in case he tried to jump or bolt or hit someone. Joel thought about his not-so-long-dead dad. Perhaps Angelica and Gilberto had lived in Urca for years, rejecting thoughts of previous marriages and lives and children – deciding to start afresh when he got out of jail, to build a new life by the bay where Gilberto once taught Joel to sail. Perhaps he had simply decided to live with a woman he loved, who was not the woman he had first married. A sad but straightforward story, a question of choices: to live loveless with a son or sonless with a love. Further each day from traumas of the past, far from potential troubles on the other side of the ocean. How much easier to let those troubles sleep. Or maybe they'd had children of their own, grown-up now, who'd made them proud. Perhaps another son had knocked a football across a square, sat on a stool and watched Gilberto work, followed him into dentistry.

Joel found it hard to adjust the image of his father from that of a gaunt man in a Flamengo shirt to a man living in a smart neighbourhood with a woman he'd known for thirty years. A man with the wits to buy paper, a pen, an envelope, a stamp; a man who was happy, not torn from the ones he loved – separated by choice, not circumstance.

Nelson kept one eye on Joel and the other on the apartment numbers. They drew closer, driving down a road with the bay shining in a gap at the end. It was just up here on the right. They paid the driver and stood on the pavement outside the block. Joel wished he still smoked. Nelson shuffled his feet with his hands in his pockets.

'Are you sure you want to do this?' Nelson said.

'Yes.'

'I'm with you, brother. We'll find that truth.'

'The truth is scaring the shit out of me,' said Joel.

'Think of all the truth we already know... an ocean of it. We haven't drowned yet.'

'No,' said Joel. 'OK, let's ring the bell.'

It was a three-storey block. They pressed a buzzer and waited. The intercom briefly fizzed then a woman's voice said, 'Hello?'

Joel paused before saying 'Angelica Branca?'

'That's right, darling. And who might you be?'

'My name is Joel.'

'Joe?'

'*Joel*. Joel Cabral.'

'*Nossa...*' said the voice.

The buzzer buzzed and Joel pushed open the gate.

'Do you want me to come up with you?' asked Nelson quietly.

'Perhaps it's better if I face this dragon alone,' said Joel.

Nelson smiled, patted Joel on the back and stuck up a little thumb. Joel entered a patio thick with palms, took stairs to the second floor and knocked. Footsteps came and the door opened.

Angelica was thin, with pale skin which was finely made-up. She wore a white shirt with a turned-up collar and a straight dark skirt. She was a little taller than he'd expected, older than in his head – she looked a few years older than his mother.

'What a wonderful surprise! The long-lost son,' she said excitedly, and touched his arm, as if checking he was real.

'I need to ask some questions,' said Joel, moving his arm away.

'Of course, darling, but let me look at you. God, you look so like Gil, darling, it's breathtaking,' she said with a gasp.

Joel wondered how much he did look like his dad – he could only tell so much from the photographs. There was no one apart from his mother who could make a proper appraisal, and she wasn't inclined to draw comparisons. It struck him then that Angelica must have been with his father for more years than his mother, which seemed unjust.

Suddenly Angelica's eyes widened, and she exclaimed, 'My God! You do know he's dead, don't you, darling?'

'Yes. I found that out about half an hour ago.'

'I'm so sorry,' she whispered. 'You must come and sit down.'

Joel followed her into a sitting room. There were a few antiques, some bookshelves, a bird cage without a bird, and black and white photographs of people leaving night-spots, though Joel couldn't discern his father in any of them.

'Take a seat, please,' she said, nodding at a sofa.

Joel didn't really feel like sitting down, especially at her behest, but standing felt awkward, so he did.

Angelica sat across from him in an armchair. She lit a long cigarette and said, 'So you came, at last. A little late to see your father, but you did find me. Do you mind if I ask you how?'

'Your name was on the death certificate,' sad Joel.

'Ahhh! Good work, *querido*!'

'Look, if you don't mind, I'd just like to know what happened – there's a twenty-year hole to fill.'

'I can tell you everything, of course, but the facts aren't very pretty, to be honest darling.'

'I'm not expecting a fairytale. How much uglier can it really get?'

'That depends how squeamish you are. But go ahead, fire away.'

Joel paused. 'OK. So what happened after we left? When did they let him out?'

'Oh, he wasn't gone that long – he was a lucky boy,' Angelica said. 'The major died of a heart attack, you see – *in flagrante*, screwing one of my friends. The irony! There was little reason to keep Gilberto in jail. No one knew why he was there. They could have killed him to answer that question – but he was a charming man.'

'What year was that?' asked Joel, in disbelief.

'It must have been early in '76.'

'Jesus Christ!' said Joel. He stood up and started to pace around. He thought of himself in 1976, sitting at a table in Brighton, writing letters and taking them to the postbox on the corner, pushing them into the slot.

'It must hurt. I'm sorry for that,' Angelica said, and for a moment a softness in her voice made Joel want to believe she meant it.

'So why didn't he get in touch?' said Joel, standing in the middle of the room. 'Was he traumatised or...?'

Angelica looked on him with curious eyes. He felt annoyed at being the object of curiosity. His dad was dead, but not long dead, and the news of that had yet to do anything like settle. Yet here he was, standing before a woman who'd played a part in amputating a limb of his life, a woman who now regarded him as if *he* was a mystery.

'The first thing you have to know about Gilberto,' Angelica said, 'is that he was a liar.'

'For all I know, you could be the liar,' said Joel, pointing at her.

'Oh, I can lie all right. What would you like me to invent?'

'I don't want you to make it up,' said Joel, trying to keep his temper in check. 'Just tell me what really happened.'

'He did a deal with a woman from a *cartório*, and sold her your flat for a good price to keep her quiet. He paid them all to lie to your mother that he was dead.'

'But why on earth would anyone do that?' said Joel. '*Why?*'

'He didn't want to live in England; he wanted to be with me. It would have been too complicated if you returned to Brazil. It was better if we all just drew a line.'

It was hard to believe it was that straightforward. Perhaps it *was*? But Gilberto had made promises to Joel, unspoken if not aloud. The fact that he was a father was a promise in itself.

Joel sat down again. 'What about the letters?' he asked. 'I wrote him dozens of letters.'

'He read them,' Angelica said. She put out her cigarette and lit another. 'If it helps to know that, then he did.'

'I'm not sure it helps at all, but I'd prefer to know.'

'He kept them in a box. I threw it out with the rest of his stuff when he died. If I'd known you were coming, I'd have kept them.'

'What about *his* letters,' said Joel. 'Why didn't he ever write back?'

'I made him choose,' Angelica said, with an apologetic look. 'That wasn't really fair of me was it? But I just didn't want him to have you. It didn't seem fair when we couldn't have a child of our own.'

'There are greater barriers,' Joel said. 'Some men move mountains for their children.'

'I couldn't have handled it. I knew what he was like, always trying to please everyone – most of all himself. Telling your mother we were nothing, telling me she was history – I could have ridden that merry-go-round for years. So I made him get off.'

'But he chose,' said Joel. 'He looked at the options and he chose.'

Joel wondered what made her want to twist the knife. Hadn't she got her man? Were there scores to settle with his mother still? Perhaps it was just a sport she loved and there were too few opportunities to play. But he didn't want to be drawn into a battle. Her machinations were not the point; his dad's choices were all that mattered. He felt angrier than ever, but knew he couldn't afford to lose control. Throwing Angelica's stuff around or pinning her to the wall wasn't going to yield answers. He refused to blow twenty years of hunting with a tantrum that might give her the perfect excuse to throw him out.

'I was only doing what was best for him,' said Angelica. 'I always acted in his best interest, and I happen to think it was best for you – '

'His best interest!' Joel interjected, incredulous. 'Don't make me laugh! You robbed the man, you sold him down the line! If it hadn't been for your lies about his prospects, he might not have gone to jail at all.'

'What a marvellous theory,' she purred. 'Tell me, Joel, what do you do – for a living, I mean?'

'What's that got to do with anything?'

'It's a simple question.'

'OK – I'm a dentist.'

237

'*Ótimo!*' she said with a clap. 'Just like dear old daddy.'

'Hilarious.'

'Do you sing too, sing like him?'

'No.'

'When you have a gift like that, it's all about luck and magic. Did I lie that he was about to make it big? Yes. Did he lie to himself that it would happen tomorrow? Every day. Are stars born every year on a diet of similar lies? Absolutely. But a thousand burn out every day. Should I have talked to him of *probability*? Yuck! What are the chances of a João Gilberto or a Tom Jobim? But they exist. Miracles, nothing less.'

'So you did it all for his benefit,' laughed Joel sarcastically. 'Pure altruism.'

'Believe me, don't believe me. I couldn't care less, darling. I'll tell you one thing, though: your mother never really believed in *him*.'

'That's not true,' snapped Joel. 'That much I know is not true.'

'OK, maybe I am a little biased – she was my nemesis, you understand.'

'I'd like to know what right you think you have to attack my mother? You won, didn't you?'

'Did I?' she said, her eyes bright.

'He's buried up the road.'

'That doesn't sound like much of a victory.'

'You know very well what I mean,' said Joel.

'I paid for the gravestone. Not the way I imagined triumph, but it means something, I guess.'

'Forgive me if I don't find it so gratifying,' spat Joel, rising to his feet again. 'We're talking about my mother here, and you helped fuck up her life.'

'Maybe that's stretching it a little – I mean, I didn't marry her, did I? What loyalty did I owe her?'

'My mother always said you were a snake.'

Angelica looked delighted. 'Every woman would like to be a serpent – so sleek and sexy, don't you think?'

238

'I'm not interested in your twisted outlook,' said Joel, his finger raised. 'I want to get to the bottom of why he changed.'

'You should count yourself lucky, darling, rather than blaming me,' Angelica said. 'Look on the bright side: twenty years you had without that *malandro* before he died.'

'He was a good father to me!' Joel said, jabbing a finger into his chest, anger inflating his voice. He could feel the wires pulling in his veins, like times of old.

'But he wasn't good to your mother, was he?' Angelica asked, eyes wide.

'He wasn't a saint, but he wasn't a devil either.'

'Perhaps you think the devil is just a character in an old book?'

'I don't remember a devil,' said Joel.

'You were young. When you're ten you can't see what's really going on,' Angelica said. 'But do you think you'd have liked it at fourteen – to know your father beat your mother twice a month? At seventeen, would you have liked to catch Daddy fucking the maid?'

'I didn't come thousands of miles to hear – '

'You wanted the truth, didn't you?'

'The plain truth, not the bitter, twisted truth,' said Joel.

'There is only one truth about that man! I thought it would all be roses – with his wife gone and his ankles clear of a child. But I just took her place, waiting for him at night while he dined out on exaggerated torture stories and screwed every skirt that moved. Why did I stay with him? Ask your mother. Would she still be putting up with the bastard, if they hadn't put him in jail? No doubt about it. She was the lucky one. She was a million miles away by the time they let him out. Always promising to change; always getting worse – '

'Enough!' said Joel.

They observed one another in silence for a moment. Joel sat down.

'That's not the full picture, though, is it?' he said, presently, his voice calmer. 'I saw a different man. You did too, and so did my mother... there has to be a common thread.'

'To explain why he wanted you one minute and not the next?'

Joel shook his head. 'If you have to put it like that.'

Angelica's eyes shone. 'Do you think he loved you, Joel?'

'Yes.'

'Your mother?'

'Yes.'

'Me?'

'I guess,' said Joel.

'Wrong on all counts. He only ever loved one thing, and one thing alone.'

'Himself?'

'Not even that,' said Angelica.

'Then what?'

'Singing, music, singing his music. Nothing else ever reached his heart.'

'But that *still* doesn't explain it,' said Joel, exasperated. 'I mean, he was a good father.'

'One of his teachers told him to be a dentist, so he became one. Your mother made him a father, and he embraced that too. He always tried to solve the riddles life set him, but he never hungered for anything except to sing – except perhaps to drink and screw. He did his best as dentist and father – he had to get up each day and do something. But singing was the only thing about which he really gave a damn. Everything else could go hang.'

'OK, I've heard enough,' said Joel. 'I'm not listening to any more of this.'

He stood up, ready to leave, then turned and asked, 'Didn't it ever bother him, to have turned his back?'

Angelica looked up at him and he had the impression she was deciding which would bring him more pain: the truth or a lie.

'Well?' Joel asked again.

'It did bother him, in the early days, that he'd cut you off,' Angelica said. 'But he consoled himself with the fact that your chapter together had a wonderful ending.'

'A wonderful ending? Jesus!'

'You fled together, dodged the cops, climbed the mountain, were flown across the city in a helicopter. His parting words were a fitting close to an episode in your life. He hoped that, after the initial upset and anger, you would come to see Brazil as a wonderful chapter with a dashing end. To you he would be dead, but remembered like an action hero. He couldn't give you the rest of his life, but at least he'd given you a decent tale to tell.'

Joel stood motionless. He wondered if this was really the way his father had seen their bond, or if it was Angelica's twisted notion of a poor father's misguided notion of a child's needs. Her notion of the truth was evidently fluid. He had a feeling she'd make up a different story every day of the week. Only with time could he know if her versions would bring greater comfort than the hundred variations he'd dreamt up over the years. One thing was certain: however you twisted this kaleidoscope of lies and secrets, the image always looked like shit.

Finally Joel asked, 'How did he die?'

'I found him dead in our bed, darling, eyes bulging, reeking of cachaça. Drowned in his vomit, they said.'

Joel went to leave. There was no sense listening to any more. A good word wasn't going to pass her lips. There probably wasn't a good word to be said.

'I keep a picture of him by the bed,' she said, standing up. 'It's the only place he was any good. You can have it, if you want. That's all there is. I burned the rest.'

She left the room and returned with a silver photo frame. The picture was a copy of one Joel had in his shoebox, the one of him and his dad on the beach with coconuts, except the picture had been cut in half, leaving only Gilberto.

Joel imagined him sitting on Angelica's bed with a pair of scissors.

'It's all right,' said Joel, walking away. 'Keep it.'

Angelica followed Joel to the door, and as he reached it she took his arm and said, 'I'm glad you came.'

'Oh, yeah?' said Joel, with a bitter laugh.

'I've always wondered what you'd be like. It's lovely to see a little piece of him again.'

'Go to hell,' Joel said.

Joel and Nelson walked to the end of the block. They sat on a low wall looking across the bay. A couple of fishermen were sorting out their lines. Joel stared over the smooth swell of the water. He told Nelson what had happened, the things Angelica had said. He told it all in the wrong order, but what did the order matter? Whichever way you dropped them, the facts landed the same way up.

Nelson watched Joel, as Joel watched the bay. Joel was bent forward, leaning on folded arms. He pushed his face towards the water, as if he was urging his eyes to run away. Not being able to think of anything to say, Nelson remained silent. What could you say to a person with a heart that had just been scrambled? He laid an arm on Joel's back, and felt him shuddering beneath his hand.

Joel looked up at him, after a while, and said, 'One more stop to make.'

'São João Batista cemetery?'

'Yes.'

They walked through the streets of Urca, past the Yacht Club and into Botafogo, where they turned away from Sugarloaf and the bay, so that suddenly Christ was high above them on the hill, arms spread and looking almost square down upon them, head a touch inclined as if finally watching. They walked a few blocks until they reached the entrance to the cemetery, where they found a man who knew the layout of the graves. He looked up Gilberto's name, and Joel and

Nelson set off up the hill, turning to the right and picking their way through the stones. They read names and dates as they passed along the rows, until, just when they thought they might be looking in the wrong place, they saw a stone which read:

> *Gilberto Cabral de Oliveira*
> *Born on the 12th of May 1938*
> *Passed away on the 21st of December 1995*
> *Até a Morte, Pé Forte!*

Joel knelt and ran his fingers over the white marble. The air seemed still. Sound had been turned down. He looked at his dad's name written in stone. It had been a long time since he'd seen it written anywhere. He wondered who had carved the letters and wished he could have watched. He stood up and looked around: one white stone in a forest of graves on the side of a hill with a view of Sugarloaf and the bay. What a beautiful place to be buried. He looked down at the earth in front of the stone. I thought I knew a bit about life, Joel said to himself. I thought I knew about people. But it wasn't till someone pissed all over your picture of the world that you got close to understanding its nature. The devil did not just live in an ancient book. The devil could be your dad. It oughtn't to be that way, but it was. Joel wondered if life was better for knowing it. Innocence was all very well, he supposed, until you got kicked. Joel hoped he would see it coming next time. There were far worse people in the world than his dad, though hopefully he wouldn't meet too many of them. Perhaps he'd be better able to spot them if they did come along. He suspected it wasn't as simple as that, but he'd certainly keep his eyes peeled.

When Nelson and Joel arrived at Bar do Paulo, Zemané was standing behind the bar. Joel sat on Nelson's stool, said little and thought a lot. He kept thinking about the letters. Nelson had been right – he must tell him as much – that behind one truth another lay hidden. He wasn't going to search for any more truths.

Nelson chatted quietly and kept an eye on him. Soon the bar became busy and Joel took Nelson across the road, where they stood under a tree. Joel took out the envelope and gave it to Nelson.

'Thank you,' said Nelson.

'Aren't you going to count it?' said Joel, trying a smile.

'You're right,' said Nelson, clasping a hand on his shoulder. 'I mean, how do I know if I can trust you?'

'There's three thousand there.'

'That's way too much!'

'Not by much, not if you count all the days,' said Joel.

'Well, I owe you, then, I won't forget.'

'You can save me a stool at the bar, for when I come back.'

'It's a deal.'

Nelson put a wad for Adolfo in one pocket and the rest in the other. Let this be the end of it, he said to himself, and prayed to the Marvellous City itself for some clear time before the next trouble started. He swore to go back to the house to replace the fat man's money, to tidy the place and mend the door, and even to pay Edinho the concierge by the lake – who after all was not expecting ever to see the rest of the money – if only his skin could be saved.

Before long a black car drew up. Vasco stepped out and opened the boot. The bar went quiet. Adolfo strolled over and said, 'Do you have the money?'

'Yes, I do,' said Nelson.

'All of it?' said Adolfo.

'Every *real*.'

Nelson counted bills into Adolfo's hand. Brown notes with Jaguars on them, smooth from the cashpoint. He hoped each note he laid upon another would make a little impression upon Adolfo, but he feared the bills would not be enough – even if they did add up to the correct amount – because honour or pride or respect or one of those concepts serious men always claimed as their right would still be owing. Men who weren't used to guys like Nelson escaping their clutches.

'Adolfo,' Nelson said when he'd counted the last note, 'I'm sorry I ran from you and sold your furniture – except the big chair, which I confess I only didn't sell because I couldn't force it through the door. And let me assure you I'll never owe you a single *centavo* again as long as I may live.'

Adolfo put the money in his pocket and looked up into Nelson's eyes. 'Considering how long you're likely to live,' he said, 'that's not much of a promise.'

Vasco looked at Adolfo. Adolfo looked at Zemané and shrugged, then turned and climbed back into the car. Nelson walked slowly to his stool, sat down with his back to Vasco and the street, and ordered a beer, half expecting a hand to grab his shoulder and haul him through the air. Zemané poured a beer and Nelson watched bubbles swirl in the glass. He heard the boot slam, a door open and close and the sound of ignition. The regulars watched the car depart.

'Why don't you come and give me a hand?' said Zemané.

Nelson ducked under the bar and started to pour beers. He took the regulars' money and tried to tempt them with golden pastries. Zemané sat on his stool and Joel sat on Nelson's. They bought beers for one another for the remainder of the evening while Nelson served and changed the barrels and switched the radio to a new station. At the end of the night Joel and Zemané were the last remaining patrons.

Joel stood up and stretched. 'You up to anything tomorrow?' he asked Nelson.

'Moving house,' said Nelson.

'Need a hand?'

'Sure,' said Nelson.

'Moving anywhere nice?'

'I haven't worked that part out yet.'

245

'Take Paulo's room for the time being,' said Zemané, handing him some keys.

'Thank you!' said Nelson, though he had to admit he felt a little uncomfortable sleeping in the bed of a man so freshly killed. He wondered if Fat Paulo had a fat Orixá of his own who might sprinkle curses in his dreams. But he knew that Zila would tell him the dead have plenty of space to sleep without taking beds from the living, and he was sure Yemanjá would be sure to defend him in his hour of need.

Joel found a cluster of taxis bunched across a pavement. As he watched the city night slide by, the world did not look much different, except that he knew that across the city his dad was not asleep. He thought of the grave sitting silent in the dark, its flowers wilting. He wanted to use every word in the dictionary except any words for father. He guessed it might be a while before he could escape the word entirely. But as the taxi sped closer and closer to Tiffany's, he swore to himself, to Debbie, to Jackie, to Nelson, to Liam, to Eva, to every god and spirit he could name, that he would try bloody hard.

Ten

On Friday morning, Joel waited until Liam had gone to work, then made a coffee and sat by the phone. He called Jackie.

'Do you want the good news or the bad news?' he asked.

'Don't tell me, I don't want to know.'

'You do want to know.'

'Tell Debbie,' said Jackie. 'She can send me smoke signals, I'm heading for the hills.'

'Look, it's all right. I've only got good news, really.'

'Good for who?'

'Good for you,' said Joel.

'You've always had odd ideas of what's good for me.'

'Just listen for a minute. Are you ready?'

'No,' said Jackie.

'He's dead.'

There was silence on the line. 'What do you mean, dead?'

'No longer living.'

'You've said that before.'

'I've been to his grave.'

Silence again.

'Oh, Joel, my love. I'm so sorry. I never meant – '

'It's all right, Mum, it's all right. It's over now. It's good.'

'Are you all right? Oh, Joel! Are you all right?'

'Right as rain,' said Joel. 'Look, I have to go and help someone move house. If you see Debbie, tell her I'll call later. Tell her I'm all right. I am all right.'

Joel walked round the lake to the Botanical Gardens. He found a bench in a row of weeping cypresses where the scented air in the shade was dark. He watched squirrels hop and an elderly woman practising tai-chi. He wandered a forest path, inhaling tropical smells, pausing to watch monkeys play high in the trees. He sat by a pond and watched birds scoop insects from the surface, cream and brown butterflies flit over giant lilies, iridescent dragonflies hover, dart and hover. You could see the red train, tiny from this distance, riding up Corcovado, taking tourists to the feet of Cristo. Joel reached into his pocket and took out his silver compass. He looked at it for a while, feeling its weight in his palm. He flipped open the lid and watched the needle spin back and forth. Doing a quick sum in his head, he fixed a bearing to Brighton. Northeast at 39 degrees.

At two o'clock, he met Nelson at the bar. Nelson gave instructions to one of the regulars then he and Joel took off through the streets, climbing with the sun hot on their necks, until they were following the *bonde* tracks through Santa Teresa. They hopped on a yellow tram and rattled up the hill. They walked a couple of hundred yards until they stood before a house with a high wall.

'My former residence,' said Nelson. 'Give me a leg-up.'

'I thought you wanted a break from trouble?' said Joel, linking his hands into a stirrup.

'Two steps forward, one step back.'

'Robbing the rich to give to poor Nelson?'

'This time Nelson is giving,' he said, and slipped over the wall. 'I just hope Adolfo hasn't cleared the place.'

Nelson opened the gate. Joel wanted to look at the view, but Nelson led him to Ganesh. After a few minutes persuading Joel they weren't about to be arrested, they climbed on to the balcony and into the house. Nelson was pleased to find Adolfo had left the place alone, so far, so he set about removing traces of himself and restoring the house to a pristine state: plumping cushions, washing up, emptying bins.

Joel hoovered and they did their best to fix the broken door to the balcony. They tried on the owner's enormous trousers and clowned in front of the mirror, then counted *real* notes into a crisp wad and put them back in the fat suit pocket.

'It hurts me, Zila,' said Nelson looking up. 'Just because it's right doesn't mean it feels good.'

Finally, Nelson showed Joel the music room and he stood in wonder before the windows. Nelson played the guitar and sang 'Undiú' to Joel, who thought about his father as he gazed at a view which seemed to have been stretched wide across his vision. There was the vast blue of the sky, the sliced peaks of mountains trimming the edges of the city, the glimmering flood of the bay. There were the skyscrapers of Centro, the cone of the cathedral, disappearing miles of smoking suburbs. And below the house, in front of everything, sat a *favela*: dense and unignorable, alive with objects flashing in the sun. Joel traced a figure weaving through a maze of paths, followed two kids chasing after one another. Nelson sang and Joel watched. When the sun was low, Nelson put the guitar into its case and closed the lid. It would be painful to be without an instrument for a while, but he had some money, and if Zemané would give him a permanent job at the bar then maybe he could invest in a beautiful specimen. Now he had a taste for the best, it was no good buying just any guitar.

Joel and Nelson checked the house a final time, closed the door to the balcony, set the alarm and left. They caught a tram to Carioca station and walked to the bar, where Nelson took over for the night. Liam and Eva came by. Liam lost three times on the ants and Zemané talked to Eva about her new job in the office of his warehouse near the docks. He might have told Nelson he could stay in Paulo's room, but he'd said nothing about a permanent job. Nelson didn't want to ask, assuming his last favour had already been used up.

Debbie went round to Jackie's on Saturday afternoon. Jackie produced a magnum from the fridge, fetched flutes and a bowl of Bombay mix, then turned on the television and played the clip. Debbie wondered if the man looked any different, now they really knew he wasn't Gilberto. She wondered if Joel would see a counterfeit where once he'd sworn it was the real thing.

Jackie finished her glass and filled it again.

'So did Joel give you all the ghastly details?' asked Debbie.

'Pretty much.'

'Do you feel any different? Now that you *know* he's dead.'

'I suppose I must,' Jackie said.

'Were you ever in any doubt?'

'No.'

'Honestly?' asked Debbie.

'I knew he was dead, I knew it... and yet... you could never tell with Gilberto. Give him half a chance and he'll jump right out of that grave.'

'Did Joel tell you about Angelica?'

Debbie waited for Jackie to speak but she just smoked, her eyes on the screen.

'Will it really be over?' asked Debbie. 'You know, for Joel?'

'There's nowt more certain than a gravestone, that's what Miriam said.'

'As long as he's buried in Joel's head.'

They switched channels and watched the racing. Jackie's horse was pipped on the line. Then, taking the bottle, glasses, a rug and snacks, they walked to Queen's Park where they sat on a slope with their faces pointing at the sun and talked about Brazil, Joel, the presents he might bring back. Families picnicked under the trees and kids kicked a ball around at the bottom of the slope. At the end of the afternoon, as they lay on their backs, the bottle empty, Debbie asked, 'Any news from Tony?'

'Not a sausage, darling.'

250

'What the hell does he think he's playing at?'

'I should have known better, I suppose,' said Jackie.

'But why won't he give you a second chance? It was hardly the crime of the century.'

'I don't know.'

'We deserve answers!' Debbie declared.

'Why don't you ask him?'

'Would you like me to?

'He's getting off far too easily,' said Jackie.

Debbie stood up too suddenly, which made her head spin. She walked home, drank some juice, took a couple of pills, smoothed her crumpled skirt and called a cab, which dropped her at the gate of a house in Hove. She crunched up the drive. Bloody gravel, she thought. She rang the bell. A shadow moved inside and a shape came to open the door.

'Debbie?' said Tony. 'Is everything all right? Is Joel – '

'I haven't come about him,' she said. 'I've come about you.'

She sat at the kitchen table while Tony made them a coffee on the stove. Tony sat down across from her. 'So…?'

Debbie hadn't thought what she was going to say. 'I want you to give Jackie another chance.'

Tony's eyes widened. 'Don't beat about the bush, then.'

'There's not much point dancing around the issue.'

'No. Well, what can I say… I respect your concern. She's very lucky to have someone like you to stick up for her, but…'

'But?'

'But, I'm not sure it's really any of your business.'

'I'm not sure that's a good enough excuse,' said Debbie.

'It's not an excuse at all – '

'It's an excuse of sorts – a poor one.'

'Look, I don't want an argument – ' said Tony.

'Then tell me why you won't give her a chance.'

'I did give her a chance.'

'Half a dozen dates and an *adios*?' said Debbie.

'It seems they weren't the only dates she had.'

'You're a bit old to hope for virgins.'

'Christ!' Tony said.

'She was going to end it. It didn't mean anything.'

'Well, it meant something to me.'

'Did somebody break your heart, Tony? Did somebody hurt you?'

'Amateur psychology to boot!'

'She's one in a million,' said Debbie. 'You should thank the lucky day she even thought of you.'

'I'll bear that in mind,' he said.

'This could be the greatest time of her life, you know. He's dead – Gilberto, I mean – Joel has found out he's dead.'

'I'm sorry to hear that – '

'Think what you're saying, will you? There's no harm in wishing a bad man dead. Especially a bad man that's responsible for the pickle you're in.'

'Look, I know the history, some of it anyway, but that was years ago – '

'But he's really dead. Don't you see the difference that makes? Not to you, but to her? I know she thought he was dead, "knew" he was dead, but now he's really *dead*. You catch my drift?'

'But I don't see how that makes a difference to what happened between us.'

'Why must you be so *rigid*? That man put her through the mill and she's coped the only way she's known how. But he's gone now, and she's found you. You've got the power to put everything right. How many men on earth have that power – to give someone's story a happy ending? And you're going to deny her – and yourself – the chance of that because of a bit of pride?'

'From what I hear, your own affair could do with a happy ending.'

'That's not the point. I gave it my best shot for twenty years.'

252

'But Gilberto is dead now, right? So that changes everything, doesn't it – I mean, that's what you're saying?'

'Maybe it does, maybe it doesn't.'

'But you want me to give second chances?'

'I've given Joel a million chances, and I'll give him plenty more. That way I'll never have to think, "What if…?" The rest is up to him.'

Debbie crunched back down the drive and stood at the bottom. She rolled a cigarette with shaking fingers. I can't believe I did that, she thought.

On Sunday, Nelson and Eva came over to Liam's and they all went to Ipanema beach. They picked a spot near Posto 9, hired low-slung deck chairs and formed a circle on the crest of the sand. They stood and observed the world, drinking beers and eating *biscoitos* as passing vendors shouted out their wares: '*Sanduíche natural!*' '*Abacaxi! Abacaxi!*' They watched serious men and women dive skilfully around volleyball courts by the lifeguard station, then went for a swim, hopping over the hot sand between bathers who wore tight costumes over all manner of flesh: flabby, toned, brown, pink, black. As their skin dried in the sun, they stood and talked. 'Maybe we should float flowers into the sea,' said Joel.

'We could ask Eva to dress up like a big Bahian,' said Nelson.

'Don't joke, Nelson, don't joke, friend,' said Eva. 'If I eat any more of that barbecued cheese I'm going to need a big white dress before I can show my face on this beach.'

'Be careful what you say by the sea about women in white dresses,' said Nelson. 'A real goddess might be listening.'

'Oh! So you're saying I'm not a real goddess now, are you?' teased Eva.

'There are goddesses and goddesses, obviously.' Nelson winked.

'So how come you're so hung up on Yemanjá?' asked Liam.

'Subtle as a brick,' said Joel.

'Zila said there were only two things I needed to know about my father,' replied Nelson. 'He was a fisherman and he was a son of a bitch. She said Yemanjá was my Orixá, like it or not, because my blood was the blood of the sea. Zila liked her too because, when she was young and slim with long black hair, a man she once loved who was also a fisherman – but not a son of a bitch – called her his goddess, saying she looked like Yemanjá.'

'And you're supposed to float flowers out to sea towards her to gain her favour, isn't that right?' asked Joel.

'She likes gifts,' said Eva. 'There's nothing wrong with that. She owns the oceans, Joelinho; she's a rich lady, a commander of storms, a mother of life on earth.'

At the end of the afternoon they strolled along the seafront road, which was closed as on every Sunday. Rollerbladers wove stretching legs through the walkers and joggers, bikers passed up and down the inner lanes, muscular men did pull-ups on gymnastic frames, women in shorts and bikini tops power-walked with headphones, chewing gum. As they sat chatting at a kiosk with a beer, a darkness touched the air and, looking up, Joel saw mist creeping over the shoulders of the apartment blocks. With a shiver the mist enveloped them all, as scattered whoops rose from the crowd.

The next day, Joel rode buses around the city and watched the world. He sat in cafés, ate *salgadinhos* and drank beer from iced glasses. His face and hands made Brazilian shapes as newly discovered words flowed through his lips when he chatted with those he met. In the evening he went to the bar, to find that its black and red sign now read 'Bar do Nelson'. Nelson polished the bar more frequently than it needed and the regulars said he should've been a shoeshine boy. 'I was once,' he said, 'and the toe-caps shone like spoons.'

Zemané turned up and sat with Joel at the bar. 'So when are you going?' he said.

'In a couple of days,' said Joel.

'Well, whenever you want a stool at the bar...'

'As long as he lets me win on the ants, I don't mind standing.'

'What are you doing tomorrow afternoon?'

'A bit of sightseeing, probably.'

'Got a surprise for you and Nelson,' said Zemané. 'Take the cable-car halfway up Sugarloaf. Be there at four o'clock.'

The next afternoon, Joel and Nelson rode the cable-car. Assorted tourists jostled for position near the outside of the bubble as views of Rio rose like scenery flats. They could see Copacabana's curve, Cristo rising on his hill, apartment blocks like a million teeth in the valleys, flesh-pink *favelas* on the slopes. They arrived at the first station, on the Morro da Urca, where passengers scrambled towards views over the bay. Zemané found them as Joel was snapping photos.

'Are you ready for the ride of your lives?' he said.

He showed them to a helipad where a grinning pilot shook their hands and strapped Joel and Nelson into the back of a small helicopter. Up they tilted into the sky, as the ground and a shrinking Zemané fell away from them. Joel gripped his seat while Nelson screamed and cheered as they swooped down over the bay, then above the towers of the city, sighting the white viaduct far below. Over the snaking streets of Santa Teresa, above *favelas* and *favelas*, then catching a glimpse of a tiny yellow tramcar not far from where the house must be. They rode over a ridge at the edge of a sea of forest which stretched over folds of mountains as far as the eye could see. Then, rising on a peak above the trees, rushing to meet them now with his arms spread wide, was Cristo Redentor, balancing on his hill, and Joel thought what an amazing idea it was, to build such a beautiful thing so high up – think how hard it must have been – just so a statue could wave its arms across the sky in the hope that out there, in the reaches beyond the visible shit of the world, there might be something that made it all make sense.

High above the arms of Christ, Nelson and Joel hung turning in the air, and the lake and the city and the sea and the forest all spun in the blue of the afternoon. They lurched towards Ipanema beach where they turned right, high above the surf, skirting the flattened peaks of Dois Irmãos, over the edge of the mighty *favela* Rocinha, until before them, rushing head-on, sitting like a sphinx on the crown of a ridge with its face staring straight towards them, was Pedra da Gávea. Joel felt a tightness in his chest as over the slope they flew and he saw the steep rocks which he and Gilberto had scrambled up all those years before. Soon they were hovering over the summit, and the helicopter sank towards the ground where it rested with a tilt and a bump.

Nelson and Joel climbed out, ducking the blades. They picked their way across the scrubby summit to the edge of the plateau, slowing to inch forward. Nelson grinned at a silent Joel as they peered towards the drop of the cliff. They sat together near the edge and looked at the view up and down the coast. They could see tower blocks far below and the snake of a golf course between the forest and a strip of beach. Beyond the peaks of Dois Irmãos were the lake and the paperclip curl of the Jockey Club, and Joel thought of how this trip had started with the hijack not far from that very spot. And he thought of Sandro, wondering if his body was lying in one of those metal drawers you saw in films, with a tag on his toe and a cloth across his face of lead. They hadn't been able to bury him, Joel had read, because the DNA test said Elza wasn't his mother after all, and there was no one else to vouch for him, no certainty who he really was. And Joel thought how the hijack story was fading now, with Sandro lying silent, a hostage still struck dumb, cops refusing to testify, the governor failing to meet the dead girl's family, and four hundred children still sleeping in the corners of the Marvellous City.

As Joel looked at the view he thought of the day he'd been here years before with his dad, a man whose story had also died. How pure his love for his father had been. He didn't want to feel dirty when he thought of him; after all, who really knew how his story might have turned out if he hadn't been put inside? But the truth was: there was no invisible number to make their family add up. His father had closed the eyes of his heart to Joel long ago, no matter how much Joel had wanted to be seen. His dad wasn't hidden but dead, dead beneath the land and dead beneath Joel's skin. His genes might be there in bone and tooth, but the rest of Joel was not much like his father, and, while it didn't make him happy to realise this, neither did it make him sad.

When Joel and Nelson emerged from their thoughts, they wandered the top of the rock together, pointing out this or that feature, marvelling at how high up they were. In places people had written their names on the rock in thick black letters, and the two men pledged to return to write their names the next time Joel was in Brazil. When it was time to go, the helicopter lifted them across the dying afternoon and dropped them in the heart of the city.

That night, they all went to the Bar das Terezas, and Joel had a word with the manageress, and whatever he said to her worked – because she let Nelson borrow a guitar and play a few songs, even though he was not on the bill. In truth she was happy to see him play – especially when he played 'Dindi'. She let Nelson invite her for a dance and after her bar shut she changed out of her suit and into a skirt and told them all her name was Belinha. They hit other bars where they drank caipirinhas from plastic cups as thick-thighed women shook their legs like earthquakes. Belinha drank cachaça like water and danced with Nelson until her skirt was a blur, and Joel danced too and Nelson watched him and thought: if some goddess had told me in a dream that a stranger would come from afar and change my life, I wouldn't have believed them. But they didn't tell me, and I don't really think they knew, which just goes to show they don't know everything – or if they did, perhaps they chose to keep quiet about it, reasoning that if I became too excited I just might blow it. But

I didn't – so here I am: not in trouble, with a steady job and only lacking a guitar, which will come to me, I have no doubt, because music could never keep its hands off me for long.

Joel drank spirits from street vendors under the white arches of the viaduct, laughed at Liam's clowning in an antique bar, slapped hands and backs and kissed cheeks and sucked in the smell of the streets, until finally the night was crowned as an old man watched him dance, grinned, looked into his eyes and said, *'Tá sambando, meu filho!'* You're sambaing, my son!

Joel picked his bag up off the conveyer belt at Heathrow, was relieved not to be searched by Customs, and looked for Jackie as he emerged into the the gallery of people waiting to pick up fares and loved ones. His eyes roved through hugging couples and pick-up signs until he was surprised by a cardboard placard which read 'Burns' – held by Debbie.

'Your usual driver is feeling poorly,' she said.

They drove round the M25 exchanging small talk, both of them wanting to move on to larger subjects, both thinking them too big for a trip in this little car. Debbie listened for clues that his measured words hid broken feelings. There must be fractures, but it was difficult to read his voice. She wondered what Brazil would mean to him now. Joel remembered the drive from the airport the last time he'd arrived. How different the world looked now from that night of grey and concrete. He observed the green of England in late June, a notch or two quieter than the green of Brazil, but no less pleasing.

The flowerbed by the roundabout on the edge of town spelled 'Welcome', and soon they were passing Preston Park and driving under the red-brick viaduct. Debbie parked outside Jackie's house. They knocked but there was no reply, so they let themselves in. On the sofa was a postcard of the Palace Pier on which was a written, *'Gone to Tony's for dinner. Don't wait up.'*

'Tony!' said Joel.

'I'll tell you about it later,' said Debbie.

'She's seeing *Tony*?'

'It's a good thing, believe me.'

'Tony!'

Debbie laughed.

They walked though the streets of Hanover, pausing at the top of Albion Hill to view the sun descending towards rooftops, past high-rises. They walked past the police station, across St James's Street, cutting down to the seafront by the Palace Pier. The evening was thick with people on the promenade. They walked west, their eyes straying over the sea towards the same old place, except it wasn't the same any more. They walked further, past the basketball court and the sagging West Pier, until they reached Hove Lawns, where they sat on a bench overlooking the sea.

'Talk to me,' said Debbie.

'What do you want me to say?'

'Tell me what you're thinking.'

'About my dad?'

'About him, yes.'

'There's nothing to think. He's dead. End of story.'

'I'm really sorry, baby, I really am.'

'I don't know if *I'm* sorry,' Joel said.

'You don't mean that, really...'

'Wasting all that energy on a good-for-nothing.'

'You weren't to know,' said Debbie.

'Wasn't I?'

They got up and walked in silence for some minutes. The wind had risen and the sea swished pebbles over one another, rolling them into a regular boom. People passed by walking dogs, rollerblading, calling to their kids. Tentacles of rain swept down to the sea not far to the west. They walked past the end of the Lawns. The wind had a chill to it and normally Joel would have put his arm around Debbie. They passed bathing huts and upturned fishing boats, stray cafés and

Victorian shelters spaced along the promenade. Raindrops started to fall. Debbie and Joel walked faster and cast a glance at one another. Larger drops fell on their hair, bouncing off their foreheads, darkening patches on their clothes. Harder and harder the rain fell, breaking up the surface of the sea, pelting them now, making their faces cold and wet. 'Shall we run?' Joel said. They sprinted, laughing, soaking until they reached a shelter. They sat on a bench painted the green of old steam engines. Huddled close, they watched the rain. It made the skin of the sea look prickly, like the stem of a nettle. Back-spray swooshed thin clouds of mist over the surface.

The rain stopped and the sky turned half a dozen shades of grey. An evening sun made the pavement shine. The arms of grey cranes stood flexed on the western horizon where the storm had gone. They looked at one another, then sat together in silence, their eyes on the sea. Far off, angled sails slid over glittering water.

'So how do you feel now about Brazil?' said Debbie.

'What do you mean?'

'You waited all that time to go back.'

'I love it as much as ever,' Joel said. 'Brazil isn't to blame. The world is full of rats.'

'You know, you were right in a way. We didn't believe you, but you were right. I mean, he *was* alive, until not very long ago.'

'True,' said Joel and laughed.

'What's so funny?'

'So many years wishing he was alive. Now I wish to God he'd just been dead.'

'D'you regret not going before?' asked Debbie. 'If you'd gone ten years ago you could have seen him.'

'I'm glad I didn't see him now,' said Joel. 'He died to me in '75.'

'Do you really feel that?'

Joel pulled his eyes from the sea and looked at Debbie.

'Yes, I do,' he said.

'Perhaps Angelica exaggerated?'

'Maybe.'

'Perhaps prison just broke him,' said Debbie.

'Perhaps a lot of things happened I'll never know about – there could be a million reasons. But it's hard to argue with twenty years of silence.'

The sun went down over the sea. Joel felt the smooth metal of his compass in his pocket but he didn't take it out.

'We could go to Rio for Christmas, if you like,' said Joel.

'Is that a proposition?'

'One last shot. Make or break.'

'I guess it's about bloody time,' said Debbie.

'It'll be hot as hell.'

'The hotter the better.'

'We can travel around or stay in the city, whatever you like.'

'The city, the beaches, the forest – I want to see everything.'

'In the evenings we can prop up Nelson's bar, then go dancing in Lapa.'

'Sounds good to me.'

'I know a restaurant in Santa Teresa where you can sit with a view of the bay as they play *chorinho* in the garden. I know a kiosk where they mix the best caipirinhas on Ipanema beach. We can catch the tram, ride the buses, hire bikes and cycle round the lake. And I'll show you the most beautiful graveyard you've ever seen.'

So I came back to my first note,
As I must come back to you,
I will pour into that one note
All the love I feel for you,
Anyone who wants the whole show,
      Re mi fa sol la si do,
He will find himself with no show,
      better play the note you know.

'Samba de Uma Nota Só'
(Antonio Carlos Jobim and Newton Mendonça)

Acknowledgements

I would like to thank everyone who has encouraged, critiqued and cajoled me over the last ten years – indeed anyone who has remembered to ask about my writing and managed to listen without evident bemusement.

In particular, I would like to thank the following people for their input and support: Ben Siegle, Carey McKenzie, Tim Lay, Amy Riley, Derek Parkinson, John Quin, Rob Smith, Stephen Silverwood, Louise Del Foco, Rob Pratten, Ken Barlow, Simon Munk, Rachel Thackray, Vittoria D'Alessio, Kathy Davies, Sophie Orme, Lee Sims, Adam Whitehall, Janette Fowler, Rob Paraman, Phil Cain, Alison MacLeod, Susanna Jones, Linda Siegle, Jon Siegle, Charlie Siegle, Lucy Siegle, Becky Siegle, Henry and Jo Harrison, Christina Daniels, Victoria Hobbs, Celia Hayley, Daneeta Jackson, Amanda Schiff and Wayne Milstead.

Particular thanks to my wife Louise for love, support and incisive critique.

A big thank you to Kathryn Heyman for mentoring me brilliantly through the writing of *Invisibles*, to Kate Lyra for checking the Brazilian content past and present, to Anna Morrison for her beautiful cover design, to Linda McQueen for sharp and sensitive copy-editing, to Dawn Sackett for spot-on proofreading, and to Melina Herrmann for her support checking Brazilian copy.

Finally, extra special thanks to Vicky Blunden, Candida Lacey, Corinne Pearlman, Adrian Weston and everyone at the wonderful Myriad Editions for backing me and *Invisibles*, and for all their continuing hard work and support.

AFTERWORD:

THE books and films identified here all helped to shape elements of *Invisibles*.

Bus 174 (Ônibus 174), dir. José Padilha and Felipe Lacerda

The hijack described in *Invisibles* was a real event, which happened in Rio on June 12th 2000. This excellent documentary analyses the incident through interviews with parties involved, from policemen to hostages, and traces the history of the hijacker, Sandro Rosa do Nascimento. It sheds a shaming light upon the plight of street children – often criminalised and occasionally murdered for the sin of being homeless orphans – and the hideous conditions in Rio's jails. Padilha does not seek to justify the hijack of the bus, but the documentary goes a long way towards explaining why the hijacker was driven to such an action. It's a great piece of work, and deeply thought-provoking regarding the roots of social violence. The opening sequence provides a stunning snapshot of the medieval inequalities of the modern world.

Tropical Truth, A Story of Music and Revolution in Brazil (Verdade Tropical), by Caetano Veloso

This wonderful book charts the development of *Tropicália*, an avant garde musical movement in 1960s Brazil, which unfolded against the backdrop of the military dictatorship. An icon in the music field, Veloso writes with a distinctive and engaging voice on that startling era. The book was important to the depiction in *Invisibles* of '60s and '70s Brazil and its music and political worlds, and to the details of Gilberto's time in prison, for which Veloso's own account of his incarceration was an important source.

Samba, by Alma Guillermoprieto

This book is an exuberant guide to samba in all its forms – from its history, to its importance in everyday life, to how to dance it (as a man or a woman). But it was of most value to the writing of *Invisibles* through its description of the lives and locales of ordinary Brazilian people, those living in and out of *favelas*. It brims with colourful characters and stories, and is highly informative regarding not just samba but facets of life such as the Candomblé religion in which Yemanjá is an important Orixá (spirit-deity), as well as everyday details such as money, clothes and food.

Carandiru, dir. Hector Babenco

A film based on the novel *Estação Carandiru* by Dr Dráuzio Varella, which dramatises life in a notorious São Paulo prison, location of an infamous revolt and massacre in 1993, when 111 prisoners died, almost all of them gunned down by the police. Partly using novice actors and former inmates, the film was shot in the prison itself shortly before its demolition. More than simply being the story of the massacre, it shows the hierarchies and relationships that characterise this sad and surreal world, one rife with disease and devoid of basic rights. By following the stories of distinctive characters, it brings a human face to the inhuman reality still experienced in many such prisons.

Bossa Nova, The Story of Brazilian Music that Rocked the World, by Ruy Castro

This meticulous book looks at the origins and pioneers of bossa nova leading up to its 1960s explosion in Brazil. For *Invisibles*, it was particularly helpful in painting the backdrop to Gilberto's attempts at musical breakthrough in the '60s, enabling me to refer to specific artists and venues and to develop a feeling for the style, dynamics and preoccupations of the music scene at the time.

For more information on the locations, music and characters from *Invisibles*, please see www.edsiegle.com.

MORE FROM MYRIAD EDITIONS

FROM THE AUTHOR OF *GLASSHOPPER*

It's more than twenty years since Sarah Ribbons last
set foot inside her old school, a crumbling Victorian
comprehensive on the south coast of England. Now, as she
prepares for her school reunion, Sarah has to face up to the
truth of what really happened back in the summer of 1986.

August 1985: As she embarks on her final year at Selton High,
Sarah's main focus is on her erratic friendships with Tina and
Kate: her closest allies one moment, her fiercest opponents the
next. When her father is unexpectedly taken ill Sarah is sent to
stay with Kate's family. The girls have never been closer – until,
a few days into her stay, events take a sinister turn, and Sarah
knows that nothing will ever be the same again.

In her eagerly anticipated second novel, *Mail on Sunday* Novel
Competition winner Isabel Ashdown explores the treacherous
territory of adolescent friendships, and traces across the
decades the repercussions of a dangerous relationship.

ISBN: 978-0-9562515-5-8

Catherine has been enjoying the single life for long enough to know a good catch when she sees one. Gorgeous, charismatic, spontaneous – Lee seems almost too perfect to be true. And her friends clearly agree, as each in turn falls under his spell.

But there is a darker side to Lee. His erratic, controlling and sometimes frightening behaviour means that Catherine is increasingly isolated. Driven into the darkest corner of her world, and trusting no one, she plans a meticulous escape.

Four years later, struggling to overcome her demons, Catherine dares to believe she might be safe from harm. Until one phone call changes everything.

This is an edgy and powerful first novel, utterly convincing in its portrayal of obsession, and a *tour de force* of suspense.

ISBN: 978-0-9562515-7-2

SHORTLISTED FOR THE GREEN CARNATION PRIZE

'Fast-moving and sharply written.'
Guardian

'There is a deceptively relaxed quality to
Kemp's writing that is disarming, bewitching
and, to be honest, more than a little sexy.'
Polari Magazine

'An interestingly equivocal and quietly questioning début.'
Financial Times

'Kemp's language is beautiful; his characters are carefully
drawn and the dialogue engaging. The narratives overlap
and are all the more moving for their subtlety. Drawing
inspiration from the life and work of Oscar Wilde, just as
Michael Cunningham's *The Hours* drew from Virginia Woolf,
London Triptych is a touching and engrossing read.'
Attitude

ISBN: 978-0-9562515-3-4

SHORTLISTED FOR THE WRITERS' GUILD
OF GREAT BRITAIN AWARD

'When you try to protect someone from grief, do you
prevent them from feeling anything at all? A beautiful début
about a son trying to break free from his father.'
Financial Times

'A warm coming-of-age story that tackles family
relationships, secrets, belonging and self-acceptance.'
Coventry Telegraph

'Lyrical, warm and moving, this impressive début
is reminiscent of Laurie Lee.'
Meera Syal

'Passages in this novel made me laugh out loud and others were
extremely moving. I silently gave three cheers for Ellis when I
reached the end. This is a poetic, moving and evocative read.'
The Bookbag

ISBN: 978-0-9562515-2-7

MORE FROM MYRIAD EDITIONS

SELECTED FOR WATERSTONE'S NEW VOICES

'This reads like an author on their fourth or fifth book
rather than their début novel. The prose is masterly,
the characters are fully drawn.'
Savidge Reads

'Every single page is full to bursting. Yet every single
word earns its place... The whole novel is breathtaking
in its scope and originality. This is a multi-layered
literary read. Thoroughly recommended.'
The Bookbag

'Hillyer's meticulous research and gift for atmosphere
brings London and its rich history to life; his handling
of Brippoki's hallucinogenic episodes is skilfully done
and his use of Dreaming is sensitive and understated.
The result is a charming, unusual and poignant book.'
All About Cricket

ISBN: 978-0-9562515-0-3

MORE FROM MYRIAD EDITIONS

'Imagine Brighton in chaos. Communities are divided – socially,
economically and physically. The council is all-powerful,
inconvenient people are "dealt with", children are controlled
and tolls strangle the transport system. Robert Dickinson
creates a world that only vaguely resembles our own. This
intriguing story brings the issues of political influence, red tape
and corruption to the fore – if only by making us relieved
that it seems improbable it could come to this.'
Liverpool Daily Post

'I loved the structure of *The Noise of Strangers* – it flits between
standard narrative, transcripts of phonecalls and meetings,
inter-departmental memos, sinister notes, and articles from
an underground newspaper. As a satire, it works well, and
is completely believable as a nightmare present scenario.'
The Bookbag

'I was pleased to find myself rapidly becoming engrossed
in the strange world which Robert Dickinson has created.'
A Common Reader

ISBN: 978-0-9562515-1-0

MORE FROM MYRIAD EDITIONS

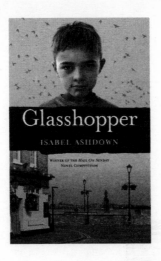

'Tender and subtle, it explores difficult issues in
deceptively easy prose. Across the decades, Ashdown tiptoes
carefully through explosive family secrets. This is a wonderful
début – intelligent, understated and sensitive.'
Observer

'An immaculately written novel with plenty of dark family
secrets and gentle wit within. Recommended for book groups.'
Waterstone's Books Quarterly

'Isabel Ashdown's first novel is a disturbing, thought-
provoking tale of family dysfunction, spanning the second
half of the 20th century, that guarantees laughter
at the uncomfortable familiarity of it all.'
'Best Books of the Year', *London Evening Standard*

'An intelligent, beautifully observed coming-of-age story,
packed with vivid characters and inch-perfect dialogue.
Isabel Ashdown's storytelling skills are formidable;
her human insights highly perceptive.'
Mail on Sunday

ISBN: 978-0-9549309-7-4

MORE FROM MYRIAD EDITIONS

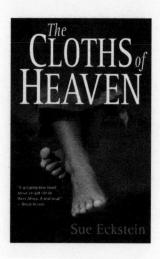

DRAMATISED FOR RADIO 4 WOMAN'S HOUR

'*The Cloths of Heaven* is a wry, dust-dry character-observation-rich gem of a book with one of the most refreshing comic voices I've read for a long while. This book is a bright, witty companion – values and attitudes in the right place – acute, observant but also tolerant and understanding and not afraid of a sharp jibe or two.'
Vulpes Libris

'Graham Greene with a bit of Alexander McCall Smith thrown in. Very readable, very humorous – a charming first novel.'
Radio 5 Live Up All Night

'Populated by a cast of miscreants and misfits, this début novel by playwright Eckstein is a darkly comic delight.'
Choice

'Fabulous... fictional gold.'
Argus

ISBN: 978-0-9549309-8-1

MORE FROM MYRIAD EDITIONS

WINNER OF THE PEOPLE'S BOOK PRIZE FOR FICTION

'Lesley Thomson is a class above, and
A Kind of Vanishing is a novel to treasure.'
Ian Rankin

'Thomson skilfully evokes the era and the slow-moving
quality of childhood summers, suggesting the menace
lurking just beyond the vision of her young protagonists.
A study of memory and guilt with several twists.'
Guardian

'This emotionally charged thriller grips from the
first paragraph, and a nail-biting level of suspense is
maintained throughout. A great second novel.'
She

'A thoughtful, well-observed story about families and
relationships and what happens to both when a tragedy
occurs. It reminded me of Kate Atkinson.'
Scott Pack

ISBN: 978-0-9565599-3-7

MORE FROM MYRIAD EDITIONS

'Imaginative, clever and darkly claustrophobic.'
The Big Issue

'An exquisitely crafted début novel set in a
post-apocalyptic landscape. I'm rationing myself
to five pages per day in order to make it last.'
Guardian Unlimited

'Martine McDonagh writes with a cool, clear confidence
about a world brought to its knees. Her protagonist,
a woman living alone but battling on into the future,
is utterly believable, as are her observations of the
sodden landscape she finds herself inhabiting. This book
certainly got under my skin – if you like your books dark
and more than a little disturbing this is one for you.'
Mick Jackson

'This is a troubling, beautifully composed
novel, rich in its brevity and complex
in the psychological portrait it paints.'
Booksquawk

ISBN: 978-0-9549309-2-9